WAIT UNTIL DARK

KAREN
ROBARDS
WAIT UNTIL DARK

ANDREA
KANE

LINDA
ANDERSON

MARIAH
STEWART

POCKET BOOKS
New York   London   Toronto   Sydney   Singapore

An *Original* Publication of POCKET BOOKS

POCKET BOOKS, a division of Simon & Schuster, Inc.
1230 Avenue of the Americas, New York, NY 10020

"Manna from Heaven" © 2001 by Karen Robards
"Stone Cold" © 2001 by Andrea Kane
"Once in a Blue Moon" © 2001 by Linda Kirchman Anderson
"'Til Death Do Us Part" © 2001 by Marti Robb

ISBN: 0-671-03655-6

First Pocket Books printing May 2001

10 9 8 7 6 5 4 3 2 1

POCKET and colophon are registered trademarks of Simon & Schuster, Inc.

Front cover illustration by Lisa Litwack; photo credits: Yuen Lee/ Photonica; Tony Stone Images

Printed in the U.S.A.

CONTENTS

MANNA FROM HEAVEN
Karen Robards 1

STONE COLD
Andrea Kane 111

ONCE IN A BLUE MOON
Linda Anderson 259

'TIL DEATH DO US PART
Mariah Stewart 389

MANNA FROM HEAVEN

KAREN ROBARDS

1

THE GREEN GLARE OF THE INSTRUMENT PANEL was the only illumination in the pitch-dark cockpit.

"Ready?" Skeeter Todd stood by the door of the small Cessna, tightening the harness of his parachute. At his feet, perhaps three dozen duffel bags slumped, each equipped with its own parachute.

"Yeah." Jake Crutcher rose from the copilot's seat and moved toward Skeeter, checking his own parachute as he went. Then, in a gesture as automatic as a breath, he rubbed a hand over his chest to make sure that his Glock was still securely holstered. It was.

Skeeter opened the door. Cold night air rushed through the plane's interior. Bracing himself against the sudden gale, Jake went to work helping Skeeter toss the duffel bags out into the night sky. They were flying low, and the specially designed search light was on, making it easy to identify their target, a narrow line of grassy fields in the midst of a heavily forested section of western Tennessee. A river ran nearby, and landing their cargo in that would be a disaster.

"Just think, in about six hours from now I'll be sippin' a cold brew and sittin' in a hot tub with my baby." Skeeter stopped working to grin at Jake. Jake didn't grin back. His expression was grim.

"Like I told you, I don't think dragging your girlfriend into this was a good idea." Jake kept on heaving bags out the door, his booted feet planted wide apart so that he wouldn't slip. Skeeter was twenty-five years old, little more than a kid, a feckless, reckless fool who had no idea of the magnitude of what he'd gotten himself into.

"Laura's okay. I'd trust her with my life. Anyway, I didn't want to leave my truck parked out here for a week. Somebody might have stolen it."

That was so damned stupid that Jake didn't even bother to reply.

"There she is, right on time." Jake's silence either didn't register, or it didn't bother Skeeter. He sounded as cheerfully unconcerned as if he'd arranged for his girlfriend to meet him at a movie. Together, they tossed the last couple of bags over the side. Then Skeeter straightened and gave Jake a mock salute.

"See ya on the ground," Skeeter said, and stepped out the door. At the last second Jake noticed that a duffel bag was tied to Skeeter's waist.

Damned stupid kid, Jake thought, and stepped toward the door. Hanging onto the edge, he glanced down. Skeeter was nowhere in sight. Of course, it was dark as hell, and the kid would have been blown back behind them by the force of the wind. But far below he could see two tiny pinpricks of light that could only be the headlights of Skeeter's approaching truck with the unknown Laura at the wheel.

To get mixed up in something like this, she had to be as big an idiot as Skeeter, Jake thought, and that was saying a lot. Shaking his head, he looked up at the pilot.

"I'm outta here," Jake mouthed, knowing the man wouldn't be able to hear over the roaring wind. He waved, and the man waved back.

Then Jake jumped into the vast emptiness of the night, enjoying the sensation of free-falling for the few precious seconds he allowed himself before he jerked his rip cord.

2

THE LOW, HISSING GROWL was enough to make the hair stand up on the back of Charlie Bates' neck.

Curled on her favorite blue velvet cushion in the passenger seat, Sadie whimpered in sympathy.

"It's okay, girl." Charlie glanced over at the tiny Chihuahua whose liquid brown eyes stared anxiously at her through the dim glow of the reflected headlights. "It can't get out. We're safe."

The cage door rattled violently. Charlie and Sadie exchanged mutually apprehensive looks. Charlie gritted her teeth, forced herself to focus on her driving, and tried not to think about what she was hauling in the back of the Jeep.

Another threatening growl caused her shoulders to rise in an instinctive bid to protect the nape of her neck. Sadie lowered her head, covered her muzzle with both paws, and whimpered again.

The critter in the back was one ticked-off raccoon. As she barreled down the pitch-dark highway toward the state park and animal preserve that was her goal, Charlie listened to it growling and rattling the bars of its cage with growing dismay. At the end of this journey, she was going to have to let the thing out. And she was really, really fond of her slender white fingers with their perfectly manicured nails. To say nothing of her long, creamy and all-too-vulnerable neck.

The things she did to earn a living! She was a singer, for God's sake. Not an animal wrangler. Especially not a wild animal wrangler. A country and western singer, trying her best to make it in Nashville, the New York, New York of the country music world.

An only modestly successful country and western singer, she had to admit. Otherwise she would never have allowed herself to be cajoled into doing this.

"All you have to do is drive the Jeep about a mile inside the park and let the animals in the back go free. What's the big deal about that?" That was how the job had been broached to her.

"And for this I get paid two hundred dollars?" Charlie had responded skeptically.

"Yep."

The persuasion had come from her sister Marisol, who was also her sometime singing partner—when they performed together, they billed themselves as the Sugar Babes—and the new owner, by way of a day job and about ten thousand dollars of carefully saved earnings, of County-wide Critter Ridders. The fledgling business billed itself as being able to rid residences of any and all unwelcome species of wildlife that had for one reason or another decided that sharing a home with humans was not half bad. Usually the humans disagreed, which was where Critter Ridders came in. For the right price, they (at the moment, *they* consisted of Marisol, her boyfriend Mark Greenberg, and Howie Stubbs, the previous owner, who was training them) would remove and relocate anything. Not kill, but move to a new home in a sylvan setting where creatures of the wild *should* live. The usually well-to-do homeowners who availed themselves of Critter Ridders' services liked the idea of that. They didn't want to kill Bambi. They just didn't want him living in their garage.

"So what's the catch? We're not talking bears or anything, are we?" Charlie had known her sister long enough to be cautious. Marisol had a talent for trouble—or, more properly, for getting Charlie into trouble—that she had been honing since they were toddlers.

"Squirrels, chipmunks, maybe a bird or a raccoon—no man-eaters, I promise," Marisol had said airily. Then, with a wheedling smile at her sister, she'd added, "Come *on*, Charlie. Mark and I just want the one night off to celebrate his birthday. Howie's going to pick up the animals and load them for us. All I need you to do is drive. It's not like you have anything better to do. You and Rick go out for Sunday brunch, and then on Wednesday and Friday nights, world without end. This is Thursday. So please?"

Put that way, Charlie's love life sounded positively dull, which she supposed it was. Rick Rozen was a big blond who coached football at St. Xavier High. Their dating schedule had long since settled into a comfortable groove dictated by Rick's need to have everything in life be on a schedule. Charlie was starting to find Rick and his schedule a little boring—all right, a whole lot boring—but he was good-looking and had a good job and, as Marisol pointed out, wouldn't be lacking for offers if Charlie cut him loose. Charlie hadn't even realized that she was thinking about cutting him loose until Marisol said that, but Marisol had, because she knew her little sister pretty darn well, as she frequently pointed out. Charlie's elder by two years, Marisol was, at twenty-nine, a tall, voluptuous, redheaded beauty with the personality of an army general and the determination of a bulldozer. As far as facial features went—oval-shaped, high-cheekboned faces, big blue eyes, delicate noses, wide, full-lipped mouths—Charlie and Marisol looked enough alike to be twins. But Charlie's build was far more slender than her sister's, even taking into account the D-cup implants that Marisol unashamedly admitted to, and Charlie's thick mane of shoulder-length hair was a quieter honey blond. And her personality was nowhere near as forceful as her sister's. Charlie could generally be counted on to go along to get along, a trait which (unless it was benefiting someone else at her expense) Marisol thoroughly approved of.

Only Charlie was getting tired of it. She had always been the good girl in the family to Marisol's bad one, and now everyone expected her to behave that way, and the role was getting old. A touch of excitement in her life would be a good thing. An exciting *man* in her life would be a good thing. Put it this way: If one suddenly dropped into her lap, she wouldn't turn him down.

Or would she? The truth was, she probably would. If a truly exciting man came into her life he would probably strike her as being too much of a risk. Her choices tended to be safe ones, and exciting was something that happened to someone else, not Charlotte Elizabeth Bates.

Tonight was a case in point. Hanging onto the steering wheel with both hands and leaning slightly forward as she strained to see through the darkness, Charlie cursed her own people-pleaser nature. Even if she ended up getting her throat ripped out by a wrathful raccoon, as at the moment seemed entirely possible, she had no room to complain, she scolded herself. She deserved exactly what she got.

After vowing not to, she'd given into Marisol's entreaties *again*.

The raccoon snarled and rattled the bars of its cage as forcefully as a convict demanding release. *Maybe a raccoon,* Marisol had said, oh, so casually. Well, this thing was as big as a bear cub and as mean as a badger. Charlie couldn't help it: Shivering, she glanced in the rearview mirror, which, as the raccoon's cage was wedged in with the others in the cargo area behind the backseat, allowed her to see precisely nothing.

The creature could be loose, and she wouldn't know about it until it leaped on her.

Sadie moaned. Charlie knew just how she felt.

"Just a little bit farther." Charlie realized as she said it that she was trying to comfort herself as much as Sadie. Not that the idea of reaching her destination was precisely comforting. Once there, she had to don the special gloves and mask and overalls that Marisol had provided, lift the cages from the rear cargo compartment of the Jeep, set them on the ground and open the doors.

And then leap back inside the Jeep until the animals chose to vacate the premises, at which point she was supposed to load the empty cages up again and return to home base.

What had she been thinking? Marisol's offer of two hundred dollars for a simple drive into the countryside was beginning to make sense. It was really more in the nature of combat pay.

There were other animals in the back besides the raccoon. A skunk, for one. A ticked-off skunk beat a ticked-off raccoon for sheer unadulterated unpleasantness any time, as Howie had told Charlie with a cackle when she had accepted the keys to the loaded Jeep from him. But this one was tranquilized—Howie informed her proudly that he'd hidden the dose in a section of apple—and peacefully asleep.

So what was she supposed to do when it came time to set it free, Charlie wondered for the first time with a touch of hysteria: Upend the cage and tip the poor drugged creature out beside the road?

She would, she decided, cross that bridge when she came to it.

The rest of her cargo—a possum and its kits, a barn owl, and an eight-foot long black king snake that made her shudder every time she thought about it—were awake, but more or less behaving themselves. Only the raccoon was throwing a hissy fit.

It was just after midnight. The song on the radio crackled, then sputtered away into static. After fiddling with the dial for a moment without success, Charlie turned the radio off. From past visits to the area, she knew that the surrounding mountains blocked all transmissions from here on out, including those of cell phones. Hers, in her purse on the floorboard beneath

Sadie, was now useless, which was, she reflected, something she was better off not dwelling on. A small green rectangular sign flashed by: CHEATHAM WILDLIFE MANAGEMENT AREA, ten miles. Thank God, she was almost there.

The two-lane highway was deserted. Although the mountains rose up to scrape the sky to the north and east, this particular stretch of road was relatively flat. Grassy fields interrupted only by the occasional stand of trees stretched endlessly all around. The fast-flowing Cumberland River ran parallel to the road perhaps a half mile away, visible occasionally when a bend in its course brought it closer. The last sign of civilization had been a self-service gas station some fifteen minutes back. Which meant, essentially, that she and Sadie and the zoo in the rear were alone in the wilderness.

Except for the light in the southern sky, that is. Charlie had first noticed it when the Jeep had topped that last rise. At the time, it had been distant, noticable only because the October night was so very dark, threatening rain, with clouds obscuring any hint of a moon or stars and fog creeping in from the river to cover the low places in the road. The light was beneath the clouds, way low for an airplane if that's what it was, and way bright.

Too bright? she wondered, watching as it drew nearer. And didn't airplane lights shine straight ahead? It almost seemed as if this light was directed at the ground, like a spotlight or a searchlight or something.

The rattling of the raccoon's cage reminded her that she had more immediate problems than a too low, too bright light.

Sadie whined. A glance showed Charlie that the six-pound dog was sitting up now and looking anxiously at her.

"I know. I should keep my eyes on the road."

But with the best will in the world to do so, Charlie could not ignore the light. She barely had to lift her eyes from the gleaming surface of the asphalt to see it now. It was closer, brighter, and seemed to be coming straight toward the Jeep.

Could it be a UFO?

The thought popped into her mind from the part of her brain that enjoyed *X-Files* and Stephen King novels, only to be immediately dismissed. She did *not* believe in UFOs. At least, not when it was daylight and she was within shouting distance of another human being. Tonight, on this deserted stretch of foggy highway with only her tiny dog and a bevy of disgruntled forest friends for company, the existence of UFOs suddenly did not seem quite so farfetched.

It occurred to her that the shining twin beams of her headlights made her about as visible to the craft in the sky as its light made it to her.

Charlie was possessed of a sudden, almost irresistible impulse to douse her lights. Don't be an idiot, she scolded herself. She was not going to spook herself into a crash.

But no matter how hard she tried to focus on the highway to the exclusion of all else, the light was now impossible to ignore. Whatever the flying object was—an airplane or a helicopter were the only possibilities, of course—it was heading straight toward her. In just a few minutes the Jeep would be illuminated by the beam.

Alien abduction were the two words that popped into her head.

Which was ridiculous. She knew it. Casting a nervous glance at her instrument panel to make sure none of the dials were gyrating wildly—she would have had a heart attack there and then if they were—she stepped on the gas. From experience she knew that a thick stand of trees lay not more than two miles ahead.

If she could just scoot beneath the trees before the light reached her, she would be safe—wouldn't she?

She wasn't going to make it. Her speedometer read sixty, seventy—an insane speed for this stretch of road—and yet the Jeep suddenly seemed to be moving in slow motion. The light was close now, just a couple of hundred feet away and closing fast, its blinding beam illuminating the tall grass in the fields beneath it. The light was beside the Jeep, *on* the Jeep, its brightness lighting up the inside of the vehicle as if it were the middle of the day.

Ridiculous or not, all she could think was: tractor beam. Designed to pull her and her vehicle up inside the craft. Any minute now, she would be paralyzed, and the Jeep's wheels would leave the road.

Sadie whimpered in sympathy.

Charlie's heart pounded. Her mouth went dry. She stomped the gas, pressing the pedal to the metal with a vengeance. The Jeep's rear wheels squealed as she peeled away from the light.

Something crashed into the roof of the Jeep with the force of a falling boulder. There was a sudden loud thud just above her head. Charlie cried out, ducked and instinctively hit the brake. The tires shrieked. Though she fought to keep it on the road, the Jeep went out of control. It shot over the gravel shoulder and into the adjacent field, jerking and bouncing and sliding sideways as it went. For one blank, horrible moment as she wrestled the steering wheel, all Charlie could think of was that she could no longer see where she was going. Then she realized that the reason she couldn't see was because a black-clad body—a human body—was plastered across her windshield. A pale face rested almost directly in front of hers. Blood poured from its mouth. Its wide open eyes stared at her through the glass.

Charlie screamed. The Jeep crashed with an ear-shattering bang, and she was thrown forward as it came to an instant, jarring halt. The body flew off the hood, vanishing into the tall sea of grass beyond the vehicle.

For a moment after the Jeep stopped moving, she simply sat where she was, stunned. Her face rested in a smothering pillow; the world had turned white. It took just seconds for her to realize that the air bag had inflated. Then it deflated, leaving her leaning limply against her seat belt and staring out through the windshield into a field of tall golden grass that was partially illuminated by the one working headlight. The other, like the entire right front of the Jeep, had plowed into a tree.

A pitiful-sounding whine drew her gaze sideways. The blue cushion was no longer on the seat beside her. Neither was her dog.

"Sadie!" Charlie called in an unsteady voice. The passenger compartment seemed to be intact, although the impact had severely damaged the Jeep's exterior. Sadie had been flung forward with no seat belt or air bag to cushion her flight; please God she wasn't hurt. Charlie called her again.

Looking as shaken as Charlie felt, Sadie clambered out of the passenger side footwell into her arms. Charlie did a quick check. The dog was trembling, but seemed unharmed.

Oh my God, Charlie thought, gathering Sadie close and burying her face in the dog's satiny coat as she remembered the body on the windshield. I've run over someone!

At that moment there was a brisk tap on the driver's side window. Startled, Charlie glanced around to discover a face peering in at her. A black-gloved hand gestured imperatively at the lock button. Automatically, before she had time to think the action through, she released the lock.

The door was yanked open.

Still shocked and seat-belted into near immobility, Charlie found herself gaping at a tall, broad-shouldered, black-clad man with a black knit cap pulled down over his head almost to his eyebrows. One of his hands gripped the door. In the other he held a pistol, which was, thankfully, pointed at the ground.

He surveyed her out of hard, narrowed eyes.

"Laura, isn't it? Think you might have been going a little fast?"

3

FROM THE SAFETY OF CHARLIE'S ARMS, Sadie yapped at him hysterically.

"What the hell is that?" His voice was a menacing growl. His expression was grim. Charlie realized that with the door open and the interior light on he could see her and Sadie clearly: a slender blonde with a dazed expression wearing black cowboy boots, jeans, a black T-shirt with Sugar Babes written across the front, and a fringed suede jacket, holding a tiny, shivering dog the same shade as her hair. He, meanwhile, remained in deep gloom, rendered all but invisible by his black clothes. As her gaze met his, it occurred to her that he was not, perhaps, overly friendly. She hugged Sadie closer.

"Oh, my God, I think I ran over somebody." She ignored his question. It was stupid anyway. Anyone could see that Sadie was a dog. The pale face so recently plastered against her windshield was all she could think about, with its wide eyes and the dark stream of blood spilling from its mouth.

"Ya think?" The words dripped sarcasm. "That was Skeeter. You were supposed to pick him up, remember? Pick us up. Not run him the hell over."

Most of what he said didn't make sense, but she was too upset to notice.

"We've got to try to help him—he's got to be somewhere right in front of the Jeep. He flew—he flew off the windshield when the Jeep hit the tree." Charlie shuddered in remembrance and scrambled out of the car, Sadie in her arms. Her knees almost buckled as she stood upright, and he caught her by one elbow, steadying her.

"Are you hurt?" His voice was rough. The hand around her elbow was large and strong.

"No. No, I don't think so." She was trembling, she realized, with reaction no doubt, but within seconds her leg muscles seemed to firm up and her knees no longer threatened to collapse. Pulling free of his grip, sliding Sadie beneath her arm, she began to move toward the front of her car. "I didn't even see him."

He followed her. She was so busy scanning the weeds for some sign of the man she had hit that she was only peripherally aware of the presence of the stranger behind her.

"Yeah, well, he was probably cutting it pretty close. The damned fool never did like to walk farther than he could help. But that still doesn't let you off the hook. Damn it to *hell,* you were supposed to stop when you saw our lights, not go rocketing down the road like a Nascar driver. Oh, yeah, I saw you speed up. What the hell were you doing?"

His words still barely registered. She followed the

beam of light forward on the theory that it was the path
the body would have taken, wading through the shoulder high grass, looking down and all around and
scarcely attending to the furious-sounding man behind
her.

A pair of black combat boots, toes pointing down-
ward, were just visible at the far edge of the light. They
were attached to black-clad legs; the rest of the body was
concealed by the grass.

"There he is." She choked and stopped, pointing. Her
companion broke off his diatribe to move swiftly past
her. Charlie found that she could not, for the space of a
couple of heartbeats, follow him. The horror of what
she had done was suddenly all too real.

She had run over someone. Killed him, probably.

"I didn't even see him," she said again, pitiably, to no
one in particular as she forced herself finally to move
and join the man who crouched at her victim's side. He
was turning the dead man over—there was little doubt,
from the open, staring eyes and the blood running from
the mouth, that he was dead—and checking his pulse.
His gloves were off now, and she saw that his hands
looked large and brown and capable. He certainly did
not seem overly concerned about the other man's fate.
There were no gasps, no groans, no rendering of first
aid, no rush to summon assistance.

Charlie frowned as he began to rifle through the victim's pockets. His manner just seemed—off.

Both men were dressed identically, Charlie registered, in solid black from head to toe. Black knit caps,
black army jackets, black gloves, black pants, black
boots. A black backpack lay on the ground beside the

dead man, a tangle of what looked like white silk and strings spilling from its partially open top. A black duffel bag was tied to his waist.

It hit Charlie then that there was something mighty peculiar about all this. Suddenly cold, she wrapped her arms around herself, and must have made some small sound, because the live man in black glanced up at her. His eyes gleamed, reflecting the light. They looked black, too, just like his thick brows, but after a moment she saw that they were a deep, coppery brown. His skin was tan, his nose straight, his jaw square. It was, weighed objectively, a handsome face, she supposed. But the set of his mouth looked ruthless, and the glint in his eyes was hard.

Charlie took a tiny, instinctive step backward.

"Don't have a breakdown," he recommended impatiently, his gaze already returning to the assortment of items he had spread out on the victim's chest: a set of keys, a wallet, a Chapstick. "You didn't run over him. Or at least, if you did, that's not what killed him. His parachute didn't open. He would've been dead wherever he hit."

Parachute? Charlie barely stopped herself from saying it aloud. Her mind, still slightly sluggish with shock, was nonetheless beginning to sound an alarm. This man was no rescuer, as she had assumed; he was not a passing motorist who had seen the accident and stopped to help; he was not a fireman or a policeman or even a forest ranger. Except for her wrecked Jeep, there were no vehicles in sight.

Where, then, had he come from? He did not look like a camper, or someone out for a nocturnal hike. Anyway, the area was too remote to make either plausible.

Charlie regarded the mass of white protruding from the backpack on the ground with fresh eyes. A parachute: The man—both of the men, she guessed, although the live one wore no backpack—had jumped from the plane, helicopter, or UFO (choose one) that had pinned her with its light. The blow the roof had taken just before the wreck had been the dead man landing on top of the Jeep.

Charlie watched with widening eyes as he opened and upended the duffel bag. Perhaps a dozen shoebox-sized bundles of a plastic-wrapped white substance tumbled out, along with a large quantity of cash, bound into bricks with rubber bands. Both hands rose to cover her mouth as she realized what she was looking at.

His next words, uttered without a glance at her, confirmed it. "Coke's all here. Money, too."

"Um, good," Charlie said, trying to sound enthused, or at least not as horrified as she felt. She must have succeeded, because he didn't pay her any particular attention. Instead, he pulled a wicked-looking stiletto out of his boot, and used it to saw through the rope that bound the duffel bag to the dead man's waist.

Her stomach began to churn at the sight of the stiletto. A deadly knife in his boot, a pistol in his hand—the pistol was no longer in sight, she realized, but didn't doubt for a moment that he still had it—the way he was dressed, the coke, the money, the parachute, all begged the question: Who *was* this guy?

The answer came to her instantaneously: nobody she wanted to know.

Everything he had said to her since she had first unlocked her door for him scrolled in double-fast time through her mind. He had called her Laura. He'd been angry because she hadn't stopped when she'd seen the approaching light. He had said that she was supposed to pick him and Skeeter up.

He clearly thought she was someone else. And, just as clearly, he was engaged in something she wanted no part of.

Could anyone say "drug smuggling"?

Had she really just been thinking that her life needed a little excitement? An exciting man, to be precise? God, she thought, if you're listening, I take it back. An encounter with an alien would have been preferable. According to the tabloids, people usually survived those.

Fright cleared her mind, and rendered it suddenly sharp. If he discovered who she was—or wasn't—it wouldn't be a good thing, to say the least. She had to get away from him and back to civilization. The gas station she had passed sprang to mind. From there she could call the police and wait in safety for them to arrive.

Her first order of business was to discover if the Jeep was still drivable.

Subtly. Without alerting him to her intent. Without letting him know that she was not, in fact, Laura.

She shivered artistically. No real acting required there. She was suddenly so nervous that her palms were sweating. The only surprise was that her knees didn't knock. Sadie whimpered as if sensing her distress. The dog, Charlie thought as she had many times before, was a mind reader.

"I'm freezing," she said, in a tone that sounded slightly squeaky to her own ears. The night was growing colder, although under normal circumstances she would have been perfectly comfortable in her jacket. Still, he had no reason to disbelieve her. "I think I'll go wait in the Jeep."

"Mmm." Engaged in returning the cash to the bag, he didn't even glance up. Lightheaded with relief, clutching Sadie tightly to make sure she stayed put—all she needed about now was to have to go chasing the dog across night-dark fields—she headed for the Jeep. It was still running, she realized as she reached it. She had never turned the engine off. Surely that was a good sign?

The door was open, too. Sliding in behind the steering wheel, Charlie closed it—very gently so that the sound would not attract his attention—and pressed the button that locked all the doors. The resultant emphatic click made her feel a little safer, but locking herself in the Jeep was useless if she could not get away, she knew.

Set free, Sadie clambered across her lap into the passenger seat, where she remained standing as if poised for action. From the rear, a faint hiss and a rattle reminded Charlie of the raccoon. The wreck had apparently simmered it down some, not that it mattered. The creature was now the least of her worries.

A live, armed drug smuggler trumped a riled-up raccoon as a source of terror any time, she reflected.

Pushing the limp white carcass of the air bag out of the way, Charlie shifted into reverse. Heart thumping, eyes fixed on the black figure she could just see through the veil of golden grass, she stealthily trod on the gas.

At first she didn't think the Jeep was going to respond. But then, with a screech of metal that made her wince, the vehicle disengaged from the tree and began to back up. It stopped abruptly. Charlie realized that something, the front bumper, the undercarriage, who knew, was hung up. Oh, God, what could she do? A quick, panicked glance revealed that the man was still crouched in the grass, although his position had altered. Was he looking at the Jeep? She couldn't tell.

"It's okay," she said to Sadie, trying to calm herself as much as the shivering dog and not much liking the quaver she heard in her voice. Panicking would not help, she told herself sternly, taking a deep, steadying breath. Then, gritting her teeth, she shifted into drive. Maybe she could rock the Jeep free.

Oh, God, he was on his feet now, heading her way. She could see the tall black shape of him through the grass, walking swiftly toward the Jeep. Panicking for real now, gripping the steering wheel so hard that her knuckles showed white, she shifted into reverse again and stomped the accelerater.

The engine roared. The tires spun with a sickening slithering sound. The Jeep strained backward to no purpose: It was still stuck.

"Oh, God," Charlie groaned aloud. Sadie whimpered. Her eyes were as big and shiny as black olives, and she looked as scared as Charlie felt.

Disappearing behind the tree to reappear on the passenger side, he reached the car. He glanced in at her, then knocked peremptorily on the window. Charlie's heart pounded. Her breathing came in short, sharp pants. Her foot ground the pedal to the floor.

The engine roared. The tires spun. The damned Jeep didn't shift by so much as an inch.

He knocked again, more demandingly, frowning at

her through the window. She might as well face it: The Jeep was not going anywhere. She was breathing so hard that she feared she might hyperventilate. Oh, God, she was trapped! What should she do? What could she do?

Charlie remembered his gun. He could break the window. He could shoot her through the glass. Locked doors would not protect her. She was as easy a target as one of the caged animals in the back.

Sadie moaned. It was all Charlie could do not to join in.

He thought she was on his side. The thought steadied her. She just must play along.

Taking her foot off the gas, Charlie swallowed convulsively and unlocked the doors. The click sounded as loud as a gunshot to her ears. The comparison made her shiver.

He pulled the door open and looked in at her. Charlie realized that she was sweating. The breeze blowing in through the open door felt icy as it hit her damp skin. She pinned a questioning smile on her face, and hoped it didn't look as fake as it felt.

"It's stuck on a tree trunk. Put it in reverse and hit the gas when I tell you," he said, seeming to notice nothing amiss in her demeanor. "I'll push."

Charlie clamped her teeth together to keep them from chattering and nodded, not trusting herself to speak. Then he slammed the door and walked around to the front of the Jeep.

Charlie almost melted into a puddle of quivering jelly right there in the driver's seat. She felt like a death row inmate who had just been granted a reprieve.

"Get a grip," she ordered herself fiercely, watching

mesmerized through the windshield as he braced a
shoulder against the hood. He waved. Meeting his gaze
for a brief, trauma-filled instant, terrified that he
might somehow be able to read her intention in her
eyes, Charlie recognized that the wave was a signal and
put the transmission into reverse. Then she stepped on
the gas.

4

THE ENGINE ROARED. The wheels spun. He lifted and pushed from the front. The Jeep rocked—and came free. It shot backward in an arc, cutting a wide swath through the tall grass that swished past the windows. As she rocketed away from him, Charlie kept her foot to the floor. She dragged her gaze from his surprised expression to look over her shoulder—just in time to get a split-second glimpse of a second tree before she hit it.

Fortunately it was only a glancing blow. The gray-barked trunk scraped along the left rear of the Jeep with a scream like bear claws on a blackboard. But there were more trees behind her, crowded together, blocking the way. Panting with terror, she hit the brake. She had traveled as far as she could in reverse.

If he caught up with her . . .

Licking her lips, she glanced wildly around to try to determine if he was anywhere near. She could see nothing in front except the narrow path illuminated by the single working headlight. For all her sight told her, the world might have consisted of no more than a golden carpet of mown-down grass, the trees beside and behind her, and the foggy night.

The thought that he might be racing toward her unseen, or even getting ready to shoot her through the glass, acted like a cattle prod on her fear-disordered reflexes. Slamming the transmission into drive, she stomped the gas.

The wheels spun out over the slippery grass. Just as they found a purchase and the Jeep started to move, the passenger door was jerked open and he dived into the seat beside her, dislodging Sadie, who leaped into the back with a high-pitched yelp.

Her foot stayed on the floor. The Jeep flew in a bumping, jolting beeline toward the road. He clung grimly to the edge of the seat with both hands, swinging his long legs inside as the door flapped like a wing beating the air. Charlie knew she was in deep trouble even before he managed to haul himself into a sitting position and grab at something inside his coat.

The gun. Of course. Casting a terrified glance at him, she discovered it pointed straight at her and realized with a fatalistic sense of calm that she was going to die.

"Stop the god-damned car!" he roared. If ever murder blazed from a man's eyes, she thought, it was blazing from his at that moment.

In a display of obedience that she doubted he was going to appreciate, Charlie stood on the brake. At the same time she spun the wheel, hoping to throw him out again through the open door or at least injure him enough to enhance her prospects of escape.

He was flung forward, but managed to catch himself

with a hand on the dashboard before any damage was done. Charlie, hanging onto the steering wheel for dear life during the double doughnut that ensued, saw with dismay at the end of it that he was still aboard and unhurt. Her desperate gambit had served about as much purpose as swatting futilely at a hornet: It had just made him mad.

Curses poured from his mouth in a steady stream as the Jeep shimmied to a halt just a few feet shy of the highway, facing back the way she had come. Charlie looked at the beckoning trail of asphalt with burgeoning despair. So near and yet so far, she mourned inwardly, following the road home with her eyes. She thought of leaping from the Jeep and running for it, but a single glance at him dissuaded her. The door was closed now, which meant the interior of the vehicle was once again dark. But there was no mistaking the pistol pointed straight at her, shining with a dull black gleam that was no more menacing than the evil glint in his eyes.

"What the hell *is* this?" His voice was lower than before, but no less furious. "Are you fucking nuts?"

Before Charlie could reply, headlights from an approaching vehicle caught her attention. If she leaped out just as the car passed them, she calculated frantically, and hurled herself in its path, it would surely stop.

"Don't even think about it," he growled, grabbing her wrist just as if he could read her mind. Charlie felt the strength of his grip and abandoned all hope. No way could she break free.

But, miracle of miracles, the vehicle seemed to be slowing down without any help at all from her. Yes, it *was* slowing down. The driver had obviously seen the

Jeep with its smashed right front. Maybe he or she was the kind of Good Samaritan who would stop to see if there'd been an accident.

Please God let it be a he. A big, burly he, preferably complete with gun. A cop would be good. Yes, please let it be a cop. A pair of cops.

It wasn't. It was a couple—no, a trio—in a mid-sized SUV. It was too dark to be precise about make or model or even color, although like the Jeep it was some dark shade, but she was clear on the number of people because the SUV pulled off the road right in front of the Jeep, stopped and turned off engine and lights. Then the trio got out. For a moment, as the SUV's door opened, Charlie saw the occupants clearly: The driver was a blond woman several years younger than herself, and with her were two men. All of them were dressed in black, and, like the man beside her, the men brandished pistols.

God, it seemed, had a sense of humor. When she'd started wishing for a little excitement, he'd sent her enough to cure her of the hankering for the rest of her life.

Beside her, her captor was staring at the newcomers, too, with an arrested expression. As they approached the Jeep, stepping momentarily into the full beam of the single headlight, his gaze swung to Charlie.

"God damn it to hell and back," he said bitterly. "You're not Laura, are you?"

Charlie shrank away from him. Having been taught from an early age that discretion was the better part of valor, she chose not to reply. His hand tightened painfully around her wrist.

"If you have the sense God gave a gnat, you'll pretend you're supposed to be here," he said through his teeth. "What's your name?"

The urgency of his manner compelled her.

"Charlie. Charlie Bates."

He swore, his gaze raking her. "I should've guessed. The clothes, the damned dog. You ever hear the saying, up shit creek without a paddle? Lady, that's where you are right now. Get out, keep your mouth shut, play along with whatever happens and stay the hell close to me. My name's Jake Crutcher."

The trio had almost reached the Jeep by this time. Giving her a final inimical glare, he reached across her, doused the lights, turned the ignition off, pulled the keys from it, and got out. When she didn't immediately follow suit, he ducked his head back inside the open door and said *get out* in a tone that made her jump. Though she would by far have preferred to stay where she was, Charlie did as he ordered. Not to do so might well be a fatal mistake, she thought, although she didn't know whether to be more afraid of him or them. He was a solid black shape in a world full of charcoal shadows as he moved toward the front of the Jeep. Stomach quaking, hands icy with fear, she joined him, not seeing any alternative. As she did, he glanced down at her, and caught her hand in a grip that hurt.

Jake. His name was Jake, and apparently, as far as she was concerned, he was the good guy now, she reminded herself in a panic, discreetly wriggling her crushed fingers in an attempt to loosen his grip. Oh God, would they kill her if they discovered she was not one of them? It seemed very probable that they would: They were drug smugglers, after all. Heart thumping, the dry, tinny taste of fear in her mouth, she pondered her options. Running for it was out of the question; his hand held hers in what she was certain was an unbreakable hold, as if he feared she might try to do exactly that. Besides, she would never be able to get away, and to run would be to reveal her fear. That might very well prove fatal. Already the newcomers were looking her up and down in a way that made her shrink closer against the dark bulk of Jake's side.

Suddenly he truly did seem more like an ally than a threat. If he meant to kill her, her guess was she'd know it by now.

Instead he'd told her to stick close to him, and was even now holding her beside him with a death grip on her hand. For whatever murky reason, this particular drug smuggler was prepared to protect her, it seemed. Not exactly the protector she would have chosen if she had been doing the selecting, she reflected, but the old saying about not looking a gift horse in the mouth definitely applied in this case. He might appear menacing, and be every bit as much a criminal as the others, but every instinct she possessed screamed at her that he was the only chance for survival she had.

"Who the hell's she?" One of the men—the shorter, stockier one—was looking her over in a distinctly non-friendly fashion as the newcomers reached them. "And where's Skeeter?"

"This is Charlie. She's okay. I told her to meet us out here because I thought we might need a backup vehicle. Skeeter's dead. His chute didn't open." This last was said without emotion.

"Shit." The stocky man sounded annoyed rather than grieved. The woman gave a little choked cry, and her hand flew to her mouth. The stocky man's head turned toward her. "Shut up, Laura." His tone was brutal. Then, to Jake, he added, "What about the stuff?"

"It's here. All you have to do is pick the duffel bags up. Skeeter kept the cash with him. He's over there." Jake nodded in the general direction of Skeeter's body.

"Hel-*lo*, seventy-five million," the taller man chortled.

The woman—Laura—made another small sound. Despite her drumming heart, Charlie felt a stirring of sympathy for her. No one else seemed to care so much as a snap of his fingers that a man was lying nearby, dead.

"I said shut *up*, Laura." The stocky man sounded positively menacing. Laura seemed to shrink.

Jake's hand tightened again on Charlie's fingers. Charlie had just managed to wriggle them into a state of near comfort, and it was all she could do not to wince.

"What are you and Denton doing here, anyway? Skeeter told me that Laura was the only one coming to meet us."

"Yeah, well, change of plan." The stocky man looked at Laura again. "You get back in the Blazer and pull it over there by those trees. I'll be with you directly."

"Sure, Woz. Whatever you say." Laura looked at Charlie for an instant, her face pale and her eyes wide with what Charlie took for fright. Then she turned and walked back toward the Blazer without another word. The stocky man—Woz—and Denton exchanged glances. Charlie frowned. Before she could figure out what it was in the atmosphere that suddenly caused her sixth sense to go on red alert, Woz was addressing Jake again in a voice that sounded almost amiable compared to his earlier harshness.

"Good idea, about having a second truck. We can throw Skeeter in the back, and keep Laura from having to see him. God, women! Well, we all have to live with 'em, don't we?" He nodded significantly at Charlie, as if commiserating with Jake for having to live with her, then looked around as Laura pulled the Blazer's door open. As the interior light flared briefly, Charlie was able to make out Woz's profile silhouetted against the distant windshield. His forehead was low, his nose large, his lips thick, his chin pugnacious. *Not* a pleasant face, she thought. Then, as a corollary, came the companion thought: not a pleasant man. "Come on, let's get a move on. We'll retrieve Skeeter and the coke first. Babe, whatever your name is, you drive."

"Sure." Charlie was proud of how cool and collected she sounded. Inside, she was as jittery as a pain-phobic patient on a first visit to the dentist. Jake released her hand—under the circumstances he had no choice—and they all headed for the doors. She and Denton were on one side of the Jeep, Jake and Woz on the other. The night was cool and full of mist and eerily quiet except for their footsteps. She was just reaching for the handle when she heard a muffled *thunk,* followed almost immediately by a grunt and the sound of something heavy hitting the ground. Glancing across the top of the Jeep, she saw no one. Before that could even start to alarm her, something hard was jammed painfully against the base of her spine.

"You really think we were going to buy that backup vehicle crap, Blondie?" Denton asked as Charlie, realizing that the "something hard" was his gun, froze in horror. "Get your hands up and let's see if you're packin'."

This was bad. The fact that she could no longer see or hear anything of Jake was worse. Dry-mouthed, Charlie lifted her hands in the air, and was shoved hard against the side of the Jeep for her pains. Her legs were kicked apart as Denton patted her down with an enjoyment that made her sick to her stomach. Woz popped into view like an evil jack-in-the-box, glanced in her direction, smiled, then disappeared again, leaning over something on the ground. The something was, presumably, Jake.

Oh, God, had they killed him? If so, she was almost certainly next. But she was too young! This whole insane episode was a mistake. And she didn't—really didn't—want to die.

God, she was taking that excitement thing back right now.

"She's clean," Denton called to Woz as he completed his search and straightened.

"Put her in the car." The Jeep's interior light came on as Woz opened the passenger side door. Denton grabbed Charlie's arm, opened the driver's door, and pushed her inside. Woz wrestled Jake's limp body inside and belted it into the passenger seat. Jake was missing his cap, and his head, covered with ruthlessly short black hair, lolled limply on his shoulder. For a horrified moment Charlie was sure he was dead. Then she saw his chest rise, and with a flood of relief she realized that he was merely unconscious. Sadie leaped nimbly between the seats and into her lap as Denton got into the back. Absurdly comforted by the dog's presence, Charlie nevertheless wasted no time in thrusting her into the footwell out of sight. These men would not, she felt sure, hesitate for so much as an instant over killing a dog.

"Watch 'em. I'll be right back. If he moves, hit him again. But don't kill him. Not till after I get done talking to him." Woz slammed the door. Charlie jumped reflexively, only to feel Denton's gun nuzzle her cheek.

"Remember, ol' Woz didn't say nothing about killing you."

Charlie sat very still. Through the windshield, she watched Woz open the door to the Blazer as Laura, illuminated now by the vehicle's interior light, turned to look at him.

Then, just like that, Laura's head exploded. *Blam.* Blood coated the inside of the Blazer's windshield before the door was closed again, shutting off the light.

Charlie was still in shock when Woz jerked open the door and climbed into the backseat.

"I ain't cleaning up that bloody mess you just made," Denton said as Woz shut the door again. "Why the hell didn't you do it on the grass?"

" 'Cause we're going to lose the car, dumbass," Woz replied. "Just like we're going to lose this one. Nobody's going to have to clean up nothing."

Denton grunted. "Good. 'Cause I ain't."

Jake made a slight sound. Terrified, Charlie cast him a sideways look. Would they blow off his head, too, when Woz was finished with him? And hers? Oh, God, and hers?

5

SHE WAS GOING TO HAVE TO TAKE A CHANCE on making a break and running for it. It might be a long shot, but it was the only shot she had, Charlie knew.

"You got the cuffs? Get 'em on him before he wakes up," Woz said to Denton.

Denton leaned an arm against the back of Charlie's seat and stroked her cheek with the pistol again. She shivered at the touch of the cold metal, remembered Laura's head exploding against the windshield, and almost vomited where she sat. Only the fear that it might cost her her life kept her from doing exactly that.

"What about her?" The pistol still touched her cheek.

"Cuff her, too."

"I just got the one pair. Besides, she's got to drive."

"Yeah." Woz seemed to ponder. "Cuff 'em together. That way neither one of 'em's going anywhere."

Charlie's eyes widened in horror as she realized that her last chance of escape was getting ready to fly right out the window.

"Give me your hand, Blondie."

When Charlie didn't comply fast enough—she was still mentally dithering over whether or not to attempt a run—Denton reached between the seats and grabbed her right arm, twisting it toward him painfully. A cold metal handcuff snapped closed around her wrist. Seconds later, the second cuff was fastened around Jake's wrist. Charlie glanced at Jake's big body, sprawled limply now in the seat with only the seat belt keeping him semiupright, with despair. There was no longer any hope of running for it. She'd just been shackled to a two-hundred-pound deadweight.

Woz passed her the ignition keys, which he had presumably taken from Jake. They jangled as she took them, and Charlie realized that her hand was shaking.

"Pull up on the road nice and easy, and head on into the forest," Woz directed as Charlie started the Jeep.

"And don't fuck with us, Blondie, or you're dead," Denton added as, forgetting that the Jeep was still in park, she nervously stepped too hard on the gas, causing the engine to rev. He punctuated this remark with his gun, with which he prodded the back of her neck.

Charlie shrank, shivering. She was breathing hard, and her left hand was clammy as it grasped the wheel. Her right, rendered useless by being tethered to Jake, felt sweaty, too, as it rested on the console between the seats. At her feet, Sadie pressed up against her legs in sympathy. The dog was shaking. Or maybe the shaking was coming from her own legs. Charlie was so scared it was hard to be sure.

She kept seeing Laura's head blow up. Oh, God, she didn't want to die. She and Marisol had a really important singing gig on Saturday, and she'd just bought a killer new dress that she hadn't even had a chance to wear yet, and . . . and . . .

They were moving now. The cages rattled in the back as the Jeep bumped up onto the road. Jake moaned, stirred, and sat up, shaking his head.

Apparently feeling himself tethered, his eyes opened and his gaze slashed sideways. Charlie cast a frightened glance at him just in time to see a loop of rope descend over his head and tighten around his neck, yanking his head back against the headrest. Jake grunted, grabbing at the rope, and at the same time the muzzle of Woz's gun jammed into the hollow just below his ear.

"Welcome back, asshole," Woz said softly.

"What the hell?" Jake's whole body seemed to stiffen. Before he could say or do anything else Woz slammed the butt of his gun into Jake's temple. Charlie winced in terrified sympathy as Jake made a pained sound.

Blinking against incipient tears, Charlie forced herself to refocus her attention on the road. Although she was driving an as-slow-as-she-dared thirty miles an hour, the forest already loomed in front of them, its gravelike darkness as ominous as an executioner. Would they die in that forest? It seemed likely.

Charlie shuddered. In the footwell, Sadie pressed closer against her legs. The dog rubbed its head against her calf in silent sympathy.

"What the hell is your problem, the both of you?" Jake spoke in the tone of a reasonable man sorely tried. The rope around his neck pinned him back against the headrest, and his voice was raspy. A lightning glance in the rearview mirror showed Charlie that Woz had the ends wrapped around his fist.

Woz snorted. "Come off it, asshole. We know you're a cop."

"What?" Jake gave a derisive laugh that ended in a choked cough as Woz twisted the rope. "You're crazy."

A cop? Charlie felt a wild burbling of hope. He was a *cop*? Surely that was a good thing—if it was true. But he didn't sound like it was true. That laugh had sounded incredulous. And maybe it wasn't a good thing anyway, under the circumstances. A cop at the mercy of a pair of drug smugglers was kind of like a bird at the mercy of a pair of cats.

And she was with the cop.

Denton's gun nudged her in the back of the neck, and she cringed. "Take a left up here at the fork in the road."

They were in the forest now. Outside, the night was dark as a cave. Mist floated in front of the Jeep. She might, Charlie thought desperately, be able to blink the one remaining headlight if another vehicle came into view. Or honk the horn. Or drive head-on into the other car. The operative principle was, whatever it took. Anything would be better than what she feared would happen to her once the pair in the back ordered her to stop the Jeep.

But there was no other vehicle in sight. And, frightening as it was to face the truth, they were not likely to encounter one. This area had been chosen by Critter Ridders as an ideal place to release their captives for one primary reason: It was remote.

Charlie groaned inwardly. Why, oh, why, when Marisol had asked her to do this tonight, hadn't she decided in favor of pleasing herself instead of her sister and *just said no?*

Woz was still talking to Jake. "You know what? Blowing your brains out will be my pleasure. I never liked you anyway."

"Yeah, well, you're not going to get a marriage proposal from me any time soon either, but this cop shit is the stupidest thing I ever heard."

"Liar! You're going to tell us everything you know, believe me. Or maybe your friend will. She a cop, too?"

"No!" Charlie squeaked in horrified protest.

"Shut up." Woz growled. Charlie shut up. Protesting her innocence would not save her, she realized with despair. Indeed, it might even hasten her end. If they thought she was a cop, they might try to torture information out of her. Once they knew that there was no reason to keep her alive, however, she was pretty much toast.

"Turn here," Denton ordered.

Trembling so hard that she had to grit her teeth to keep them from chattering, Charlie turned. Gravel crunched as they left the paved road. Denton's gun brushed the back of her neck almost caressingly. Short of a miracle, there was no chance of any kind of encounter that might save them. They were as good as dead. Charlie realized that she was starting to hyperventilate, and deliberately slowed her breathing down. Breathe in, breathe out, in, out ...

Sadie was behind her legs now, rubbing against them, offering what comfort she could. If she didn't think of something, fast, poor innocent Sadie would die along with poor innocent her and who-cared-if-he-was-innocent Jake. Charlie thought frantically, but could come up with nothing that might save their lives.

Running the Jeep into a tree would not help. If she did that, and survived, she would almost certainly be shot for her pains.

She was going to be shot anyway. Oh, God, would it hurt? Had it hurt Laura to be shot like that? With a sense of deepening horror, she realized that Jake did not even know that Laura was dead. He'd been out cold when it had happened. She glanced at him, burning with an urgent need to acquaint him with Laura's fate. But she didn't dare so much as open her mouth.

Sadie rubbed against her leg again, twining around her left ankle almost like a cat. Poor, dear Sadie. Beloved Sadie.

"Is Jerry Colina working with you? He is, isn't he? I always hated the bastard." There was a certain grim pleasure in Woz's voice, Charlie realized, that told her that he was enjoying the situation. Out of the corner of her eye, Charlie saw him grind the mouth of the pistol into Jake's neck. She could see the gleam of Jake's teeth as he grimaced. She could see something else, too, she realized: the gleam of Sadie's eyes.

Sadie was huddled in the footwell on Jake's side.

Charlie froze. If Sadie was on Jake's side, *what was rubbing against her leg?*

She glanced down. Something black was twining around the paleness of her jean-clad calf. Something twisty and ropelike and alive. A triangular head was slithering up the pale blue column of her leg toward her knee.

Charlie screamed. No, she shrieked. The sound was earsplitting, window-shattering, heart-attack inducing. No horror film in history had ever recorded a more bloodcurdling screech. Completely forgetting that she was at the wheel of a vehicle traveling at thirty miles an hour over a narrow bumpy track, completely forgetting that there was a gun pointed at her and two armed murderers in the back and a strange man cuffed to her wrist, she shot out of that seat like a ball out of a cannon, flinging herself over the console and onto Jake in an insane effort to dive through his closed window, screaming all the while.

"What the hell!" Jake grabbed her.

"Shut the bitch up! Shoot her!" Denton lunged between the seats. Without even meaning to do it, Charlie kicked him in the face. He fell back.

"Snake! Snake, snake, snake, snake, *snake!*" The snake swarmed toward her crotch, then undulated past her pelvis, moving up her body like it had somewhere to go. Charlie screamed like a steam whistle, kicked like a demented mule, then grabbed the writhing, leathery thing and flung it as hard as she could. Two plus yards of twisting, ropelike reptile flew into the air, smacked against the roof, and disappeared into the backseat.

"Snake!" Woz screamed as horribly as she had done seconds earlier, and kept on screaming to the sound of beating fists and stomping feet.

"Shit! Snake!" Denton was screaming, too, as they both engaged in panic-stricken battle with the snake. A hideous smell suddenly exploded in the air.

The Jeep smacked into a tree. Charlie, still screaming for all she was worth, was thrown forward, hit the side of her head on the dash, and was still seeing stars as she found herself hauled bodily across the seat and out into the cold night air.

"Run, damn it!" Jake yelled as he dragged her upright. Head spinning, gasping now rather than screaming, Charlie needed no further urging. With visions of that hideous black snake slithering after her to spur her on, she ran like the hounds of hell were on her heels. Jake pounded beside her, his hand tight around hers.

Behind them, she could hear the sound of the Jeep's doors opening and Woz and Denton spilling out.

"There's a fucking skunk in there!" Woz shouted, coughing and cursing at the same time.

"And a snake! God, I hate snakes!"

"You fucking pussy, Denton! *I hate snakes!*" Woz mimicked Denton's voice, all the while coughing his lungs out.

"I'm going to puke! That smell. . . ." There was a gagging sound.

"What are you, some sort of pansy-ass? Come on, we can't let them get away."

"Jesus, I'm gonna be sick."

The voices faded as Charlie found herself sliding on her backside down a steep, vine-covered embankment. Jake was slightly in front of her, sliding, too, his hand clamped around hers, his weight pulling her down.

"Sadie," Charlie gasped.

"We've got more to worry about than a damned dog," Jake said as they reached the bottom. He dragged her to her feet. "They've got guns, remember. Be as quiet as you can."

"But they'll kill her."

"Why would they? She's a fucking dog. It's us they want to kill."

With this grim reminder, Charlie found herself running again, dragged along in Jake's wake. The woods were so dark Charlie could barely make out the outlines of trees as they flashed by. The ground underneath was slippery with fallen leaves. The smell of damp was everywhere, and here and there small points of light glowed through the darkness.

Eyes, Charlie thought with a shiver, trying not to think about the kinds of nocturnal creatures they might belong to. The next thought that popped into her head brought faint comfort: nothing, *nothing,* could be as bad as that snake.

Something was behind them, giving chase. Charlie could sense it more than feel it, sense rather than hear the pant of their pursuer's breathing, sense rather than feel the weight of their pursuer's gaze.

It could not be Woz and Denton. They could not have found them so easily in the dark. And they would make more noise, with heavy thundering footsteps and the crashing of their bodies through the undergrowth.

To say nothing of the firing of their guns.

"Jake! Jake!" She tugged on his hand to warn him. Head lowered, he was burning up the ground in front of her, leading the way, either knowing where he was going or giving a good imitation of it.

"What?" It was a growl thrown over his shoulder. His pace never slackened.

"There's something behind us."

He glanced over his shoulder again, and his hand tightened on hers, but before he could respond in any other way a bullet smacked into a tree not two feet from Charlie's head.

"Shit!" Jake altered course, propelling her in a right angle to the shot as another one was squeezed off. This one went thankfully wide, whistling harmlessly through the trees in the same direction as the first.

"Over there!" The voice was Denton's, and it was still some distance behind them. Whatever she had sensed chasing them had been far closer. The crack of a shot and the whoosh of a bullet passing terrifyingly near Charlie's ear put all thoughts of a second pursuing party out of her mind. The first was bad—and close—enough.

"Keep your head down, and move your ass." It was a roar. Jake raced through the trees, leaping over the underbrush and fallen logs that were suddenly underfoot, practically pulling her arm from its socket as he towed her behind him. Bent over like an old woman with a dowager's hump, feet barely touching the ground as she ran and jumped and stumbled and was dragged until she was on her feet and running again, Charlie gasped for air and prayed harder than she had ever prayed in her life. Bullets spat through the air around them, tearing through the leaves, smacking into trunks.

"Get 'em, get 'em, get 'em, get 'em!" Woz howled. Charlie barely heard him over the odd roaring in her ears.

Ahead of her, Jake suddenly stopped, and jerked her up beside him. His hand gripped hers tighter than ever even as her free arm windmilled for balance. Looking ahead, Charlie saw to her horror that they teetered on the brink of a cliff. Some twenty feet below, pushing deep into undercut banks, was a shining black ribbon of rushing water: the Cumberland, Charlie guessed.

No wonder she'd heard a roaring in her ears.

In that instant she realized what he meant to do. Charlie tried to back up, shaking her head in protest.

"I can't—" she began, even as he growled, "Jump!"

She had no choice. He leaped with a death grip on her hand, and, willy-nilly, she went with him as bullets peppered the place where, seconds before, they had stood. Charlie fell like a stone, plummeting through the darkness, limbs flailing as she completed what she had been going to say in a hapless wail.

"—swim!"

6

CHARLIE BELLY FLOPPED with a tremendous splash. Cold dark water closed around her, blinding her, choking her, shooting up her nose, filling her mouth. The shock of submersion galvanized her. Shutting her mouth with a snap, Charlie fought for all she was worth, kicking and thrashing against the life-stealing depths. Still she tumbled like a sock in a washing machine, helpless in this element that had terrified her from the moment she'd fallen into a neighbor's swimming pool as a five-year-old and nearly drowned. That time, just as she'd given up hope, she'd seen an angel, a lovely winged angel dressed all in white, and heard a heavenly chorus sing.

This time there was a big black shape rising like a giant bat beside her and a sudden vicious yank on her arm. She felt as if it was being wrenched from its socket as she was hauled ruthlessly upward. Seconds later her head broke the surface, and she gasped for air.

"Help!" she croaked, or tried to croak, but icy water

spewed from her mouth like flow from a fountain as she struggled madly to keep her head up. Her own saturated hair blinded her and she still had trouble breathing because of all the water she was coughing up. Then she was once again sinking, slipping back down into the liquid abyss that terrified her more than anything in life. Despite her frantic efforts her head went under. She fought the amorphous enemy like a wild thing, kicking and clawing to no avail, only to find herself dragged to the surface again through no effort of her own.

"Hold still!" It was a roar. It had to be a roar, for her to hear it over the sound of her own heart pounding in her ears and the deep gurgle of the water as it rushed past. Charlie realized that Jake was there, right beside her, holding her hand in a steely grip as both of them were swept ruthlessly downstream by the strength of the current. She surged desperately toward him, free arm windmilling, kicking with all the strength left in her legs. They felt heavy, so very heavy, as if lead weights were attached to her feet, pulling her down. Nevertheless, she managed to reach him with that panic-stricken lunge, and locked onto him as the only solid thing in a terrifyingly unsolid world, wrapping her free arm around his neck, trying to climb on top of him in a blind panic that left no room for rational thought.

"God damn it," he began, trying to pry her off him, but whatever came after that she didn't hear. She sank like an anvil. Rather, *they* sank like an anvil, because the death grip she had on him wasn't being shaken off this side of the grave. She clung to his neck like a giant squid to a battleship, and for all his superior strength he couldn't budge her.

Within a minute or so he managed to break the surface again anyway, dragging her up with him. With her mouth and nose above water, she gulped in air. They were cheek to cheek, she discovered, and his was wet and cold and rough as sandpaper.

"Let go of my neck." He was somehow keeping them both afloat despite having her battened onto him like a barnacle and only one free hand to work with. Wrapping her legs around his waist for good measure, she choked and gasped and sucked in lifesaving air as they were swept downstream. "Damn it, you're going to drown us both."

"You're the idiot who jumped in the river." Her hold on him tightened as, using him for a ladder, she tried to climb a little higher out of the maelstrom. Her efforts plunged his head under. She went down, too, despite her best efforts to save herself, and tumbled head over heels as the current spun her around like a child with a ball. Having managed in the course of the past hour to survive two car crashes and the same number of armed killers and a hideously close encounter with a snake, she realized with the kind of mental clarity reserved for only the most extreme situations that she was now face-to-face with a death that was the stuff of her worst nightmares: She was going to drown.

She would never, ever, ever wish for excitement again, she thought despairingly, and managed by dint of pressing down on the closest submerged object—boulder-hard and covered with human hair, she suspected it might be the top of Jake's head—to win through to the surface, and draw air into her tortured lungs.

The surface exploded right in front of her, and Jake's

seal-sleek head shot into view. Coughing, sputtering, he caught both her wrists in a crushing grip as he took a few gasping breaths. Without the boost of his body beneath hers to keep her up, she felt herself being sucked down again, and made a despairing sound just before her head submerged.

As she went under, his grip shifted. Somehow she was spun around, then hauled upward. When her head broke through again, and she coughed and gasped and sucked in air, she found that he was behind her, wrapping their shackled arms around her waist, supporting her with his body.

"All you have to do is lie still!" he yelled in her ear. "Do you hear me? Quit fighting and lie still. I can swim well enough for the both of us if you'll quit trying to drown me."

"Oh, God." Charlie had no strength left to fight anyway. The lead weights dragging her down seemed suddenly less oppressive, and she realized that one of her boots had fallen off. Enlightenment dawned, and she kicked off the other one. Never mind that they were her best boots, made of ostrich skin and costing over five hundred dollars; if she had to lose them to live, lose them she would. Even without them she wouldn't call herself buoyant—she was about as buoyant as a slab of marble—but her body definitely felt lighter.

Bye-bye, boots.

"Just relax. Lie back against me and relax. I won't let you go, I promise. Hell, I can't, remember?" His voice was soothing now—well, as soothing as it was possible for a near-shout to be. With his arm around her waist and his back against hers, Charlie found to her surprise that she was not sinking. The water stayed at chin level, and she could breathe. She could feel his legs moving beneath hers, and his free arm seemed to be moving, too. He was swimming and keeping her afloat.

"I never even go out on boats," she moaned through chattering teeth, unable to believe the situation in which she found herself.

"I've got you. As long as you don't panic, we'll be fine." His tone was reassuring. So was the knowledge that he was handcuffed to her wrist. No matter what happened, he wouldn't be letting her go.

Something that glowed faintly in the darkness floated into her line of vision, rising and falling with the motion of the water. It was pencil thick, and semicircular. . . .

"Hold onto this," Jake instructed, distracting her by shoving a branch the size of an oar in front of her nose. Charlie took one look, and thought *thank you, God!* With his help, she wedged it under her arms, and felt marginally more secure. Between Jake and the branch, she just might survive this nightmare after all.

"Okay, we're heading for dry land. We'll be out of this in just a few minutes. Hang on."

He was towing her steadily toward shore, Charlie saw with a quick glance around. Although it was so dark she could barely differentiate the solidness of the branch from the inkiness of the water, she could tell where shore was: It was that place where the white line of foam bubbled against a grayer shade of night. Looking closer, she realized that the grayer shade belonged to a wall of sheer rock. Even if they reached the riverbank, getting out might prove difficult if that wall of rock was as straight up and down as it looked.

"Jake. Jake, they killed Laura." The imminent prospect of drowning had knocked the horror of it clear out of her head. Now that she felt fractionally more secure, her brain was able to function enough for her to remember.

"What?" He sounded startled.

"They killed Laura. After Woz knocked you unconscious, he shot her. Her head—it—it exploded."

"Jesus." She could feel the arm beneath her breasts tighten. "Stupid sonofabitch, I told him not to get his girlfriend involved. Now they're both dead."

Charlie took deep breaths, trying to expel the hideous image once again. For a few moments both of them were silent, as Charlie did her best to erase her memory banks and Jake concentrated on keeping them afloat. The glowing thing bobbed into view again, closer this time. Successfully distracted, Charlie frowned at it, then realized with a burst of pleased surprise what it was.

"Sadie!" The little dog was swimming valiantly in their wake. The glow Charlie had seen was from the reflector strip on her collar. Now that Charlie knew what to look for, she could see her distinctly. Sadie was stretching her neck, holding her head as high above the surface as she could, her eyes round and black in her pale face. She looked about as drowned and desperate as Charlie felt.

Without thought, Charlie reached out toward her. The branch immediately tried to dislodge itself from beneath her arms, and she grabbed it with a sudden fresh upsurge of panic and clamped it back into place.

"What the hell are you doing? Lie still." Jake sounded breathless. "This is like swimming with a ton of bricks on my chest as it is."

"Sadie!" Charlie tried to coax the dog closer. "Come on, Sadie!"

"Are you deaf? I said *lie still.*"

"It's Sadie! Here, girl!"

"I don't give a damn if it's Madonna. You keep wriggling like that, and we're both going to go under."

The warning terrified her anew. Charlie made a conscious effort to relax her muscles as best she could, letting her head rest back against his broad shoulder while her lower body floated, but she kept her eyes on her dog.

Sadie paddled determinedly, but whether her efforts or the force of the current brought her nearer Charlie couldn't tell. She was almost close enough to grab.

"Look at the damned dog's damned collar." Jake sounded so alarmed that Charlie stiffened instinctively. His arm tightened, and she was reminded to relax. "Look at it! It glows in the dark! No wonder they were able to track us through the woods. The damned dog was following us the whole time. They'll be able to find us in the river, too. Don't call it any closer. Damn it to hell, anyway! Grab it, and let's . . ."

His words were interrupted by what sounded like a firecracker going off. A sudden splash of water hit Charlie in the face.

"Shit!" Jake said. "That was close."

Even as she looked in the direction he was looking in, Charlie heard what sounded like a whole string of firecrackers exploding. Water shot up all around them in frothy white mini-geysers, showering her with spray. From the top of the rocky wall that lined this section of the river, a baseball-size circle of light shone in their direction: a flashlight, she realized. Its beam was a puny thing as it reached over the dark water toward them, but its impact couldn't have been greater if it had been the spotlight that had mesmerized Charlie earlier: Woz and Denton had clearly found them. The geysers were caused by bullets hitting the water. Her pulse, frozen into near nonexistence, began to race anew. Had she thus far survived drowning only to be shot? Or maybe she would be shot, and then drown?

What was this, a hundred and one ways to die? Charlie moaned.

Out of the corner of her eye, she saw Jake grab Sadie, pulling her in. His savage kicks and her death grip on the branch was all that was keeping them afloat. Bullets smacked the water in a sharp, staccato rhythm, kicking up water all around.

At least, she thought semihysterically, she wouldn't die alone. Not that there was much comfort in that.

"Let go," Jake said in Charlie's ear, and to her horror the branch was wrenched from her grasp. She gasped, stiffened, flailed and sank, swallowing what felt like half the river in the process. Jake sank right beside her, but instead of hauling her up again he kept her beneath the surface, holding her down and pulling her along as he swam. He was careful to keep just enough distance between them so that she couldn't latch on to him as she was desperate to do. Lungs aching, eyes wide open but unable to see anything in the frigid darkness, Charlie kicked and clawed at the water with her free hand even as she mentally surrendered to the inevitable: One way or another on this hideous night, she was going to die.

When they surfaced at last, she was so limp with terror and exhaustion and lack of oxygen that she couldn't even latch onto Jake. She gasped and coughed and wheezed, filling her lungs with air, letting him do with her as he would. Once again she found herself with her back to his front and their connected arms beneath her breasts. He was treading water, supporting her, and she leaned her head back against his shoulder and just breathed. None of her senses seemed to be working properly. Even her sense of fear was numbed, which she realized vaguely was probably a good thing. Otherwise she would, by now, probably have been literally scared to death.

However, she could, she realized after a moment or two in which air was the most important thing in the world, still hear. More specifically, she could still hear gun shots, although the sharp pop-pop-pop was fainter than before. That realization caused her to lift her head, brush the soaked hair from her eyes and look around. She could see, too, she discovered, and feel, and even smell. The wind was brisk and cold against her face. The muddy smell of the river was all around her. The intense blackness of the water and the slightly lighter darkness of the shore was interrupted by the faint beam of the flashlight which was now moving away from them. She and Jake had surfaced, Charlie judged, almost in the middle of the channel, and the flashlight seemed to be chasing a pale, glowing semicircle that bobbed up and down as it fled downstream.

Realization was sudden and terrible.

"They're shooting at Sadie!" Charlie gasped with horror, stiffening in spite of herself.

"God damn it." It was a warning growl in her ear as they started to sink, reminding her of the need to remain limp. "They're shooting at the branch. I put the damned dog's collar around it. With any luck, they'll follow it clear into the next county."

"But Sadie . . ."

"Right behind us," Jake said, sounding as if he was talking through clenched teeth. "What is the thing, a damned bloodhound? The way our luck is going tonight, we couldn't lose it if we tried. Think you could kick your feet a little without sinking us both? I'm getting kind of tired here."

That news was so alarming that Charlie found that she could, indeed, kick her feet. Meanwhile, her gaze fastened on Sadie's knobby head stretched cobralike above the water. The killers had been, for the moment at least, thrown off the trail. Now if they could just survive the river . . .

The current was far stronger where they were, Charlie realized after a few minutes. With the water rushing them inexorably downstream, they managed nevertheless to make progress toward the opposite shore. Jake's breathing grew increasingly labored, rasping its own warning against Charlie's ear. Now that she had the hang of it, she kicked fervently, although she could no longer feel her legs. Her teeth were clenched to keep them from chattering. She was so cold that she would have felt warmer sitting in a freezer, and the sad thing was that being cold was the least of her problems.

Thankfully Sadie remained near, fighting the current just as they were, sometimes drawing closer, sometimes being forced farther away. Charlie could not do much to help her pet under the circumstances, but she kept her gaze on her, almost as concerned for Sadie's safety as she was her own.

Another oar-size branch floated past, and she managed to grab it despite Jake's snapped warning to stay still. Wedging it beneath her arm, she felt marginally better. It provided an extra degree of buoyancy that might prove to be the difference between life and death. For Jake as well as herself, she realized. With their wrists handcuffed together, their fates were inexorably entertwined.

In a strange way, she found the knowledge almost comforting—until she considered that it was Jake the bad guys were primarily trying to kill.

She was just, with the worst luck in the world, along for the ride.

7

"TELL ME SOMETHING: What the hell kind of normal adult human being doesn't know how to swim?" Jake growled in her ear, sounding very tired. Charlie had thought his movements were feeling more and more sluggish, and his tone confirmed her estimate of his exhaustion. Their bodies were definitely riding lower in the water, too; her chin was more or less resting on the undulating surface. Her fear was already so acute that it could scarcely grow worse, but it definitely gave off a new, very sharp, pang. Sort of like an appendix that intermittently flared up, warning that it badly needed to come out, before it finally gave up the ghost and burst.

"One who never, ever planned to dip so much as a toe in a river," she said, and swallowed a mouthful of muddy-tasting water for her pains as a surge slapped her in the face. Clinging to his encircling arm for dear life, she coughed the water up. They seemed to be sinking lower with every movement, she realized. Among other problems, most notably her lack of swimming skills, their waterlogged clothes were dragging them down. There was nothing to do about it. Handcuffed as they were, they could not shed the soaked jackets that now seemed heavy as anchors. The only thing they could lose—their pants—didn't weigh enough to make their removal worth the near-death experience that would almost certainly be involved.

"I suppose you'd rather have been shot back there."

"At least I would have died quick."

They were being swept downstream at a far faster pace than they were progressing toward shore. Still, they were getting closer to safety, Charlie saw, twisting around to cast an assessing look over his shoulder at their destination. They had, roughly, another four hundred yards to go. Maybe—please God, please God—they would make it after all.

"Are you *trying* to sink us? Quit squirming."

Something else she had seen in that one quick glance registered on her consciousness: a faint, luminous line on the horizon dead ahead. For a moment Charlie puzzled at it; then, absolutely unable to resist the temptation to do so, she sneaked another, sideways glance that required just barely moving her head. The puzzling white line was still visible. There was no bank in that direction for the river to break against. The banks, a sheer wall of rock behind them and a more forgiving wooded shore ahead, were to the north and south. The new line of foam was to the west. Suddenly the increasingly louder roar which had been filling her ears for some time began to make a certain, terrible sense. The sound, which she had put down to a combination of the normal murmurings of the rain-engorged river and the thundering of her own blood in her ears, had a far more terrifying source.

"There's a waterfall ahead!"

"Just figuring that out, are you?" He sounded as if he were fighting for breath. "If you want specifics, it's about a thirty-foot straight drop onto rocks. I saw it when I checked this place out a couple of weeks back. Think you could kick a little harder?"

"We're going to die," she moaned, kicking so vigorously that the splash she made hit her in the face.

"Not that hard!"

She moderated her kick so that no more water was displaced, but kept her foot action vigorous. They were making steady progress toward shore, another eyeball-rolling glance informed her, but at the rate they were going they weren't going to make it. Already the current was much faster, pulling them along just like the debris swirling past. Its force made simply staying afloat while gaining scant inches per stroke about as much as they could hope for. There was no way to swim any harder. Both she and Jake were doing the best they could. Even Sadie was desperately fighting the current. Close behind them now, pushed against their bodies by the force of the water, Sadie was swimming almost backward, her muzzle pointing upstream. Her eyes were big as quarters and she looked terrified—almost as terrified as Charlie felt.

"Look at it this way," Jake said, his arm tightening around her rib cage as an entire tree rocketed past them, missing them by less than a yard. "Nobody lives forever."

"Oh, that made me feel better." She kicked for all she was worth, muttering every prayer that she, the daughter of a Baptist preacher and a gospel singer, had ever learned in her life. After a moment or two spent praying and kicking, she was interrupted by an amused sounding grunt in her ear.

"You sure know a lot of prayers."

"You should try saying some."

"I don't know any. But yours seem to be working, so keep it up. There's a rock dead ahead. I'm going to let go of you, and we're going to spread out and latch on to it. All you have to do is stay afloat. Ready?"

"No!" He was going to let go of her? No way! No how! She would sink like a stone. She would drown. She would . . .

But he had already let go and was swimming out from underneath her, pushing her away from him so that suddenly she found herself facing forward with him beside her but as far away as the chain would allow him to get. Panicked, Charlie churned her feet like a duck in its death throes, pawed at the water with her chained hand, and prayed as she had never prayed in her life. She was going down. . . . But no. No. She still had the branch, wedged under her left armpit. It was keeping her up. All she had to do was not let go.

At that point, the combined plagues of the Four Horsemen of the Apocalypse couldn't have forced her to let go.

Caught up by the current, she—they—were heading straight for what was to all intents and purposes a tiny island. The centerpiece of it appeared to be a large rock, visible because it was a solid, unmoving charcoal triangle above the oil-black water, and because of the foam that leaped and curled against its base. Logs and a variety of miscellaneous debris had been trapped against it, making it into a small, precariously put together oasis—and their only chance. Latching onto it in their previous position would have been almost impossible. But in their present butterfly formation, they might, just might, be able to snag it.

Another strand of the current caught them up, carrying them wide. Suddenly they were being swept too far to the left.

"No!" Charlie cried.

"Kick! Kick!" The roaring of the water all but drowned out Jake's words. He surged toward the rock with a mighty one-armed stroke, towing her after him. She kicked frantically in an effort to do her part. All at once, while still about three feet short, they were level with the rock, passing it, going to miss it altogether. . . .

Jake hurled himself across the surface of the water like a flying fish and latched on to the outermost branch of the outermost log. Charlie could see the paleness of his hand closing around the dark wet bark as, despite kicking for all she was worth, she was carried on downstream. Would his one-handed grip be strong enough to hold them? Would the forearm-sized branch break? The falls were so close she could have thrown a rock and it would have gone over, she discovered with a single terrified glance over her shoulder. She could feel the current tugging at her like a giant vacuum, intent on sucking her down.

Sadie, still paddling frantically upstream, swept past.

"Sadie!" Without thought, Charlie lunged for her pet, knowing the dog faced almost certain death if she did not catch her. Her clutching hand closed over one fragile front leg. The branch wedged under her armpit shot free and was gone, just as quick as that. Charlie didn't even have time to feel horrified. Gasping, kicking, flailing, hanging onto Sadie with every scrap of determination she possessed, she sank. The water was merciless, swallowing her up like a giant mouth, shutting off air and hope. She clawed for the surface, for air—and felt a powerful jerk on her right arm.

Jake! Thank God for Jake! He was reeling her in. Her head broke the surface, and she gulped in sweet, blessed, lung-filling air as he pulled her toward him. Kicking for all she was worth, still maintaining her death grip on Sadie, she wrapped her fingers around the reassuringly thick bones of Jake's wrist and then, when she was close enough, practically swarmed atop him, locking her free arm around his neck. He felt reassuringly big and solid, her own private rock, and she was never, ever going to let him go again this side of dry land.

"You almost got us killed! Over a damned dog!" With one arm hooked over the branch, he kept them both afloat as she pressed her shaking body to his. He was as wet and cold as she was, and in as precarious a position, too, but his shoulders were broad and his chest was wide and his arms were strong, and, reasonably or not, Charlie felt safe in his hold. She pressed her cheek to his wet bristly one and clung, coughing and sputtering, as she fought to clear her lungs. Sadie, dear Sadie, scrambled free of her grip and up over her arm and shoulder to stand, trembling, completely clear of the water, on the uprooted tree which had saved them.

"She would have drowned if I hadn't grabbed her."

Each word was punctuated by a choking cough. She was numb with cold and boneless with exhaustion, and if he hadn't been holding her up she feared she would have just slithered down into the water like not-quite-set gelatin.

"Better the dog than us. For your information, when you grabbed her, I almost lost my grip on this tree. If I had, we would have gone over the falls." His voice was grim, but his breath fluttering past her ear was surprisingly warm and comforting.

"I'm sorry, okay?" Charlie coughed some more, pressing her cheek closer to his, greedy for even the meager warmth generated by this small area of skin-to-skin contact. Sadie, secure in the knowledge that the worst of the ordeal was now behind them, chose that moment to shake the water from her coat. Unfortunately, Jake got the brunt of the shower right in the face. When he opened his eyes again, he was scowling.

"I think that's called adding insult to injury. You're pushing your luck, dog."

This was addressed to Sadie, uttered half under his breath and on such a sour note that Charlie, feeling safer than she had for some minutes, almost smiled.

And why not? The situation wasn't good, but it was at least stable. The man she clutched was reassuringly solid, the thugs were off on a wild-goose chase somewhere downstream, and suddenly the odds of surviving the night appeared to have improved to something at least a little better than zero. As ridiculous as it seemed, that combination of factors made her suddenly feel almost euphoric.

The thought that she might actually be going to live was intoxicating. Maybe she would get a chance to wear that new dress and sing with Marisol at the Yellow Rose after all.

Or maybe not. Reality hit right along with a cold splash of water in the face. Charlie was reminded that her nonswimming self was still trapped in the middle of a rushing river only a few hundred yards above a deadly falls, hanging on for dear life to a stranger whom a pair of really bad guys were doing their best to kill.

If her odds of survival had increased, it was only because they had been so low to begin with. They were still so bad that no gambler worth his salt would touch them with a ten-foot pole.

"What now?" she asked, pulling her head back so that she could look at him. She couldn't see much of him in the darkness, but what she could see—and feel—gave her a tiny spurt of hope. He was exactly the kind of hard-muscled man's man who would know what to do in all manly situations. She bet he knew how to fix car engines and repair roofs and grill steaks outdoors. She knew for a fact that already tonight he'd jumped out of a plane, dodged a hail of bullets and swum more than halfway across a river with her dead weight attached. Right at this very moment, he was probably formulating a plan for their salvation.

"Got me," her hero answered.

"Great." Her bubble of burgeoning hope deflated like a pricked balloon.

"If you've got any suggestions, I'm all ears."

Charlie glanced around. The utter impossibility of remedying their situation was clear. "I don't."

"Look on the bright side: We're not dead yet."

"*Yet* is the key word here, I think."

"Regular little optimist, aren't you? All right, let go of my neck and hold onto the tree instead. I want to see what's on the other side of this rock, and to do that we have to move."

8

CHARLIE WASN'T HAPPY about letting go, but it was beginning to occur to her that hypothermia could probably be added to the list of ways she might reasonably expect to die tonight, right up there along with being shot and drowning. They had to get out of the water soon. She wasn't even shivering much any longer, and that, she knew, was a bad sign. With Jake's support she turned, hooked the arm that had been around his neck over the branch, then inched herself along in his wake. The tree seemed to be solidly wedged, she noted gratefully. It didn't budge despite their shifting grip, or the force of the water pushing against it. Sadie trotted along above their heads, careful to stay well clear of the water while keeping pace.

"Are you really a cop?" Charlie asked, grasping at any straw of hope she could think of as they made it to the other side of the pile of trapped debris. Jake was looking toward the bank as if he were contemplating the possibility of swimming for it. Not in this life, Charlie thought, and definitely not with her attached. No way. No how. In her opinion, dying of exposure was better than drowning. Anything was better than drowning.

"DEA." His tone was absent. He was still looking in a measuring way toward shore.

"Then don't you have any little DEA buddies around here somewhere who might come charging to the rescue about now?"

"Nope." He glanced around at her then, and grinned suddenly. She could see the faint gleam of his teeth through the darkness. "Sorry, Charlie."

"Oh, funny." She had heard that one so often that it had ceased to amuse about ten years back. "Why not?"

"Because none of my little DEA buddies, as you call 'em, has any idea that anything's gone wrong here. As far as my guys know, this operation is going down exactly as planned."

"Fantastic," Charlie said. "Were you supposed to be undercover or something? What were you going to do if something went wrong—as it obviously has? Didn't you have a Plan B?"

"Working on it."

"Care to share your thoughts?"

"You ever hear that old saying about curiosity killing the cat?"

Charlie snorted, and glanced meaningfully around. "Curiosity's going to have to get in line."

He grinned again. "Yeah, well, being in the wrong place at the wrong time works, too. Do you always drive alone through remote areas of the country in the middle of the night, by the way? It's just a suggestion, but you might want to rethink that."

"I was working," Charlie said through lips that were starting to feel alarmingly stiff.

"What do you do, run a traveling animal act? Not that I'm complaining, mind you, but driving around with a snake and a skunk—to say nothing of that pitiful excuse for a dog—doesn't sound like any job I ever heard of."

"I was releasing animals into the wild." That sounded commendably noble. It was also the literal truth. But Charlie had been brought up to tell the whole truth, so she reluctantly continued. "My sister just bought a company called County-wide Critter Ridders. People hire them to rid their houses, or barns, or whatever, of wild animals that have somehow managed to get in. Tonight Marisol—my sister—had something else to do, so she asked me if I'd drive the animals to Cheatham Wildlife Management Area and let them go. That's what I was doing. Getting involved with this—with *you*—was just bad luck."

"Yeah, well, your luck doesn't seem to be getting any better." Surprisingly, his voice was grim again. "Look upriver."

Charlie did, and her eyes widened. A bright light, the same kind of light that had first attracted her attention on the road, was just visible through the trees. It obviously came from some kind of aircraft, and it was just as obviously scanning the river.

"Could somebody have called the police?" she asked on a last, forlorn hope.

" 'Fraid not. Woz must have called for reinforcements. That's a helicopter."

"Looking for us?"

"Yep. They can't afford to let us get away, you know. We know too much, and they'll do whatever it takes to make sure we don't live to tell the tale. I wouldn't be surprised if there isn't a boat coming, too."

Charlie glanced wildly all around. Where they were, the river was about a quarter of a mile wide. The light seemed to be moving methodically from side to side. There was no way it wasn't going to see the rock jutting up from the glossy black surface of the water—and if it found the rock, it would find them.

"Oh, my God, what do we do?" Panic sharpened her voice.

"Only one thing to do: Swim for it."

"No! Oh, no!" She shook her head vigorously. "You know we can't make it to shore. The waterfall's too close and . . ."

Her voice broke off abruptly as Jake took a deep breath and disappeared underwater. For a moment Charlie could only stare in horror at the place where he had been. At any second she expected him to yank her down, too. There were several tugs on her handcuffed arm, but they were relatively benign, as though he was moving around. After the first one, she stopped paying attention anyway. She hung onto the branch like a monkey in a hurricane while her gaze fastened on the spotlight which was drawing ever closer. As she watched, wide-eyed, the helicopter itself appeared around a bend in the river. It was flying low, perhaps only a few hundred feet above the surface, and the whirr of the blades could now be heard distinctly even above the rushing water. The spotlight moved from side to side like a great all-seeing eye. In minutes it would be upon them. With her heart pounding so fiercely that she could feel each slamming beat, Charlie gave a sharp tug on the chain linking her to Jake. Seconds later he popped back into view, shaking water from his head and sucking in air.

"Jake, Jake, look! They're getting really close. There's no way they're going to miss us. We're out of time."

"Yeah, I see." He barely glanced at the oncoming helicopter. Instead, his gaze fixed on her face. "Charlie, listen: There's a tree wedged against this one that stretches out toward the bank. We're going to go underwater and hang on to it as far as we can, and then we're going to shove off hard with our feet and hope that the little extra boost that gives us brings us close enough to the bank so that we can make it. We're going to stay under until the helicopter passes, and we're going to have to take the dog under with us. If we leave it here, they'll spot it and it will give us away. All I want you to do is hang on to the dog, and leave everything else to me."

"I really don't want to do this." The prospect of leaving their safe haven terrified her. The shore was close, but the falls were closer, and the current was strong and swift.

"We don't have any choice."

He was already scooping Sadie up and handing her over. Charlie accepted her blissfully ignorant pet because there was nothing else she could do, and cradled the shivering dog close. A glance upriver and the increasing volume of the roaring in her ears confirmed that the helicopter was still there, its spotlight sweeping pitilessly from side to side.

Clearly, somebody upstairs was having a huge laugh at her expense.

"Here we go. Take a deep breath, hang onto the dog, and trust me, baby. We're going to make it."

With that he submerged. Charlie only had time to take a terrified breath that wasn't nearly as deep as she'd meant for it to be before he was pulling her under after him. The icy depths claimed her once again. Her heart was pumping so fast that a heart attack seemed like a foregone conclusion. She could feel Sadie's heart thudding, too. She had the little dog tucked under her arm like a football with her hand clamped over her muzzle. Did dogs know to hold their breath? Sadie seemed to. Caught up by the current, Charlie's hair wrapped sea-weedlike around her face, covering her eyes, her nose, her mouth. Not that there was any need to use any of those organs. She could neither see, nor breathe, nor speak. She could only hang onto Sadie and trust in God and Jake as he pulled her with surprising speed through the water. She kicked, and gripped the slippery wood of the submerged log with the hand that was chained to his, but on her own she would have been swept away, she knew. The river was just too powerful. The current sucked at her feet, her legs, her body, drawing her toward the falls and certain death.

A sudden brightening of the depths made her eyes widen. It was only then that she realized they were open, and had been all along. The water around her was lit from above, turning a clear golden brown that was aswirl with twigs and clumps of mud. She could see Sadie's bug-eyed and terrified expression as her tiny paws paddled frantically, and Jake's big black shape in front of her, his hair standing on end as he pulled them along the log, and the solid gray cylinder of the fallen tree itself. All that she glimpsed in an instant, as if a camera had flashed, illuminating the scene. Then the light was gone, moving on, and she realized that the spotlight, and the helicopter with it, had just passed them by.

Without warning, Jake pulled her close, and his arm locked around her waist. An instant later she felt his legs bunch and then give a powerful thrust as, having reached the root of the tree, he abandoned their protector and launched them defenseless into the maelstrom. Hanging grimly onto Sadie, she kicked, but there was no doubt that Jake was propelling them both. Not that he seemed to be accomplishing much. They were being swept sideways despite everything he could do. The river had them at its mercy now; their best efforts were puny against its strength. Any minute, any second, she feared to feel the world dropping away beneath her, and herself going with it, shooting out into space, falling, falling, to drown or be crushed at the foot of the falls.

In seconds fear took a backseat to a more immediate need. Her lungs were bursting. She needed air. She had to breathe or die. Sadie, obviously in like distress, was struggling in her arms. Thrashing her legs, tugging frantically on her shackled wrist in an attempt to signal Jake, Charlie fought to surface. Her side crashed into something hard, and then her head was above water and she was gasping, coughing, drinking in air, lifting Sadie so that the little dog, too, might breathe. They had fetched up against another rock, she saw, blinking, and saw too that Jake stood—stood!—no more than chest deep in front of her. He grabbed the back of her jacket and hauled her to her feet. Knees shaking, still clutching

Sadie, Charlie threw herself against him, clutching the soaking front of his coat in both hands as if she never meant to let go again.

"Hey, we made it." His arm came around her waist, hugging her close. Charlie's head was bent, and her forehead rested against his broad shoulder. It was a luxury, a wonderful, unimaginable luxury, to feel solid ground beneath her feet, and be able to breathe. A sideways glance showed her that the rock she had hit jutted like a finger about three feet out from the bank, and that without it they probably would have been swept over the falls, which were now no more than a hundred yards away. The helicopter with its spotlight was still visible, but it was moving away from them, continuing the search downriver. For the moment, at least, they were safe.

"Thank you, God," she muttered devoutly.

"Come on, let's get out of here." Taking Sadie from her, gripping her hand tightly, he started sloshing toward shore, pulling her behind him. Even with the rock to lean against, the current was strong and the footing was uneven. Her knees were still unreliable, and her stocking feet slithered and slid. It was hard to keep from falling, but Charlie managed it. If she could help it, she was never going to be submerged in water again, not even in the bath.

"Did we time that right or what?" Jake was climbing the rocky bank now toward the thick pine woods beyond, hanging onto Sadie and pulling Charlie behind him. He paused to nod upriver. Charlie looked, and felt her heart give a great leap of fear. Just as he had predicted, a boat was on the river. Its running lights and the powerful hum of its motor were unmistakable. It was small, an aluminum fishing boat perhaps, and coming downstream fast. Undoubtedly it was looking for them.

"They're better equipped than an army." Despair almost dropped her to her knees. She had no strength left to struggle on. Her muscles were as limp as wet shoelaces. Her bones seemed nonexistent. Her soaked jacket and jeans were unbelievably heavy and cumbersome. She was so wet water poured from her in streams, so cold goose bumps were racing along every square inch of her skin, and suddenly totally devoid of willpower. Jake the indefatigable dragged her on, hauling her up the slippery bank in his wake until the scent of pine replaced the muddy smell of the river and the first few feet of a thick growth of old forest stood between them and the unseen eyes of those on the boat.

Then he pulled her to him, and let her rest against his strength while she caught her breath.

"They are an army. A renegade army with one purpose: to make money. We're talking billions and billions of dollars here. This group is just one small branch of an enormous tree. And with what I know, we can start chopping that tree down."

"Always hoping you live to tell it."

He grinned. "Yeah, well, there is that. If we can keep alive until morning, though, we've got a shot. Come six A.M., my guys are staging a raid on the farm where the stuff we dropped tonight was supposed to end up. When they find out I'm not there, they'll come looking. I figure it'll take 'em maybe two, three hours after that to get out here, tops."

"So all we have to do is survive for, what, another

eight hours?" Charlie's tone made it clear that she thought it was an impossible task.

He lifted the wrist that was manacled to hers, and checked his watch. The faintly luminous blue glow as he pushed a button drew her eyes.

"No more than five or so. It's three seventeen."

"Piece of cake." The sarcasm was unmistakable.

He chuckled. "You're still alive, aren't you? I mean to keep us both that way. Trust me."

Charlie sighed. Under the circumstances, what choice did she have?

"Okay, I trust you. So what do we do now?"

9

WALK WAS THE ANSWER TO THAT, it seemed. Walk until Charlie had lost all sense of time and direction, until she was staggering like Frankenstein's monster through the tangled growth that covered the forest floor, until she wished her poor abused feet were once again numb as they were bruised and pricked and stubbed by countless rocks and sticks and brambles and who knew what else underfoot. Walk up a slope that was growing ever steeper. Walk until she was gasping with every breath she took, until the muscles in her legs ached, until she was ready to collapse with exhaustion. The only good thing she could say about all that walking was that it was probably keeping her from freezing to death. The temperature was in the forties, the wind was strong enough to intermittently shower them with dislodged pine needles, and the water weighing down her wet clothes seemed to have turned into about two tons of icy slush.

"Do you have any idea where we're going?"

"Maybe." He didn't even glance back, just strode

relentlessly on. He was in his stocking feet, too, his boots having been lost to the river just as hers had been, but if his feet were being systematically tortured he gave no sign of it. His fingers were entwined with hers and the warmth of his hand was appreciated, but that hold she could have broken. It was the unbreakable link of the thrice-cursed handcuffs that kept her on her feet. That, and the knowledge that Woz and Denton and who knew how many others were fanned out behind them, pulling out all the stops to find and kill them before they could make it to safety.

"Is it a secret?" There was an edge to her voice when he didn't elaborate.

"Are you always this sarcastic, or am I just getting lucky tonight?"

"Look, pal, I'm scared out of my mind and soaking wet and freezing to death and hurting in places I didn't even know I had and I lost my brand-new, five hundred dollar ostrich-skin boots in the river, which means I'm tromping around here next door to barefoot and my feet are being cut to ribbons and the whole thing is basically all your fault, so if I were you I wouldn't mess with me."

"I figured that sooner or later you'd get around to blaming all this on me." The long-suffering-male tone of his reply made her long to bop him in the back of the head. Lucky for him she didn't have the energy.

"If the shoe fits . . ."

"You're the one with no better sense than to go driving into a deserted area all by your lonesome in the middle of the night."

"Well, *you're* the one who parachuted out of an airplane and crashed into the roof of my car and made me wreck and . . ."

"That was Skeeter," he interrupted mildly.

"Oh, that's right," she said with bite. "*You* just mistook me for poor Laura, and dragged me into a fouled-up drug bust I'd much rather not know anything about, and nearly got me murdered, and . . ."

"I'm also the one who saved your life. Who towed your fanny all the way across that river, hmm?"

"Who made me jump into it in the first place? And anyway, I saved your life first. Remember the snake?"

"Oh, yeah, I remember it. Does screaming and wrecking a car because a snake is crawling up your leg count as saving somebody's life, do you think?"

"You're alive, aren't you?"

"So are you. So I'd say we're even."

"Well, I wouldn't. And I'm tired of walking. My feet hurt, and I need to rest."

Having come to an overturned tree, Charlie plopped down upon it without further ado. She was tired and cross and frightened and freezing times about a thousand each, and all she wanted to do was go home.

Fat chance.

The handcuffs worked both ways, she discovered. He was forced to stop walking when she sat. He backtracked, and Sadie was abruptly plopped into her lap. He'd been carrying the little dog, because Charlie needed all her energy to walk and he feared, despite Charlie's assurances to the contrary, that Sadie might go running off and somehow give them away. Fed up with his attitude toward her and her dog, Charlie cuddled Sadie close. In a burst of mutual feminine pique, they both glared up at the man who towered over them.

"Damn it. . . ." He broke off, snapped his teeth together, and ran his hand through his hair. "Charlie, look: There's a cabin around here close. Just over the top of this ridge, I think. When we get there, you can rest. If we're really lucky, there might even be a telephone. We can call for help."

Charlie's eyes widened as she took that in. A fresh little bud of hope surfaced inside her like the earliest crocus nosing up against a still-thick layer of crusty snow. Cabin, rest, phone—it all sounded amazingly good—in fact, too good to be true.

"How do you know?" she asked suspiciously. It was probably just a ploy to get her on her feet again, and make her keep walking. She was beginning to know how he operated.

"Because I had this whole area scoped out as soon as I found out they meant to use it as a drop zone. Aerial photos, maps, the whole works. Sometimes knowing the lay of the land can mean the difference between life and death."

That was so obviously true in this case that Charlie didn't reply. Instead she rallied her uncooperative body enough to stand up. The lure of a cabin was irresistible.

"Lead on," she said.

"Attagirl."

He scooped Sadie up, his hand closed around hers again, and he was off, once again pulling her through the dark woods at a killer pace while she hobbled along in his wake as best she could. If there was pursuit, she could neither see nor hear it. The darkness was breached by no more than an occasional glowing pair of eyes, and the only sounds besides the ones they made were the wind rustling through the treetops and the cries of nocturnal animals.

Just when Charlie thought she could not take another step, there it was in front of them, just as Jake had promised: a cabin, foursquare and solid, nestled at the foot of a trio of tall pines. It was small, dark, and deserted-looking, about the size, perhaps, of a one-story detached garage, with a dirt road or track approaching it from the north and ending right in front of where they stood. As eager as a starving man suddenly presented with a feast, Charlie was all for rushing right inside. Jake, curse him, had to circle the place twice, staying well back in the trees, studying it from every angle.

"I'm dying here," Charlie finally protested through chattering teeth when he seemed ready to begin the circuit yet again.

"Not if I can help it." His hand gripped hers more tightly, and he glanced down at her, then relented. "All right. Come on."

To her relief, he headed straight toward the front, and only, door. Two wooden steps led onto a narrow covered porch. The door, which seemed to be made of wood with a glass insert, was in the center. He passed Sadie over, then, while Charlie waited, jiggling with impatience, he knocked softly, then tried the knob. When that didn't work, he turned, and without a word drove his elbow through the lowest of the six glass panes. The sound of shattering glass made Charlie jump. By the time she recovered, he had already thrust his hand through the hole he had made, and was unlocking the door.

"Watch the glass," he said, opening it and heading inside.

"Isn't this called breaking and entering? What if there's a burglar alarm?" she asked nervously, not having previously considered this aspect of it. Shivering, wet clothes squelching with every step, stepping carefully because the last thing her poor feet needed was to be cut by broken glass, she followed him inside.

"We couldn't get so lucky."

Good point. The idea of a convoy of police cars converging on the cabin was enough to make her heart go pitter-patter. But it wasn't going to happen, of course. Frowning, she put Sadie on the floor. The little dog stayed close at her heels.

"Is there a phone?" Charlie asked, straightening.

"How can I tell? It's darker than hell. But I don't think so. In case you didn't notice, there weren't any utility lines around outside." He had stopped just a few feet inside the door, and seemed to be working on getting his bearings in the nearly pitch dark. Charlie was, perforce, right behind him.

A faint musty smell enveloped her, and it was even darker inside than out, but at least the cabin was warmer than the woods. Now that she was out of the wind, Charlie realized just how strongly it had been blowing. She shivered, then found she couldn't stop. If she didn't already have hypothermia, it would be a miracle. Never in her life could she remember being so cold. What she wanted more than anything else on earth—except to go home—was a hot bath and dry clothes.

"I don't think there's any electricity either." Her hand had been groping the rounded log surface of the wall beside the door, instinctively searching for a light switch, but she found nothing.

"I'm not surprised. I think whoever owns this must use it as kind of a hunting camp. I doubt if there's even running water, or any heat except maybe a woodstove."

"Can we . . . ?" At the alluring image this brought to mind, she momentarily perked up.

"Nope. Smoke."

"Right." She drooped, wrapping her free arm around herself in a futile attempt to seek warmth. Since her arm was as wet and cold as the rest of her, it didn't help.

Jake closed the door, and started hauling her about the cabin after him as he subjected the premises to a search with the aid of the luminous blue dial of his wristwatch. It was no more than a single room, perhaps twelve by fourteen feet, lacking even a bathroom and furnished with what seemed to be the barest of necessities. Stumbling blindly in his wake, Charlie finally stubbed her toe on a metal furniture leg, cried out, and decided to call a halt right there. Feeling for the cause of her pain, she discovered a bed, and sank down on the corner of it, already anticipating the jerk on her wrist as he was forced to stop. She could sense rather than see his frown as he turned.

"That's it," she said, narrowing her eyes at him although she was aware that it was too dark for him to see her expression. "I'm not moving another inch. I stubbed my toe, and I'm putting you on notice right now that you owe me a pair of five hundred dollar, black, ostrich-skin cowboy boots."

"You want to blame me? Fine." His impatience was obvious in his tone.

Ignoring his looming presence, no longer caring one whit if he didn't like what she was doing, she pulled the thin trouser sock from her damaged foot and massaged her throbbing toe. Jake loomed for a second or two longer, then apparently abandoned all thought of intimidating her into motion and moved toward the head of the bed. He stopped before he had quite reached the end of his tether but far enough away to cause her arm to hang in the air. Ignoring this indignity, Charlie heard the sound of a drawer being opened. Not that she cared. Her toe really hurt.

"Bingo," he said.

A sudden brightness made her blink. Startled, Charlie glanced around. Jake had found a flashlight, and was aiming its beam at the floor. By its light, she could see several things: cheap gray-flecked linoleum rendered even more unappealing by Jake's muddy footprints smeared across it, his big feet in their black socks, and part of the metal bedframe, box spring and thin ticking-stripe mattress of the bare bed on which she sat.

"Oh, goody." If her response was unenthused, it was because she felt unenthused. She'd gotten excited when he said *bingo,* expecting some really momentous discovery such as a working telephone, and in that context a flashlight just didn't cut it. Looking at it disparagingly, she bethought herself of something and felt a renewed upsurge of fear. "Won't they see the light?"

"It's not bright enough. Anyway, the windows all have blinds." He had already moved on to a chest beside the bed. Charlie gave a long-suffering sigh as her arm was stretched in a different direction, and pulled the sock from her other foot. This one tingled and throbbed too, and ached as if deeply bruised when she rubbed it.

"Hey, look at this."

Something landed on the bed behind her. Charlie glanced around. After the flashlight, she didn't expect much. Jake was already walking toward her, and the flashlight played over his find: a pair of oversize brown plaid bermuda shorts, some ratty-looking gray sweatpants, a faded green flannel shirt big enough to serve as a tent, and a moth-eaten blue blanket.

"Feel like slipping into something more comfortable?"

Her upsurge of enthusiasm suddenly fell flat.

"You're forgetting the handcuffs," she said. Showing her dry clothes when she couldn't get them on was rather like strewing seed just outside a hungry bird's cage: cruel.

"No, I'm not. How could I?" He crouched in front of her, placing the flashlight on the floor so that the beam provided just enough illumination to allow them to see each other and the small circle of their immediate surroundings. With a flicker of surprise, Charlie watched him pull a screwdriver and a hammer from the pocket of his soaked black coat.

"They were in the drawer with the flashlight," he said in answer to her look. "There are more tools, too, but these are what we need. Get down here on the floor, and let's see if I can get these handcuffs off."

The thought was so alluring that, for the first time in quite a while, Charlie moved with alacrity. She slid off the bed onto her knees. Sadie, who'd been sitting at her

feet, sidled under the bed, where she lay down, propping
her muzzle on her paws and watching the proceedings
with apparent interest. Jake paid no attention to their
audience as he positioned Charlie's hand flat on the
linoleum, then maneuvered the screwdriver until the
business end was wedged into the place where the chain
was linked with the cuff.

"Don't move now."

Before Charlie had quite worked out the implications of that, he brought the hammer down on the head
of the screwdriver with enough force to jar her bones all
the way from her wrist to her teeth—and split the link
cleanly in two. She snatched her newly freed hand out of
harm's way, shook it in an attempt to get rid of the
tingly feeling that ricocheted back down from her teeth
to the ends of her fingers, and stared at him with real
approval.

"Jake," she said, impressed. "You're a god."

"Well, I like to think so," he replied with becoming
modesty, then grinned and stood up, stretching his arms
wide. She stood up, too, and immediately shrugged out
of her soaked suede jacket. It landed on the floor with a
wet-sounding plop. Getting rid of it felt wonderful. She
had not realized how heavy it was until her shoulders
were suddenly free of the burden.

Jake had stopped stretching and was frowning at her.
"You're as blue as a Smurf."

"Yes, well, freezing to death does seem to have that
effect on people, I've heard."

Paradoxically, the tartness of her voice seemed to
ease his concern.

"Here, get those wet clothes off and put these on." He

reached behind her, picked up the shirt and sweats, and thrust them at her.

Charlie took them with fingers that felt clumsy because they were still so cold, then hesitated, glancing up at him. What was left was slim pickings. "What about you?"

"I'll make do with the shorts and blanket. That way, if we end up hitchhiking, it won't be any trouble for me to stick out a leg." He smiled then, a funny, charming smile, with his mouth turning up crookedly and his eyes crinkling. It occurred to Charlie with some force that he was one hot, sexy guy. "Don't argue. Strip."

She frowned. "Turn around."

Dazzling as the idea of dry clothes was, she was not stripping with him just standing there watching. Especially not after the unsettling little epiphany she'd just had.

There was the way he was looking at her, too. His gaze was moving over her with an arrested expression as if he were really seeing her for the first time. Glancing down at herself, she realized that her black T-shirt with the Sugar Babes legend was wet through, and clung to the firm globes of her breasts like a second skin. Her nipples were hardened and puckered from the cold, and thrust boldly through the stretchy cotton and the flimsy nylon bra that covered them. His gaze lingered on her breasts for a moment, she noticed, then slid swiftly down over her slim waist, narrow hips, and long, slender legs.

Charlie's eyes widened and her mouth went dry as it occurred to her that her partner in extreme survival was checking her out.

When his gaze lifted seconds later and their eyes met, the expression in his made her heart skip a beat. Raw sexual heat flared out at her before he abruptly turned his back.

"So strip already," he said in a tone that was faintly grim. "And hurry up. Under the circumstances it's not smart to spend too much time in one place."

10

"WANT TO EXPLAIN *SUGAR BABES?*"

It was the first thing he'd said to her in the minute or so that had passed since he'd started undressing. During that time, he had shed his coat and shirt—it was a pullover sweatshirt, Charlie had discovered, watching with fascination as he tugged it over his head—and he was currently in the process of unbuckling his belt. The question was directed at her without his ever looking around. Charlie was so mesmerized by the striptease taking place in front of her that it took her a couple of seconds to realize that he was talking about the writing on her T-shirt.

"Oh—I'm a singer. My sister and I perform as the Sugar Babes." His back was magnificent, she thought. Really, really magnificent. Broad shouldered and deeply tanned, with muscles that flexed every time he moved, it was mouthwatering enough that just looking at it made her forget that she was supposed to be removing her own wet clothes as well.

"Older or younger sister?" His biceps flexed as he stood on first one foot and then the other to pull off his socks. They were great biceps, she thought. The kind of biceps that women salivate over.

"Older. There are only the two of us. And my mom. My dad died five years ago." Realizing that he was almost finished undressing and she hadn't even started, Charlie hurriedly pulled her T-shirt over her head and dropped it on the floor. Unbelievably, she was even colder without the soaked shirt than she had been with it. Fortunately her hair was very nearly dry. Shaking it back from her face, rubbing her hands briskly up and down her goose-pimpled arms, she cast him a quick look to make sure that his back stayed firmly turned—not that the idea of being naked in front of him didn't turn her on, because it did, but she barely knew the man, after all, and she didn't think she was quite ready to take that particular step—then discarded her bra and pulled on soft, dry flannel.

It was pure bliss.

"So how old are you?" he asked.

"Twenty-seven. What about you?"

"Thirty-four."

"Old man." She said it teasingly.

With another quick look at him, she shed her jeans along with her panties, then quickly pulled her knees up to her chest inside the voluminous shirt, which covered her well enough in that position so that only her small bare toes peeked out.

"Try thinking of it as experienced."

Was that a subtle come-on? Charlie wondered, and at the idea her heart rate increased. She discovered that she liked the idea of him coming on to her. Then an unmistakeable sound distracted her, and she looked up to find that he had unzipped his pants, and was shucking them with as much nonchalance as if he'd been alone, revealing an athlete's toned physique. He was wearing a pair of dark colored boxer briefs that clung to his narrow hips and muscular thighs like a second skin. Of course, they were probably as wet as the rest of him, she realized, which would account for how very faithfully they molded his flesh. He moved then, stepping out of his pants, and she had an excellent view of a tight, well-muscled masculine backside in motion.

She was, she realized, starting to feel a little warmer.

"Charlie." He glanced around then, frowning, and Charlie realized that he must have asked her a question she hadn't heard. She was, in fact, staring at his tush, and he had caught her at it. His eyes narrowed at her, and she frantically searched her mind for what he had last said. Whatever it was, if she had even heard it, it eluded her now.

"What?" she asked, defeated. She *definitely* was feeling warmer.

"I thought you and your sister trapped wild animals, or something." He was stepping into the oversize Bermudas.

"*I* don't. She does. I was just helping out for tonight," she said, hurrying to finish buttoning up the shirt before he could turn around and see that she was not quite done and guess the reason why. Really, getting all those little buttons into their holes was not easy with fingers made clumsy by—well, she preferred to think it was the cold. "Marisol—my sister—asked me to cover for her tonight so that she could celebrate her boyfriend's birthday."

"So you actually make a living by singing?" The Bermudas were so big that they threatened to drop straight back down to the floor the minute he let them go. Charlie looked on with interest as he bent to retrieve his belt from the soaked black pants. Really, watching all those muscles ripple was entertainment worth paying for.

It was only when he straightened and started threading his belt through the loops on the Bermudas that she remembered that he'd asked her a question. Exhaustion had to have something to do with her lack of concentration, she told herself. And her racing pulse and the weakness in the pit of her stomach that happened when she looked at him, as well. His wasn't the first male body she had seen, after all.

Although she had to admit that it might well be the best.

"Nothing very lavish." She grimaced, thinking of the small amount she actually took home each week. "I sing backup for various studio bands during the day, and at night I perform wherever I can get a gig, or wherever Marisol and I—the Sugar Babes—can get a gig. We're singing Saturday at the Yellow Rose."

A hint of pride touched her voice as she said that last. Along music row, a job at the Yellow Rose was considered pretty prestigious. Then she remembered that she might not be around to sing on Saturday at the Yellow Rose, and that effectively distracted her from the sudden attack of the hots she seemed to be experiencing for Jake.

"Maybe I'll come see," he said, turning around. The Bermudas clung to his hips by nothing more than the grace of God and the good offices of his belt and reached well below his knees. He would have looked utterly ridiculous if it had not been for his truly gorgeous physique. Just looking at his chest was enough to infect her with the hots for him all over again, Charlie discovered. Wide and well-muscled, with a thick wedge of black hair, it tapered in a classic vee-shape from his shoulders to his narrow athlete's hips.

She wanted to touch it, to run her hands over the firm muscles, to thread her fingers through the mat of hair so badly that her toes curled.

"Always assuming we'll be alive Saturday." She said it flippantly, partly to remind herself of the direness of their circumstances and partly to remind him. His words, plus the heated glint in his eyes as they moved over her, told her pretty conclusively that she wasn't the only one dealing with a sudden bad case of lust.

Not that good girl Charlie Bates was going to do anything about it, of course. It just wasn't in her to jump a sexy stranger's bones. She hadn't been raised like that.

Why did nothing in her life ever work out the way it was supposed to? This gorgeous guy had practically been handed to her on a plate, and there were half-a-dozen good reasons why she wasn't going to do anything about it.

"You forgot to put your pants on," he said, draping the blanket over his shoulders and picking up the sweatpants. Charlie was horrified to discover that he was right. She'd been so involved in salivating over him that she had totally forgotten that she was freezing, exhausted—and only half dressed.

He moved around in front of her and bent, holding the sweatpants open for her as if she'd been a child.

"Put your foot in," he said, with a lurking half smile and that carnal glint in his eyes.

She did, first one, then the other, sliding her long legs into the cavernous depths of the wide-load fleece, conscious of his gaze on the slender curves of her calves and thighs all the while. He swept her with a single hot look as, kept decent by the length of the shirt, she stood to pull the pants up. Then he turned away to scoop the flashlight from the floor.

She watched him, and her heart pounded. Her mouth went dry. She was totally turned on, she realized, and the man hadn't even touched her.

Yet.

She'd wished for excitement, hadn't she? Well, tonight she'd gotten excitement in spades.

The terrifying kind of excitement that came with stumbling across murderous drug smugglers she could do without, she thought. But the kind of charged sexual excitement that was sizzling between her and Jake— well, now she knew what had been missing from her life.

She had never, ever, even when they had first started dating almost a year ago, felt that kind of excitement with Rick.

This was what she wanted.

"There must be kids in your life," Charlie said, glancing around to find Jake going through drawers behind her and striving to keep the conversation light until she could figure out what to do about him. The question about kids had sprung from the way he had held out the pants for her, as if it was a natural thing for him to do.

Then she realized what she had said. *Kids in his life?* Oh, God, she thought fervently, don't let him be married.

"Six nephews. I have three brothers, and they have two boys each. Actually, when I'm home I baby-sit a lot."

"Where's home?" Without even thinking about it, she moved a little closer to him, caught herself doing it, stopped, and crossed her arms over her chest.

"Memphis."

"That makes you a local boy." What she was really trying to find out was whether or not he had a wife, but so far she couldn't quite seem to phrase the question subtly.

"Close enough."

"So are you married?" Right, Charlie, just blurt it out.

He glanced around at her, smiling faintly, and again she was aware of the smoldering quality of that look. "Nope. You?"

Thank you, God, she thought, but managed not to say it aloud. "No."

"Good."

Without warning, the flashlight went out. The cabin was plunged into total darkness.

"Shit."

"Jake!" Charlie moved toward him, reaching out for him in sudden alarm. Her fingers encountered the soft hair on his chest, and brushed over the warm hard muscles beneath before being reluctantly withdrawn. The contact produced a tingling electricity that shimmied along every nerve ending she possessed. The strength of her own reaction made her catch her breath.

"It's okay. Nothing to worry about. Damn batteries."

"We don't really need it, do we?" It was an effort to make her voice sound normal. She had to resist the urge to touch him again. It was too soon, she didn't know him, the situation was about as inappropriate as one could get. . . .

She could hear him doing something that involved metal, shaking it until it rattled, screwing and unscrewing a lid.

"If we do, we're out of luck, because it's not coming back on. Here, wrap this around yourself. It's cold out there, and we've got to get moving. I wish to hell we'd managed to hang onto our boots."

"Ostrich leather, black, size seven. If we get out of this, you owe me a pair." Her tone was severe, but Charlie was smiling faintly as she said it.

"Yeah, okay. Fine. Blame me. I don't care." He sounded as if he might be smiling, too. Charlie felt something settle over her shoulders: the blanket. The gift of it touched her. For all his obvious physical toughness, he was as human as she was and he would freeze outside without it. It also settled something: However unexpected her attraction to him might be, it was something that deserved to be explored.

For once in her life, she meant to take a chance. And good girl Charlie be damned.

"Jake." She reached out for him again, and this time touched his arm. Her hand curled around one of the biceps she had so admired. It felt warm and hard beneath her fingers. "You know what? I think you're a pretty great guy."

Heart pounding, she took a step closer, rose up on tiptoe and kissed him. His lips were warm, and firm, and tasted faintly of the river they'd just left behind. For a moment, as she pressed her lips to his, he did nothing, just stood immobile as if he would absorb the touch of her lips.

"God, I've been wanting to do that." He said the words against her lips. Then his arms came around her hard and he pulled her to him and bent her backward over his arm and slanted his mouth over hers with a greedy hunger that made her quake.

By way of a reply, she wrapped her arms around his neck and put her tongue in his mouth and kissed him back for all she was worth. But it was he who controlled the kiss now as his tongue thrust urgently into her mouth and his hand came up to cover her breast. Charlie thought she would die at how good it felt to have his hand there. Her loins clenched and throbbed. Her breasts swelled, and the one fortunate nipple thrust boldly against the palm of his caressing hand. Quivers raced up and down her thighs as he pressed his knee between them. Her knees went weak. The bed was pushing against the back of her calves as he turned her around, and she swayed against it, wanting to be horizontal with him in the worst way.

Whether she pulled him down or he pushed her she didn't know, but suddenly she was on her back on the mattress and he was coming down on top of her, pulling up her flannel shirt, cupping her breasts, running his thumbs lightly over the distended nipples, kissing her ravenously all the while. Charlie moaned into his mouth, sliding her hands over his chest, tugging at his ridiculous shorts, so hot her legs were already wrapping around him and she wasn't even naked yet, hotter than she could ever remember being for a man in her life.

"Let's get your clothes off." His voice was thick as he lifted his head to yank the huge shirt over her head. His mouth returned to claim her breast; he slid his tongue over her nipple, then sucked it. At the same time he reached down between their straining bodies to slide his hand inside her pants and caress the cleft between her legs. His thumb found the place where she most wanted to be touched, and pressed.

"That is so—incredibly—good." She was panting, squirming beneath the ministrations of his mouth and that knowing hand, on fire for him, wanting him inside her so badly that she felt like she'd die if he made her wait.

She couldn't wait. Her hands slid between them to caress him through the soft cotton shorts. He was huge and hard and so hot that she could feel the heat even through the cloth. Her hand closed around him and he groaned.

"Charlie. God, Charlie." He jerked down her pants, baring her to the knees, and she kicked the offending garment the rest of the way off. Her legs parted, eager for him to come inside her, but instead of shedding his own pants he bent his head and pressed his mouth to her. She cried out as his tongue found the very center of her, gasping his name and digging her nails into his shoulders. His mouth was wet and scalding hot and well versed in the ways of women, and Charlie thought that she would die with the sheer pleasure of what he was doing to her.

"Oh, Jake!" It was a shuddering sigh as she let go of the last of her inhibitions and clutched at his hair.

"Gently, baby," he murmured. She was arching herself against his mouth and trembling and begging silently for release.

"Please don't stop," she gasped when his mouth didn't return to finish what it had started. But then, before she could even really begin to miss him, she felt something even better, the thick burning length of him sliding against her, pushing inside her, filling her to bursting, causing her body to pulse with a million fiery tremors as he sought his own pleasure at last. She clung feverishly to him as he took her with hard deep thrusts until she was striving with him, until she came, until her body exploded into a fireball of sensation that rocked her world.

If there was such a thing as sexual nirvana, that was where she landed.

She was just floating back to earth when the cabin door opened and two men carrying flashlights and God knew what else stepped inside.

11

A NUMBER OF THINGS HAPPENED almost simultaneously.

Sadie erupted barking from beneath the bed. The flashlights found them. Jake hissed, "Get under the bed!" and shoved Charlie over the far edge, then launched himself off the mattress toward the newcomers in a low, fast dive. A gun boomed.

Charlie hit the floor hard on her hands and knees, and screamed as a bullet tore through the mattress to lodge with a thud just inches from her fingers.

The men were now engaged in a desperate struggle. They were cursing and grunting and thumping around, and to her horror Charlie recognized the voices of Woz and Denton. Oh, God, if she and Jake had left just a few minutes earlier, they would have escaped.

The most mind-blowing sexual experience she had ever had in her life was going to lead to her death. How ironic was that?

The sickening sound of blows came fast and thick.

Sadie barked frantically. Both flashlights had apparently hit the ground at around the same time Charlie did, dropped in the newcomers' surprise at Jake's assault. One was rolling away across the room, casting weird shadows as it went. The other lay near the men's feet. Its beam pointed toward her, illuminating the floor, the underside of the bed, her and Jake's abandoned clothes—and the screwdriver.

With no very clear idea of what she meant to do but knowing that in a crisis of this nature any weapon was better than none, Charlie snatched up the screwdriver and, crawling on her hands and knees, rounded the foot of the bed. The men were very near. It was easy to tell which one was Jake because he was barefoot and naked. Jake was grappling with Denton, who was taller and thinner than Woz. Jake had a choke hold on Denton's neck and a grip on his gun hand and seemed to be using him as a shield against Woz, who circled the writhing pair, darting this way and that and lashing out with his fists and feet in a kind of deadly dance, looking for an opening. Woz had his pistol ready, but unless he wanted to risk hitting Denton it was obvious that he was going to have to be careful how he used it. It was, however, clear to Charlie that it was just a matter of time before Jake went down. Naked and weaponless, he couldn't best two armed men.

"Get the girl!" Denton grunted. Woz glanced around....

"Damn it, Charlie, run!" Jake roared.

But it was too late. Even as Charlie backpedaled frantically, then tried to roll under the bed, Woz was upon her, knotting a fist in her hair, locking an arm around her neck, hauling her to her feet. Charlie didn't bother to scream, or fight. She hung limply in his hold, letting herself be dragged toward where Jake and Denton still struggled.

"Hey, asshole, I got your girlfriend!" Woz said in a taunting voice. His arm, in a bulky twill coat, was wrapped around her neck. He held her so that there was no possibility of escape, with his pistol pointed at her head.

Charlie clutched the screwdriver and prayed.

Sadie came running up, yapping frantically at this assault on her mistress, and launched herself at Woz's leg.

"Get out of here!" Sadie was too small to do much damage, but Woz glanced down, and angrily shook his leg. The pistol wavered and fell. . . .

Charlie took a deep breath, and drove the screwdriver with all her might into his thigh. It pierced his pants, and sank deep, feeling like a fork going into tender meat.

He screamed, and let her go, and dropped his gun, clapping both hands to his punctured thigh and falling writhing to the ground.

"Bitch! Bitch! Bitch!"

"That was for Laura," she said, and went diving after Woz's dropped gun.

Jake did something violent to Denton, but Charlie didn't know exactly what because she was sliding across the floor just about then. When she came up with the gun, scrambling to her feet and gripping it in both shaking hands, it was to discover that the fight was over.

Denton was on the floor near Woz, and Jake, gun in hand, was taking careful aim. . . .

"Oh my God, don't kill him!" Charlie gasped, knowing that she couldn't be a party to cold-blooded murder even though Woz and Denton deserved it. Jake didn't even look at her before he fired. Denton screamed, clutched his leg, and rolled around on the floor.

"I'm not going to kill them, just make sure they won't be coming after us," Jake said grimly, glancing at her before repeating the exercise with the already shrieking Woz. Then he turned to Charlie, and held out his hand. "Here, give me that gun, and grab us some clothes. Time to get the hell out of here."

It was only then that Charlie realized that she, like Jake, was as naked as the day she was born. Trying not to listen to the cries and curses of the men writhing on the ground, she snatched up what clothes she could find— the flannel shirt and sweatpants, both of which were still on the bed—and pulled the one over her head and tossed the other to Jake. As he juggled the guns in one hand and yanked the pants on, she scooped up Sadie. Then the three of them headed cautiously out the door.

Only to find, parked neatly in the driveway beside the cabin, Critter Ridders' own Jeep, smashed front end and all. Charlie was embarrassed to realize that she and Jake had been so engrossed in what they were doing at the time that they'd never even heard it pull up.

"Yee-haw, I think we're in business," Jake said when he saw it. "Let's go."

The bad news was, the smell of skunk was still so strong that, after stopping to call the state police and Jake's boss from the convenience store, they had to drive all the way to Nashville with the windows rolled down, and it was cold. The good news was, the snake was long gone. But the raccoon and the possums were still in their cages.

"I've got to go," Jake said, after driving her clear back home. An unmarked car was already waiting for him in front of her mother's house, where she had told him to take her after he'd refused to let her drive on from the convenience store alone. Two men in suits got out of the car as they pulled up. Jake, wearing nothing but too-large sweatpants, lifted a hand at the men in greeting and then turned to Charlie.

"Jake." But she couldn't say anything else, because she knew it was good-bye and her throat was suddenly aching. He leaned over and kissed her, quick and hard, on the mouth.

"See ya," he said, and bestowed a quick scratch on Sadie before getting out of the Jeep. Her mother came out of the house just then, standing on the porch and staring, but Charlie stayed where she was, watching as Jake slid into the back of the car, which promptly drove away.

Only then did she climb out, and, carrying Sadie, walk toward her mother, who hurried down the walk to embrace her.

Even as her mother exclaimed over her, and hustled her toward the house, Charlie couldn't rid herself of a terrible sense of loss.

She'd taken a risk, given him all she had to give, and now he was gone. The question now was, would she ever see him again?

12

By NINE O'CLOCK SATURDAY NIGHT, Marisol was still trying to explain to her insurance company exactly what had happened to her Jeep. Parachuting drug smugglers and undercover DEA agents and ticked-off skunks did not seem to fit into any categories that would ensure a prompt payout. Marisol was growing increasingly exasperated, and, though she knew it was not Charlie's fault, some of that exasperation naturally was vented at her little sister. Especially since Charlie had made the gigantic error (in Marisol's opinion) of quite firmly breaking up with Rick. Charlie had to have dog food for brains, as Marisol told her. The man was good-looking, nice to kids and animals, and had a good job.

What more could Charlie want?

Something a little more exciting, Charlie answered stubbornly. And it was so unlike Charlie to be stubborn that Marisol was truly concerned.

Whatever had happened on the night the Jeep had been wrecked—and Charlie had told her, but the whole story sounded so fantastic that Marisol couldn't help but wonder if perhaps her sister had hit her head hard in the crash and imagined two-thirds of it—the bottom line was that Charlie, sweet, sensible Charlie, had been changed ever since.

Take tonight, for instance. Charlie never suffered from stage fright—she shouldn't, she'd been singing in public since she was a little girl—but she'd been jumpy as a cat at a dog convention getting ready for tonight's performance. She'd changed costumes three times, which meant that Marisol had had to change as well, because they had to match, then in the end had gone back to the one they'd originally decided on, the new gold-sequined evening dresses with the long white gloves. This appearance at the Yellow Rose was *important*, for God's sake, it could be their big break, and Charlie was in a dither.

Charlie never got in a dither.

They were getting ready to go on, the emcee was *announcing* them, and Charlie kept peeking around the curtain, looking out at the audience as if she was searching for somebody in particular.

Charlie hadn't really told her, but Marisol knew her little sister well enough that she was willing to bet she could even guess who: this Jake guy, this DEA agent who had, in some tangled fashion that Marisol still didn't quite have sorted out in her head, been responsible for the ruination of her Jeep.

For Charlie's sake, she hoped he showed up.

Then they were on stage, breaking into their opening song. Marisol was shaking her booty along with her tamborine and looking beautiful and Charlie was strumming her guitar and singing like an angel and looking beautiful, and everything was going just as it should, when Charlie's eyes fixed on something beyond the stage and she stopped singing and broke into this absolute shit-eating grin and missed *two whole chords*.

Horrified, Marisol tried to take up the musical slack even as her gaze followed Charlie's. In just a couple of beats Charlie was with her again, but not before Marisol spotted him.

Not that it was hard. He was the only gorgeous hunk in the place with a pair of ladies size seven, black ostrich leather cowboy boots sitting on the table in front of him.

About the Author

Karen Robards lives in her hometown of Louisville, Kentucky, with her husband, Doug, and their three sons: Peter, sixteen; Christopher, ten; and Jack, four. Besides her family, books are the great passion of her life. The award-winning author of twenty-six novels describes herself thus: "I read, I write, and I chase children. That's my life!"

STONE
COLD

===

ANDREA KANE

1

"A HOUSE?"

Lindsey Hall feathered her fingers through her hair, a puzzled expression on her face. "I don't understand. Why would Harlan Falkner leave me a house?"

"A mansion, not a house," Leland Masters corrected. He regarded her steadily, whatever he was thinking masked behind a professional veneer he'd perfected over forty years. One of Providence, Rhode Island's most prominent attorneys, he'd represented the Falkners' interests since Harlan made his first million, some thirty-five years ago. Now, it was his job to carry out his client's final wishes.

He folded his hands in front of him, a formidable presence in an equally formidable office—all gleaming mahogany and polished tile—an office that Harlan Falkner's money had helped pay for. "You're aware of your relationship to Mr. Falkner."

Lindsey's smile was tight-lipped. "My relationship? If you mean my blood ties, yes, I know Mr. Falkner fathered me. But as for a relationship, we had none. I never even met the man. He made no attempt to contact me, not in twenty-six years. So why would he suddenly leave me a portion of his estate?"

Another thoughtful stare. Yes, he could see the resemblance. The same unusual coloring: fine, tawny hair, its hues ranging from gold to light brown and, in contrast, startlingly dark eyes. The same refined manner and natural grace. And the bone structure was there, although Miss Hall was slender and delicate in contrast to Harlan's larger, more towering presence. She probably took after her mother on that score.

She hadn't been at the will reading. Then again, she hadn't been invited. It was better that way. The reaction from Harlan's children would have been explosive. As it was, it hadn't been pleasant. It had, however, been predictable. Until last week, they hadn't known Lindsey Hall existed.

They knew now.

"Miss Hall, I don't think Harlan's—your father's—motives are the issue here. His provisions are. He left you the mansion in Newport, along with a sizable sum of money, to be used at your discretion."

"My discretion," she repeated, turning her palms up in noncomprehension. "What does that mean?"

"The mansion has been vacant for years. It needs to be restored. Harlan thought you might enjoy doing that. If so, a portion of your funds could be used to renovate the house in whatever manner you choose." Leland shrugged. "If not, you're welcome to sell it and keep the profit, along with the rest of the money he's left you. As I said, the choice is yours."

A flicker of anger flashed in her eyes, followed by a spark of curiosity. "Why was the mansion vacant?"

The attorney shrugged again. "It used to be a family vacation home. Circumstances changed. Lifestyles changed." He left it at that.

"I see." Obviously, she didn't see at all. Nor should she. But she changed the subject nonetheless. "What about Mr. Falkner's legitimate children? Wouldn't he leave the mansion to them?"

Leland had anticipated that question. "He thought you'd have a greater appreciation for it, based upon your career choice."

That was his second reference to her inclinations toward design, this one more pointed than the first.

It found its mark, and Lindsey Hall's delicate brows rose. "Are you saying Mr. Falkner was aware I'm an architect?"

"Mr. Falkner was aware of a great many things about you, Miss Hall. Your graduation with honors from Cooper Union, your unique contributions to the architectural firm you're currently working for in Connecticut, specifically the fine work you've done restoring classic old homes. Many things."

Lindsey's jaw dropped. "He kept tabs on me?"

"He kept abreast of your accomplishments."

She digested that with a jolt of surprise and an obvious swell of resentment. Based on her perception of things, Leland couldn't blame her. He could just imagine what she was thinking.

He didn't have to imagine long.

"Talk about too much, too little, too late," she commented bitterly. "Am I supposed to feel honored?

Honored that Harlan Falkner followed my life like one of his high-yielding stocks—no, actually not as closely. In my case, no active participation was necessary. Not until now. Now, when he's gone and my existence can no longer tarnish his family's reputation, he's throwing me a bone? How gracious. It sounds like a payoff, Mr. Masters. A payoff from a man with a guilty conscience." She rose to her feet. "No mansion can compensate for Mr. Falkner's actions. Nor can money make up for what he did—not to me, but to my mother. I notice she's not mentioned in this will."

Leland tipped back his head, met Lindsey's angry gaze with a calm, steady stare. "No, she's not." He watched the controlled anger simmer in her eyes, and thought again how much like Harlan she looked and, perhaps, was. If she knew more, she might feel differently. But she didn't know more.

"Before you tell me to go to hell, I'd suggest you think this over," he advised quietly. "Separate pride from pragmatism. Between the value of the mansion and the cash, we're talking about well over five million dollars. You can do a lot with that sum of money, Miss Hall, including anything you choose to do for your mother. She's past fifty now. She can't clean houses forever."

Lindsey opened her mouth, then pressed her lips together, a war taking place inside her. She was still gripped by questions and suppressed fury. She was also a realist—like her father. She knew Leland was right.

"Don't decide immediately," he suggested. "Take a day or two. Think it over—all of it."

"I'm going back to Connecticut tonight."

"Wait for morning." Leland reached into his desk,

extracted a set of keys and a slip of paper with an address on it. "I've made a reservation for you at a local hotel. Spend the night. Consider your options. In the meantime, use the rest of today to take a ride out to Newport. The mansion's less than an hour's drive from here. This is the address. Look it over. See what you think. Stop by my office tomorrow on your way home. You can give me your answer then." He paused, flourished a business card. "Here's my card. Call if you need anything."

Automatically, Lindsey took it, although she looked reluctant to do so.

"Looking costs you nothing other than time, Miss Hall. And a day might shed new perspective on what I know must be an emotional situation."

She nodded. "Very well." She turned to go.

"Oh, one more thing." Leland rummaged through the papers on his desk, extracted another business card. "Here."

"What's this?" She frowned, taking the card. Her frown deepened as she saw the name and phone number on it. "Nicholas Warner?"

"Yes. He's a major real estate developer in the Newport area, and a business associate of the Falkners."

"I know who he is, Mr. Masters. His name is in the newspapers almost as often as the Falkners'."

"True. In any case, he asked me to give you his number, just in case you decide to sell the house. He's very interested in buying it."

"Is he?" Lindsey's jaw tightened. "He didn't waste any time. Or is it just that he, like the Falkners, is so sure I'd prefer cash to property?"

Leland didn't respond, keeping his expression nondescript. "Whether or not you call him is up to you. As for the rest, give your inheritance some thought."

This time her nod was more definitive. "I intend to." She turned the keys over in her palm. "I'll ride out to Newport now. You'll have my decision by morning."

Leland watched her go, contemplating the ironies of life with bittersweet awareness. Then, he glanced down at the documents on his desk. "Well, Harlan," he murmured, "I did as you asked. I think you'd be pleased with the results."

2

HARLAN FALKNER MUST HAVE KNOWN she'd fall in love with this place.

Lindsey came to the end of the winding gravel driveway, flipped off her windshield wipers, and turned off the engine. Hopping out of her modest Honda Civic, she stuffed her keys into her pocket, strolling up the path and drinking in the structure before her with a combination of artistic appreciation and genuine awe.

It wasn't the most palatial estate she'd ever seen; certainly not glamorous enough to take its place on the Cliff Walk with the rest of Newport's historic mansions. Yet somehow that didn't matter. In fact, the manor's isolation and subtle grandeur gave it a distinctive flavor that enhanced rather than detracted from its beauty.

Set off by itself, the house stood amid acres of wooded land with the ocean as its backdrop. Gothic in design, it managed to combine the sophistication of a 19th-century mansion with the homeyness of a country cottage. Even the cold rain, gray skies, and restless ocean waters of the blustery May afternoon couldn't lessen its charm. It was lovely.

Lindsey pulled her windbreaker more closely around her, shivering a little as the rawness of the day penetrated her thin cotton sweater and jeans. This spring had been exceptionally cold and dismal. Not to mention that it was much chillier here by the ocean. She'd have to remember that and dress accordingly the next time she came—if there was a next time.

She climbed the five stone steps leading to the manor's front door and let herself in. The musty smells of long-time abandonment greeted her. That, and dust. It was everywhere, making her eyes water and her nose burn. She blinked away the tears that stung behind her lids, reaching over to test the light switch.

It worked.

The overhead chandelier came on. Its dozens of tiny bulbs were enough to illuminate not only the entranceway but a good portion of the main floor.

The rooms were huge, rich with mahogany floors and paneling. The walls were bare, but there were marks on the plaster indicating places where paintings had once hung. The moldings were exquisite, the lines classic and impeccable.

She turned slowly, admiring the grace and charm that no amount of dust could hide.

It was a crime that no one had cared for this beautiful home. Circumstances had changed, was Mr. Masters's explanation. Lifestyles had changed. That might explain why the Falkners no longer came here, but it didn't explain why they hadn't had the place kept up. Obviously, Mr. Masters didn't choose to provide details. Fine. But who could desert such a magnificent treasure?

The same man who'd deserted her mother.

Lindsey felt that familiar knot tighten her stomach. Five million dollars. To think what that kind of money would mean to her mother. Irene Hall had been cleaning houses for thirty years. She was worn out, partly from physical labor, partly from the emotional burden of raising a child alone and on a domestic's income.

It had improved a little these past few years. Lindsey was making enough money now to afford a decent two-bedroom apartment for her mother and herself. And her mother was only working three days a week now, instead of six. But even that was too much.

Today's announcement could change all that.

Lindsey approached the winding staircase, pausing to trail her fingers along the smooth surface of the banister, and gazed up toward the second story. Almost mechanically, she began to climb.

She couldn't help thinking how taken her mother would be by this house. Irene loved old manors. Many nights when Lindsey was sprawled out on the living room floor, working on architectural plans to restore an old mansion, her mother would sink into the sofa, exhausted from her day and yet fascinated by what Lindsey was doing. She'd watch, asking questions and expressing her admiration for the buildings' structure and design.

She'd adore this place. And if she could live here . . .

She could. *If* Lindsey kept it.

The battle that had been going on inside Lindsey's head since her meeting with Leland Masters roared back to life.

She wanted nothing from Harlan Falkner. Nothing.

Still, a little voice inside her contended, what would be gained by refusing her inheritance? What would she be proving by signing away her rights to this manor, along with the fortune that went with it? The man she'd be lashing out at was dead. He'd never feel the sting of her retaliatory gesture. So what point did it serve? How would it hurt him? More important, how would it *help* her—by salvaging her pride? Pride didn't pay the bills. Nor did it offer her mother a shred of what she'd been denied all these years. She was entitled to that money—to that, and so much more.

True, Lindsey could sell the manor. That would solve her problem neatly. It would sever all ties to the Falkners, and leave her with a fortune in cash. She had a ready buyer. From what Mr. Masters said, Nicholas Warner was eager to take the place off her hands.

Why? Did he plan to restore it himself?

She shuddered in distaste. The man was a real estate developer, not to mention a big-time entrepreneur. The only thing he could want was to transform this magnificent dwelling into some ostentatious palace he'd then sell at a huge profit. Or worse, he could opt to turn it into a tourist attraction.

Odd that Harlan Falkner hadn't sold it to him already. He and Nicholas Warner were close business associates. Their respective fortunes had been co-invested time and again, the results of which were splashed across the pages of the business section. They shared the society pages, too, she reminded herself, traveling in the same circles, mingling with the same highly visible, affluent crowd. Nicholas Warner and Stuart

Falkner, Harlan's son, had attended Harvard together. They were fast friends on the same fast track, chasing— or being chased by—a parade of fast women.

The frivolity of it all made her sick.

Still, that didn't answer her question. Why hadn't Harlan Falkner sold this property to Nicholas Warner rather than keep it only to neglect it so shamefully?

Some piece of the puzzle was missing. But what?

Lindsey had just stepped across the threshold of what had to be the master bedroom, when she heard the front door open, then click quietly shut.

She froze, standing rigidly as footsteps moved across the front hall.

Abruptly, she realized how isolated this place was, how vulnerable she'd left herself, and how stupid she'd been to leave the front door unlocked. The summer season didn't begin till Memorial Day, maybe later, if the weather didn't improve. That was three weeks away. Which meant very few people were around. And in this isolated section of town, *no one* was around. Any troublemaker or criminal could walk in and . . .

Reason intruded, stifled that thought. This neck of the woods might be isolated, but it was hardly a haven for vagrants. Conversely, by virtue of its deserted state, it wouldn't attract thieves. So, whoever had just walked in must have a purpose. Plus, her already-existing presence was hardly a secret. The first floor lights were on. The door was ajar. Her car was in the driveway.

Squaring her shoulders, she marched to the stairway, loudly making her descent. "Hello?"

"Hello," a cultured baritone replied.

Definitely not a criminal.

She descended the rest of the way, her visitor revealed by bits and pieces as she did. He was a walking advertisement for J. Crew, she observed, seeing first his docksiders, then his khakis, and finally his navy crewneck sweater. His arms were folded across his chest, one broad shoulder propped lazily against the wall as he watched her approach. His features were patrician, his raven-black hair thick, glistening with droplets of rain, his eyes a probing dark blue.

That probing gaze took her in from head to toe. "I hope I didn't frighten you."

Lindsey walked across the foyer and shook her head, tilting it back so she could meet his gaze. "You didn't. Although I am a little surprised to see you. Mr. Masters mentioned that you were interested in the property. But he didn't say you were chomping at the bit to the point where you'd follow me out here."

His lips quirked. "You obviously know who I am."

"I read the newspapers, Mr. Warner. You photograph accurately."

"And here I thought my pictures didn't do me justice."

"Newspaper shots rarely do anyone justice. But I'm sure you didn't ride out here for reassurance of your good looks."

She hadn't meant to sound quite so harsh. Clearly, her curt retort startled him. His dark brows rose ever so slightly, though he seemed more puzzled than offended.

"It's obvious we started out on the wrong foot, although I'm not sure why," he stated bluntly. "If it's because I frightened you when I walked in, I'm sorry. If it's because you resent my driving out here to talk to you, I didn't. I drove out to look over the property. I had no idea you'd be here. Actually, I'd planned on calling your hotel later and making an appointment to see you before you left for Connecticut."

"I see." She couldn't get angry at that. It was too honest—something she hadn't expected.

He extended his hand. "Let's try again. You must be Lindsey Hall. It's a pleasure to meet you. I'm Nicholas Warner."

Lindsey acknowledged the formal introduction with a polite smile and a handshake. "What gave me away— my Connecticut plates or my key in the front door?"

"Both. That and your striking resemblance to Harlan."

She'd noticed that, too, if only from photos. Still, her stomach tightened at hearing the observation spoken aloud.

"I'll take your word for it. Mr. Falkner and I never met." The strain was back in her voice. But she couldn't help it. This subject was her Achilles' heel.

"I know," Nicholas Warner replied quietly. "Harlan regretted that."

"Did he?" Skepticism laced her tone.

"Yes."

She averted her gaze, stared into the empty mahogany living room. "You knew him well."

"Almost twenty years. He gave me my first break, backed the real estate investment that launched my career. He was a complex man, a brilliant businessman. He built his reputation deal by deal and dollar by dollar."

"And his wife? His children?" Lindsey forced her gaze back to his. "Where did they factor into things?"

Nicholas Warner studied her for a moment, that probing blue stare boring through her. "Stuart and Tracy meant everything to Harlan. They were his legacy, his reason for building an empire. As for his wife, Camille is a lovely, fragile woman. I'm sure you know about her situation. It's hardly a secret. If you've scoured the newspapers enough to spot my picture, then I'm sure you've read about Camille's difficulties."

Slowly, Lindsey nodded. "She's confined to some estate-like psychiatric facility."

"Rolling Hills. And, yes, she's been there for about seven years."

"That's quite a while. Does her family visit her?" Lindsey had no idea why she was asking these questions. Each detail she learned cut through her like a knife. But somehow she had to know.

"They visit frequently, yes." Nicholas's tone was cautious, as if he were sifting through his information and providing only those facts he felt Lindsey was entitled to. "Tracy lives in Boston. She runs a division of her father's company there. She drives down every chance she gets. Stuart goes more often, usually several times a week, since he lives right in Providence. Harlan used to go with him."

"Mr. Falkner's death must have come as a horrible blow to his wife."

"It did. As I said, Camille is fragile. Harlan was her world. His visits were her lifeline."

Lindsey swallowed hard, thinking of her own

mother's reaction when she'd read of Harlan Falkner's death. Her lips had trembled, and her eyes had filled with tears—tears she'd made sure were gone by the time she folded and put down the newspaper. She'd dismissed the subject and pretended to go about her business, as if what she'd just read had been any upsetting but impersonal item. Lindsey hadn't been fooled. Late that night, she'd heard her mother's muffled sobs as she'd privately mourned a man she'd never really had but never stopped loving.

So, yes, Camille Falkner had undoubtedly been shattered by her husband's death. But at least she'd been allowed her grief. And at least she'd been bound to him, legally and emotionally, and, as a result, had lost something tangible. What had Irene Hall lost? A dream. A wisp of memory that was almost three decades old.

The injustice of it made Lindsey's heart wrench.

"He really did wish he'd known you, Lindsey," Nicholas murmured, watching her face. "Honestly."

Emotional shutters descended inside her. She didn't even know this man. She certainly wasn't going to bare her scars to him. "It wasn't me I was thinking of. In any case, I appreciate your candor, Mr. Warner. I hope my questions weren't intrusive."

"They weren't. And it's Nicholas." He reached out, touched the sleeve of her windbreaker. "It's only natural that you'd be curious about your . . . about Harlan. I'd be happy to fill in whatever blanks I can. Why don't we go somewhere and grab a cup of coffee? We can talk. I'll tell you if you're overstepping."

He certainly knew the right things to say. And the right times to say them.

Perhaps *too* well.

He'd gone from being pleasantly impersonal to warmly empathetic in a matter of minutes.

Lindsey had the uncomfortable feeling she was being manipulated.

And she could think of just one reason why.

"There's one blank you can fill in right away," she tested. "And that's your role as prospective buyer of this house. I've been racking my brain, and I've come up empty. Why didn't Mr. Falkner sell the manor to you before now? Clearly, he didn't want it. It's been vacant for years. So why wait?"

The barest hint of a pause. "That's easy. He wanted to give you first dibs."

"*After* he was dead."

"After it was too late for Stuart and Tracy to try talking him out of his decision. A will is binding. It made the choice of whether or not you owned the manor solely yours to make. If you sell, it won't be because you were deprived of the opportunity to own this place. It will be because you don't want it."

Another honest reply. Maybe she was being overly suspicious.

Maybe.

"Okay, suppose that's true," she conceded. "My next question is, why would *you* want to buy it? You're a successful real estate developer. You work on projects that yield huge profits. Why would you want a single, neglected Georgian manor? Restoring it would be a huge undertaking and a minimal profit-maker."

This time the pause was longer, more pronounced, and Lindsey had the feeling she was about to find out what it was about Nicholas Warner that made her so uneasy.

"Because I have plans for the land," he said at last. "Plans that could give lots of people a chance to wake up to a view of the ocean each day."

"The land?" Lindsey blinked. "Lots of people? I'm not following you."

"I'm not going to restore the manor, Lindsey. I'm going to build condos. A cluster of luxury townhouses nestled in the middle of the thirteen acres—"

"*Condos?*" Lindsey spat out the word as if it were poison. So that was it. He wanted to demolish something he knew she'd want to preserve.

She backed away, whatever camaraderie there had been developing between them blown to bits. "You want to destroy this magnificent manor so you can build some condos?"

"You make it sound as if I said prisons. I'm talking about tasteful structures of wood and cedar shakes, constructed so they blend in with the natural setting—"

"I don't care if you said miniature Taj Mahals." Lindsey's palm sliced the air, effectively cutting off whatever else he'd been about to say. "The answer is no. Absolutely no. You're not razing this beautiful house to the ground. You're not tearing down one brick, not one wooden tread. And you're definitely not replacing it with some garish, high-priced townhouses."

She flipped up the hood of her windbreaker, marched around him, and headed for the door. "You can keep your cup of coffee, Mr. Warner." She paused, facing him as she twisted the doorknob. "Oh, and thank you for making a difficult decision very easy. As of now, this manor is not for sale. Not at any price. I'm keeping it."

She stormed out of the house.

Nicholas listened to the crunching sound of tires on gravel, and then her car driving away. His smile faded, his lips tightening into a grim line.

Lindsey Hall was going to be a problem.

3

By the time Irene Hall got home from work the next night, Lindsey had just finished preparing a chicken casserole and popped it into the oven.

"Hi," she greeted her mother, tugging off her oven mitts and tossing them to the counter. She walked out of the tiny kitchen, giving her mother a tired smile.

Petite and slight of build, Irene appeared much younger than her fifty-one years—at least at first glance. It was only when one looked closer that one could see her chapped, overworked hands and the world-weariness in her eyes. Still, with her diminutive size, flaxen hair, and cornflower blue eyes, she looked all the world like a china doll—one that had been dragged around rather than allowed to sit on a shelf and be admired.

"You look exhausted," Lindsey said gently, walking over to give her mother a hug. "Sit down and relax. Dinner will be ready in less than an hour."

Irene smoothed a strand of pale hair off her forehead and studied her daughter, her fine features tightening with concern. "An hour," she repeated quietly. "Good. That gives us a chance to talk."

Lindsey averted her gaze. "There's not that much to talk about. I can recap the past day in about five minutes."

"I beg to differ with you. There's a lot to talk about. And I don't only mean the past day. I mean the past twenty-six years. This talk is long overdue." Irene's firm tone surprised Lindsey. Her mother was always soft-spoken and gentle, her personality as delicate as her appearance. Now she sounded adamant.

"Lindsey, I was here when Mr. Masters called and asked you to come to Providence. I might not be aware of the specifics, but I am aware of what, or rather *who*, prompted the call. I'm also aware that you purposely got back here this morning with just enough time to shower, change, and rush off to work. You didn't want to talk then, and you don't want to talk now. Well, that's not going to fly. Not this time. I realize you're trying to protect me. But I don't need protection. I'm not some fragile piece of glass that's going to shatter if you mention Harlan's name." She broke off, a troubled expression darting across her face. "Quite the opposite, in fact. We need to have this talk—for more reasons than one. I should have insisted on it years ago."

She pointed at the cozy alcove that was their living room. "So let's both sit. Tell me what Mr. Masters said. Obviously, Harlan made provisions that involve you. What are they?"

Lindsey shot her a startled look. "Why would you assume that? I never even met the man."

"I'm right, though, aren't I?" her mother returned, a statement rather than a question.

"Yes. You're right." Lindsey walked over and settled herself on the sofa, waiting for her mother to follow suit. "The whole situation is pretty cut and dried," she went on to report. "The official reading of the will took place days ago. This was a post-reading arrangement made in advance by Harlan Falkner." She inclined her head, gazed quizzically at her mother. "Did you know he had a manor in Newport?"

A nostalgic smile. "I remember it, yes."

"Well, he left it to me. That and a huge chunk of cash. That's what Mr. Masters announced at our meeting." A bitter edge crept into Lindsey's voice. "I guess it was Mr. Falkner's way of rewarding me—sort of a payoff for not causing a family scandal."

"Is that what you think?"

Lindsey gave an exasperated sigh, letting her head fall forward and massaging the back of her neck. "What else is there to think? I could have shown up on his doorstep years ago, DNA evidence in hand, and announced that he was my father. I didn't. I guess that impressed him. It certainly relieved him of a lot of embarrassment and explanations. According to Mr. Masters, he followed my life and my career. He knew I loved restoring old homes. So, he left me his. Along with a few million in gratitude. End of story."

Irene sank back against the cushions, her shoulders sagging with regret. "This is my fault."

"Your fault?"

"Yes. I thought that filling in the blanks would make things worse. I was wrong." She twisted around to face her daughter. "Lindsey, did you turn down the manor? Because if you did, it was for the wrong reasons."

"I don't understand."

"Did you turn down the manor?" Irene pressed.

"No. Ironically not. I accepted it. It was either that or see it torn down and replaced with condos." Briefly, Lindsey filled her mother in on her meeting with Nicholas Warner, told her what he'd intended. "I can't allow that. The house is far too beautiful to be destroyed. Oh, I realize that accepting it is hypocritical, given how I feel about Harlan Falkner, but I have no choice. I won't let it be torn down. Besides," she added quietly, watching her mother's face. "I have another reason for wanting to keep it. I want you to have it. I want you to make it your home."

Irene swallowed, her lips quivering a bit. "My home . . ."

"I don't know how well you remember the manor," Lindsey rushed on, determined not to let her mother refuse this well-deserved gift, "but it's elegant and homey all at once. The ocean is close enough to wake you in the morning and lull you to sleep at night. Right now, the house is barren, with no furniture or decorations to enhance its charm, but even so there's something so special about—"

"I remember every detail of the place," Irene interrupted quietly. "You were conceived there."

Lindsey went very still. "Oh," she said at last. "I had no idea."

"You had no idea of many things," Irene replied. "All you know is that I was a maid in Harlan's house, that he slept with me, got me pregnant, then gave me enough money to take care of the problem and sent me off.

That's all you ever *wanted* to know. But I should have insisted. I should have forced you to listen."

"To listen to what? The fact that you were in love with him? That you're *still* in love with him? Mom, I didn't need to hear that. I knew it."

"What you didn't know, what you never wanted to hear, is that *Harlan* was in love with *me*, too. Maybe not enough to turn his back on Camille, certainly not enough to alienate his children and blow his family to bits, but he did love me, Lindsey."

Lindsey spread her hands in a gesture of disbelief. "Then why didn't he come to you? Why didn't he offer you something, anything, besides enough cash for an abortion? Why didn't he—"

"He did."

A start of surprise. "What?"

Irene folded her hands in her lap, stared sadly down at them. "He came to me several times. First, when I announced I was going through with the pregnancy and having his child, not getting rid of it. Next, after you were born, to lay eyes on his daughter. And again, when you were about ten. Each time he offered me money, help, his influence in finding a better job. Anything. Anything but what I really wanted: him."

Irene wet her lips with the tip of her tongue. "Each time he came, I refused his offers and sent him away. I told him he'd given up any rights to you and certainly any rights to me. I was proud in those days. The way I saw it, either he loved me enough to leave his family and marry me, or I wanted nothing to do with him. I wouldn't take his money. And I wouldn't publicly acknowledge him as your father—although on his last visit, he pushed me to do that, and damn the consequences. But I refused, and not because I was trying to spare him or his family. *You're* the one I was worried about. It was hard enough for you as it was, being the child of a faceless, nameless man who'd abandoned me. But being Harlan Falkner's bastard? That would have ruined your life. I finally managed to convince him of that, and he went away for good. But it doesn't surprise me that he kept track of your life and followed your career. I'm not even shocked that he left you the Newport estate. I'm just glad you accepted it."

Lindsey glanced away, trying to process all her mother had just said, feeling equal amounts of pain and relief at the realization that Harlan Falkner wasn't the total monster she'd believed him to be.

It was true that she'd resisted any discussion of him. She hadn't wanted to hear anything personal about him, especially not the details of his relationship with her mother. It was too hurtful to think about how he'd used and abandoned Irene, how easily he'd cut her and his unborn child from his life. By knowing nothing more about him than that, other than what the media provided, Lindsey could reciprocate in kind. She could wipe him from her mind and her heart. He was genetically responsible for her conception. Period.

Until now. Her mother's explanation had just given Harlan Falkner dimension, made him a flesh-and-blood man—a man who'd taken steps to reach out to her mother and acknowledge his child.

"I realize this is the last thing you wanted to hear," Irene murmured. "You were more comfortable hating him."

"Okay, so he loved you. He offered you help. But ultimately you ended up raising me alone," Lindsey pointed out faintly, feeling vulnerable and hating the fact that she did.

"That's true. And I resented Harlan for that, at least at the beginning. Actually longer. I resented him until a few years after the last time I sent him away. Then life stepped in. I got older. I gained perspective and set aside pride." Irene covered Lindsey's hand with her own. "Life's not black-and-white. In a perfect world, Harlan would have divorced Camille, married me, and the two of us would have raised you together. But he already had a family—including two small children he loved and was committed to. Stuart was only eight when you were conceived, and Tracy was five. What should he have done—deserted them? He was torn. And I wouldn't so much as entertain a compromise. I shut the door in his face—literally—not once, but three times. He had no choice but to accept my decision."

"There's always a choice, Mom." Lindsey ran a shaky hand through her hair. "But it doesn't matter anymore. He's dead. The what-ifs might as well die, too."

Irene cleared her throat, indicating that she thought Lindsey's suggestion was impossible, and that she realized Lindsey knew the same. "What about the manor?" she asked. "What arrangements have you made?"

"I told Mr. Masters I was keeping it. I have an appointment with him later this week to sign the necessary papers." Lindsey faced her mother, the enthusiasm that had accompanied her plans for Irene's move tempered by what she'd just learned. "You and Mr. Falkner . . . I didn't know it happened there. If I had the place not only restored but completely redone, would you be able to live there? Or are the memories too strong and too painful?"

A wistful smile touched Irene's lips. "I know you can't understand this, but when I think of my time with Harlan, I don't feel pain. I feel joy. We didn't have a sleazy affair. He didn't take advantage of me. I was a grown woman of twenty-four, trying to save up enough money to go back to school and make something of myself. I didn't plan on falling in love with my employer. He didn't plan on falling in love with me. It just happened. What's more, out of our relationship came the greatest treasure of my life—you. So, no, the memories wouldn't keep me away. But, my goodness, a house of that size . . . restoring it will cost a fortune. Not to mention keeping it up . . ."

"I have more than enough to do both, and then some. If you add up what Mr. Falkner left me, it's worth five million dollars. And you're the one who deserves to enjoy it." Lindsey's heart grew lighter as she spoke, delivering an announcement she'd dreamed of making for years. "You can stop working, Mom. Right away. The money will be transferred to my account by next week. Give notice to all the families you work for. Tell them you're going back to school—finally—*after* you take the summer off. For the next few months, you'll be a lady of leisure. Sleep late. Read the newspaper. Go to museums, restaurants, the theater. Take a trip. You always wanted to see Paris. Now you can."

Irene looked dazed, a glow of anticipation staining her cheeks.

"If Harlan Falkner cared for you as much as you say, he'd want you to have this," Lindsey added. It was speculation, meant as leverage. Still, she couldn't help but wonder if it was true. "Maybe that's why he left me the manor and the money to begin with. If he truly did keep track of my life, he knew how close you and I are. And he'd realize I'd share my inheritance with you. Wouldn't he?"

Before Irene could answer, the doorbell rang.

Squeezing her mother's hand, Lindsey rose. "I'll get that. You start making plans. Begin with the trip to Paris."

She went into the hall. "Who is it?" she called, simultaneously peering through the peephole.

"Stuart Falkner."

She stiffened. Her narrow field of view revealed an impeccable silk tie and white shirt. Great. Stuart Falkner. What did he want?

There was only one way to find out.

She flipped the latch and opened the door.

Just as she'd recognized Nicholas Warner from his photos, Lindsey did the same with Stuart Falkner. He was tall and lean, his toned physique the obvious result of work-outs at the gym. His suit was an expensive European cut whose fit screamed custom-tailored. And his light brown hair was cut short, brushed off a high forehead, which made his already aristocratic features seem even regal, his dark eyes even more intense.

Lindsey wished she didn't, but she saw the resemblance between them.

So did he. She read it in his expression as he studied her in amazement, assessed her from head to toe. "Lindsey Hall?"

One pale brow arched. "I think you've already

guessed as much, but yes. What can I do for you, Mr. Falkner?"

He managed a wry grin. "That seems like a stupid formality, wouldn't you say?"

She couldn't dispute that. "I suppose so."

"Then let's get past it. As for what you can do for me, how about inviting me in?"

With an uncertain nod, Lindsey stepped aside. "Of course. Come in."

He stepped inside, looking off-balance and unused to being so. "This is bizarre," he blurted out. "I was half-prepared to find out you were a fraud. Not that my father makes mistakes like that. He doesn't. But one look at you . . ." He drew in his breath. "You're my father's child. My half-sister. And I never even knew you existed."

Lindsey hadn't expected this. She'd assumed Stuart had come to put her in her place, maybe to announce he meant to contest her inheritance, certainly to make sure she didn't intend to squeeze a dime more out of his family than was absolutely necessary. Emotions never factored into her thinking.

"On the other hand, you *did* know about me," Stuart added. "And about Tracy. Weren't you ever curious? Curious enough to look us up?"

Lindsey maintained her composure. "I didn't have to look you up. Anything I ever wanted to know I could read in the papers. Other than that . . ." She feathered her fingers through her hair. "It's complicated . . . Stuart."

"I'm sure it is." The scent of the casserole wafted out from the kitchen, and Stuart turned, sniffing. "I've interrupted your dinner. I'm sorry."

"Don't be. It's just a casserole. And it won't be ready for another twenty minutes." Lindsey gestured for him to go into the living room. "Have a seat. Our liquor cabinet is limited, but I could fix you a drink."

"Just some water would be great." He waited while Lindsey got two bottles from the kitchen fridge. He started following her into the living room, then halted when he saw Irene rise from the sofa. "This must be your mother."

Irene nodded, a kind of faraway sadness in her eyes. "Hello, Stuart. You've certainly grown since the last time I saw you. You were eight. You were just learning how to play lacrosse."

He smiled, but the smile didn't quite reach his eyes. Then again, how could Lindsey blame him? Irene was the "other woman"—a woman who'd slept with his father and given birth to his father's child, none of which Stuart had known about until a few days ago. "I haven't played lacrosse since college," he replied with forced cordiality. "But, yes, I did learn that summer. Forgive me, I don't remember you."

"I didn't expect you to." Putting an end to the tension, Irene headed toward the kitchen. "I'll check on the casserole. You and Lindsey stay in there and talk."

"Thank you. I'd appreciate that." Stuart waited until she'd gone. Then, he turned to Lindsey. "I didn't mean to be rude. It's just that this whole situation is damned uncomfortable, to say the least."

"I understand." Lindsey took a gulp of water and perched at the edge of the sofa cushion. "I doubt you came all this way just to introduce yourself."

"No, I didn't." He cleared his throat, lowered himself to the armchair. "I'm here about the manor."

"Just the manor, or the money, too?"

Stuart's bottle of water halted halfway to his lips. Slowly, he lowered his arm, turning to give Lindsey an incredulous look. "You think I want to challenge your claim?"

"Do you?"

He shook his head. "It's pretty obvious you're his child."

"*Pretty* obvious. To a man as prominent as you, that wouldn't be enough. You'd want *definitely*. You'd want proof."

"What I want is to keep this from becoming a field day for gossip columnists. I want my father's name protected."

"In other words, you'd prefer this stay quiet. My stepping forward with proof would support your father's belief that I'm his daughter, but tarnish his image."

"Something like that, yes." A pause. "Lindsey, I'll be blunt. I want to buy you out."

Lindsey swallowed hard, as the impact of what he was saying sank in. "You're not just talking about the manor. You're talking about buying my silence. Your plan is that my paternity stay our little secret."

Stuart shifted uncomfortably. "I'm sorry if that sounds cold or conniving, but I have to think of my family. So tell me, how much would it take?"

A cool stare. "I'm not for sale, Stuart. Not at any price. I'm afraid you've driven a long way for nothing." She came to her feet with an air of finality. "If it eases your mind, I don't intend to make any public statements. In fact, I plan to avoid the press altogether. I'm not interested in proclaiming my identity to the world.

If people wonder why Harlan Falkner left part of his estate to me, that's their problem. However, if the truth does manage to leak out, I'm afraid that's *your* problem. I realize you have family to consider, especially your mother. But I have to think of *my* mother. She's been denied a great deal. I'm giving the manor to her as a gift. Your father . . . *our* father . . . wanted us to have it."

Lines of tension tightened Stuart's mouth, and he, too, stood. "You mean he wanted your mother to have it. Well, you're wrong. If that were the case, he would have transferred title to her years ago. The place has been vacant for ages. We never use it."

"Then you won't miss it." Lindsey set down her water with a thud. "I'm sure you think I'm being spiteful. I'm not. But, with all due respect, a scandal pales beside a lifelong injustice. You have a name, financial security, established family ties. You've never done without. Not a day in your life. I have. More important, my mother has. She's scrubbed floors for twenty-six years to make enough money to provide for the child your father helped create."

"I'm prepared to offer you millions. When you add that to the millions Father left you, you can buy your mother two mansions and a staff of servants for each, then hand her a pension the size of Connecticut. That's a great deal of financial security."

"You haven't been listening. This isn't only about money." Lindsey hesitated, choosing her words carefully. She wasn't about to divulge the intimate details of her conception. "My mother has a special fondness for that manor. Your father knew that. That's why he made it part of my inheritance. That, and the fact that he found out I love restoring old mansions." A sudden thought struck. "Are you aware that Nicholas Warner wants to buy the house and tear it down to build condos?"

A muscle in his jaw flexed. "I'm aware of it."

"Of course you are. And you'd sell it to him in a New York minute before you'd let me have it." She pressed her lips together. "Well, unfortunately, you don't have that option. I'm keeping the manor."

The finality of her words sliced the air, and Stuart made a frustrated sound, averting his gaze as he did. Lindsey could have sworn she saw a flash of panic there, but it was gone by the time he looked back at her. "I respect your feelings," he said evenly. "I'm asking you to respect mine. Your appointment with Leland isn't for three days. Use that time to think."

It was no surprise that Stuart knew her timetable for returning to Providence. Lindsey had the feeling the Falkners knew everything that concerned them. "I'll think over what you said. But, I'm giving you fair warning. I don't expect to change my mind."

"I hope you do—for everyone's sake."

4

LELAND MASTERS WASN'T ALONE when Lindsey arrived at his office that Friday. Pacing near the windows was a tall, slender woman in her early thirties. Her chin-length blond hair was cut in a blunt, fashionable style, her slate gray eyes were highlighted with just the right amount of makeup, and she was wearing a suede suit that screamed money.

Tracy Falkner.

"So you're Lindsey."

It didn't take long for Lindsey to deduce her half-sister's state of mind. Tracy marched over, scrutinizing her as if she were a piece of jewelry being considered for purchase.

"Yes," Lindsey replied coolly. "And you're Tracy."

Mr. Masters rose from behind his desk. "I agreed to delay our appointment for five minutes," he informed Lindsey, silently conveying that their transaction, when it was held, would indeed be private. "But Tracy wanted to meet you."

"That's fine." Lindsey nodded.

Tracy smoothed a strand of hair off her forehead. "Stuart was right. You do resemble Father, in a fragile sort of way." She gave an offhanded shrug. "As for why I wanted to meet you, it was to stop this ridiculous idea you have of taking title to the Newport manor. You work in Connecticut. The commute would be impossible. You'd be gone fifteen hours a day. That would leave your mother virtually alone. The house is over ten thousand square feet, with thirty rooms. She'd get lost in it."

Pausing, Tracy walked over to the chair, pulled some papers out of a briefcase she'd placed there. "According to my private investigator, you owe two thousand five hundred thirty dollars in various loans," she announced, scanning the pages. "Your car still isn't paid off. Your mother earns a daily sum of one hundred twenty dollars—and that's if she doubles up and cleans two houses a day rather than one. As for you, your salary is laughable. You should be earning four times what you do. You would be, if you worked in Stamford or Greenwich, rather than that poky little town you live in. Actually, you have the talent but not the resources to start your own architectural firm."

Lindsey was shaking with anger. "You had me investigated?"

"Of course." Tracy sounded surprised she'd be asked. "Did you honestly think I'd just accept you as my sister, no questions asked?" She tossed the papers aside without waiting for an answer. "When Stuart came to see you, he didn't mention a figure. I will. Eight of them, in fact. How does ten million dollars sound to you? Enough to make you walk away?"

Leland Masters was on his feet. "Tracy, for heaven's sake . . ."

She waved away his protest. "I won't cut into your time, Leland. My business with Lindsey is almost over."

"Correction," Lindsey returned, so outraged she could scarcely think, much less speak. "Our business *is* over—now. I don't want your money. I don't want your approval. In fact, I want nothing from you. So, if you'll excuse me, I have a meeting scheduled with Mr. Masters."

Tracy's jaw dropped. "You still intend to go through with this?"

"Without batting an eyelash."

Before Tracy could retaliate, Leland Masters intervened, his tone stiff. "It's time Miss Hall and I got started, Tracy. I'll be in touch later today."

Twin spots of red stained Tracy's cheeks, and Lindsey had the distinct feeling no one had ever refused her anything before now. "Fine. You can reach me at Stuart's house." An icy stare. "I'm not going back to Boston until this ludicrous situation is resolved."

She whisked out of the room, shutting the door firmly behind her.

Mr. Masters gave an awkward cough. "I apologize for that scene. Tracy is used to getting what she wants."

"So I gathered," Lindsey returned dryly. Her chin came up, and she met Mr. Masters's gaze. "I'm ready to sign those papers now."

Two hours later, Lindsey turned onto the private road leading to what was now her estate. She was still bristling from the altercation with Tracy, the drive to

Newport having done nothing to quiet her outrage. *Relax,* she chided herself as she made her way down the winding driveway. *There's a lot of work to do and no time to dwell on the tantrums of a spoiled snob.*

She'd purposely chosen a Friday to take title and ride out to the manor. It gave her a whole weekend to spend taking notes, making detailed sketches, and placing the necessary phone calls to contractors. She'd already made a huge dent in the process. Her sketchbook was brimming with potential floor plans she'd burned the midnight oil drafting over the past three sleepless nights. Not only that, but her mother's European trip was booked, her itinerary set. She'd be leaving in ten days, and spending a month abroad—two weeks in Paris and a week each in Rome and London. If Lindsey had her way, Irene would get back to find her new home well on its way to completion.

As if on cue the manor came into view, and Lindsey felt a surge of anticipation as she studied it. The exterior was mostly stone and brick, needing only the most minor repairs to renew it. And the interior, a great portion of which was mahogany and oak, needed only a good cleaning and polishing to restore its natural beauty. After that came the redesigning, the minor structural changes, and the—

Abruptly, Lindsey's thoughts broke off, and she frowned as she spotted another car parked in front of the door—the *open* door. She didn't have to guess who the car belonged to. She recognized the silver BMW from when she'd stormed out of here the last time.

Nicholas Warner.

He appeared in the doorway as she turned off her

ignition and climbed out of the driver's seat. "Hello again," he said, descending the steps, his navy sports coat and crisp open-necked shirt indicative of the fact that he was in the middle of a business day.

"What are you doing here?" Lindsey asked, her voice tight.

He shoved his hands into the pockets of his slacks, his hooded gaze flickering over her, then settling on her face.

She'd forgotten how intense those probing blue eyes were.

"Looking for some papers I had with me last time I was here. I have a key; I thought I'd mentioned that."

"Did you? I don't recall. But it won't matter after today. I'm having the locks changed." Lindsey wasn't feeling in a charitable mood—not after her earlier scene with Tracy.

Nicholas's brows rose. "Aren't you overreacting a bit?"

"Why? Because I want to make sure only my mother and I have access to our home?"

"No, because you're taking my head off. I'm a friend of the family, checking to see if I left my notebook here. You're acting like you just found a thief ransacking the place."

"Maybe that's the way I feel." Lindsey broke off, realizing she sounded irrational. True, she didn't like what Nicholas Warner stood for, whom he associated with, or what his plans had been for this manor. But that didn't justify venting the fury she was feeling toward the Falkners at him.

"I'm sorry," she said, feathering a hand through her

hair. "I'm taking my foul mood out on you. It's been a rough couple of days."

"So I gathered. Is this all the result of your inheritance?"

She gave him a measured look. "More or less. Let's just say I'm making a tough transition." A wary pause. "I assume you know I took title to the manor today?"

"Now how would I know that?"

"Do I really need to answer that?"

A corner of Nicholas's mouth lifted. "Are you always so difficult?"

The blunt question caught Lindsey off guard and, despite her tension—or maybe because of it—she found herself giving a rueful laugh. "I never thought so. But when it comes to the Falkners, yes, I guess I am."

"Then let's not talk about the Falkners. Let's talk about something else—like that cup of coffee we never had." He slipped easily into the role of social orchestrator, studying her intently as he did. "I know a place that serves great cappuccino, iced or hot. And a great sandwich, too, if you happen to be hungry."

Which she was, Lindsey realized suddenly. She glanced at her watch, surprised to see that it was nearly one o'clock. As if to confirm that fact, her stomach gave a purposeful growl.

Nicholas chuckled. "Ah, I see I've struck a chord. I might not measure up to your principles, but I managed to appeal to your more basic instincts. Come." He gestured toward his car. "I'll feed you."

Lindsey hesitated, as uneasy as she'd been at their first meeting, *and* as uncertain of Nicholas's motives. True, she'd turned him down flat on his offer to buy the manor. That didn't mean he'd given up trying. This second conversation was no less highly-charged than the first, fluctuating from tense to friendly to adversarial, ricocheting from one to the other like a stray bullet. Okay, so part of the reason for that was her defensiveness toward him—who he was, his relationship to the Falkners. But part of it was also skepticism with regard to his sincerity. What exactly was he after? Had he really given up his notion of buying the house? He seemed genuine enough, as if his only goal was to make her transition easier. So was it just his natural magnetism speaking, or did he have a more backhanded agenda, like softening her up for the kill?

She stopped in her tracks, eyeing his car but not making a move toward it. "I really can't take the time for lunch. I have so much to do, so many details to work out. I've only got a few days."

"You can't work on an empty stomach," he reasoned, and Lindsey noticed he didn't ask for any specifics about her initial restoration plans. Could that be because he didn't expect them to happen?

It was time to check out her suspicions.

"True," she agreed. "But we can accomplish both— filling my stomach and letting me get started. I could stay here and work. In the meantime, you could ride into town, buy me a sandwich and a cappuccino, and bring them back. Now *that* would be a godsend."

Silence.

"Not what you had in mind, is it?" she asked, a caustic edge to her words.

"No," he returned flatly. "It's not."

"And why's that? Could it be because you want an

hour to try winning me over again? Could you be looking for another chance to convince me to sell you the manor?"

Nicholas's jaw set.

Lindsey sighed, massaging her throbbing temples and feeling overwhelmingly weary. "Let's not play games, Nicholas. I'm not up for it. Just lay your cards on the table. I deal much better with honesty than with manipulation. Is all this about charming me into selling you the manor?"

"In part. Most of it is about charming you into bed."

Her head snapped up, and she stared at him in amazement, wondering if she could possibly have heard him right.

The watchful expression on his face told her she had.

"A bit too honest, huh?" he murmured. "I'm not surprised. I got the feeling you weren't exactly used to the direct approach."

For the life of her, Lindsey couldn't think of a thing to say.

"Are you offended, furious, or still convinced I'm playing games?"

Visualizing the number of women she'd seen draped on his arm in newspaper photos, Lindsey slowly shook her head. "None of the above. I'm just stunned. Then again, I shouldn't be. I might not be your usual type but, then again, maybe that's the appeal. A conquest from the other side of the tracks; variety is the spice of life, and all that. I guess it's ridiculous for me to be surprised. Picking up women is standard operating procedure for you."

For the first time he looked rankled, tiny sparks of

anger darting in his eyes. "Thanks for the assessment. Do you know, for a woman who keeps herself at arm's length so no one will get too close, you have no trouble inserting yourself in other people's lives. You don't want to be judged, but you're pretty quick to judge others."

Lindsey was taken aback, not only by his annoyance but by his appraisal of her. It was true she kept herself at arm's length, but she normally wasn't intrusive or judgmental. Yet here she was being both. And as for the touchiness he'd picked up on . . . "What makes you think I'm concerned about being judged?"

"The fact that you're so incensed by the Falkners' reaction to you. The defensive way you're responding to the knowledge that you're Harlan's daughter. The way you're sheltering your mother like she's some eighteenth-century mistress who's being whispered about at quilting bees. This is the twenty-first century, Lindsey. No one cares that your mother had a child out of wedlock, or that that child happens to be Harlan Falkner's. The tabloids will have a field day, sure, but they have a field day with everything concerning the Falkners. It'll blow over. It always does."

Lindsey drew a slow breath and turned away, feeling unnerved and off-balance, and not totally certain why. "You're probably right. But I'm a lot more provincial than the crowd I assume you're used to. My values are different. So are my priorities. I'm not used to being the center of a scandal, or to subjecting my mother to one."

"I guessed as much."

Lindsey stared at the ground, pondering his original admission. "With regard to the manor, I'm not going to change my mind. It's not for sale."

"I guessed that, too. But I'm a good businessman. I had to try." A whisper of a pause. "As for the rest, don't be so shocked. Okay, so I'm frank. I don't like playing games any more than you do. Yes, I want you. That shouldn't come as a surprise. You're a beautiful woman—a *very* beautiful woman."

"Thanks—I think." She'd be lying if she denied being pleased by the compliment. It wasn't one she heard often. By her own choice, she didn't date much. She had neither the time nor the trust when it came to men. Being admired by a charismatic guy like Nicholas Warner felt surprisingly good.

Maybe *too* good.

"Just to clarify those values I mentioned, I don't jump into bed with a stranger, no matter how charming and well-known he might be," she announced, setting the record straight for both their sakes.

"At least you think I'm charming." He didn't sound put off by her clearly stated boundaries. To the contrary, he sounded warm, teasing, whatever anger he'd been feeling having dissipated. He took a step closer, until she could smell the woodsy scent of his cologne. "As for being a stranger, I'd like to change that. So, tell me, am I charming enough to have lunch with?"

"As long as lunch is served in a public place and I'm not dessert," she heard herself quip.

My God, she'd just agreed to have lunch with Nicholas Warner. She must have lost her mind letting him get to her like this. But the truth was, it was more than his compliment, more than the knowledge that he wanted her, more even than his natural charm. None of those things would have been enough to sway her. There was something surprisingly real and down-to-earth about Nicholas, neither of which she'd expected and both of which she found appealing.

Laughter rumbled in his chest. "Fair enough. A busy restaurant and seven-layer-cake for dessert. Got it." His hand curved around her elbow and he propelled her toward his car. "Let's go."

"Just for an hour," she qualified. "I need to call several contractors before they disappear for the weekend."

"I'll have you back by two." Nicholas opened the passenger door, waited politely while she slid in. Then, he walked around to the driver's side, reaching into his pocket for the ignition key as he did.

He cast a quick glance at the house.

One hour.

He had his work cut out for him.

5

ROLLING HILLS LOOKED MORE LIKE A COUNTRY CLUB than a sanitarium.

With lush, sweeping grounds, an eighteen-hole golf course, an indoor swimming pool, and an enormous clubhouse—with one large room dedicated to bridge players, another to social gatherers—Rolling Hills was a resort-lover's dream, the uniformed staff and heavily secured front gates being the only indicators that this was indeed a place of confinement.

Stuart Falkner took an absent bite of his turkey club, watching as the nurses escorted a new patient over to the group playing croquet. The RNs introduced her around, encouraging her to join in. She was about forty, Stuart noted, wearing the same dazed, jittery expression all patients wore when they first arrived at Rolling Hills.

This place worked wonders.

"Sweetheart? Are you all right? You've scarcely touched your sandwich."

Stuart turned, smiling at the fragile-looking woman

sitting in the lawn chair beside him. She was over sixty now, but with her soft brown hair, artless gray eyes and flawless complexion, she looked like a young, uncertain girl. She still *was* uncertain, in so many ways. The memory lapses, the occasional periods of fading out and retreating to her own little world—all that was still there, though greatly diminished in frequency and severity. The doctors had cautioned that chunks of her memory might never return. To Stuart's way of thinking, that was just as well. Bringing certain things to the surface would cost her nothing but pain, and she'd had more than enough of that to last a lifetime. She'd come such a long way from the broken woman he'd brought here seven years ago. Thanks to the incomparable treatment at Rolling Hills, she hadn't had a drink in ages or swallowed any pills other than those prescribed by the doctors in order to ensure her continued mental health.

Yes, Camille's physical and mental state had been on an upswing—until two weeks ago when her husband died. True, she'd known he'd had a heart condition. She'd also known his strength wasn't what it used to be. Not to mention that she hadn't truly lived as his wife for years. None of that had mattered. She'd fallen apart.

Stuart had expected it. Besides his own sense of grief and guilt, he'd been sick with worry over his mother's reaction to losing her beloved Harlan. He knew he had to be the one to tell her, but he'd dreaded it.

The doctors had been on hand. He'd told her gently, with as few details as possible. It hadn't helped much. She'd gone to pieces right in front of him. She'd lived on sedatives for the first few days, with Stuart spending every waking moment by her bedside. She'd alternately wept, stared endlessly off into space, and murmured endearments to Harlan.

It took a full week before she finally started to come out of it. And now, these past few days, she'd been almost herself again. The worst of the setbacks were over, the doctors assured him. She was eating her meals again, sleeping without the aid of sedatives, even doing a little reading. Those were all good signs.

The best sign of all was seeing her sitting beside him, enjoying the fresh air and sunshine.

"I'm fine, Mother," he assured her, covering her hand with his. "Just not terribly hungry. I ate a huge breakfast with Tracy."

Camille's face lit up. "Tracy's in town?"

"Um-hum. And she'll be over to visit with you later. This way we don't have to share you. I have you as a lunch companion, and Tracy gets to spend dinner with you."

"How lovely." Camille squeezed Stuart's hand. "You both take such good care of me. I'm very lucky. Of course, Harlan always took good care of me. He watched over me like a hawk and made sure that—" She broke off, her lips trembling as she did.

"I know." Stuart looped an arm around his mother's narrow shoulders. "And he's watching over you still. I'm sure of it. He knows you're in good hands. Tracy and I will be here for you no matter what."

"Especially you," she whispered. "You've never let me down."

"And I never will." For the umpteenth time, Stuart thanked the heavens that he'd managed to keep his mother from finding out about Lindsey Hall. If she had any idea Harlan's bastard daughter had inherited the house in Newport . . .

She didn't. And she wouldn't.

Besides, it would soon be a moot point. After Nicholas worked his magic, the house would be theirs again.

Stuart shifted in his seat. Judging from the fact that lunch trays were being collected, he guessed it was sometime around two.

He wondered how the lunch in Newport was going.

"I've got to get back." Lindsey glanced at her watch, frowning as she saw the time. "It's late."

"Ah, the contractors." Nicholas set down his cappuccino mug, leaning back in his chair and crossing one long leg over the other. "I wouldn't worry; many of them are reachable all weekend long. Depending on the size of your project, of course."

Lindsey met his gaze, resting her elbows lightly on the table where her own cappuccino sat, still half-full. "The size of my project," she repeated. "Meaning that huge condo projects take precedence over small restoration ones."

"No, that's not what I meant." A sigh. "Are we back to verbal warfare again? I thought we'd gotten past that by now."

Studying him thoughtfully, Lindsey replied, "I'm not sure we'll ever get past that. I like you, Nicholas, but the truth is I don't quite trust you."

He looked more intrigued than bothered. "Trust me about what? That I've really given up trying to buy the manor, or that I haven't given up trying to take you to bed?"

No longer shocked by his directness, she shrugged. "It's not as cut and dried as that. Let's just say I have the distinct feeling there's more to you than meets the eye. What you do say I believe is candid. It's what you *don't* say that worries me."

"So now it's not only honesty you require, it's openness. Fair enough." He signaled to the waitress, turning back to Lindsey as the young girl hurried over, took Nicholas's credit card, and vanished.

Waiting only until they were alone, Nicholas shifted forward, folding his hands and looking Lindsey straight in the eye. "Here's openness for you," he stated abruptly, the easy banter that had accompanied their meal replaced by a quiet intensity Lindsey could actually feel. "I really want that manor. I'm determined to build those condos. Newport is one of the East Coast's hottest vacation spots. There's a growing need for luxury housing, not for the year-rounders or the mansion-buyers, but for those who want low-maintenance retreats that are theirs, not rentals. This way, they can get the tax benefits of ownership and use the place whenever they want. The rest of the time they're free to leave their unit vacant or rent it out. The project is a gold mine. I want to be the one to supply it. Is it ego? You bet. A desire to make money? Sure. But it's also more. It's good for the economy. It's good for the job market. It's good for the vacationers who've been priced out of the Newport housing market until now. So there you have it—my cards on the table, faceup."

Lindsey swallowed, feeling Nicholas's blue eyes boring into her, gauging her reaction. She knew full well what that reaction was, and she made sure to hide it even as she berated herself for feeling it. In a word, she was deflated. "So this whole lunch was about—"

"No." He cut her off. "This whole lunch was about getting to know you. That's the second part of this full disclosure you were looking for. I want the manor, yes. But I also want you. Don't confuse the two. I planned to make one last pitch for the house whether or not you agreed to come out with me. Consider this that pitch."

It wasn't that she didn't believe him. It was just that the whole thing felt so sordid.

Then again, he wouldn't understand that. He was raised in a different world, by different rules.

"I wasn't so wrong in my judgment of you after all," she murmured.

Nicholas's hand shot out, captured hers. "To the contrary, you were very wrong. You assumed I was some vapid jet-setter who regards life as a big party and who roars through it without morals, scruples, or principles. None of that's true. Okay, I'm ambitious. That's not a crime. I'm also tenacious as hell when it comes to business. But I don't live in a vacuum, consumed only by my own needs and wants. Fine, I'm rich. I'm successful. But I'm not shallow. I'm not a spoiled brat who's used to getting whatever he wants and who'll manipulate things, and people, until he does." A small flicker of amusement. "Oh, and I also don't sleep with every woman you see me photographed with. I'm thirty-five, not eighteen. My hormones took a backseat in my decision-making a long time ago."

Lindsey wanted to yank away her hand almost as much as she wanted to leave it where it was, the heat of his palm burning through her.

What was there about this man that confused and affected her so?

"Fine," she said tersely. "I stand corrected. I shouldn't have judged you. But I'm not selling you the manor. From what I saw, there's a lot of undeveloped land near the coast. Build your condos there."

His brows drew together. "Why?" he demanded. "Just answer me that. Is it because you're resentful toward me, or the Falkners—or both?"

"None of the above." She gulped down the last of her cappuccino. "I've already told you. It's because I believe Harlan Falkner wanted my mother to have the manor. I told the same thing to Stuart when he came to my apartment. Call it sentiment; call it whatever you want. I'm not expecting you to understand. But that house is going to remain hers. And, Nicholas, I won't change my mind."

For one long, silent minute he scrutinized her face. Then, he nodded. "All right." He paused to sign the bill and rip off his copy. "Consider the subject dropped."

She eyed him suspiciously. "Just like that?"

"Just like that."

"No strings?"

He grinned. "Just one. Take a stroll with me. Along the Cliff Walk. Just the first half mile or so. We won't have time to cover more than that—*this* time. The view is incredible, especially now that the rain has finally stopped and the sun is out. I won't bring up the subject of the house," he added quickly. "And . . ." He whipped out his cell phone in anticipation of her next objection. "I'll call the contractors myself, ask them to meet with you over the weekend. That will free up your afternoon."

"You'd do that?"

"Watch." He punched up a few numbers, and spoke to people whose names Lindsey recognized as among those she'd scribbled down to call. It was clear from Nicholas's tone that he had solid working relationships with these men, and that they were more than willing to do his bidding.

Ten minutes later, he pressed END and slipped the phone back into his pocket.

"Done," he announced. "I'll write down the particulars for you. Plan on a busy weekend."

Lindsey pursed her lips, a few doubts still nagging at her. "I assume these contractors won't be coached between now and then?"

He stiffened, annoyance and resentment tightening his features. "If you mean, will I call them later and tell them to turn down the jobs you offer, no. I also won't call and ask them to talk you out of keeping the place. In fact, I won't be calling them at all. Satisfied?"

She felt a stab of guilt. After all, he'd just done her an enormous favor. And she was repaying him with accusations. "Yes. I'm sorry for that question. It was rude and unwarranted. I appreciate what you just did. Your making those calls will set things in motion much faster than if I'd cold-called the contractors myself. Thanks."

His tension vanished, an inquisitive look taking its place. "Does that mean you'll take that walk with me? I could show you the view your mother will be able to enjoy in a few months."

"Can you spare the time away?" A challenging twinkle. "After all, you have a lot of research to do to site your condo development."

"Don't worry about my research. It's very thorough." Decisively, Nicholas pushed back his chair, extending his hand to her as he did. "As for my being able to spare the time away, that's one of the perks of being my own boss. I answer only to myself."

"All right." Lindsey placed her fingers in his, and she couldn't help but start at the rush of palpable energy that surged between them. She shot a quick glance at Nicholas, but his lids were hooded, his expression enigmatic. He looked pensive, as if he were in deep thought about something. Was that something her, and whatever was happening between them? Or was it the unexpected monkey wrench she'd thrown in his path—the task of having to check out new land for his project?

Either way, he'd made it clear he wanted her.

What was becoming less clear was what she wanted to do about that.

6

Lᴉɴᴅsᴇʏ's ᴜɴᴇᴀsɪɴᴇss ᴡᴀs ᴛᴇᴍᴘᴏʀᴀʀɪʟʏ sɪᴅᴇᴛʀᴀᴄᴋᴇᴅ by nature in all its magnificence.

She stood on the Cliff Walk, leaning up against the fence, taking in the spectacular view of the ocean and inhaling the salty air. She tilted her face up to the sun, shutting her eyes and letting the breeze waft through her hair.

"You were right," she informed Nicholas. "This is amazing."

"Um-hum." He joined her at the rail, gazing out across the water with a look of pleasure and pride. "And this is just the Memorial Boulevard section of the walk. The view gets better and better."

Lindsey's eyes opened, and she shaded them from the sun as she peered down the coast as far as she could see. "How long is the Cliff Walk?"

"It starts where we came in and runs south along the coast for about three-and-a-half miles. The terrain changes along the way. In some spots, navigating can get tricky."

"Really? It seems tame enough."

"Where we're standing now it does," he clarified. He pointed south as the paved footpath rounded the bend and disappeared from view. "It gets rougher as you go along. The hike becomes much less civilized and a lot more dangerous. You need good shoes and a good head on your shoulders. In some sections, the vegetation runs right up to the edge of the cliffs. The drops are steep. Wandering off the path without knowing what you're doing could be fatal."

Nicholas stared off in that direction, a fine but distinct tension coming over him. "I've seen a few close calls," he continued, his tone and expression grave. "People get careless. Or foolish. They put their lives at risk."

Lindsey shuddered at his somber words, the image they conveyed. "How horrible. Remind me to stay away from those sections."

"Why?"

"Why?" she repeated. "I think that's obvious. I'm not big on risking my life. I'd assume most people feel the same way."

"They do. So they keep their wits about them. But that doesn't keep them from exploring."

"They're not dissuaded by the danger?"

"Actually, they're enticed by it." Nicholas's entire demeanor changed. He turned toward her, taking a step closer, those probing eyes fixed on her face, heated sparks glimmering in their depths. "The wilder sections of the Cliff Walk are exquisite, Lindsey. They take your breath away. They make you feel alive and vibrant. They ignite your senses. What would life be like without that kind of cutting edge excitement?" He reached out, brushed a strand of hair off her face, then let his knuckles trail lightly across her cheek.

A tiny shiver rippled through her. "I'm not an expert on cutting edge excitement."

"Then let me introduce you to it."

Lindsey was well aware they were no longer discussing the Cliff Walk and, instinctively, she stepped back, breaking the contact. "Another time," she replied, averting her head and taking in the jagged edges of the cliffs that sloped down to the beach. "Today's not the day."

"When is? Pick it and it's yours."

"I don't know," she returned pointedly. "I've learned to be cautious when dealing with unfamiliar and dangerous situations. Otherwise things get out of hand. And, as you just said, that can lead to disaster."

"In certain cases, yes. In others, where the stakes aren't as dire and the possibilities are limitless, the pleasure is well worth the risk." It was clear Nicholas had heard Lindsey's message loud and clear—and that he meant to ignore it.

She cleared her throat. "Is it always so quiet here?" she blurted, changing the subject abruptly.

"Nope." He shook his head. "That'll end in a few weeks when vacation season gets under way. Then this area will be crammed with walkers, joggers, sightseers—you name it." A knowing grin. "Why? Looking for safety in numbers? If so, you don't have to wait for Memorial Day to explore the Cliff Walk. There's a two-hour tour given here every morning. We can take it. Although, frankly, I'd rather be your private tour guide. We can explore on our own, going at whatever pace makes you comfortable."

"You don't let up, do you?"

"Not when I want something, no."

Lindsey blew out her breath. "It's a moot point anyway. I'll be tied up with contractors all weekend, remember?"

"I remember." Nicholas paused, staring out over the water again, his expression nondescript. "Once the renovations get started, you'll be overseeing them, I assume?"

"Of course. I oversee all my projects. And in this case I own the house I'm restoring. I'll be out here for as much of the work as possible."

"What about your mother? Will she be driving out with you?"

"No, she's leaving for Paris in ten days to start the trip of a lifetime. As for me, I've got almost a month of vacation time saved up. I plan to spend it out here."

"Really." Nicholas propped his elbows nonchalantly on the fence. "Where will you be staying?"

Lindsey's shoulders lifted in a shrug. "We passed three or four inns on our way here. Any one of them will do."

"Not if you haven't made reservations by now, they won't. They'll all be booked for the summer."

She frowned. "I never thought of that. Fine, I'll stay outside Newport and drive in."

"You don't have to."

"Why? Do you have a better suggestion?"

"Um-hum." He gave her a lazy smile. "My first choice would be to ask you to stay with me. But I suppose that wouldn't fly."

"No," she retorted, shooting him a sideways look. "It wouldn't."

"I've got a huge place."

"One of many, I'm sure."

"This one's just a ten minute drive from the manor. Or, if you prefer, I've got a yacht right down there." He pointed. "We could use that."

"I get seasick. And I'm a lousy roommate. I snore."

Nicholas chuckled. "That I doubt. But, okay, I'll move on to my next suggestion—one I think you'll find more to your liking. You take my house. I'll take the yacht."

She gave an incredulous laugh. "Just like that."

"Just like that."

"That's a very selfless offer. Tell me, how often will you be dropping by, unannounced?"

"Never."

Her eyebrows rose. "Why don't I believe that?"

"Believe it. The house will be yours. No strings." Once again, Nicholas reached out, his knuckles brushing her cheek. Abruptly, he shifted, his thumb tracing the curve of her lips, first in one direction, then the other. The action caught her off guard, and Lindsey felt her body react before she could steel herself.

Nicholas felt it, too. "I'm not going to manipulate you into bed, Lindsey," he murmured, his gaze darkening as it followed the path of his caress.

This time Lindsey didn't pull away.

"If we make love, it will be because you want it as much as I do." He tipped up her chin, slid his palm around to cup the nape of her neck. "Do you believe me?"

Her nod was shaky.

"Good." He drew her close, lowered his head, and covered her mouth with his.

The kiss was electric, and Lindsey felt its effects like a jolt of adrenaline slamming through her system. Nicholas wasn't slow or tentative. His lips opened hers, and his tongue claimed hers in a hot, deep caress that told her exactly what he wanted. Her response came with a will all its own, her hands gripping his lapels as she leaned up, met his kiss head on. He didn't stop until she was kissing him back with the same intensity, until he knew it was her desire and not his seduction that was propelling her.

Then, he raised his head.

"Have dinner with me," he demanded, his eyes smoldering.

Lindsey swallowed, trying to steady her senses. "Just dinner," she qualified. "Then, I'm going back to my hotel—alone. I'm not ready for breakfast."

"Fair enough. I can wait."

She searched his face, trying to determine how seriously he was taking her. "I mean it, Nicholas," she said, forcing herself to be honest even if it meant coming across like a sheltered child. "Don't push me. As it is, I'm out of my league."

An odd expression crossed his face, and Lindsey got the feeling he was struggling with an unexpected conflict. "Funny, I was just thinking the same thing."

7

"WHAT DO YOU MEAN SHE DIDN'T SELL? You spent the whole damned weekend with her!"

Stuart Falkner paced across Nicholas's office, regarding his friend with a mixture of incredulity and apprehension.

"Exactly what I said. She didn't sell." Nicholas leaned back in his leather desk chair, deceptively calm as he fiddled idly with a paper clip. "And I hardly spent the whole weekend with her. Most of the time, she was lining up contractors." He leveled a hard stare at Stuart. "I don't know why you're so stunned. You told me yourself she was dead set on keeping the manor for her mother."

"Yeah, but you were supposed to seduce that idea right out of her head."

"No, I was supposed to convince her to sell," Nicholas corrected, his tone as hard as his gaze. "I tried. It didn't work."

"How could that happen? Did you forget how important this is?"

"I didn't forget anything. Obviously, you overestimated my powers of persuasion. You also underestimated Lindsey's commitment to her mother. She wants that manor. If I look at it objectively, I can understand why. You should be able to, also. You're trying to protect your family. She's trying to protect hers. Unfortunately, those goals conflict. Someone has to lose."

"Well, that someone can't be me." Stuart stalked over to the sofa, and dropped onto the cushion. "My mother won't survive."

"Camille is stronger than you think. You just finished telling me she was well enough to leave Rolling Hills yesterday."

"That was for a drive. Not to hear news that would tear her apart. She can't handle this, Nick. You've got to do something." Stuart raked frustrated hands through his hair. "When's Lindsey heading back out to Newport?"

"Her workmen are starting next week. She'll be here then."

"Did you at least make plans to see her again? Maybe change her mind before it's too late?"

Nicholas stared at the paper clip he was holding. "Actually, she'll be staying at my place."

Stuart's head shot up. "What?"

"Don't get too excited. We won't be roommates. She'll be staying alone. I've been relegated to the yacht."

"Right." A flicker of hope registered in Stuart's eyes. "That arrangement will last about an hour. Especially after you show up on her—*your*—doorstep, and pull out all the stops. Taking her out to dinner is one thing. Arranging it so she's sleeping in your bed is another.

Even a woman as virtuous as Lindsey Hall won't be able to resist your charms. Not under those circumstances. I don't care what our private investigator's report said about her girl-scout lifestyle. Good. Some cause for hope."

Nicholas didn't reply.

"Nick." Stuart gripped his knees, lines of tension tightening his mouth. "Don't let me down. I don't know how you got Lindsey to agree to stay at your place, and I don't care. It gives us another shot at making things right. Do this any way you have to. Get her into bed and keep her there long enough to delay the start of her renovations. Use that time to soften her resolve. Then, when she's feeling more compliant, persuade her to sell you the manor."

Slowly, Nicholas unfolded in the chair, leaned forward. "I'll take care of things at my end. Now let's talk about *your* end. Back off. Tell Tracy to back off. Neither of you has the slightest idea how to handle Lindsey. You think dangling dollar signs in front of her eyes will do the trick, and Tracy thinks she can browbeat Lindsey into giving up the house."

Stuart shifted slightly, looking more than a little uncomfortable. "What does that mean?"

"You know damned well what that means. First, you drive out to her apartment in Connecticut and try buying her off. Then, Tracy goes to Leland's office and lies in wait like some predator ready to strike, ripping into Lindsey and trying to shove ten million dollars down her throat."

"Lindsey told you all that?"

"Um-hum. Friday. Over lunch, and not happily.

What you did was stupid and counterproductive. Here's a news flash. Lindsey doesn't take well to being exploited. She's got every bit of Harlan's pride and backbone. She stands her ground. She's not impressed or scared off by the Falkner wealth and power. She wasn't raised on a diet of business hardball, but that doesn't mean she's a pushover. What Tracy pulled backfired completely. If she thought Lindsey would be intimidated by that verbal assault, she was wrong. All she succeeded in doing was pissing Lindsey off enough to intensify her resolve."

"I hear you." Stuart nodded, making a steeple with his fingers and resting his chin atop them. "And, yes, Tracy can be overbearing. Especially now, with this situation making her crazy. I'll talk to her. We'll both back off. But Nick, I want that manor."

Nicholas's brows rose. "*You* want it? I thought you wanted *me* to have it."

"That's what I meant." Stuart came to his feet. "The important thing is that Lindsey *doesn't* have it." He glanced at his watch. "I've got a meeting. Then, I've got to run out to Rolling Hills, do my daily damage control. I've got to make sure no word of this reaches my mother."

"Sounds good." Nicholas studied him thoughtfully, his expression neutral. "I have a phone call to make, anyway." He picked up the receiver, began punching in a number. "Send my regards to Camille."

"Will do. And, Nick—keep me posted."

Nicholas gave a terse nod. "When there's something to tell."

Preoccupied, Stuart left the office, headed straight

for his Jaguar XKR convertible. He climbed in, turned over the motor, and pulled out of the parking lot. He'd go straight home. Tracy would be there, waiting for him. They had to think this through, revise their strategy. Buying Lindsey off hadn't worked. Neither had threatening her. And so far, Nick hadn't managed to charm her into selling.

They needed a new plan. And they needed it now.

Behind his desk, Nicholas waited for the sound of Stuart's Jag zooming out of the lot. Then, he finished pressing the digits of the private line, leaning back in his chair as the number rang through.

"Hello?"

"Leland, it's me," Nicholas said without preamble. "We need to talk."

8

A WEEK LATER, Lindsey put her mother on the late night flight to Paris. After seeing the plane take off, she drove straight home from the airport, packed the last of her things, and turned in so she could get an early morning start. The contractors would be arriving at eight A.M. She wanted to beat them there.

The ringing of the telephone jolted her out of a deep sleep.

Her bedroom was pitch black. She blinked, trying to focus on the digits of the alarm clock as she groped for the phone. Three thirty-five. Who in God's name would be calling at this hour?

Abruptly, the cobwebs in her mind cleared, and her gut clenched. Her mother's flight. It had taken off six and a half hours ago. It couldn't have arrived yet. Oh, God, could something have happened?

She snatched up the receiver. "Hello?"

"Sell it," a gravelly voice commanded.

"What?" Whatever Lindsey had expected, it hadn't

been this. She sat bolt upright, her heart slamming against her ribs. "What did you say?"

"The manor," the gravelly voice continued. "Sell it. Cancel your plans. Forget about Newport tomorrow. Keep quiet about your bloodline. You'll get rich and stay healthy. Do yourself a favor—sell."

Click.

Lindsey stared at the receiver for a long moment. It was only when it began beeping stupidly at her and a computerized voice droned, "If you'd like to make a call, please hang up . . ." that she reached over, put the phone back in its cradle. Her mind was reeling, and she leaned back against her headboard, waiting for her breathing to return to normal and her hands to stop shaking.

Part of her reaction was relief that her mother was fine. A middle-of-the-night call when her mother was on an overseas flight—Lindsey's imagination had run wild. On the other hand, her own well-being had just been threatened. And while she was sure it was all an ugly bluff, she still felt unnerved.

She pulled her knees to her chest and wrapped her arms around them, propping up her chin as she pondered what had just occurred.

Whoever was responsible for that call knew she was leaving for Newport in the morning. They were getting desperate. So they'd decided to go for the jugular and threaten her safety if she didn't sell the house.

She tossed off the blanket and got up, all semblance of sleep having vanished. She was unnerved, yes, but she was also furious. The voice at the other end of the phone had been unfamiliar—some dirtbag paid by the Falkners, no doubt. Which one of her loving stepsiblings was desperate enough to arrange for that call—Tracy or Stuart? Or was it both of them? Were they so intent on forcing her out of their lives that they'd resort to scare tactics to accomplish their goal? And did they honestly think she was stupid enough not to guess they were the ones behind the call? Who else knew she'd inherited the manor? Who else cared if she kept it? No one but the Falkners had an interest in the place.

Wrong. There was one more person. Nicholas Warner.

An uneasy shiver darted up Lindsey's spine, although her mind was already screaming its denial.

Or was it her hopes doing the screaming?

Nicholas had called her three times since she left Newport eight days ago. And not only to make arrangements for her stay at his house. They'd talked for almost an hour each time, about nothing and everything, until Irene had started giving her daughter knowing looks and leaving the room so she could have some privacy.

Lindsey wasn't sure she needed privacy. In fact, she wasn't sure what she was feeling when it came to Nicholas. Excitement. Attraction. Desire.

Not trust. Not yet.

Could he possibly be the one who'd arranged for that phone call? He hadn't brought up the manor since their lunch two Fridays ago, except to ask an occasional question about the contractors she'd hired. Not over the weekend, and not during any of their subsequent phone calls. Nor had he made a single attempt to convince her to sell him the manor for his condo development. Was he still hoping to accomplish that?

Even if he was, would he stoop to threatening her into selling?

No. She didn't believe it. She *wouldn't* believe it.

She walked across the room, turned on the light, and began packing some last minute things.

Whoever had arranged for that call was going to be sadly disappointed. Their theatrics had failed. She was going ahead with her plans. In fact, since she was wide awake anyway, she'd leave for Newport immediately.

Nicholas stood in the doorway to his bedroom, staring at his bed and trying not to picture Lindsey lying naked on the sheets, her body intimately entangled with his. Unfortunately, it was an image that came to him a lot these days. And it was bad for his concentration. He had a job to do. Getting involved with Lindsey Hall was going to make it tougher for him to do it.

That wasn't going to stop him from accomplishing his goal.

He'd made a promise to Harlan—one he intended to keep.

Newport was exquisite at dawn.

Lindsey stopped her car at the entrance to the manor's driveway, easing her gear shift into park so she could turn and admire the view. The sun was just starting its shimmering ascent, and she rolled down her windows so she could truly drink it in. She gazed out toward the ocean, watching as slices of lemon and orange tinged the sky, glistened on the water.

Feeling a sense of peace that had eluded her since last night's phone call, she drew a slow, appreciative breath, letting her mind and body relax. She'd needed that tension release. She hadn't realized how much.

Leaving her windows down, she shifted back into drive, the ocean breeze rippling through her hair as she continued the rest of the way to the manor. She pulled around front and stopped.

The house looked regal at this time of day, the rays of the sun hovering over the manor like a golden crown.

The workmen wouldn't be here for two hours. That gave her tons of time to review her designs, to polish off the extra-large Styrofoam cup of coffee she'd picked up down the road, and to imagine her mother's face when she moved into her new home.

She let herself in, flipping on the lights and wandering through the hallway. It was odd to think she'd been conceived here, in one of the bedrooms upstairs, or maybe in the staff quarters behind the kitchen. Odder still, that that thought didn't bother her, but somehow gave her a sense of validation. After the history her mother had relayed of the love affair she'd shared with Harlan Falkner, Lindsey was having a harder and harder time viewing the man as an intangible entity, much less one to be despised. He'd obviously loved Irene enough to try to find some way to stay in her life and to offer something to their child.

If circumstances had been just a little different—if Harlan Falkner had been less integrally tied to his family and his high-visibility world—she might have gotten to know, or at least to meet, her father.

To Lindsey's surprise, tears stung at her eyes. She hadn't let herself walk down this road before, to contemplate these deeply personal might-have-been's. Not in any one of the handful of times she'd walked through the manor. Then again, she hadn't had any quiet time here, time to be alone with her thoughts.

She wished she knew more about Harlan Falkner. Not the business mogul, and not the fervent lover her mother described. But the man—the man who'd struggled between loyalties, who'd opted to leave her this manor with the full realization of what the consequences would be.

When had he made the decision? Before or after his wife's breakdown? Did Camille know about his affair with Irene? Was her drinking the result of that knowledge, or was it the other way around?

"A penny for your thoughts."

Lindsey whipped around, stunned to see Nicholas standing in the front hall. She'd never heard him come in. And the last thing she wanted was to have him see her in this vulnerable state. She wasn't ready for that.

Especially after the nagging question of who was behind last night's phone call . . .

"What are you doing here?" she managed, blinking the moisture from her lashes and trying to keep her voice steady.

He frowned, walking toward her. "You're crying. Why?"

She took an inadvertent step backward. "It's barely past six o'clock. Why are you out here?"

"I could ask you the same thing."

"I couldn't sleep. I rode out early."

"I know. I called your apartment to see when you were leaving. I got the answering machine. So I drove out to surprise you. I planned to be waiting when you arrived. It never occurred to me you'd be here already." He reached her, his forefinger tipping up her chin. "Are you okay?"

"Did you think I wouldn't be?"

His frown deepened. "Lindsey, what is it? What's wrong?"

She searched his face. He looked tired, lines of weariness etched around his eyes. As for guilt, he was either the best actor she'd ever seen, or he had no idea what was bothering her.

With that in mind, she took the risk.

"I'm tired and on edge. I got a pretty upsetting phone call at three in the morning." Seeing no flicker of comprehension register on Nicholas's face, she continued. "I was warned to sell the manor and stay away. Oh, and to keep my parentage a secret. Or else."

Nicholas's eyes narrowed. "Or else what?"

"The caller wasn't specific. He just suggested I stay healthy by following his advice."

"Did you recognize the voice?"

Her gaze was steady. "No. Then again, rich, powerful people don't usually do their own dirty work. Do they?"

Her point got through, loud and clear, and Nicholas's jaw clenched. "You think *I* had something to do with it?"

"Did you?"

"No. Then again, if you have to ask me that, I doubt you'll believe me."

"Frankly, Nicholas, I don't know what to believe. It's hard for me to imagine your being that cruel. On the other hand, you told me yourself how much you wanted this manor."

"I also told you I'm not the self-indulgent hedonist

you think I am. I don't always get what I want. When I don't, I live with it. I don't resort to the kind of tactics you're describing."

"How about your friend Stuart Falkner? Does he resort to those kind of tactics? Or what about his sister, Tracy?"

Nicholas rubbed the back of his neck, clearly uncomfortable with her question. "I can't speak for Stuart. Or for Tracy. I can only speak for myself." He reached out, gripped Lindsey's shoulders, his probing stare boring through her. "Look at me," he commanded, waiting until she'd complied. "I realize we haven't known each other long. Whatever it is that's happening between us is happening fast. That scares you. Who I am, how I live, scares you. I can accept all that. But I can't accept suspicions like the ones you're battling now. Trust your gut, Lindsey. Do you honestly think I'd threaten you just to get this house?"

Lindsey released her breath on a sigh. "No. I don't." She felt frustrated, unsettled, and just plain drained. "But someone would. And I'm getting a little sick of this cat-and-mouse game. It's starting to get out of hand."

"I agree."

Something about Nicholas's tone struck her, a hard decisiveness that was new.

"Why is it I can't get past the feeling that you know a lot more than you're willing to say?" she asked. "Are you protecting someone—Stuart, for example?"

"Nothing like that." Nicholas weighed his words carefully. "Whatever I might or might not know has nothing to do with you, or with last night's phone call. Let's leave it at that."

Puzzled, Lindsey inclined her head, studied

Nicholas's unreadable expression. She felt more curiosity than suspicion, an indication that, with or without any logical basis, she believed him. Whatever was troubling him clearly related to the Falkners, but in what way, she didn't know.

"You still think I'm lying," Nicholas stated, watching the speculative look on her face.

"Actually, no. I think you're telling the truth."

"Then what is it you're so deep in thought about?"

"I'm trying to fit together the pieces. How do you factor into the Falkners' lives? How close are you really, and what is it about them you're hiding?" She waved away the evasive reply she knew was coming. "Never mind." Just as quickly—before she had time to chicken out—she added, "Would you answer just one question for me—one that has nothing to do with your relationship with Stuart and Tracy?"

"All right," Nicholas agreed warily.

Now came the hard part. Lindsey wet her lips with the tip of her tongue. "You told me you knew Harlan Falkner for twenty years, that he gave you your first business break. What about personally? How well did you know him?"

Nicholas never averted his gaze. "He was like a father to me. My own father died when I was in my teens. Harlan took over from there. He was both mentor and friend. Why are you asking? Is this about his commitment to his family again?"

"No, this is about my getting to know my father," Lindsey managed to say. "I never had the chance before. I wouldn't have taken it if I had. But now . . . I had a very enlightening talk with my mother. Things have changed."

"I see," Nicholas murmured. He studied her with a delving intensity that was unnerving. It was as if he could see inside her, read her thoughts, and her emotions.

Gently, he reached out, caressed her cheek, wiped away the lingering traces of moisture near her eyes. "So that's why you were crying." He didn't wait for a response. "I tell you what. The contractors won't be here for almost two hours. That pathetic Styrofoam cup of coffee I see sitting in the corner must be ice cold by now. I brought a whole thermos of it with me, hot and freshly brewed, along with a half-dozen of the best doughnuts you'll ever taste. Why don't we sit outside, eat some breakfast, and talk? This time we'll get past the superficial questions. This time we'll *really* talk about your father."

Over the next hour Nicholas talked, and Lindsey was a rapt audience. He told her about Harlan's driving ambition, his dry sense of humor, his mile-wide stubborn streak. He got into Harlan's commitment to the environment, his aversion to shellfish and his affinity for classical music. He spoke of a man who prided himself on his people skills, who pushed himself to excel at everything he tackled—from investments to golf—and who tried a dozen different methods to get over his chronic seasickness, all unsuccessfully.

"He couldn't even look at a boat," Nicholas chuckled. "Not even when it was docked. The mere sight of it rocking from side to side made him lose his lunch."

"So that's where I get it from," Lindsey noted aloud. "Oh, I'm not quite as bad as that. I'm fine on kayaks, rowboats, canoes, even an occasional sailboat. But anything bigger than that?" She shuddered. "I went out on a friend's yacht once. The minute we dropped anchor and the boat started bobbing around, my insides started churning. I dived into the ocean and alternately swam and treaded water until it was time to head back. I love the water, but only as a spectator, a paddler, or a swimmer. *Not* as a passenger on anything serious enough to have a motor."

Nicholas shot her a sympathetic look. "Hearing that, I'm glad you're staying at my house and I'm using the yacht. I guess I won't be offering you any moonlight cruises."

"Not unless you're dying to send our clothes to the cleaners."

"I see your point." A wicked grin. "On the other hand, that would mean having to take our clothes off. Maybe we should try out my yacht after all."

Lindsey rolled her eyes. "You're impossible."

"Um-hum. But am I making headway?"

Averting her gaze, Lindsey wondered how the conversation had gone from teasing to intimate. "I don't know how to answer that."

"You just did."

Electricity crackled in the air.

Lindsey's cell phone rang.

She jumped, startled by the sound, and stared blankly down at her side where the phone lay. Recovering, she snatched it up. "I hope none of the contractors is canceling," she muttered, punching the talk button. "Hello?"

A slight pause, after which a male voice inquired, "Lindsey?"

"Yes?"

"This is Stuart Falkner. I need to speak with you. It's important. Can I buy you breakfast?"

Her gut tightened. "I've already eaten."

"I see. Lunch, then. Say, about noon? There's a great restaurant overlooking the Cliff Walk that . . ."

"That won't be possible. I've got contractors coming any minute. They'll be here all day. I can't get away."

A heavy sigh. "I realize you're leery of me, and my motives. The truth is, Tracy and I feel very bad for the way we've treated you. We'd like to make amends. Plus, we really do have something important to discuss with you. Can you just break away for an hour?"

"So now it's you *and* Tracy." She wished she knew where Stuart's head really was, what he was and wasn't guilty of. "Honestly, Stuart, I really can't. I don't have time for lunch. I don't know my way around Newport, and I don't have time to ask directions—"

"I'll drive you," Nicholas interrupted.

Her head whipped around. "What?"

"Wherever it is Stuart wants to meet, I'll take you there."

"Is that Nick?" Stuart jumped in eagerly. "He knows where the restaurant is. He can join us."

Lindsey was on the verge of refusing when Nicholas plucked the phone from her hand. "Stuart? Where and when?" A pause. "We'll be there." He pressed END and handed Lindsey the phone.

Resentment simmered through her. "Why did you do that? I have no desire to meet with—"

"Because I want to find out if either of them had anything to do with that phone call you got last night,"

Nicholas broke in. "I can read them better than you can. Plus, I think you should hear what they have to say. We both should—for different reasons, maybe, but equally valid ones." He met and held her gaze, although he didn't elaborate on that statement. "The contractors I referred you to are all pros. They don't need you here every minute. Trust me. Let's have this lunch."

Her indignation slowly abated. "You have some kind of agenda. I wish I knew what it was."

"Trust me," he repeated.

Slowly, she nodded, wondering if she was going to regret this. "I do."

9

THE RESTAURANT WAS CHARMING, elegant in a Newport-vacationer kind of way. Lindsey was glad she'd stopped off at Nicholas's house long enough to drop off her bags, freshen up, and change out of her jeans and into a pair of linen slacks and a blazer before heading off to this farce of a meal.

Nicholas seemed to sense her tension, because he wrapped a steadying arm around her waist as he escorted her through the lounge and up to the reservations desk.

"Hello, Henry," he greeted the maître d'.

"Mr. Warner, how are you?" Henry waited politely for Nicholas to respond before he plucked out two menus and gestured for them to follow him. "Mr. and Ms. Falkner are already here. I'll show you to your table."

They made their way to a quiet corner table near the open French doors that had a magnificent view of the ocean and plenty of privacy. Stuart and Tracy Falkner were seated there, drinking wine and having a heated discussion.

From the corner of his eye, Stuart spotted them, and cut short whatever he'd been saying. With a cordial smile he rose, his gaze lingering on Lindsey as if he still couldn't believe her resemblance to his family.

Tracy followed her brother's gaze, angling her head in their direction and watching them approach, her expression closed and emotionally contained. But the tight, arrogant set of her jaw told Lindsey that the restraint she was demonstrating was costing her, and that it was all an act.

Then again, this whole lunch was probably an act.

"Thanks for coming," Stuart said, addressing Lindsey but shooting a grateful look at Nicholas. "I know you're busy."

"Yes. Busy supervising the work you're doing on the family vacation house," Tracy added.

"I am." Ignoring the accusation lacing Tracy's tone, Lindsey slid into the chair Nicholas held out for her. "But whatever you needed to see me about sounded important. And Nicholas offered to drive me. So here I am." In response to the waiter's quiet request, she turned and ordered a glass of sparkling water.

"You don't drink either?" Tracy inquired, arching a brow. "I'm beginning to think you don't have any weaknesses."

Steadily, Lindsey met her gaze. "I have several. One is a bad temper—which I lose when my privacy is invaded, when I'm bribed, and when I'm patronized. By the way, I do drink—just not in the middle of a workday. I'm an architect, not a figurehead CEO. I do designs, not business lunches."

A tight smile curved Tracy's lips. "You certainly have the cutting Falkner tongue," she noted. "I'll try to remember that." At Stuart's warning glare, she continued, forcing out the words as if they pained her. "I apologize for the private investigator, for my brother's and my attempts to buy you off, and for that scene in Leland's office. I came off as a pushy bitch. The truth is, I'm just very protective of my family."

"Of which you're now a part," Stuart jumped in. He cleared his throat. "Why don't we order lunch? Then, we can talk."

"Good idea." Nicholas signaled the waiter, who was on his way over anyway. The round little man picked up his pace, hurrying over to place Lindsey's sparkling water and Nicholas's glass of merlot on the table. He then whipped out his pad, jotted down their order, and scurried off to the kitchen to have it filled.

"How's the construction going?" Stuart asked. "Has it started?"

"Barely," Lindsey replied. "I won't see major progress for a few days."

"What exactly have you planned to renovate?" Casually, Tracy set down her glass, inclining her head in question. "The place is in excellent condition. I'm sure it's dusty from lack of use, but I can't imagine it needing much more than a little sprucing up."

"It doesn't. What I'm doing is restoring the manor, making it consistent with its original Georgian style. As for major renovations, the only ones I've planned are to have the plumbing and electrical systems modernized. And I'm having a couple of structural changes done to make the house more suitable to my mother's lifestyle—

taking down a few walls to enlarge certain rooms, adding some windows for sunlight. I'm also having landscaping done, creating a front and backyard garden. Gardening is a passion of my mother's—one she's never been able to indulge in, since we've always lived in an apartment. Now, she can plant and prune to her heart's content. The contractors will be digging around the foundation to waterproof it, anyway. I'll have the landscapers do their work after that."

"It sounds very ambitious," Stuart said with another of those practiced smiles. "No wonder you plan to spend every waking moment of your vacation there."

"I don't recall saying that," Lindsey replied slowly. "But, yes, I will be at the manor most of the time. More out of interest than to supervise. As Nicholas pointed out, the contractors he recommended are pros. They don't need overseeing. I'll probably drive out each morning, stay as long as I choose to, then drive back at night."

"At night?" Tracy asked. "Why?"

"Because I like to look over my projects when it's quiet and there are no distractions. That way, I can evaluate my ideas, see if they look as good in reality as they did on paper."

"Really." Tracy's tone actually contained a tinge of admiration. "You're certainly dedicated. And thorough."

"You obviously know what you're doing," Stuart concluded.

"I should. I specialize in the restoration of historic homes." Lindsey paused, wondering where this in-depth discussion of her skills was leading. She was beginning to feel distinctly uncomfortable. "None of this is news to you. You know everything there is to know about me, thanks to your investigator."

"We know only facts. You're giving us nuances." Stuart cleared his throat again. "In any case, you're clearly top-notch in your field. Your mother must be very proud."

Warning bells sounded in Lindsey's head.

"She is." It didn't take a genius to guess that Stuart was steering the conversation in a specific direction. And whatever that direction was, it was the basis for this lunch.

Their food chose that inopportune moment to arrive, and everyone at the table fell silent until all the entrées had been served, the water glasses had been refilled, and the waiter was satisfied that he'd done all he could to make his renowned customers comfortable.

"That'll be all," Nicholas told him quietly.

"Very good, Mr. Warner." He took the hint and vanished.

"I hope you enjoy your salad, Lindsey," Stuart said, trying to dispel the tension. "The food here is quite good."

"I'm sure it is." She had no more desire to eat than she had to be here. But she dutifully tasted her chef's salad, chewing and swallowing automatically.

Another prolonged silence, presumably so they could savor their meal.

Lindsey's nerves were frayed to snapping, when Nicholas put down his fork and gazed steadily at Stuart. "You mentioned that this lunch was important," he prodded.

A slow nod. "It is."

"Then let's get to its purpose," Lindsey demanded with quiet intensity. "We've had enough small talk and food."

Stuart dabbed at his mouth, then refolded his napkin on his lap, and leaned forward, angling his body toward Lindsey. "You're very direct. I appreciate that. So I will be, too. Tracy and I have been less than honest with you. It's time we cleared the air, laid all our cards on the table."

"Meaning?"

"Meaning that, as you know, neither Tracy nor I knew of your existence before the will reading. What we didn't realize at that time is that our mother did. She knew that one of her maids, Irene Hall, was involved with our father. She knew that Irene became pregnant, and that it happened right here at our Newport manor. She knew that my father paid Irene Hall to disappear. Needless to say, that discovery took a huge toll on my parents' marriage and on my mother. The marriage recovered. My mother never really did—not completely. Not even after Father assured her the affair was over for good. She started drinking. She couldn't bear the sight of the manor, and that aversion got worse as the years passed and her emotional and physical state deteriorated. She tried to curb her reaction, for Tracy's and my sake. But eventually it became too much for her. We stopped visiting the summer house altogether. After that, Mother coped the only way she could—she blocked out all memory of anything relating to the affair."

"Blocked it out," Lindsey repeated woodenly. She wished she hadn't eaten. Her stomach was lurching, threatening to return its contents. "If your mother doesn't remember any of this, then who did you get your information from?"

"Mother's doctor. I went to him right after Leland told us about you. I wanted him to advise us how best to break the news to my mother. As it turned out, Dr. Farley already knew the whole story. It seems Mother confided in him. It was during one of those rare sessions when she experienced a flash of memory. When I divulged the situation to him—about you and Father's provisions for you—he told me he already knew. He cautioned me that my mother was protecting herself by forgetting, that it could be dangerous if she learned of these new developments. He believes it might push her over the edge. She's fragile. He wants to shield her. So do we."

A heartbeat of a pause. "I understand my mother is not your problem," Stuart clarified. "But *your* mother is. Dr. Farley went on to explain that he adamantly believes it would be psychologically harmful for Father's mistress to make her home in a place that can conjure up nothing but painful memories. He suggested we get rid of the house altogether, start anew—for everyone's sake."

Taking a deep swallow of water, Stuart leaned closer, determined to drive home his point. "I'm not trying to intimidate you, Lindsey, nor am I trying to buy you off. I'm simply asking you to do what's best. Sell Nicholas the manor. Let him raze it to the ground. Let the past be laid to rest. Who knows? Maybe we can start over. Maybe we can actually get to know each other, form some kind of relationship. Tracy and I are willing. But not with this albatross hanging around our necks."

If that wasn't emotional blackmail, Lindsey didn't know what was.

"This relationship we form—will you tell your mother about it?" she asked.

Silence.

"That's what I thought." Lindsey waved away whatever Stuart had been about to say. "Let's skip the mending fences. It's clearly never going to happen. I don't do clandestine relationships. And I certainly won't expose my mother to one."

"Fine," Tracy said a little too quickly. "What about the rest of what Stuart said—are you agreeable?"

Lindsey wasn't sure what she felt. Nor did she give herself time to consider it.

"Let's say I believe everything you just told me," she said. "You're desperate to protect your mother. Well, what happens if the press gets wind of my existence? What if they find out I'm Harlan Falkner's illegitimate daughter? It's more than likely, given the world's fascination with your family. The media will have a field day. News of my identity might even get through the fortress you've built around Rolling Hills. What will happen to your mother then?"

"She'll be reminded of a past she already knows but has buried in her subconscious." Stuart's comeback was so fast that it had to have been rehearsed. "Yes, it'll be difficult. But not nearly as devastating as what will happen to her if she's forced to learn that the manor harboring all her emotional ghosts is now home to Father's mistress and illegitimate child. I'm sorry to be so blunt, but let's face it, Lindsey, if you're nothing more than a news story, if the house is leveled, you'll be an upsetting but obscure memory, not a blatant slap in Mother's face. Now let's turn the tables. What happens to *your* mother if the press finds out about you? Let me assure you, her best bet is to be as far away from Newport as possible. Otherwise, she'll find herself directly in the line of fire."

Everything inside Lindsey went cold, and her suspicions over last night's phone call surged to the forefront. "Is that a threat? Because today seems to be a big day for my getting those."

Stuart frowned. "I specifically said this wasn't meant to intimidate you. It was meant to—"

"I'm not talking about now. I'm talking about last night. Somewhere around three A.M."

"You've lost me."

Nicholas spoke up for the first time since Stuart had begun his explanation. "Lindsey got a phone call in the middle of the night. She was warned to sell the manor, to stay away from Newport, and to keep her mouth shut about her blood ties to Harlan. She didn't recognize the voice." He took a sip of merlot, gazed steadily from Stuart to Tracy. "Neither of you knows anything about that phone call, do you?"

"What kind of question is that?" Stuart returned, a flush stealing up his neck.

"I think we're being accused of something, Stu." Tracy entered the conversation flippantly, taking another bite of her filet of sole as she did. "Our new stepsister doesn't trust us."

"Obviously, neither does our old friend." Stuart leveled an icy stare at Nicholas.

That stare didn't seem to phase Nicholas a bit. "I can't think of many people who would benefit from scaring the hell out of Lindsey. The three of us are definite choices. And I know *I* had nothing to do with it. I'm simply asking if either of you did."

"No," Stuart bit out.

"Tracy?"

She dabbed at the corners of her mouth with a napkin. "Three A.M.? I'm generally asleep around then. I save my threatening calls for morning."

"So you had nothing to do with it?"

"No, she didn't," Stuart answered for her. "Neither of us did."

"Interesting." Nicholas polished off his merlot. "That doesn't leave many suspects."

"It must have been a reporter. Word of Lindsey must have already leaked out." Stuart raked a hand through his hair. "Dammit."

"A reporter?" Lindsey echoed in disbelief. "Why would a reporter threaten me?"

"You're pathetically naïve," Tracy announced, that arrogant glint back in her eyes. "A reporter would do that to get a reaction. A reaction would mean a story. Why else?"

Lindsey digested that bizarre possibility. A story? The idea had never occurred to her. But knowing the press's fixation with the Falkners, anything was possible.

She studied Tracy and Stuart's reactions, thinking how ironic the world they lived in was. They were more worried about bad publicity than they were about potential bodily harm being done to another person. Still, Lindsey couldn't help but note Stuart's very genuine concern. His values might all be screwed up, but she doubted he was behind that phone call. Not unless he was one hell of a fine actor.

As for Tracy, she was impossible to read. She looked upset, her jaw clenched tight and her expression icy. What that meant was anyone's guess.

There was no way to prove anything.

The whole scenario was just too sordid for Lindsey's tastes. She'd had enough.

Tossing down her napkin, she rose. "I think we've said all there is to say."

Stuart's head snapped up. "What about the manor? Will you think about what I've said, maybe change your mind? That phone call should have clinched it for you."

Her brows arched. "Why? You just said whoever called was probably with the press. Which would mean I'm not in any danger, right?"

"Not physically. But if that was the press, it's just the first of many crank reporters who'll be on your doorstep night and day when this story leaks out. Your life will never be your own."

Lindsey pressed her lips together. "I'll take that chance. As for our mothers, mine is like me. She's strong. She's been through too much not to be. She'd thumb her nose at the world and say keep the manor. And yours? My guess is our father thought his wife could handle this. Otherwise, he never would have left me the manor." She scooped up her purse. "Honestly, Stuart, I think you're overreacting. But I'll give you the benefit of the doubt, just to put your mind at ease. I'll give this Dr. Farley a call, explain my position, and hear what he has to say. If anything changes my decision, I'll let you know." She pushed back her chair and stood. "Tell him to expect my call. Now, if you'll excuse me, I've got to get back." A quick glance at Nicholas. "I'll catch a cab."

"No need." He rose, his expression pensive. "I'll drive you."

"Nicholas, talk to her," Stuart hissed, as Nicholas went to follow Lindsey out.

Nicholas paused, his brooding stare shifting from Stuart to Tracy and back. "I intend to."

Stuart stared after Nicholas's retreating figure, muttering a curse under his breath. "We have a problem. Farley's never going to go along with this."

"We have a bigger problem," Tracy commented, resting her elbows on the table. "It seems our dear friend Nicholas has defected."

10

LINDSEY WAS GLAD THE CONTRACTORS were experienced, because she was in no condition to supervise their work. In fact, she was in no condition to deal with anyone.

The drive back to the manor was silent, with Nicholas leveling frequent probing glances in her direction. She felt his scrutiny, knew he was eager to talk. But she had too much to digest before she did. So she averted her face, letting him know she wasn't ready to discuss what had happened at lunch. He respected her wishes, at least for the time being, and bit back his thoughts. He even went so far as to drive her around to the manor's front door, and yet make no move to accompany her inside. He said nothing when she thanked him for the ride, but he did stop her as she groped for the door handle, holding her arm long enough to say he'd call her later. She nodded, feeling his brooding stare as she jumped out and darted up the stairs and into the house. He gazed after her for a few long minutes before finally driving off.

She hung around long enough to chat with the project foreman, who was covered with plaster as he stood under the scaffolding positioned in the manor's two-story foyer, directing traffic as his workers tore down the wall that separated the front sitting room and the salon. The house was bustling, with the electrical contractor checking out the wiring he needed to reroute, and construction workers retrieving tools and equipment, or clustered around the walls designated to come down, breaking off chunks of plaster.

Seeing how smoothly everything was running, Lindsey left, driving directly to Nicholas's house. She felt unusually jumpy, and she kept looking in her rearview mirror to see if she was being followed. Nope. Only the steady flow of residential traffic. Too many spy movies, she chided herself wryly. And too little sleep.

Then again, that wasn't a surprise under the circumstances. After all, she wasn't used to receiving threatening phone calls and attempted payoffs. No wonder her nerves were shot.

She drove up Nicholas's driveway and around to the front of the house, reflexively checking over her shoulder as she got out of the car to see if she was being watched. Nothing and no one. She walked up the stairs and let herself in, leaning back wearily against the door. Time to think of something pleasant.

She forced herself to focus on her surroundings, taking her first really good look at Nicholas's home.

It was a class act, just like its owner, she mused. All subtle tones of brown and beige, and refined touches she suspected were a combination of Nicholas's tastes and a decorator's skills. The lower level, complete with a winding staircase, contained a massive great room, and an equally impressive dining room and kitchen. The upper level, as she'd seen earlier when she changed clothes for lunch, held the bedrooms. The house had an open, airy feel to it, its polished oak floors and marble fireplace adding an elegant touch to its clean-lined, uncluttered furnishings. Cozy accents like a thick-cushioned futon and twin leather recliners in the great room—not to mention an impressive sound system—made the place feel lived-in, more like a retreat and less like the high-priced piece of real estate Lindsey's practiced eye told her it was.

She climbed the stairs, peeking into the huge master bedroom suite before turning in the opposite direction. When they'd dropped by earlier, Nicholas had urged her to make herself comfortable, to treat the place as if it were her own. Regardless, she wasn't about to use his room. Instead, she'd selected the second of the other three bedrooms—a sizable guest room done in shades of teal, with lots of windows and an adjoining bathroom. She went there now, cutting across the bedroom to hover in the bathroom doorway. The tub looked too inviting to resist, and she reached for her suitcase, tugging out what she needed and changing into a robe before heading off for a long, hot soak.

Five minutes later, she sank into the tub, letting the warm water envelop her, wash the tension from her muscles.

While she relaxed, she reviewed everything that had happened at lunch, more confused than ever by her half-siblings and their motives. Correction: not the motives themselves, but to what extremes those motives would drive them.

They wanted her gone. That much was as obvious now as it had been from day one. Were they behind that phone call she'd gotten? Was today's lunch simply a ploy to see if their scare tactics had worked? And, as a backup plan, had they elicited the help of a doctor to gain her compassion and send her packing?

It was sickening to think that anyone, even the Falkners, could convince a doctor to compromise his ethics and lie. Then again, they had untold wealth, power and influence. They probably contributed millions a year to Rolling Hills. That kind of money bought a lot of loyalty.

On the flip side, Stuart hadn't looked happy when she'd called his bluff, announced she'd be contacting Dr. Farley. So maybe the doctor wasn't involved. Maybe Stuart had made up the whole story.

She'd find out soon enough. She'd call Dr. Farley the minute she got out of the tub. If she jumped on this, Stuart wouldn't have time to prep the doctor for her call. She'd checkmate her half-brother, beat him at his own game.

That idea was scrapped a half-hour later when she phoned Rolling Hills, only to learn that Dr. Farley was off this week and wouldn't be available until Monday. Coincidence? Maybe.

Feeling restless and out of sorts, Lindsey pulled on a pair of jeans and a tee-shirt, then glanced at the bedroom clock. Five-thirty. Most of the workers would be gone, but a few of them, including the foreman, would still be finishing up. She'd kill some time before heading over there.

She perched at the edge of a chair and wrote a post-card to her mother in Paris—a cheery note that didn't so much as hint at anything unpleasant. She stamped it and scooped up her purse. She'd drive to the post office and drop the postcard in its outside mailbox. After that, she'd grab a sandwich, stroll around the more touristy area of Newport, then drive back to the site and check out the day's work. By that time she'd have the solitude she needed to properly assess how things were going. Hopefully, she'd also have worked off her restlessness, and would feel renewed and calmer.

It was almost eight o'clock when she rounded the drive to the manor. Dusk was settling over the area, but the sky wasn't completely dark yet, and there was more than enough light for her to see her surroundings. The top of the driveway was devoid of trucks, and the house was quiet, a sign that all the workers had gone home.

Good. She'd look over the place, see where the restoration was heading and if it coincided with the fin-ished product she visualized in her mind's eye.

Again, she paused when she got out of the car, glanc-ing around to see if she was alone. But the sensation of being watched was no longer there. Thank heavens.

She let herself in, for once grateful that workers always seemed to leave a slew of lights on when they went home at day's end. In this case, walking into a brightly lit manor was a welcome relief. It made her feel less vulnerable. Just to be safe, however, she locked the door before strolling through the entranceway and across the main level.

To the layperson's eye, the place was in shambles. There was plaster dust everywhere, along with wood planks, nails, and tools. She ignored the mess, stepping over everything and scanning the area, studying it through narrowed eyes. The work had progressed beautifully for day one. The kitchen had been ripped out and was down to bare studs. The plumbing fixtures in the downstairs bathrooms had been removed. And the wall separating the sitting room and salon was completely gone, the scaffolding having been moved to the other side of the house where the wall dividing the conservatory into two smaller greenhouse-type rooms was scheduled to be torn down first thing tomorrow.

Lindsey walked in that direction, imagining her mother's excitement when she saw the grand, fabulous conservatory that would soon be hers. She'd be in her glory. Starting this year, she'd be able to indulge in her beloved gardening even during New England's most brutal winters.

The door leading to the first greenhouse was shut, and there was no light peeking out from under it, almost as if the room had yet to be disturbed. That was odd. Usually, an experienced construction crew set up the next area in which they'd be working before they left, so everything would be ready to go when they arrived in the morning. She hoped the crew wasn't running behind schedule, although she saw no signs that they were. The sitting room wall was already down, and the scaffolding had been moved into its new position.

She eased open the door and peeked inside. Ah, false alarm. Everything was as it should be. All the necessary tools and drop cloths had been lined up neatly for tomorrow's leveling project. For whatever reason, someone had just thought to turn off the light and shut the door behind him.

She was just about to retrace her steps when she felt the vibrations above her, heard the sound of grating metal. Her head jerked up, and her eyes widened as she saw the oncoming disaster.

She turned and lunged into the hall, barely clearing the point of impact. Dropping into a squat, she curled close to the wall, covering her head for protection.

An instant later the entire scaffolding crashed to the floor.

Lindsey didn't move until the deafening noise had stopped. Then she rose, her legs shaking as she pivoted to survey the damage. The floor was a mass of wood and metal. A few seconds earlier and she'd have been part of that mangled heap. The whole structure would have caved in on her.

She squeezed her eyes shut, whether to shut out the sight or her thoughts, she wasn't sure.

Had this been an accident, or an attempt to hurt her? She'd never seen scaffolding give way like that, certainly not from the mere vibration of a door.

A door she'd been puzzled to find shut.

Sell the manor, her ominous phone caller had demanded. *You'll get rich and stay healthy.*

Dear God, had that actually been a threat on her life?

She had to get out of here.

The drive back to Nicholas's house was a blur. Lindsey's hand shook as she unlocked the door, and she double-bolted it behind her.

She went into the great room, dropped onto the futon. Maybe she should call the police. But what would she report? That she'd been the victim of a threatening phone call and a near-miss? One could be a crank, the other a construction accident.

No. There wasn't any proof. And they'd ask lots of questions—questions that would open up a big-time can of worms that would result in scandal and social embarrassment for the Falkners. She couldn't be responsible for that, not without hard evidence.

But in her gut she knew what had just happened was no accident. Skilled and experienced professionals such as the contractors she'd hired didn't make these mistakes. That scaffolding had to have been tampered with for it to collapse like that.

Which meant someone was setting a trap for the next person who touched the greenhouse door.

Tracy and Stuart both knew that someone was she.

Today at lunch, she'd specifically mentioned her intentions to go back to the manor tonight. Then she'd sensed that someone was following her. Had either one or both her half-siblings hired someone to keep track of her whereabouts and leave a surprise welcome for her when she dropped by the manor this evening?

If so, this was no longer a game of cat and mouse. This was a cold-blooded attempt to hurt her. To hurt her—or worse.

The phone in the kitchen rang, and she nearly jumped out of her skin. Bolting to her feet, she whipped around and stared at the telephone, trying to decide whether or not to answer.

It continued to ring.

Sucking in her breath, she crossed over and lifted the receiver from its cradle. "Hello?" she said tentatively.

"Lindsey?" It was Nicholas's voice, and it was taut with strain. "Are you all right?"

"Yes. No. I don't know." Her voice sounded shaky, high and thin to her own ears. At the same time, she wondered how Nicholas knew she was in trouble. Had he found out about the accident already? "What have you heard?"

"Heard? Nothing. It just took you forever to answer the phone. I know you're not asleep; I saw you go inside a few minutes ago. And I know what kind of shape you were in this afternoon. Now you sound worse. What's going on?"

She blinked to clear her head. "What do you mean you saw me go inside a few minutes ago?"

A brief pause. "I'm parked down the street. I was waiting for you to get back. I need to talk to you. But I know I promised not to show up on the doorstep. So I waited to be invited in." Another pause. "Am I invited in?"

Lindsey felt tears of relief burn behind her eyes. "Yes. Please. Come in."

There was another hesitation, then a click and a hum as the connection was broken. By the time she replaced the receiver and started for the front hall, she heard Nicholas's BMW roar up the driveway. She unbolted the door and yanked it open.

Nicholas was striding up the walk. His gaze swept her as he mounted the steps, stepped inside the house.

"You're white as a ghost," he announced tersely. "You're also covered with plaster. And you've been crying. Sweetheart, what is it?"

Maybe it was the endearment. Maybe it was her frazzled state of mind. Either way, she didn't think. She simply went to him, seeking some measure of comfort. "I was at the manor. The scaffolding collapsed. It missed me by inches."

His fingers bit into her shoulders, his worried stare delved inside her. "Are you hurt?"

Mutely, she shook her head.

He gathered her close, his embrace tightening as if to offer her his strength. "Tell me what happened."

She was too strung out to censor her words. She simply poured out the entire story, omitting nothing. "I don't think it was an accident," she concluded.

"I agree. Accidents like that don't just happen."

Lindsey swallowed. "Stuart and Tracy both knew I was going back to the manor tonight. They were the only ones I told."

"Not quite." Nicholas drew back, tipping up her chin with his forefinger. "You also told me. I was at that lunch, too, remember? Which means I could just as easily have rigged the scaffolding as Tracy or Stuart. I could also have been part of their whole lunch setup. Don't forget, if you caved in to Stuart's wishes, you'd sell me the manor, and I'd get to build my condos there. I've been torturing myself about that since we left the restaurant, wondering if I was back on your list of suspects. I need an answer—now more than ever. Do you think I'm involved? Or do you know in your heart I'd never hurt you?"

She shook her head slowly, seeing the anguish on Nicholas's face and wanting to erase it. "I know you'd never hurt me," she replied softly. "This morning when I said I trusted you, I meant it. When I heard your voice on the phone just now, I almost wept with relief. All I wanted was to run to you—for help, for comfort. I don't know why, but—"

"Don't you?" His tone was husky now, his expression still intense, but in an entirely different way. "Funny, I know exactly why."

He cupped her face and slowly lowered his head, giving her more than enough time to pull away. She didn't. She rose up to meet him, tiny shivers rippling through her as his mouth covered hers. The kiss was deep and drugging, Nicholas's lips nudging hers apart, wasting no time on preliminaries, demanding what she was more than willing to give. Whatever reservations she harbored based on who he was, how he'd lived, none of them mattered now. All she wanted was to lose herself in this unnamed emotion that had been building between them from the moment they'd met. She was tired of fighting. She just wanted to feel.

Nicholas sensed the change in her instantly, knew she'd abandoned her emotional suit of armor. His fingers sifted through her hair, tightened around the nape of her neck and, with a discernible effort, he dragged his mouth away, raised his head. "Lindsey." His eyes were smoky with passion, his breathing unsteady. "You've got to want this. *Really* want this. Not only to escape. And not only for tonight. Once we're together—I don't plan to let you go."

"That's convenient," she murmured, a soft smile touching her lips. "Because I'm staying at your house." Her hands glided up his shirtfront, slid around his neck. "And tonight, so are you."

He caught her wrist, brought her palm to his lips. "You're sure?"

She knew exactly what he was asking. This wouldn't be a one-night stand. It would be a whole lot more. "Very."

Without another word, he scooped her into his arms and headed purposefully toward the stairs. Those he took two at a time, rounding the landing and veering toward the master bedroom. He laid her on his bed, following her down and capturing her mouth for another hungry, searching kiss. He paused only long enough to drag her T-shirt over her head and throw it carelessly to the carpeted floor.

"I've wanted this from the first moment I saw you," he muttered, burning a trail of kisses down her throat, his fingers shifting to unhook the front clasp of her bra. "Keeping my hands off you has been hell."

He pushed the scrap of silk aside, visually drinking her in for a brief minute before lowering his head, surrounding one taut nipple with his lips. Lindsey gasped at the jolt of pleasure that speared through her, arching reflexively closer. He anchored her with his arm, brought her more fully to his mouth, and began an unbearable rhythm that drove her wild. His tongue lashed across her nipple, his lips tugged and released, tugged and released, until Lindsey heard herself cry out, her loins clenching tighter with each pull of his lips.

"Nicholas." Blindly, she reached for him, yanking at his shirt until he sat up, tore it off and threw it aside, then drew her up and against him.

Lindsey's breath caught in her throat. The contact was excruciating, his bare skin against hers, and she rubbed herself against him, her nipples contracting further at the warm, abrasive feel of his chest hair rasping across her skin. Her head came up, and she stared at him in wonder, seeing the heat in his eyes, the muscle working violently in his jaw. He wanted her every bit as much as he'd said. And he was trying to slow down, for her sake.

His palm slid around the nape of her neck, and he brought her mouth back to his, kissing her deeply as he lowered her to the bed. He unzipped her jeans, hooked his fingers inside her panties, and pulled them both down and off, taking her socks and shoes with them. His hands skimmed up her legs, caressed her thighs, his palm covering the tawny nest between them. His fingers eased lower, slipping inside her and touching her in a way that nearly brought her off the bed.

Lindsey's heart was slamming against her ribs, her body drunk on sensation. Vaguely, she wondered if it was always this wonderful. She doubted it. There was something electric between her and Nicholas. Something that made her lose her mind.

Lose her mind . . . God, she was being careless.

That awareness triggered a semblance of reason, and she acted on it now, before reason slipped entirely away.

"Nicholas?" Even as she spoke, her hips were lifting, seeking more of his touch. His fingers responded to her unconscious plea, gliding in and out in a prolonged, tantalizing rhythm, his thumb caressing her just where she needed him most.

"You're perfect," he told her fiercely, those amazing eyes blazing with desire, sweat dotting his forehead as he watched her face.

"I . . . not yet . . . wait . . ." she managed, barely able to speak.

"I can't." He stopped only long enough to yank off the rest of his clothes. "I want to, but I can't." He settled himself between her legs, bracing his arms on either side of her head. "Next time, I'll go slower. This time—" He must have seen the reservation in her eyes, because, with a supreme effort, he stopped. "What is it?"

"I'm not taking anything."

A flash of self-deprecating amazement crossed his face. "Lindsey, I'm sorry. Damn, this isn't something I forget." Leaning past her, he hauled open his night table drawer, groped around until he found a box of condoms. He pulled one out, dealing with it with the expertise of a man who was used to doing so. Vaguely, she realized that the implications of that should bother her. They didn't. Somehow she knew what the two of them had together was different.

She studied his body as he loomed over her. He was all power and sheer masculine beauty, and her palms explored him, feeling the hot, hair-roughened texture of his chest, the corded muscles of his shoulders and arms.

He shuddered beneath her touch, moved urgently back into position. "I want you," he ground out, pressing her into the pillows. His chest was rising and falling with each breath, and he lifted her legs to hug his flanks. "I'm about to explode. That's how much I want you." He kissed her again, his tongue taking hers as his body began its penetration.

Her body was screaming for his. She wrapped her arms around his back, and her eyes slid shut as she felt him crowd into her. His hands gripped her bottom, angling her toward him and, with one hard thrust, he pushed all the way inside.

They both felt the resistance give, but Lindsey was so lost in sensation she scarcely winced.

Nicholas was another story. He froze. "Lindsey?"

"Don't stop," she protested weakly. Her nails dug into his back, and she urged him on, shifting to ease his way inside her.

His breath emerged in a hiss, but he fought the instinctive motion of his hips, which were already propelling him deeper. He turned his lips into her hair, his words a harsh rasp of sound. "Why didn't you tell me?"

"Later," she whispered. "Please."

Nicholas sucked in his breath, the muscles in his arms bulging with the strain of holding back.

"Please," she repeated. "I'm dying. Make love to me."

It was enough.

"I'll go slowly if it kills me," he vowed in a voice that was thick with passion. He circled his hips against hers, giving her a taste of what was to be. "Which it might."

He withdrew, pressed forward one tantalizing inch at a time. But Lindsey would have none of it. She wanted the pleasure that hovered just out of reach, and she wanted it now.

Instinct guided her. She arched when he pushed, forced their bodies into a deeper joining. She knew the instant Nicholas's control snapped, because a hard tremor racked his body, dragging her name from his lips. His fingers bit into her thighs and his strokes became fast, deep, driving him farther and farther into her clinging passage.

Lindsey couldn't breathe, the pleasure was so intense.

She just clung to him, matched his rhythm, and felt her body coil tighter and tighter as it escalated toward an unknown pinnacle of sensation.

She found that pinnacle, and she heard herself cry out Nicholas's name as her body unraveled in a series of pulsing contractions too exquisite to bear.

Nicholas went rigid, pushing into each rhythmic spasm, letting her body milk his until holding back became an impossibility.

He came powerfully, his orgasm as overwhelming as hers, and he threw back his head, grinding out her name through clenched teeth as he gave in to the sensation.

He collapsed on top of her, too exhausted to move, blanketing her with his weight for long, languorous minutes.

At last, he managed to lift himself away, rolling onto his back and pulling her against him. "Are you okay?" he asked, his voice rough, unsteady.

She nodded, even that gesture almost too difficult to muster. "Very okay."

His lips brushed her hair. "Why?"

"Which why? Why was I a virgin? Or why didn't I tell you?"

"Both."

Lindsey swallowed. This wasn't easy to talk about. Her mother's life, the way it had impacted her own, the decisions she'd subsequently made—she wasn't sure anyone who hadn't experienced her background could understand. But she had to try. Nicholas deserved an answer.

"Why was I a virgin? An emotional reason, not a

moral one. After seeing what my mother went through—letting her involvement with a man ruin her life—let's say I've always kept men at arm's length. Until now. Why didn't I tell you? I guess it never occurred to me that it would make a difference. Does it?"

"Yes," Nicholas returned fervently. "I said I'd never hurt you. I did."

She smiled, propping herself on one elbow and gazing at him. "I forgive you. You were wonderful."

"So were you." He drew her mouth down to his, kissed her tenderly. "I meant it, Lindsey. I don't intend to let you go."

"I don't want to go," she heard herself say.

An odd expression crossed his face. "I never expected this. But I'm beginning to think Harlan did. In fact, I think he was counting on it."

Lindsey blinked. "You think he wanted us together?"

"The more I consider it—yes, that's exactly what I think. Now that I remember some of the comments he made, some of the conversations we had with Leland . . . I never gave them much thought before, but now that I do, it makes sense. Your father was a brilliant, tactical man. He never did anything that wasn't part of some bigger plan. My guess is, you and I are part of that plan."

She tucked the sheet around her, sat up. "You'd better explain."

"Yes, I'd better." Nicholas pushed himself to a sitting position, and drew Lindsey around to face him. "I wasn't ready to talk about this yet. But, under the circumstances—what's happening between us, that supposed accident at the manor—my subtle poking around is no longer enough. Not when I believe the threats on your life and Harlan's concerns are related."

Lindsey gave an exasperated shrug. "Nicholas, you're talking in riddles."

"Not anymore. It's time I filled in the blanks. You wanted to know my agenda? Well, here it is."

11

Lindsey watched Nicholas's expression, knowing in her heart that what she was about to hear was going to greatly impact her frame of reference, if not her life.

She wasn't wrong.

"I told you how I felt about Harlan," Nicholas began. "He was like a father to me. We were very close, closer in some ways than he was with Stuart or Tracy. Oh, he was crazy about his kids. But neither of them thought quite the way he did. Our minds were very much in sync. Between that and the fact that he needed an impartial ear, he opened up to me about several things. One of those things was his children." Nicholas frowned, staring off into space. "Harlan had a heart condition, a bad one. The last year of his life, it deteriorated to the point where even his medication didn't help. He knew he was living on borrowed time. Unfortunately, so did Stuart and Tracy."

"Why unfortunately?" Lindsey asked, puzzled. "I'd think they'd want to know so they could spend as much time with him as possible." *Time I never had,* she added silently to herself.

"They did. Stuart was glued to his father's side, and Tracy came in from Boston for half a week at a time. But it wasn't the gentle time of closure it should have been. The three of them argued, constantly. The doctor cautioned Harlan to keep calm, but something about his kids was eating him up inside. I tried to get him to talk to me, but he wouldn't. Not until the end. The week before he died, he called me into his office, said he was changing the allocation of his estate."

"The manor," Lindsey murmured. "He was leaving it to me."

"That would be my guess. He said Stuart and Tracy knew nothing about these changes, just as they knew nothing about your existence. But he was worried. And not only about their reaction when they found out about you and the steps he'd taken to provide for you. He was worried that they were involved in something unethical, maybe even illegal, under the guise of protecting the family. Whatever that something was, it wasn't tied to his businesses. He'd checked that out himself, and then had Leland and a staff of financial experts do the same. All his companies and the individual departments were operating on the up-and-up. All his assets were intact. Which made him worry all the more."

"Why? What else could they harm?"

"You. You and your mother. Harlan was determined to provide for you, but he was worried sick about how that would factor into whatever Tracy and Stuart were up to. He begged me to get to the bottom of this, to find out what they were doing, to protect them from themselves. More important, he wanted me to protect you. He asked that of both Leland and me. No matter what, he wanted you kept safe."

Lindsey tasted salt, and realized she was crying. "I . . . I didn't realize."

"I know you didn't. That's why I told you how sorry Harlan was that he'd never known you. It was one of the greatest sorrows of his life. He loved you, Lindsey, whether or not you believe it."

"I'm beginning to." Lindsey wet her lips, stared at the sheets. "You said my father opened up to you about a lot of things. Obviously, that includes his children—*all* his children. Does it also include my mother?"

"To some degree, yes." Nicholas caught her chin between his fingers, gently lifted her gaze to meet his. "I don't know details. Harlan kept those to himself. But I do know he was tormented with guilt. He believed he should have found a way to help Irene, and to be there for you. He talked about your future, and how he wanted to make it secure and happy. But his hands were tied. Camille was sick. She was drinking herself into oblivion. More and more so as the years progressed."

Painful memories darkened Nicholas's eyes. "Sixteen years ago, right after Stuart and I finished our freshman year at Harvard, we drove down to spend a week or two at the Newport manor. A few days into our vacation, Harlan showed up. He looked terrible, almost haunted. Later, I found out he'd just come from visiting your mother."

Slowly, Lindsey nodded. "When she opened up to me about how things had really been between them, my mother said that my father had tried several times to get through to her. The last time was when I was about ten. She sent him away—again."

"Well, it tore him up pretty badly. He barely spoke to Stuart or me, just wandered around the house looking miserable. We realized he wanted to be alone. So we packed up to leave. We were about to head out, when Camille exploded in. She'd followed Harlan to the house. Apparently, she thought he had arranged some kind of rendezvous with Irene. I'm not sure what made her think that; she was irrational by that time. She went a little crazy, shattering crystal and sobbing accusations. She downed half a bottle of vodka, then took off. Stuart jumped in one car, Harlan and I in another. We split up so we'd have a better chance of finding her. Stuart got to her first. He found her car at the entrance to the Cliff Walk. By the time Harlan and I showed up, she was staggering around on that rough section I pointed out to you. She nearly fell and killed herself. If Stuart hadn't grabbed her when he did . . . I shudder to think what would have happened."

"So that's why you got that strange look on your face when you showed me the wilder portions of the Cliff Walk," Lindsey murmured.

"Exactly. And it wasn't the only near-miss Camille had there. There was another one, about nine years later. That time it was a blatant suicide attempt. I don't know what prompted it, or why Camille was there in the first place. The doctors felt that the amount of pills and alcohol she was consuming by then made her delusional. Stuart was terrified she'd try again—and succeed. He and Harlan did some research. They found Rolling Hills. Camille was admitted a few weeks later."

Lindsey swallowed. The situation was tragic. And what she was about to ask would probably sound horribly insensitive. Still, she had to know.

"Nicholas, from the way you describe Camille's condition, it was much worse than I imagined."

"That's because Harlan managed to keep most of it from the media. If he hadn't, the whole sordid story would have been splashed on page one of every tabloid in America."

"I understand. He was devoted to his family." Lindsey searched Nicholas's face. "Is it possible that's the only reason he stayed with her—out of duty?"

Nicholas didn't look offended by her question. On the contrary, he looked as if he'd expected it. "It's more than possible. At the time when Harlan was involved with your mother, his children were young. He would never have traumatized them with a divorce. But later? When they were grown? If he'd met Irene then, things might have been different. He might have taken the risk—*if* Camille's mental state hadn't been so fragile. Regardless, if you're asking if he was happy, the answer is no. He was committed to Camille's well-being, but he wasn't a husband, not in any real sense. Does that help?"

"I don't know." Lindsey ran a hand through her hair. "If he was still in love with my mother, then, yes, it helps."

A brief hesitation. "He never said it aloud, but my guess is, he was. The way he spoke of her—not the words, but the tone—the pride he took in your accomplishments . . . as I said, I can't be sure, but I suspect his feelings were still there."

Lindsey's mind was reeling. "You said he asked you to look out for me."

"Not just to look out for you. To make things right. To stay close by as you made your adjustment, to talk to you about him, to help you with your inheritance. At that point, I suggested that Leland, as Harlan's legal adviser, would make a better choice. But Harlan nixed that idea, saying your inheritance and how it should be handled was right up my alley. I guessed that meant it included real estate. So I agreed. Still, when I met with him and Leland, I thought it was strange how involved in your life they wanted me to be. Now I'm not so sure it was as strange as it seemed."

"You think they were playing matchmaker?" Lindsey asked incredulously.

A slow smile curved Nicholas's lips, and he reached out, traced the curve of her bare shoulder. "Pretty good matchmaking, wouldn't you say?" His knuckles caressed her cheek. "Yeah, I have a hunch that's what they were doing. But we'll have to get confirmation from Leland."

Lindsey's brows drew together. "How much does Mr. Masters know?"

"Everything. He's been working with me to figure out what Stuart and Tracy are up to. Whatever it is, they're desperate to make you go away."

"Desperate enough to kill me?"

Nicholas's smile faded, and he gave a troubled shrug. "I don't know. Stuart was pressuring the hell out of me to seduce you into selling me the manor—to the point of being irrational. So, yes, I think he's out of control. But to rig a scaffolding to fall on you? That's another story. I've known Stuart for twenty years. Yeah, he'd do just about anything for his family, especially Camille. But violence? I never would have believed it."

"Unless whatever he's involved in is serious, maybe criminal—and I'm a threat to it."

"Right. Or unless it's Tracy who's behind this."

Lindsey drew a slow breath. "You think she's more capable of violence than her brother?"

"I think she's harder and colder than her brother. Other than that . . ." Nicholas shrugged again. "I don't know her as well as I know Stuart." His jaw tightened. "But I intend to get at the truth."

"How?"

"It's time to pull out the stops and back those two into a corner. You and I will head out to the manor first thing tomorrow for cleanup and questions. I'll call Stuart and Tracy, presumably so they can ward off the press. They'll come tearing over. I'll leak enough of what I know—what their father suspected—to knock them off-balance. Then I'll issue an ultimatum. That'll do it."

"I'm sure it will," Lindsey agreed. "Okay, so that's tomorrow. What do we do in the meantime?"

"In the meantime, I stick to you like glue, from now until whenever we resolve this insanity."

"Like glue, huh?" Lindsey attempted a smile. "That could be interesting, especially since my plans for the rest of the night involved staying in bed."

"How convenient." Nicholas's eyes turned that heated shade of dark blue, and he tugged the sheet away from Lindsey's body, eased her onto her back. He groped for the box of condoms, tossing the entire box on top of his night table. "I guess I'll be confined to bed, too. After all, I did promise to take excellent care of you, to stay close by while you adjusted to your new life."

She wrapped her arms around his neck, drew him closer. "I like the sound of that."

"Me, too." He tunneled his fingers through her hair, lowered his mouth to hers, and kissed her deeply, reluctantly pulling away while he still had the presence of mind to do so. "Give me a minute."

"Okay—*one* minute."

He took less, returning to cover her body with his. "Better?"

"M-m-m . . . much."

"Good. Now, tell me when you feel adjusted." He settled himself between her thighs, pressed slowly forward. "*Fully* adjusted."

Lindsey's breath caught, and she arched to bring him more fully inside her. "That might take a while."

He shuddered, his chuckle emerging as a hoarse groan. "Somehow I doubt it. But we'll test your adaptation in every way possible—just to make absolutely sure."

The man stood outside the heavy oak door, bracing himself for the less-than-chipper reception he was about to get. He didn't have the news she wanted. This conversation wasn't going to be pleasant.

Sucking in his breath, he pushed open the door and stepped into the room. "Ms. Falkner."

Her head snapped up the minute he walked in, and she put down her fountain pen, rose from behind her desk. "Mike. Finally." She raised her chin, scrutinizing him intently. "Well? I've been on pins and needles all night. Is it done?"

He shifted, shoving his hands into his pockets. "Yes and no. I rigged the thing like you asked."

"And did she show up?"

"Yup. Around eight o'clock. She went in by herself. Everything went just like you said it would. Except that she's quicker than we thought. She got out of the way before the thing collapsed."

"Damn." A frown. "We were supposed to be rid of her—permanently."

"*That* we might be," the man said brightly. "She drove away from that place like a bat out of hell."

"Did she drive all the way back to Connecticut?"

"No. At least not yet. She drove to Warner's house."

"Then maybe you should have taken care of her there."

"I thought of it. But I didn't know if you wanted me to be that obvious. Right now, there's still no proof anyone's trying to hurt her. If I break in and attack her outright, the whole accident theory goes out the window. Besides, she's not alone. Warner's with her."

Her eyes glittered bitterly. "Comforting her, no doubt. As only Nicholas Warner can." A contemplative pause. "Fine. Maybe we can use this new attachment she and Nicholas have for each other to our advantage. A few subtle moves, an unfortunate accident, and Lindsey Hall will be wiped from our lives for good."

12

It was eight a.m., and the construction crew had already begun its cleanup when Stuart Falkner's car came racing up the driveway. He jumped out, strode up to the front door and into the manor. A few paces in, he stopped, taking in the whole scene at once.

Nicholas tapped Lindsey on the shoulder to let her know her half-brother had arrived. She nodded, not bothering to turn around—yet. They'd agreed that Nicholas should take the lead in dealing with Stuart.

Stiffly, Nicholas walked over. "Stuart," he acknowledged. "Where's Tracy?"

"H-m-m?" With an effort, Stuart tore his stare away from what was left of the scaffolding. "Oh—she must be tied up with something. I couldn't reach her last night or this morning." His gaze wandered back to the huge pile of wood planks being removed from the floor. "You weren't exaggerating," he muttered. "Christ, the whole damned thing crashed down."

"It sure did," Nicholas agreed. "It missed Lindsey by inches."

Stuart dragged a hand through his hair, his entire body tensing as Lindsey broke away from the clean-up crew and came over to join them.

"Hello, Stuart."

"Lindsey." His forehead creased. "Nick said you were here when this happened. Are you okay?"

"I'm fine." She gave him a tight smile. "Just scared out of my wits. I got lucky. I managed to jump out of the way in time."

"How could something like this have happened?" Stuart demanded.

"I don't know." Lindsey kept her tone calm, detached, playing out her part as she and Nicholas had planned. "It just did. In any case, let's get to the purpose of your visit— you know, the *real* reason you came tearing out here. You can relax. Nicholas is the only one I told about the accident. So, as long as you took care of any press leaks, your family won't be subjected to ugly publicity. Okay? Now, if you'll excuse me, I have a cleanup to supervise so my construction schedule stays on track." She turned.

"Your construction schedule? You're still going on with this?" Stuart blurted out. "You almost got killed, and you're sticking to your plan to keep the place?"

"After I renovate it, yes," Lindsey supplied. "Why wouldn't I? After all, what happened was an accident. And accidents do happen, even with a top-notch construction team like the one Nicholas provided." She gave an offhanded shrug. "Anyway, it's back to work for me. I'll catch you later." She headed back to the hallway just outside the greenhouse.

"I don't believe this." Staring after her, Stuart gave a hard shake of his head. "There really is no getting through to her, is there?"

"Nope. But you're another story. I'm about to get through to you, loud and clear." Nicholas angled himself so his back was to the room and he was facing Stuart. Making no further attempts to mask his anger, he backed Stuart against the front door, planting his hand on the door jamb as if to keep him from bolting. "Now," he said his voice low and taut, just loud enough for Stuart to hear over the construction din, "you and I are going to have an enlightening talk."

Stuart studied him warily. "About?"

"About what happened here. About the fact that I'm not nearly as trusting as Lindsey. About the fact that I have a lot more years' experience with construction sites than she does, and that I know damned well the collapse of that scaffolding was no accident. Someone rigged it. So, I'll ask you bluntly: was it you, or Tracy, or both of you, who were responsible?"

Chips of ice glittered in Stuart's eyes. "That's a pretty ugly accusation."

"With a great deal of justification." Nicholas bit out the words, ripping into Stuart before he could counterattack. "Let's call it like it is. I know you. I know Tracy. I know how badly you want Lindsey out of your lives. I *thought* I knew the lengths you'd go to to accomplish that. Obviously, I underestimated how over the edge you really are. You'd actually kill to protect whatever the hell it is you're protecting. And I *know* you're protecting something, Stuart. I just don't know what—yet. But I will. Because this time you've gone too far. Consequently, you've got a helluva lot more to deal with than Lindsey. You've got me. I've just become your worst nightmare. Because I know things about your family—things I heard directly from Harlan—that will blow apart the whole damned fortress you've built around the Falkner name."

Alternate surges of shock and fear flashed across Stuart's face. "What things? What are you talking about? And what the hell is the matter with you, threatening me like this?"

"Nothing's the matter with me. It's you and your sister who've snapped. As for specifics, we'll get to those later. For now, just give what I've said some good, hard thought. Find Tracy and talk it over with her. Then decide how much you're willing to risk. Because I'm not bluffing, Stuart. I'll find your secret. And I'll destroy you both. You can bet your sorry ass on it."

Stuart blanched, realizing Nicholas was not only dead serious, but in possession of what could be a lethal weapon. "Nick, for God's sake, think about what you're saying. You're like family. My father treated you like a son."

"Yeah, he did. That's part of why I'm doing this. For Harlan."

"That's crazy. My father would never want you to hurt—" Stuart broke off, his gaze narrowing suspiciously. "*Part* of why you're doing this," he repeated. "What's the other part?"

"Lindsey," Nicholas stated flatly. "I'm in love with her. I plan to protect her—for my sake, and for Harlan's. Just as he asked me to."

That reality struck like a blow, and all the color drained from Stuart's face. "My father *told* you about Lindsey? He asked you to watch over her?"

"Uh-huh. He thought she might get hurt. He also thought you were up to something—something ugly. Obviously, his instincts were right." Nicholas's eyes blazed. "I've been digging around subtly, out of deference to Harlan and his feelings for you. But I'm through with discretion. I'm going for the jugular. I'll smoke out your sordid little secret if I have to start the fire myself. I know just where to go for help. Like you, I have the phone numbers of every tabloid in the country. And I'll use them."

With that, Nicholas leaned past Stuart to shove open the door. "This conversation is over. Go find your sister and tell her the way things are. Decide how you want to play this. It's over, any way you look at it. Whether it ends quietly or in a full-blown scandal complete with an exposé and pictures is up to you. When you're ready to talk, give me a call." A muscle worked in his jaw. "Now get out."

For a long moment, Stuart just stayed frozen in place, stunned with disbelief. Then he turned and stalked off.

Nicholas didn't budge until Stuart's Jag had disappeared from view. Then, he retraced his steps, came up behind Lindsey.

"It's done," he murmured, wrapping a protective arm around her waist.

Her nod was tight. "The proverbial trap is set."

"Yup. Bait and all."

She turned, gazed up at him. "And now?"

"Now, we wait."

*   *   *

The waiting was over by nightfall.

Nicholas's cell phone rang just as he and Lindsey were munching on the sandwiches they'd picked up on the ride home.

Lindsey's eyes widened, and slowly she lowered her turkey sandwich to the plate.

"Good," Nicholas muttered. "Maybe now we can get to the bottom of this." He punched the talk button. "Yes?"

"It's me," Stuart said without preamble.

"Where's Tracy?"

"She's not here. It doesn't matter. I need to see you." A pause. "Alone."

Nicholas wasn't surprised. He and Lindsey had discussed the probability that he'd have to meet Stuart without her. If the man planned on spilling his guts, he'd never do it with Lindsey there. "When?"

"Now."

"I'm not driving out to Providence."

"You don't have to. I'm still in Newport. Meet me at your yacht. We can talk there."

"Fine. Give me twenty minutes."

Nicholas punched END and put down the phone. "He's scared to death," he informed Lindsey, shoving back his chair and standing. "Whatever he's got to say, it's bad."

She rose as well, reminding herself to stay calm. "He wouldn't hurt you, would he?"

"No." Nicholas shook his head. "He'd have nothing to gain. He knows this thing has spun way out of control, that too many people are on to him. Besides, he realizes you're aware of everything I'm doing—where

I'm heading and why. What he wants is a painless way to get out of this. Whatever 'this' is. That's what I'm going to find out."

Lindsey nodded. "Be careful."

"I will." Nicholas reached over, pulled her against him, and kissed her. "I love you, you know."

"I know," she replied, her voice breaking. "I love you, too."

His thumbs caressed her cheeks. "Once this ordeal is over, we've got plans to make. Surprisingly, this self-indulgent hedonist is turning out to be a very traditional guy."

"Is he?" A soft smile touched her lips. "Then, happily, I stand corrected."

Mike was half-asleep in the driver's seat of his car when he heard Nicholas Warner's BMW rev to life. He ducked down as the car rolled down the driveway and turned on to the road, zipping off to parts unknown.

He grabbed his cell phone and dialed.

"Ms. Falkner, it's me. Warner just drove off in his Beamer. By himself. Yeah, I'm sure. She's still in the house. How do you want me to play this?" He frowned, listening. "Okay. I'll give it fifteen minutes. Then, I'll start the ball rolling. I'll meet you at the Cliff Walk. Fine, I'll wait for you there." He hung up, glancing at his watch. Eight-twenty.

The minutes ticked by.

At eight thirty-five, he turned over his motor and drove up to Nicholas Warner's house.

Lindsey was pacing around the great room when the doorbell rang. She nearly jumped out of her skin at the sound. Drawing a calming breath, she walked through the hall to the front door.

"Who is it?" she asked, peering through the peephole.

"Ms. Hall?" Mike answered in a crisp, professional voice. "My name is Mike Carl." He held up his ID, leaving it against the peephole long enough for her to verify its authenticity. "As you can see, I work at Rolling Hills Medical Facility. I'm a private investigator hired to pose as an orderly there. It's urgent that I speak with you."

"About?"

"You. And Mr. Warner. Both of you are in danger."

Lindsey yanked open the door. "In danger? How?"

Mike frowned. "I'm not free to discuss the particulars. Suffice it to say, this investigation you're pursuing—you're in over your heads. I need to ask you and Mr. Warner a few questions."

A tight knot of panic began forming in Lindsey's stomach. "Right now, Mr. Warner is . . . out."

Mike's frown deepened. "We'll need to find him right away."

"I'll give you his cell phone number."

"No." Mike gave an adamant shake of his head. "I don't want to call him. There's a chance he's with one of the individuals I'm investigating. Tipping that person off could be dangerous. I've got to get to him in person. Do you know where he is?"

Lindsey nodded.

"Good. Then grab a sweater and come with me. I want you out of here anyway. It isn't safe for you to stay in this house alone."

For a brief instant, Lindsey paused, her natural sense of caution surfacing. "May I see your credentials again?"

"Of course." He offered her the proof she sought.

It was enough.

She grabbed her sweater, purse, and keys and followed him out. "He's at his yacht," she said quietly. "He's meeting Stuart Falkner there."

Mike's jaw tightened. "We'd better hurry."

13

STUART WAS ON DECK, nursing a Makers Mark, when Nicholas arrived.

"Hope you don't mind," he commented, holding up his glass as Nicholas climbed on board. "I helped myself."

"No. My guess is, you need it." Nicholas propped his elbow on the railing. "Okay, I'm listening."

In one gulp, Stuart polished off his drink. "Can we go below? I'd like to keep this conversation private." When Nicholas hesitated, Stuart gave an odd laugh. "For God's sake, Nick, I'm not going to shoot you. I don't cause destruction, I clean up after it."

Slowly, Nicholas nodded. "Fine."

He gestured for Stuart to precede him, then followed down the stairs. Stuart paused to refresh his drink, then the two men settled themselves in the den off the main cabin.

"Do you remember seven years ago, the night my mother tried to kill herself?" Stuart began, staring broodingly into his glass.

"I remember."

"I don't suppose my father mentioned what prompted her suicide attempt."

"No, Stuart. Harlan didn't gossip to me about Camille."

"Right. Well, he obviously confided in you about Lindsey. Did he also talk about her mother? Did he tell you how crazy about her he was, that he was like a love-struck fool who would have taken off at a moment's notice to be with her if it weren't for his kids?"

Nicholas steepled his fingers together, rested his chin on them. "No. But it doesn't surprise me. I guessed Harlan was in love with Irene Hall. Are you saying he planned to leave Camille for her?"

"Bingo. Oh, he waited until Tracy and I were well-established adults. By that time, his heart condition was critical. I guess those two things combined made him reassess his priorities. He decided to go for it. So he broke the news to Mother, thinking she was strong enough to handle it. She wasn't. His plan was to ride out to Newport, get the summer place ready for Irene, then drive to Connecticut and surprise her. Hell, after all those years, he probably would have begged her if that's what it took. But Mother went crazy. Even I couldn't calm her down. She followed Father out here. I'm not sure what was said between them, but it had to be ugly. By the time I got here, my father was gone and my mother was wrecking the place, guzzling vodka like it was going out of style. I tried to take the bottle. She freaked. She ran out the door, jumped in her car, and sped wildly down the driveway, zigzagging from side to side like a ricocheting bullet. The only problem was, the groundskeeper was out there. He didn't stand a chance. She plowed him down like a weed."

Nicholas's head came up. "She killed him?"

"Instantly. I'm not even sure she realized what she'd done—at least not then. She kept going. She was so drunk, it's a miracle she made it to the Cliff Walk. But she did. You know what happened next. You also know that after the suicide attempt we had her committed to Rolling Hills. What you don't know is that I buried the groundskeeper, wiped that part out as if it had never happened. It was easy enough. The poor old guy was nearing seventy. He lived alone—no family, no friends, no questions."

"Who knew about this? Obviously not Harlan."

"No. Only Tracy and me. She helped me bury the body where no one would find it." Stuart's gaze met Nicholas's. "It's under some shrubbery in the back of the manor."

Nicholas's breath expelled in a hiss. "So that's why you wanted me to build those condos. To destroy any trace of . . . " He tasted bile. "All this to cover up Camille's crime? She's ill, Stuart. She's institutionalized. No one would expect her to stand trial."

"Maybe not a court trial. What about a public one? Do you have any idea what the media would do with that story? Do you realize how they'd destroy her—or whatever's left of her?"

"What I realize is how screwed up your values are," Nicholas shot back. "We're talking about a man's life, not a nasty little indiscretion you want to smother." He found himself wondering if he'd ever really known Stuart at all. "Be that as it may, your story still doesn't fit.

All that happened seven years ago. In your own sick way, you took care of the groundskeeper. Your family skeleton was safe. So what happened? Why did Harlan sense you were acting strange a few weeks before his death?"

"Because, unbeknown to him, I found out about Lindsey, and the inheritance he'd left her. I was shuffling through some papers on his desk, looking for a particular contract. And what did I find? A memo to Leland listing the provisions he was making for a bastard daughter I never knew existed. I saw red. Then, I panicked. If Lindsey moved into that house, worse, if she renovated it, she might find the body. As it turned out, my fears were justified. Her contractors are digging around the house, so the landscapers can put in a goddamned garden for her mother."

Fury glinted in Nicholas's eyes. "So you *are* responsible for trying to kill Lindsey. You made the phone calls, rigged the scaffolding—"

"No," Stuart denied instantly. "I didn't do any of that. Oh, I'd do just about anything to make Lindsey walk away from that house. Anything short of what you're accusing me of. I didn't threaten her, Nick. And I didn't try to kill her. I swear." He leaned forward, gripping his glass tightly between his palms. "I'm begging you not to leak this story. It wouldn't serve any purpose, other than to destroy my mother."

Nicholas still wasn't convinced. "Harlan specifically told me you didn't know about Lindsey."

"That's what he believed—until the end. The day before he died, he confronted me head-on about how strangely I'd been acting. He accused me of hiding something from him—pretty outrageous, wouldn't you say, considering what *he* was hiding? He pushed me too far. I lost my temper. I blurted out the whole truth. We had a huge blowup. Things got out of hand." Stuart squeezed his eyes shut, looking positively green. "That's when he had the massive heart attack. I never expected it to be fatal. I—"

"Christ." Nicholas rose, dragging both hands through his hair.

"There's nothing you can say to me that I haven't already said to myself," Stuart said woodenly. "I killed my father. It's because of me that he's dead." He opened his eyes, determination glittering through the moisture that had gathered in them. "Which makes it twice as crucial for me to protect the rest of my family. It's the only way I can make amends."

"That's a lot to make amends for, Stuart," Nicholas said in a tight voice. "Being an accessory to your mother's manslaughter and instigating your father's fatal heart attack."

"I know. I live with that guilt every day."

"Are you sure that's *all* you live with? After all, what's one more fatality after two others?"

Stuart winced. "I told you, I had nothing to do with what's been happening to Lindsey."

"And Tracy? What about her?"

"She's as innocent as I am."

Nicholas inclined his head. "Really? Then why isn't she here to make that claim herself?"

"Because she's at Rolling Hills making sure Mother's okay." A bitter stare. "Just in case you decided to jump the gun and call the tabloids."

"Or maybe she didn't want to be here because she's afraid I'd see through her and realize she's behind the attempt on Lindsey's life."

Tension crackled in the air.

Stuart's cell phone rang.

He snatched it up. "What?" he snapped into the receiver. A long pause. "What do you mean, gone? Gone where?" He listened, shaking his head adamantly as he did. "That's impossible. She hasn't driven in years. She's not mentally focused enough to get behind the wheel." Abruptly, he stopped shaking his head, the color draining from his face. "They're sure? How long has she been missing? Who? Who the hell is he?" Silence. "Pictures of . . . shit—" A sharp inhale. "I'm on my way."

He hung up, staring dazedly at Nicholas. "That was Tracy. My mother's disappeared from Rolling Hills. Security said she took a car, registered to some orderly named Mike Carl. He's missing, too."

"Do they think he kidnapped Camille?" Nicholas demanded.

"What? No. She was alone in the car. *Driving*. She was headed east. That's the direction of the Cliff Walk. Tracy called the police, just in case she plans to do something crazy. But it doesn't sound that way. The guard who saw her drive off said she seemed totally rational. Which, under the circumstances, can only mean . . . Christ—" Stuart broke off. "I've got to get out there." He took a step toward the door, then halted, gazing back at Nicholas like a condemned man who realized he had no choice but to divulge a chilling—and damning—piece of information.

A sickening premonition settled in Nicholas's gut. "There's more. What is it?"

"When they searched this Mike Carl's room, they found a book on home construction, some Post-its and a couple of photos. The book was dog-eared on some pages that had pictures of scaffolding. The Post-its are scribbled bits of information, and the photos are of a woman. Security didn't think anything of the stuff. But Tracy demanded to see every last scrap of it. She said the Post-its are in Mother's handwriting—including the one that was slapped on the book instructing Mike Carl to read the dog-eared pages. The other Post-its list dates, times, and the addresses of the manor, your place in Newport, and Irene Hall's apartment in Connecticut. As for the photos—Nick, they're of Lindsey."

"*What?*"

Stuart looked positively stricken. "I don't want to think about how all this fits together. But you'd better get to Lindsey."

Nicholas had already grabbed his cell phone, and was punching up his home number. He gripped the phone until his knuckles turned white, counting the rings and praying.

No answer.

He pressed END, and tried Lindsey's cell number.

Nothing.

"She's not picking up," he said in a strangled tone. "Something's wrong." He strode past Stuart, heading for the main deck. "Let's go," he ordered. "This Mike Carl must have Lindsey. And if he's working for Camille, if they're taking Lindsey to the Cliff Walk . . ."

He didn't finish his sentence.

He didn't have to.

*   *   *

Stuart's cell phone rang a minute after they screeched away from the docks. He propped it in its cradle, so he and Nicholas could listen together.

"Yeah?"

"It's me." Tracy sounded like a frightened child. "I'm about a half-mile from the Cliff Walk."

"We're even closer. I was at the yacht when you reached me. Nick's with me. I've got you on speaker. What's going on?"

"The police just called. They spotted two cars near the exact entrance to the Cliff Walk I suggested—that rough section Mother's always headed to in the past. One of the cars is Mike Carl's. The other's a rental, but he's the one who rented it. I guess he left his own car at Rolling Hills for Mother to use. Both cars are empty. But the police found a woman's sweater in the rental."

"What color is the sweater?" Nicholas demanded.

"Light blue with pearl buttons."

"That's Lindsey's." Nicholas's jaw clenched. "Your mother's definitely not out there to kill *herself*, Tracy. Not this time. This time she has a different target in mind." He slammed his fist against his leg, glaring from the cell phone to Stuart. "God help the two of you if she succeeds."

14

Lindsey leaned back against a tree, staring out toward the water, grateful that the night was overcast and she couldn't make out the outline of the cliffs. She didn't want to see the jagged drop to the ocean below. Not when she was horrifyingly certain that was where she was headed.

Even so, her memory was excellent. And her imagination was hideously keen.

She winced as the ropes Mike Carl had bound her wrists and ankles with bit into her skin. Her leg muscles ached from her holding them so stiffly, and they screamed for her to shift position. But she didn't dare. Not when one wrong move could mean either losing her balance and toppling to her death, or being shot down by Mike Carl, whose pistol had been aimed at her head since he'd hauled her out of the car a half-hour ago.

"Are you going to tell me who you really are and why you want me dead?" Lindsey asked, turning to peer at her captor, who was squinting into the darkness, obviously searching for someone.

"Huh?" His head came up, and he scanned the area behind them intently, as if he'd heard a welcome sound. "You know who I am," he replied, his gaze fixed on a spot off to their right. "Everything I told you was true. Oh, except the part about being a PI. I made that up. I'm really a regular orderly, although I'd be a helluva good detective. I did a great job with you, didn't I?"

"Exactly what is it you did?" Lindsey asked, picking up on a faint plodding sound and wondering if it was the wind or the arrival of whomever Mike Carl was expecting. "Other than kidnap me and drag me to the edge of a cliff?"

"I did all of it. I made that threatening phone call to you in Connecticut. I rigged the scaffolding. I tailed you around Newport. And now this. I did the whole she-bang."

"Why? Or should I ask, for whom? Who put you up to this? Who is it we're waiting for?"

"That would be me."

Lindsey twisted around as the acknowledger to her question walked out of the shadows.

Recognition was instant, even though the ethereal-looking woman who joined them hadn't been publicly photographed in years. One didn't forget those aristocratic features and china-doll looks.

Camille Falkner.

Lindsey was so stunned, she could barely speak. "Mrs. Falkner?"

"None other." She loosened the scarf around her hair, letting it fall to her shoulders. "Fine work, Mike," she commended, reaching into her pocket to pull out a folded slip of paper. "Here's a check for ten thousand dollars made out to cash. Take it, and run along. Just leave me your car. I'll park it in the lot at Rolling Hills. You can pick it up tomorrow. Oh, and I'd appreciate your pistol. I doubt I'll be needing it, but one never knows."

"Sure thing, Ms. Falkner." Beaming, he took his check and handed her the gun. With a quick glance at Lindsey, he took off.

"Now then—we're alone." Camille's hand was steady as she aimed the pistol at Lindsey. She walked over, taking Lindsey's chin between her fingers and angling her face so she could study it. "You have Harlan's coloring and your mother's bone structure," she pronounced, releasing Lindsey's face. "A striking combination. No wonder Nicholas Warner is so enchanted. He never could resist a pretty face." Anger glistened in her eyes. "I suppose the same applies to Harlan, or you wouldn't have been conceived, would you?"

Lindsey swallowed. This woman might be unbalanced, but she was completely aware of what she was doing.

"Do you intend to kill me?" she asked Camille. "Is that why you had me brought here?"

Camille sighed. "I'm afraid so. I hoped it wouldn't come to this. In fact, I actually tried to forget your existence over the past years. Of course, Harlan made that impossible with his fixation on you and Irene. He even tried to leave me for her, did you know that? I made quick work of that plan. Anyway, things seemed to be under control. Harlan was my husband, even if we weren't able to live together. Mike kept tabs on his loyalties and reported back to me at Rolling Hills. Harlan didn't go to Irene—not once. I was satisfied."

Her expression hardened, and her fingers tightened on the pistol. "Then, my beloved Harlan died. I thought nothing could be more painful than that—until Mike showed up in my room to break the shocking news to me that you'd been left a sizable inheritance, including my summer house. That wouldn't do. Not at all. Truthfully, I didn't originally plan to kill you. Not in cold blood. My plan was to make you vanish from our lives. But you refused to do that. I tried everything from threats to an ugly construction accident. Nothing worked. Which leaves only one alternative."

Lindsey fought back her fear, twisting her hands wildly in an effort to free them. But what good would that do? Even if by some miracle she managed to free her hands *and* feet, Camille had a gun. She'd shoot her down in a heartbeat.

Reason. She had to try reason.

"You're talking about murder, Mrs. Falkner. Surely you don't think you can get away with that?"

"Of course I can," Camille replied calmly. "I've killed before. I ran over our groundskeeper the night Harlan announced his plans to leave me. Stuart thinks I've wiped the incident from my mind, but I remember it quite clearly." A smile curved her lips. "Being an unstable alcoholic has some wonderful advantages. No one ever expects you to be lucid. You can get away with anything—even murder. Especially if you're a Falkner. Besides, it will be days before your body is found, and even longer before it's identified. At first, everyone will assume you went back to Connecticut. Once they realize you're at the bottom of the Cliff Walk, they'll think you went for a stroll and had a terrible accident. Tragic, but true."

"What if I put up a struggle?" Lindsey tried. "Even bound, I can manage that. You'd have to shoot me, which means the police will find a bullet hole in my body and realize my death was a homicide, not an accident."

"True," Camille conceded. "And they'll be looking for suspects. But I'll never be one of them. I'm an inmate at a medical institution, confined to the grounds—remember?"

Lindsey stared at her in amazement. "Your children think you're emotionally frail. The fact is, you have nerves of steel. What's more, you know exactly what you're doing."

"That's true." Camille frowned. "As for Stuart and Tracy, I've hated misleading them. Unfortunately, it was the only way for me to have free rein to do what I needed to do. If I hadn't created the illusion of being unfocused and unstable, Rolling Hills would have kept a much tighter leash on me. So would my children, given that they love me and would want to protect me. I needed to work closely with Mike, to have him do my legwork for me. It all played out beautifully. Someday I'll tell Tracy and Stuart the truth. They'll understand. They'll more than understand—they'll applaud my actions. They want you gone every bit as much as I do."

Abruptly, she reached out and grabbed Lindsey's arm, yanking her forward with a surprising amount of strength. "Now then, I need you to take a few more little hops. Then I'll give you one hard push. Gravity will do the rest."

"No." Lindsey began struggling, her survival instinct taking over, no matter what the cost. She twisted her body fiercely from side to side, praying that her defensive motions would force Camille into using both hands, and that she'd lose her grip on the pistol. Even if that plan failed, Lindsey wouldn't give in. Let the woman shoot her. The thought of dying that way was far less gruesome than the thought of plunging to her death. And if the bullet that killed her was traced to Mike Carl's gun, there'd be a better chance of Camille being found out.

"Let go of me!" Lindsey elbowed Camille hard enough to shove her aside.

The motion caught Camille off guard, but she recovered quickly and without dropping the pistol. Steadying herself a few feet from the edge of the cliff, she grabbed Lindsey's arm again, her nails digging into her flesh. "Damn you," she bit out. "You're going over that cliff. You're going to be erased the way you should have been twenty-six years—"

"Mother!" Stuart's shout broke through the trees, and he rushed forward, stopping fifty feet away. "Don't do this. Let her go."

Camille started, her brows drawing together in puzzlement as she angled herself toward her son. "Stuart? How did you find me?"

"Let Lindsey go," Stuart repeated. "Please. Before it's too late."

"You know I can't do that, sweetheart. She should never have been born in the first place."

"You can't erase that." It was Tracy who spoke, coming up behind her brother. "Mother, listen to me. I don't want her in our lives either. But this isn't the answer. The police are here. They've surrounded the area. I've begged them to hold their fire, but if you don't back off, they're going to sacrifice your life to save Lindsey's. Is that what you want?"

"The police?" Camille's puzzlement turned to shock. "You called the police? Why?"

"Because we were worried about you," Stuart replied. He was aware that Lindsey was taking advantage of the distraction he was providing, moving subtly away from the edge of the cliff while Camille spoke to him and Tracy. He kept talking, giving Lindsey time to put distance between herself and his mother. "You disappeared from Rolling Hills. We thought you might hurt yourself." A quick sidelong glance at a spot diagonally behind Camille, where Nicholas was closing in. "Mother, listen to me. You're not thinking clearly. Everyone understands that. So just put down the gun and everything will be all right."

Camille was opening her mouth to refuse when Nicholas lunged from behind. He grabbed her, knocking the gun to the ground with one sharp blow, and locking his arm around her waist to keep her from retrieving it. She whimpered, her head snapping around so she could see who her captor was, struggling against him even as she did.

"Nicholas, get your hands off of me!" she commanded.

"Don't tempt me, Camille," Nicholas ground out, glaring pointedly at the cliff's edge, sparks of rage blazing in his eyes. He looked furious enough to kill.

"Nick, please—don't hurt her," Stuart begged. He made his way over, even as the police began to close in. "Please."

"We'll take it from here, Mr. Warner," one of the officers assured him, his gun poised and ready.

Nicholas didn't need a second invitation. He handed Camille over to the cop, then went to Lindsey, who'd sunk down on the grass, shaking. "Are you okay?" he muttered, squatting down beside her.

She didn't trust herself to speak. She just nodded, then rested her head against him as he untied the ropes at her ankles and wrists.

"It's over," Nicholas told her, bringing each wrist to his lips. "The whole nightmare is over." He looked up, watching as the cops handcuffed Camille and led her away, Stuart and Tracy flanking her like devoted soldiers.

"We'll need Ms. Hall to answer some questions," another officer informed Nicholas.

"In the morning," Nicholas replied firmly. "Right now, she needs some rest."

"Yeah, okay, but first thing tomorrow."

"I'll be at the station at nine," Lindsey promised in a shaky whisper.

"We both will," Nicholas amended. He stood, swinging Lindsey into his arms and heading away from the Cliff Walk. "Come on," he murmured gently, pressing his lips into her hair. "It's time to go home and make those plans I was talking about."

15

"THAT THREE A.M. PHONE CALL made to your apartment was traced to Mike Carl's home phone," Leland Masters informed Lindsey, propping his elbows on his desk. "The police called me with that information today."

"Not a surprise," Lindsey murmured. She and Nicholas had dropped by Leland's office to tie up loose ends and to touch base on the legal status of the Falkners. After that, they were driving up to the Cape for a much-needed weekend away.

"Also with regard to Mike Carl, the police discovered he had a criminal record. Breaking and entering, as well as assault."

Nicholas frowned. "How did that manage to stay hidden? Wouldn't Rolling Hills have uncovered it in his background check?"

"If he'd had one, yes. Apparently, Mike Carl's association with Camille predated her stay at Rolling Hills. He worked at a local clinic, and supplied her with extra pills when she needed them. Once she was committed, she panicked, and wanted Carl close at hand, both to smuggle her pills, if need be, and to appease her paranoia by checking on Harlan's actions. She got Rolling Hills to bypass the background check. She provided Carl with a personal reference, said she knew him and his family. Based on her recommendation, he was hired, and assigned to the group of rooms that included Camille's. That gave them ample opportunity to touch base. She worked the whole thing out quite nicely. Right down to having damning information to blackmail Mike Carl with, if need be."

"And here we thought Camille was spaced out, oblivious to everything," Nicholas muttered. "She's like a barracuda."

"A very sick one," Leland reminded him. "Very sick. She was desperate to hold on to Harlan, even in death."

"I assume you'll be her defense attorney," Lindsey said. "And Stuart and Tracy's, too."

"Actually, no. I handle their business, and their trust and estate work. I've recommended a top-notch criminal attorney. I'll confer with him as needed." Sighing, Leland made a steeple with his fingers, and rested his chin atop them. "Stuart and Tracy are pleading guilty as accessories to vehicular homicide in the death of their groundskeeper. With any luck, their sentences will be kept to a minimum. As for Camille . . . I realize her crimes against you were premeditated, Lindsey, but she's insane, nonetheless. A high-security institution is the best place for her, not a prison. I'm sure the courts will agree with that." He gazed at Lindsey. "Does my sympathy for them anger you? Because if it's any consolation, their lives will never be the same. This scandal will haunt them forever."

"No, it doesn't anger me," Lindsey replied. "The Falkners are your clients, and your friends. They have been for years."

"And Harlan would want it this way," Leland added quietly.

"I'm sure he would."

Nicholas reached over, took Lindsey's hand. "Speaking of what Harlan would want, Lindsey and I have some news."

"Oh?" Leland's brows lifted.

"We're getting married. Right after Lindsey's mother gets home from Europe." Nicholas's lips twitched. "Surprised?"

"No. But very pleased." Leland rose, extended his hand first to Lindsey, then to Nicholas. "This is welcome news indeed." He smiled—a broad, genuine smile that reached his eyes. "It seems Harlan was right. Then again, he usually was."

Lindsey leaned forward in her chair. "So Nicholas wasn't imagining things. My father did do a little match-making."

"No, he did a *lot* of matchmaking," Leland confirmed. "He was absolutely sure you two belonged together." Wistfulness softened his smile. "He was also determined to give you the future he wanted desperately for your mother, but could never give her—the opportunity to spend your life with the one you love."

Feeling Nicholas's fingers tighten around hers, Lindsey smiled through her tears. "Well, he succeeded. He did more than succeed. He brought Nicholas into my life. He also brought me closure, a sense of peace, and the joy of knowing I had a father—a *real* father. I only wish I could tell him—" She broke off, emotion clogging her throat.

Leland watched as Nicholas stood, drew Lindsey into his arms, and held her there, all the love in the world shining in his eyes.

"He knows, Lindsey," Leland replied with absolute certainty. "Believe me, he knows."

ABOUT THE AUTHOR

ANDREA KANE marked her debut in the world of romantic suspense with her *New York Times*–bestselling blockbuster thriller, *Run for Your Life*. Prior to that, she was the bestselling author of fourteen historical romances, including the highly acclaimed two-book series, *The Gold Coin* and *The Silver Coin*. She lives in New Jersey with her husband and daughter. Visit her Web site at www.andreakane.com.

ONCE
IN A
BLUE MOON

===

LINDA ANDERSON

1

SILENCE CLOAKED THE OLD LIBRARY, settling over the empty aisles and overburdened bookshelves like an old friend and invisible protector. The grandfather clock struck a solemn nine gongs.

Addie Rivers glanced up from her desk in surprise, then checked her watch. "Yep. Working late again, Addie," she said to herself.

Her mother would be worried, which was a major source of irritation for her twenty eight-year-old daughter. For a brief moment, Addie missed Buck's presence and his habit of driving her home every night. Buck had become a bit smothering lately, but he did get her home early enough to alleviate her mother's anxiety. Addie, however, loved the nights when she jogged home, and looked forward to her solo run tonight.

She reviewed the material on her computer and decided another thirty minutes would do it. Tomorrow was the first day of ghost stories for the children's hour. Halloween would be here soon, and the children loved each session as she built the suspense to a higher and higher pitch.

Outside, a late October wind wailed and hurled brittle leaves against the long, slender windows. Addie shivered, and drew her sweater close around her shoulders. The converted nineteenth-century Victorian house was drafty and difficult to heat. Addie had begged the Blue Springs town council for a new heating system, but they'd turned her down.

An unfamiliar noise distracted her. She cocked her head and listened, but heard nothing and decided she had imagined it. She went back to work, then stiffened when the rustle came again. A soft, sibilant sound like a slipper sliding on a polished floor came from somewhere in the dark nether region of the history section.

"Coffee? Is that you?" She called the cat. "Coffee?"

A plaintive purr and a rub against her ankle surprised her. Coffee had been sleeping at her feet beneath the receiving desk.

"There you are. Thought you were in the stacks. The wind must have found a fresh crack in the wall to whistle through." She lifted the dark brown cat to her lap and rubbed her cheek against his thick coat. "Time for us to say goodnight. I have to go home, and you have serious mouse duty for the rest of the night."

Fifteen minutes later, she had changed to jogging sweats, had passed the familiar and impressive old houses on Elm Street, and was running along the tree-lined path that paralleled the two-lane highway out to the farm. The night was cold, and stars twinkled like chipped ice in the black sky. Headlights from an occasional passing car flashed over her bright red sweatshirt.

There was little traffic this late in the evening in Blue Springs.

Her eyes smarted and watered as the brisk air lashed against her face, but Addie found it stimulating and forced herself to breathe evenly. This three-mile run always gave her a sense of freedom. Each long stride increased her feeling of power and control, both of which she'd found little of lately. Her mother's increasing fear for her safety irritated her, and Buck's pressing for a wedding date made her feel as if he'd placed her in a box and locked the lid.

There were times when she felt like she couldn't breathe.

Exercise released her bottled up tension. With no tennis courts, golf courses, or swimming pools, Blue Springs, West Virginia, held little opportunity for exercise, so she made a point of walking to work in the mornings. She'd jogged home every night until six months ago when Buck decided it was his duty to drive her home.

Buck meant well. They had dated since high school and through college. Somewhere along the way, Buck had assumed it was his job to take care of her. Addie hated it, but he was such a kind soul that she hadn't the heart to tell him that she would prefer to get home on her own. Thank God he taught a class once a week at the community college an hour away. The time alone gave her needed breathing room.

The drowning death of her best friend, Laurel Major, a year ago, and the mysterious disappearance of a book group friend, Janelle Knight, three months ago had triggered her mother's growing paranoia and Buck's smothering protectiveness. Her throat tightened at the thought of how much she yearned for her childhood friend, Laurel, and their good times together. Laurel and Janelle were both missed by the members of Addie's compatible book circle, which met every two weeks to dine and review current books.

Slap, slap, slap. The unmistakable beat of running feet startled her. The sound of soles crunching leaves and debris on the dirt path behind her was quite clear in the quiet night. How odd, she thought. No one who lives out this way is a runner.

She turned to see who else ran this time of night, but saw nothing except dark shadows and the trembling of a bush, as if someone had just stepped behind it. *Hogwash, Addie.*

Either I really heard something, or my ears need to be examined. Maybe the runner stepped into the trees for a minute.

There weren't many joggers in the small town. Buck ran some, and Joe Bolo, their police chief, and a few others. She resumed her pace, but worried that maybe a large dog followed, or a wild animal of some sort. *Come, come, Addie. Wild animals vacated Blue Springs years ago.* Blue Springs was her birthplace. She'd grown up here, and had returned to live, work, and write here because it was peaceful, and her mom needed her.

Again, the sound came, and she jerked her head around, but there was nothing there. It's a broken tree limb rubbing against a trunk, she imagined, but ran faster. For the first time in her life she wondered if Blue Springs wasn't as safe as she'd always thought.

The white board fence coming up on her left indicated the boundaries of Rivers Farm, and she moved toward it eagerly, ashamed of her irrational fear. The scent of freshly mown grass, cut earlier in the day by farmhand Bobby Heed, filled the brisk night air. A cowbell tinkled in the distance, and Rags barked. She was home.

She skirted a white oval planked wooden sign that hung from the arm of a sturdy post. A light on the ground at the base of the post shone on quaintly painted gold letters that spelled out RIVERS FARM BED AND BREAKFAST. She gave the sign a quick thump, and it swung gently back and forth. The squeaking of its wrought iron chains in the quiet night followed her through the gate and up the long drive.

The old farmhouse, a delightful, added-onto, sprawling semicolonial, painted pastel yellow with wide verandas and large white-framed windows, beckoned warmly. Her mother's bedroom window on the second floor was dark, but welcoming lights shone from the kitchen windows.

The last sprint up the drive was always an effort, and she was breathing hard as she passed the barn and headed toward the friendly lights of the kitchen. A happy bark came from the dark, and she knew Rags raced up from the lower meadow to say hello. The border collie reached her as she passed the barn, and she braced herself for his affectionate onslaught. They fell to the ground with a lot of laughter, licking kisses, and tail wagging.

"Okay, okay, you bandit. I love you. Now let me up."

Rags rolled over on his back to have his belly scratched. Addie obliged. She glanced up and saw an expensive sports car parked near the barn. It was too dark to tell the make of the sleek machine, but its glossy finish reflected faint yellow beams of light from the windows.

The new guest must have arrived. Her mother was happiest when her three guest rooms were filled. Eileen Rivers's hosting and cooking abilities were known all over this border region of West Virginia and Virginia.

Good, thought Addie. *Having someone here will keep her mind off me.*

She gave Rags a final rub and got to her feet. A cup of hot chocolate would taste great. She jogged the last few yards to the house, crossed the planked porch to the kitchen door, and then remembered with dismay that she'd left her house keys at the library.

"Dammit," she muttered. They'd never locked their door until recently, and Addie still hadn't developed the habit of carrying keys. She hated to wake her mother, but she would have to.

She pounded on the door, hoping that her sound-sleeping mother would eventually hear her.

The door opened so quickly that she almost fell in, and a tall barefooted man dressed only in red pajama bottoms stood before her. His well-muscled chest was at her eye level, and her gaze traced a thick patch of triangular black hair up to a strong chin and found an inquiring look on his face.

"Hi. I hope you're Mrs. Rivers's daughter, Addie," he said, and smiled. "If not, then you must be a beautiful damsel in distress lost in the country and seeking shelter at a friendly farm. You found the right place."

Addie realized immediately that this was the newly

arrived bed-and-breakfast guest. What was he doing in the kitchen half-dressed?

"Eh, yes, I'm, I mean, no—I'm not a beautiful stranger." She blushed, flustered at this vibrant masculine energy confronting her in her own house and in such an audacious manner. "I'm Addie Rivers. You must be Mom's new guest."

He nodded and stepped aside so she could enter. "You may not be a stranger, but you are beautiful. Come in out of the cold," he said. Seeming very much at home, he swept his arm in front of him and bowed.

She passed by him quickly, catching an inviting scent of aftershave and rich cigar. The heat of the kitchen hit her, warming her cheeks with welcome. Sweet smells of melted butter, cinnamon, and blackberries filled the inviting country kitchen.

A pan of cornbread sat in the open microwave, and the refrigerator door hung ajar. On the big rectangular pine table sat the leftovers of a dinner Eileen Rivers had prepared for friends the evening before: containers of sweet potato soufflé and deep-fried herbed quail. Wavery ribbons of sweet-smelling vapor rose from the remains of a blackberry cobbler, which the usurper had obviously just removed from the microwave.

The coffee maker made a tinkling sound, indicating the coffee was ready. In one long stride, the man gave the refrigerator door a nudge to shut it, took the cornbread from the microwave, then poured himself a cup of coffee.

"Join me for a snack?"

She stared at him, aghast at the arrogance he displayed in offering her a snack in her own home. His heavy dark eyebrows lifted at her glare, amusement twinkling in his devastating eyes. A tiny gold earring pierced one ear.

"Sorry. I should introduce myself. I'm Will Court. I arrived later than expected, and your mother was about to go to bed. She asked if I'd like something to eat, and I declined. But later, after she'd retired, I suffered severe sugar withdrawal and came back downstairs. I didn't think your mother would mind."

Eileen Rivers wouldn't mind, but Addie did.

He waved a golden-brown quail wing at her. "Sure you don't want something? Your mother is a superb cook, isn't she?"

"Yes, she loves to cook."

Addie tried not to notice the width of his shoulders, and how they curved so symmetrically down into firm tanned arms. Suddenly acutely aware of her sweaty disheveled appearance, she jammed her hands into her pockets and wanted to shrink headfirst down into her sweatshirt. *Hey, wait a minute,* she lectured herself, *he's the one who's half-naked and ordering me around in my own kitchen. Who does he think he is, anyway?*

"I understand you're the town librarian?"

"Yes."

"Convenient for me. I'm here to do some research."

"How nice," she said coolly. "Look, Mr. Court, I just jogged three miles from town, and I planned on having a cup of hot chocolate. I'll fix it and be out of your way shortly."

"Certainly," he said. He peered at her over the rim of his mug and gulped down half of the coffee. The steaming hot liquid seemed not to bother him at all.

With great confidence, and not a whit of shyness, he sat down at the table, helped himself to more quail, a heaping ladle of sweet potatoes, a piece of cornbread dripping with butter, and proceeded to finish the meal she'd interrupted. Addie turned away, but felt his interested gaze on her as she moved about the kitchen, and remembered the blueness of his deep-set eyes.

Concentrating self-consciously on her hot chocolate preparation, Addie tried to ignore the sounds he made as he cleared his food from the table, rinsed dishes in the sink and placed them in the dishwasher.

He said, "If I've offended you, I apologize. Had no idea I would be discovered half-naked, sneaking cornbread. I have a tendency to plunge full speed ahead, damn the results."

Half-naked and not caring a fig if anyone found you, she thought.

"Not to worry," she said, aware she should be more gracious to a paying guest. "I'm tired and not very sociable tonight."

With cup in hand, she turned to say goodnight and found him right behind her. His steady regard unnerved her and an embarrassing warm flush traveled over her breasts, up her neck, and onto her cheeks. The fragrance of his light aftershave came again, and Addie wanted to inhale it, lap it up, sleep with it.

What? Sleep with his aftershave? Sleep with it?

Good Lord, what is the matter with me? I'm lusting after a complete stranger, that's what is the matter with me, came her shameful answer.

"Goodnight," she said curtly, and turned to cross the kitchen floor. She felt his penetrating gaze on her all the way.

When she reached the door, Will Court said, "Goodnight."

"If I'd known Buck was gone I'd have come for you myself," declared Eileen Rivers the next morning, setting a platter of warm blueberry muffins in front of her daughter. "I certainly hope you're remembering to lock the library up tight."

Addie poked at her scrambled eggs, her mother's words barely registering as she daydreamed out the expansive picture window. Images of the man she'd met in the kitchen last night, and his disturbing effect on her, interfered with her wandering view of the farm's meadows and creek.

"You're really getting paranoid, Mom. Relax, for heaven's sake," she murmured, but suffered a fleeting pang of guilt at the memory of the keys she'd forgotten at the library.

Her reverie drifted across the broad creek and frost-covered meadows and found the distant red and gold peaks of the Allegheny Mountains shimmering in the early morning sun.

"I think the death of two good friends in the last year is enough to make anyone worry."

Addie sighed, and finally gave full attention to her mother.

"Laurel's drowning was an accident, and Janelle was in Marysville when she disappeared. Who knows? She may have gotten bored with teaching first grade and run away to Tahiti or something. None of it puts me in any danger. Besides, I have Coffee to protect me."

"You can make fun if you want, but they're still investigating Laurel's so-called accident. She never went swimming alone, and she had marks around her neck indicating she might have been strangled."

Addie's stomach turned. "Mom, please, must we talk about this? It's a beautiful morning, and I'd rather remember Laurel alive and happy."

Her mother sniffed. "Sorry, dear, but I really think Joe should call in some superior help for the investigation of Laurel's death. And you know perfectly well that Janelle didn't run off to Tahiti. Wishful thinking, Adelaide Rivers. They found signs of a struggle and traces of her blood in the apartment and her car. Don't you think it's more than coincidence that two members of a book group in this rural area have disappeared?"

Addie sighed again. "No, Mom, I don't. Laurel was an accident, and Janelle must have met the wrong person."

"The *Real Crime* magazine I read last night said those monsters usually form a pattern and don't break it. I don't think two members gone from the same book group within a year is a coincidence. And," she said, pausing for dramatic effect, "this monster evidently likes bookish women with dark-brown hair—like yours. I'm just happy Buck escorts you home at night."

"Yes, Mom, Buck is always there. I can always depend on good ol' Buck." Addie tossed her hair in self-irritation. "And, by the way, just because I'm a writer and a librarian doesn't make me bookish. I've got to get going."

She finished her muffin, gulped the last of her coffee, and got to her feet.

"Where's our new guest?" she asked, with an attempt at casualness.

"It was late when he arrived so I told him he could come down for breakfast whenever he woke up."

"Mom, you can't run an efficient bed-and-breakfast if you let the guests wander down any time they please. I found him making himself at home in the kitchen last night."

Her mother grinned. "I thought I detected signs of a refrigerator raid. Isn't he nice, Addie? And so, well, not handsome in the classic sense, but there's something absolutely riveting about him. I think you young women would say he's . . . sexy." She blushed, and self-consciously stuck her hands into the pockets of her frilly white apron. "Besides, a bed-and-breakfast should be more about graciousness than efficiency."

Addie smiled at her mother's reaction to their guest, and kissed her on the cheek.

"You're right, darling. I promise I won't bug you about how you run the place, if you'll promise not to worry about me and mysterious deaths and murderers. After all, we take in more strangers here at the inn than I see at the library in a blue moon. I should be worrying about *you*."

Eileen Rivers sniffed indignantly, and shoved a lock of fading flaxen hair off her forehead. "We only get nice people here, Adelaide Rivers, and you know that."

"Who is Will Court, anyway?"

"*Doctor* Will Court. He isn't much of a talker, but whoever called to make his reservation said he's a history professor at Yale."

Addie slipped on her jacket.

"Don't forget your pumpkin. Bobby Heed searched the pumpkin patch for an hour yesterday afternoon to find just the right one for your children to carve."

Addie picked up the small pumpkin from the kitchen counter and settled it comfortably in her arms.

"What in the world is Dr. Court doing in this out-of-the-way place?"

Her mother frowned. "I'm not sure, some kind of research, I think."

"Yeah, research on rudeness."

"Addie!"

She kissed her mother on the cheek. "Bye, Mom. Love you. See you tonight."

Addie walked briskly across the lawn to the long tree-bordered driveway, her desert boots shuffling through crisp fallen leaves. She shifted the pumpkin in her arms and considered driving her car to work, then rejected the idea immediately. The two-mile walk into town was a discipline she'd adhered to religiously since she'd come home to live three years ago.

At the end of the drive she skirted the gleaming white and gold Rivers Farm sign, and turned onto the tree-shaded dirt path that led to town. As she walked, she remembered the sounds she'd heard on the path last night and her near panic. How silly it all seemed in the light of this beautiful fall morning.

The whip of whirling wheels rushing through the leaves behind her warned her to step aside.

"Hey, Miss Rivers." Bradley and Amy Lee Simples, neighbors from the farm next to the Rivers place, swept by on their bikes. Late for school as usual.

"Hi, Brad, Amy. I've got that Harry Potter book you've been waiting for, Brad."

"Okay. Be in after school," he called back, and waved farewell as they drew ahead of her.

There was little traffic on the highway alongside the

path, but Bradley and Amy Lee would be entering town soon and she wanted to call after them to be careful. She quelled her protective urge, but it made her wonder, as she often did, if she'd ever have children of her own to worry about.

She picked up her pace, anxious now to get the day started.

Will Court stood at his guest room window and watched the slender figure cross the lawn, go through the trees, and onto the driveway. Earlier he had put a match to the wood laid in the fireplace and it had caught nicely, but the morning chill still wasn't off the room. Shivering, he pulled a navy-blue sweater hastily over his head, ran fingers through his dark hair, then continued his interested surveillance.

Addie's hair was a coppery brown. He couldn't take his eyes off the lively shining tresses. Of medium length and wavy, her hair glinted gold and red when it caught the sun's beams. It bounced freely around her ears and off her shoulders as she hurried away into the protection of the trees. He waited impatiently until she came into sight again at the end of the drive.

He liked the way she walked with confidence and purpose, even with the burden of the pumpkin. She turned onto the path next to the highway, and he could see her profile. She was too far away for him to see her face clearly, but he wished that he could. Two children rode past her. They waved and spoke, but soon all three were out of sight.

"Well, are you going to stare out the window at beautiful women all day, Professor Court?" he asked himself. "Not a good beginning for your hideaway time."

Turning his attention to the stunning green, gold, and russet autumn landscape that enveloped the farm, he smiled and breathed a sigh of satisfaction. He'd arrived late last night, but this was the scenery he'd hoped for in this part of the country.

Blue Springs was a tiny historical town on the West Virginia–Virginia border. Because of its out-of-the-way location and the stubborn determination of old families with large land holdings, Blue Springs had miraculously escaped the evils of development and tourism. He suspected the Rivers family was holding to their land by the skin of their teeth, thus the necessity for a bed-and-breakfast.

Planning and scouting out this retreat had taken a year, but he was pleased with the results of his efforts. Not sure how long this research project would take, he decided that for a change he wouldn't be in a hurry.

He'd told Mrs. Rivers he would be here for a week, but his room was spacious, pleasing to the eye, and lushly comfortable, and judging from the food he'd sampled last night, Mrs. Rivers was a superb cook. More importantly, the Blue Springs Public Library owned a collection of Appalachian and Allegheny tales and legends second to none.

And an intriguing librarian, he reminded himself.

No one knew where he was and he wasn't expected back for a month. This looked like the perfect place to hide for a while.

Addie reached the village and ahead of her stretched Elm Street and its row of historic eighteenth-century houses, some with deep wraparound porches, others with sturdy columns and long green shutters. Lulu Murphy waved to her from the front porch of the home she'd turned into an antiques shop.

Lulu stopped sweeping and called, "Hey, Addie. Lookin' forward to seein' you and Buck Friday night. I'm makin' your favorite roast pork with sausage stuffing."

"Great. Sounds like fun. See you."

Roast pork was Buck's favorite, not hers. People had become so accustomed to the two of them together that they tended to link their likes and dislikes. Addie admired Lulu. Lulu meant well, and she had it all: an adoring husband, two beautiful children, and a business of her own.

She hurried, turning the corner onto the square. Library hours were nine to five weekdays, and nine to nine on Saturdays. It was almost nine o'clock.

A car drew to the curb next to her and stopped.

"Slow down, beautiful. That library can get along without you for five minutes."

"Oh, hi, Joe. It won't open until I get there. Any increase in the Blue Springs crime wave?"

It was an old joke between Addie and the chief of police. Joe Bolo had gone to high school with her, graduating tenth in their class of twenty. Buck had been class valedictorian, Addie the salutatorian, and they had gone on to Penn State. Joe had attended one year of community college, taken a course in criminology and town administration, then headed happily home to take charge of the Blue Springs police force of three.

He turned off the ignition of the police cruiser, and got out to relieve her of the pumpkin and carry it for her as they headed toward the library.

"Well, let's see," he said, considering her question. "Burt Manning is missing two shiny new hoes at the hardware store, Mavis thinks kids are stealing the best pumpkins from her display in front of the grocery store, and old Mrs. Tabor swears a peeping tom is staring through her bedroom window every night. Heaven knows what for."

Addie laughed. "Gee, Joe, things are really going downhill in this burg. Do you think you can handle the intrigue and danger?"

"I don't know. May have to import more manpower." He winked at her, a wistful look in his eyes. "Don't suppose you'd have lunch with me today. It'll be some warmed up by noon, and we could take a sandwich to the park, or maybe we could go to the diner. You love Dixie's meatloaf special. I'm sure Buck wouldn't care."

Addie almost said yes, but she didn't want to give him any false encouragement. Joe hadn't lost the serious crush he'd had on her since high school. She loved him dearly as a buddy, but that was as far as it would ever go.

And why did everyone want to tell her what she liked to eat? It was downright embarrassing.

"I don't really care whether Buck approves. I'm not married to him, you know," she said. "But I can't have lunch with you today, Joe. The nursery school is coming in for story hour."

"How about Friday, Ad?"

Why not? She thought. She was irritated with people taking her and Buck for granted. Maybe she would shake things up a bit. And she hadn't been to the diner for a while.

"Sure, Joe. I'd love to."

A huge grin stretched his earnest face, and his round rosy cheeks bunched in delight. His sturdy shoulders, on a level with hers, straightened and she could have sworn he walked taller. Addie was glad she'd said yes. She wished it were that easy to make everyone happy.

"Looks like this fat pumpkin came direct from the patch at Rivers Farm. Where do you want it, beautiful?"

She indicated the bales of hay and the scarecrow arranged on the front lawn of the library. "Put it next to the scarecrow. We're going to carve it tomorrow."

They said good-bye, and Addie climbed the broad stone steps to the entrance of the tall imposing old house, which had been converted to a library forty years ago. A wealthy book lover had left her home to the town, along with a small trust fund to run the library for years to come.

As she opened the double doors, Addie vowed to remember to lock them this evening. Admiring, as always, the finely etched glass panels in the heavy walnut doors, she stepped into the vestibule. The quiet soothed her immediately. Coffee usually greeted her first thing, but he didn't show this morning.

With deep pleasure she inhaled the aroma of mellowed oak floors polished to a high shine, musty old books, new fresh-leafed books, and of ink and paper. The silence and the scents always gave her an odd assurance, and a feeling of satisfaction about what she was doing.

Addie often worried whether she'd made the right decision three years ago. A year after the death of her father, she completed her master's in creative writing and came home to be with her mother. She'd reasoned that she could write novels as well, or better, in Blue Springs than she could anywhere, her mother needed her, and the town was crying for a competent full-time librarian. It had all seemed to fit together at the time, had seemed so right.

However, no matter how much she worried or wondered about her decision to return to the tiny town, being in the library always set her straight.

When she worked with books, reading, cataloging, researching, organizing events for children, she forgot about everything else. She forgot her resentment of the assumption that she and high school sweetheart, Buck Harvey, were a done deal, that they were as good as married, and that he owned her. She forgot that her novel wasn't progressing well, and that she couldn't conjure up the missing ingredient. She forgot that she still held misty, girlish dreams and notions of a deep and passionate romance—dreams and notions that wouldn't let her go.

Whistling Willie Nelson's "Crazy," she shook her head impatiently, flipped the switch that lit the dusty crystal chandeliers high overhead, and headed for the receiving desk.

As she passed the door to the cellar, she heard a long, plaintive meow. Coffee sounded unhappy. She stopped and stared at the cellar door. Coffee couldn't be in there. When she left last night Coffee had been roaming free. The cat couldn't have let himself into the cellar.

He meowed again, and she opened the door. Coffee leaped out, landing two feet past her, then sat and looked at her disdainfully, as if it was her fault he'd been closed up.

"Sorry, Coffee cat. I sure don't know how you got in there."

Dank smells from the cellar swam up the stairs and under her nose, and she slammed the door hastily. In August, a particularly rank odor, sickening to the stomach, had sifted up from the dark cellar. Donny Jim, the handyman, had searched the place, and found nothing, but whiffs of the rotten odor still remained. She hated the cellar.

"Okay, let's go, cat. Time for work."

She continued to her desk, and Coffee followed, purring at her heels. Evidently, he'd forgiven her.

An unfamiliar legal-size pad of blue paper lay in the center of her desk. A black ballpoint pen lay on top of the pad.

Interesting, she thought, *strange. They don't belong to me. They weren't there when I left last night.*

The door was unlocked, remember, Addie? But who on earth would just walk into the library and leave paper and pen? Blue Springs held a few eccentric residents, but none of them had ever done anything like this before. Donny Jim Slater, the handyman who came twice a week to clean and repair, wasn't due until later today, and Donny Jim was a deaf mute, who could barely read. He surely wouldn't be carrying around a pad of paper.

A quick look around revealed no damage had been done, so Addie relaxed. This was a small town and the library belonged to the people. One of her regulars must have returned a book after hours, then sat down to make themselves at home. That would also explain Coffee being accidentally locked up in the cellar.

Sure, she thought, *nothing to worry about.* She put on a pot of coffee and opened the inside shutters, grateful for the sunlight that brightened gloomy corners, then turned on the CD player. Bach's *Keyboard Concerto* drifted down the aisles, and wafted randomly through hidden nooks and pinched crannies of the rambling old house.

While Addie sorted books she tried to recapture the reassuring feelings she'd experienced when she first entered, but they were gone. Worry scratched at her like Coffee's paws.

2

"JANIE WAS SO SCARED SHE could hardly breathe. She ran as fast as she could, but the wailing, groaning ghost from the graveyard who collected little girls' pigtails, hovered close behind her." Addie told the ghost story with drama; using wavery tones and shuddering sighs. "She tripped over a rock and fell. A bony hand reached out and grabbed her hair."

"Oh, no," screamed a girl, and the boys laughed.

The younger children had nightmares if she told them horror stories, so she reserved the scariest tales for the older children. The fifth grade class from Blue Springs Elementary sat on the floor in front of her, wide-eyed and unusually well behaved today.

From the doorway of the children's reading room came a hideous screech. The children screamed and turned to see the principal of their school with his shoulders hunched in an awkward stance, his arms and hands all crablike, and his face scrunched up like a monster.

They all laughed and pointed their fingers. "Mr. Harvey. We're not afraid of you," said one little girl.

"Heck, no, Mr. Harvey," said Brad Simples. "We know you too good."

"Well, shucks. I thought maybe I'd help Miss Rivers scare you to death. Guess I'll have to try harder next time."

"Yeah," said Brad. "Takes more than a fake scream and an ugly face to scare us."

Buck Harvey grinned, straightened his blue striped tie, and patted his boxy, immaculate camel sports coat into place. He tried to keep up-to-date with the latest in male fashion trends, and liked to look sharp.

Addie gave him a small wave. "Hello, Mr. Harvey. How nice of you to visit."

"We needed cleaning supplies and I had to make a trip to the hardware store, so I thought I'd drop by and see how my favorite class is doing."

Addie tried to subdue the irritation that simmered in her, but failed.

Buck had developed the habit of dropping into the library at odd hours lately, and if one of his classes was visiting he always found a reason to be there. Cleaning supplies from the hardware store was just one of many excuses he'd used lately. Addie resented the interruptions, but the children seemed to love them. They loved Mr. Harvey, and they knew he loved them.

He was always cheerful and pleasant, so Addie found it difficult to protest or complain. Addie knew Buck genuinely loved her, and she'd accepted the fact that someday they would marry and spend the rest of their lives in Blue Springs, but she ached to loosen the collar she felt he'd already fastened around her neck.

"Your visits always make us happy, Mr. Harvey," she said, straining to smile. "But you've interrupted a good story. Do you mind if we get back to it? Miss Lewis will be here to walk this class back to school in five minutes, and the nursery chidren will be here at noon."

"Uh, oh. Sorry, kids, but I think Miss Rivers wants to finish your ghost tale." He smiled at them, then winked at her, and gave her a meaningful look. "Everything okay here, Miss Rivers?"

"Fine and dandy, Mr. Harvey, as it always is," she replied. She glared at him, then smiled sweetly. "Safe as little bugs in a rug, or peas in a pod, or cats in a barn, or mice in an attic, or whatever. We are *super* okay."

"Right. Good. Great." The grin on his kind face grew bigger. He knew he'd irritated her, and it amused him. Nothing ever bothered Buck. Addie could yell and scream and shake her fists at him, and he would just smile. "See you later, kids."

Buck waved and turned to leave, disappearing into the greater library area. Addie heard him speak to someone. She thought he offered assistance to whoever had come in, and she wished that he wouldn't assume responsibility where he had none. Most of the library regulars were familiar with the layout and Addie's rules, and if she was occupied with children, or otherwise not available, they helped themselves.

"Hey, Miss Rivers, you goin' to finish the story?"

"Absolutely." She heard Buck in conversation with someone, but turned her attention back to the children.

"Addie is having story hour in the back room there."

"Yes, I know," said Will.

He'd been amused at the sign on the desk. ADDIE'S
READING A STORY. HELP YOURSELF.

"You're a stranger. May I help you? I'm Buck Harvey,
principal of the elementary school."

"I'm Will Court," he said, as they shook hands. "I'm
traveling through the region gathering folk tales and
legends. A friend told me Blue Springs supposedly has
one of the best collections in the country. If it's as good
as I've been told, I'm surprised you don't have a library
full of scholars."

"It is a superb compilation, but we're a small town,
and the library's skills are limited. The computer system
is so antiquated we're not even on the Internet. So you
can see why little is known about the collection." Buck
Harvey smiled genially. "I think we'd just as soon keep
things the way they are anyway. We'd rather welcome
the few drop-ins like you, than try to handle a crowd."

"Who gathered the stories?"

"My fiancée, Addie Rivers, the librarian. Appalachia
is the setting for a novel she's writing. In her research,
she kept running into old tales and legends she'd never
heard before. She kept them and added them to the files
that were already here."

So, Addie with the smoky eyes and coppery hair was
engaged to be married. Will's sharp disappointment
surprised him. He should have known she'd be taken.
He'd come to this small town to find new material for
his books and lecture series, but found Blue Springs' real
hidden treasure was its librarian. Obviously intelligent,
with long legs, a sensual mouth, and an expressive face,
Addie Rivers would be difficult to ignore.

Will took a second appraisal of the congenial man to

whom he was talking. Buck Henry stood as tall as he, but they were of different build. If Will had to describe him briefly he would say Buck looked like an impeccably dressed wooden ruler, "a thin rectangle." Buck's slender handsome face sat on a long neck and met slim squared shoulders, and so it went all the way down to his trim cordovan wing tipped shoes. He was painfully neat, and ran a hand across the top of his severe "army-issue"-type brush-cut hair from time to time.

"How interesting," said Will. "It's nice to know Miss Rivers is available if I have questions. Could you direct me to the section I should be in?"

"Sure. Go past fiction and turn right. Most of it is on the back wall in the history area." He pointed to the rear of the library. "Addie discovered some handwritten stories, which were years old, and those are under lock and key. You'll have to ask her about those."

"Thanks for your help." Will shook hands with the man again, and turned away.

But Buck Harvey didn't move. "How long you going to be here?" he asked.

Will thought it was none of the man's business, but he stopped and turned around to say, "I'm not quite sure. Could take me two days, could take me a month."

"I see. I don't think there is enough material for a month's work."

"Well, I won't know until I get into it, and I'll probably do some traveling and story gathering on the back trails myself."

"You'd better let one of us know if you plan to do that. Some of the elder mountaineers are wary of strangers, and aren't too friendly."

Will's first opinion of this seemingly congenial man began to change. At first a friendly helpful person, Buck Harvey now seemed nosy, controlling, and perhaps even hostile.

"I'll keep that in mind. Now, if you'll excuse me, I have work to do."

"Of course," said Buck. A brief, big smile blazed across his face, then disappeared quickly. His duty to be friendly taken care of, Buck lifted a hand in farewell and headed for the door. "Good luck."

"Right," said Will, and walked toward the aisle Buck had indicated. Eager to get to work, he started down the aisle, but the sound of Buck's fading footsteps stopped, and Will looked over his shoulder to see what had halted the man.

Buck raised his hand in farewell again. "Sorry, just wanted to be sure you were headed in the right direction."

Will nodded and walked on.

When he reached the area he'd been looking for, he heard the faint sound of closing doors behind him and knew with an odd relief that Buck Harvey had finally left the library.

He swiftly surveyed the three shelves holding the work he was interested in, realizing with excitement that he'd found a treasure trove. In front of him was a veritable feast of boxes, books, pamphlets, and note pads containing tales he could use in his lecture series, and material that he needed to complete his new book.

Sorting through the books, Will chose three to start with, and gave the remainder of the material a wistful look. He couldn't wait to delve into it all. He took the books to a nearby table, extracted pads and pen from his backpack, and sat down to work. A coffee-colored cat arrived to inspect his moccasins, sniff up and down his legs, and finally, purring intimately at Will's friendly strokes, to curl under the table next to his feet as if they belonged together.

Set to begin work, he riffled through one of the books, but had an odd sensation that he wasn't alone, that some-one watched him. He looked up to find a big, brawny, middle-aged man dressed in denim overalls and red flan-nel shirt observing him. He clutched a broom and dust-pan. Will got the impression that the man was inspecting him, considering whether Will passed muster.

"Hi," said Will. "You must be the janitor. I'm Will Court."

The man said nothing, just continued to study him. Then he disappeared as quietly as he'd appeared. Will shrugged, and wondered how a huge, beefy guy wearing farm brogans could walk so silently. He shrugged again and focused on his books.

Alone with his beloved work in the quiet library, Will soon was deep into the first of the volumes he'd picked, *Forgotten Legends of the Appalachians.* Laughter, and the high pitched voices of children hurrying through the area near the receiving desk and out the doors barely registered. He worked steadily, completely enamored with stories he'd never heard before.

Thirst finally interfered with his concentration. It was time for a break, and he raised his head to look for a water fountain. He left his table to wander up and down several aisles, but found nothing, and finally entered the cleared space of the main area.

Addie Rivers worked at the desk, her head bowed over books and papers. His soft-soled moccasins concealed his approach. She didn't know that he watched her, and though it wasn't fair, he took advantage of the opportunity and drank his fill of the picture she made.

Autumn sun shone through the large window behind her, catching the coppery highlights in her hair that he'd noticed and appreciated earlier that morning. Her hair spilled softly over her cheek, hiding her smoky eyes, which disappointed him. Her eyes were what he remembered most from their encounter in the kitchen last night, her eyes and the way her graceful hands had moved so efficiently as she prepared the hot chocolate.

She raked her hand through her hair in irritation, and shook her head. "Damn," she muttered.

Ah, ha, thought Will. *The beautiful bookish lady has a bit of temper.* The flickering flames that teased and licked at his groin flared higher. *Not good, Will, not good. You're here to work, not flirt with the librarian. But this is a vacation, too, a retreat,* he reasoned with himself. *Still not sufficient reason to be playing around with an engaged woman, Will.*

She tapped her pencil on the desk and the tat-a-tat-tat echoed loudly in the vast hushed room. It was chilly in the old house. She wore a cream cashmere turtleneck sweater. His heart hammered as he watched her stroke her arm up and down, up and down, warming herself, caressing the soft cashmere sensually, soothing her arm, and perhaps soothing herself.

The phone on her desk rang, abruptly breaking the spell he'd cast around the two of them. He didn't move as she picked up the receiver and lifted her gaze to notice him.

She started and her eyes widened. "Hello, uh—Blue Springs Library."

He smiled, and her eyes grew wider.

"Oh, hi, Mavis." She listened to her caller while Will continued feasting his eyes on her face, the flawless cheeks, tinged with a faint pink now, the feathery eyebrows lifted in surprise at the sight of him, the sweep of her dark eyelashes as she closed her eyes for a second in response to a comment on the other end of the line.

"No, Mavis, I'm positive Bradley didn't take one of your pumpkins," went the conversation. "We're carving ours on Friday. Certainly. I would be delighted if you'd like to share some of your pumpkins with the children. Why don't you come and help us carve? Okay. See you then." She replaced the receiver.

Shocked at Will Court's sudden appearance, Addie realized that she had been staring at him for an embarrassing length of time.

Still as a cat about to pounce, he didn't move, didn't alter his casual stance. Propped against the front section of Fiction A–M; his arms crossed, one foot cocked over the other, he stared right back at her. The acute blue of his eyes sped across the space between them, setting every nerve ending she possessed tingling with anxiety.

She finally forced words out of her dry mouth. "Hello, Dr. Court. You surprised me."

"Sorry, Addie." With a twist of his shoulder he pushed away from the bookshelf and came toward her. She held her breath, trying not to notice the way his soft faded jeans clung to wiry lean hips and long legs. He walked lazily, as if he had not a care in the world. Coffee followed close behind, tale waving arrogantly in the air as if this, at last, was another male he could relate to. "I thought you'd be expecting me."

What arrogance, she thought.

"Oh, that's right. You said you were in Blue Springs to do some research. Anything I can help you with?"

"Yes, I think so. Your friend, Buck Harvey, said you were the curator of the Appalachian tales and legends collection. I understand you're responsible for its fine reputation."

He placed his hands on her desk, and leaning toward her, supported himself on stiffened arms while he spoke. The sleeves of his sloppy navy blue cable knit sweater crumpled down over strong wrists and hands. Crisp dark hairs were scattered over the backs of his hands. A one day growth of dark beard stubbled his jaw, and Addie found it incredibly sexy. The gold earring glinted momentarily when he moved his head.

What did he say? Oh, yes, her compilation of mountain stories. A fierce sense of ownership flared within her, which surprised her, and she found herself on the defensive. Other people had come to use the collection and she hadn't reacted so vehemently. It was as if he had come to take a child away from her. What was there about Will Court that generated such strong feelings in her?

"Why do you want to see that group of work in particular?" she asked, unable to keep the frost from her voice.

He lifted his eyebrows at the tone of her voice. He removed his hands from her desk, and stood erect.

"Perhaps I should explain. I teach American Literature at Yale, and my field of expertise is Appalachian folklore. I've written several books on the subject."

"How did you find Blue Springs, Dr. Court? Our collection *is* considered one of the best, but it is not well known."

An indolent smile made its way leisurely across his angular face, and he stuck his hands into the rear pockets of his jeans. "I like to wander, Addie, and I especially like to wander when I'm searching for material. I don't make arrangements. I discover more when I simply arrive somewhere. I spent a few weeks in Marysville last summer, and heard about the Blue Springs collection. So when it was time for my sabbatical, I came back this way."

To Addie's dismay, she suddenly recalled that a Dr. William J. Court had written several impressive textbooks on Appalachian literature, its forms, origins, and history. She'd read one of his books three years ago when she'd first started her own selections. How could she have forgotten?

This man had thrown her off-balance from the instant he'd opened the kitchen door last night. She'd been unable to think of anything except his eyes, the shock of black hair that fell across his brow, and her desire to sleep with the masculine aroma of him, to curl herself around it and hold it safe and soft around her all night long.

She cleared her throat self-consciously. "I apologize, Dr. Court. I'm rather protective of the material, only because most people don't appreciate its importance. I now remember reading one of your books several years ago. I'll try to help in any way I can."

"Actually, I'm thirsty. I was looking for water."

"Sure," said Addie. She got up from behind the desk. "Go back to your work while I fetch a bottle of water from the kitchenette."

Addie got the water and made her way back to the corner where Dr. Will Court worked, with Coffee perfectly at home at his feet. The long maple table was piled with papers and books, and he seemed already engrossed in his work. A yellow pencil was clenched between his teeth while he wrote rapidly on a blue legal-size pad of paper with a ballpoint pen. The pad was a replica of the one she'd found on her desk this morning.

Could Dr. Court have been in the library last night? Impossible. He'd arrived at Rivers Farm Bed and Breakfast while she was still at the library.

She cleared her throat. He glanced up at her, and she could tell that for an instant he didn't recognize her, and probably didn't even know he sat in the Blue Springs Library. Addie guessed that he was in the back hollows of the mountains somewhere, maybe chasing revenuers, or telling tall tales around a fire, killing a "bar," or kissing an innocent mountain lass.

"Your water," she said, and placed a paper napkin and the bottle on the table next to him.

"Thank you," he said. His eyes lightened as he focused on her and took a long swig of water. "Addie, this Bloody Mud Hollow story has a reference to a Simon Meredith, but I can't find any further mention of him. Do you have anything else on the Meredith clan?"

"Yes, I do, but it's not included here because the Meredith history is in the genealogy section. We also have microfilm you can study, but I always start with books. Come, I'll show you."

He unfolded his long lean body from behind the table and, in an ambling, lazy gait, followed her through several rows of stacks. Addie stopped in the center of a dim narrow aisle and ran her hand over volumes containing West Virginia's families' lineage.

"Here we are. The Merediths are down here, I think."

She knelt to examine books and files on the bottom shelf. He knelt behind her, and stretched an arm across her shoulder to hold onto the shelf for balance and support. His shoulder touched hers, and if he extended his other arm he would have her enclosed, she thought nervously. Their fingers brushed as he too ran a hand over the contents. A peculiar lightness at her center almost drove her butt to the floor, and she heard her swift involuntary intake of breath.

"Something wrong, Addie?"

"No," she said slowly, the word kind of falling out of her mouth like soft air.

Luscious warmth spread low in her stomach and spiraled down where it shouldn't. The lightness and warmth swelled until her inner thighs trembled. She grabbed the edge of the shelf and held on for dear life.

"Are you sure you're okay? You've turned two shades of white and back again."

He was so close behind her that his breath stirred her hair.

"Really, I'm just fine," she protested as she turned to look at him, and found his face inches from hers. He smiled that lazy, disturbing, but inviting smile again. Her eyelids fluttered and she felt light-headed.

His smile faded. With gentle fingers he explored the contours of her face. "You're beautiful, Addie Rivers."

Speechless and unable to move, Addie studied his rugged face.

He rubbed his thumb lightly across her bottom lip, and whispered, "Holy, fair, and wise is she; The heaven such grace did lend her."

The Two Gentlemen of Verona, recalled Addie hazily. *Act Four, Scene Two.*

Weak with desire, curiosity, and a heady sense of adventure, Addie didn't move as he closed the short distance between. His lips were rough and firm, and the coarseness of his stubbled chin sanded her chin. She collapsed to sit on the floor and Will went with her, never taking his lips from hers.

"Dr. Court," she said shakily, and meant to utter a ladylike protest, but found herself unable to say anything further.

"Maybe you better call me Will, Addie," he whispered against her cheek.

He drew back to give her a penetrating look, and she knew immediate loss at the lack of his warmth against her cheek. She ached to kiss him, deep, and long, and hard.

This is totally absurd, Adelaide Rivers. You're sitting on the floor of the library engaged in dangerous flirtation with a man you just met—but, dear God, it feels so very right.

Heart beating at breakneck speed, Addie leaned forward and kissed him. Will caught her to him, pulling her into his lap as the kiss deepened. His tongue prodded her lips and she drew it into her mouth, loving its demanding heat.

"Addie. Addie, where are you?" Was someone calling her?

The telephone rang on her desk up front, and someone called "Addie" again. Addie tried to fight her way to the surface of the drugged state she found herself immersed in, but was defeated by her strong craving for this man and his melting touch. She swam along through the hot, hazy, exciting currents Will created, lost in a world she'd only dreamed about.

"Addie. Where the hell are you?" It was Joe calling, and Joe never cussed. The phone rang over and over, the intrusive noise reverberating through every nook and cranny of the large house. She hadn't switched on the answering machine. She didn't care.

Will withdrew from her mouth, kissed her on the temple, and said softly, "I think someone needs you."

"Yes, I, ah, better see what Joe wants."

Will got to his feet and helped her up. Addie's head whirled and she leaned shakily against the shelves. She poked at her hair, blushing furiously all the while, and searched in vain through the pockets of her slacks for a tissue.

Will, smiling, extracted a white handkerchief from a jeans pocket and tenderly erased from her face any traces of their kiss.

"Okay?"

"I don't know," she said. Embarrassed, she tried to smile, but knew the result was lopsided.

"Addie?" Joe's voice was closer and she realized he was searching for her. The phone had stopped ringing.

"It's all right, you know. As far as I'm concerned, you haven't done anything wrong, so don't be embarrassed." Will's smile turned into a grin, a big delighted grin that creased his face from ear to ear. "In fact, I just had the best time I've ever had in a library, and I *love* libraries."

"I hear you, Joe. I'm coming," she called.

Will gave her a small wave and made his way quietly back to the Appalachia section. Addie took a deep breath, walked quickly to the front, and emerged from the aisle.

Joe paced the area near her desk worriedly.

"Joe, what on earth is so important? I was deep into some files in the back. I had to put them away before I did anything else."

He placed his hands on her shoulders, and she saw fear on his earnest face. "Thank God, Addie. I got worried when you didn't answer."

"Something the matter, Joe?"

He brought her to him briefly, gave her a quick self-conscious hug, and released her. "You'd better sit down. I have some bad news."

"Just spill it, Joe."

"Another member of your book group was found murdered last night. Jennifer Hatfield."

"No way." She sat on the desk, and grabbed its angular edge for added assurance.

"Sorry, Addie, but it's true. She left Marysville Merchant Bank about five-thirty yesterday. The teller who works next to her said Jennifer hinted that she was meeting someone for dinner and a romantic evening, but she wouldn't name her date."

"Oh, no, Joe. It can't be." The phone started ringing again, but Addie could only stare at him in horror.

"Better answer that, Ad. I'll bet it's your mom. The news has been all over television."

Shakily, Addie picked up the receiver.

"Addie, Addie, have you heard about Jennifer Hatfield? Why didn't you answer the phone when I called before? Are you okay?" Eileen Rivers's worry came through loud and clear. "Addie? Answer me."

"I hear you, Mom." In trying to keep her voice calm for her mother's sake, Addie found herself regaining composure. "Joe is here with me, and I'm great."

"Addie, this proves that what I've been saying all along is true. Someone is after the women in your reading circle."

"I'll have to admit you might be right this time, Mom, but I'm fine. Really, I am."

"You be sure Buck brings you home tonight."

"Okay." She said good-bye and punched the disconnect button.

Joe handed her a glass of water and she sat in her desk chair.

"Where did they find her?" she asked Joe.

"Out by the lake."

"Near where they found Laurel?" she asked with dread.

"Yes. They called me right after I saw you this mornin'. I've been out there. It wasn't pretty, Addie. You know I've done all I can to find the truth about Laurel's drowning. Up until now I was pretty sure that Laurel had too much to drink that night, as she did sometimes, and that it was an accident. Janelle's disappearance, of course, isn't in my jurisdiction."

"What happens now?"

"Now, there are no more coincidences. I used to think your mother was being paranoid, but she's been right all along. We're looking for a serial killer." He grimaced, and took her hand in his. "Addie, you're going to have to be mighty careful. Me or Buck will take you home at night, and bring you to work in the morning. I'll devise some sort of alarm system for you here in the library. Donny Jim thinks the sun sets and shines because of you, and he's here twice a week, so that's good. Promise you will alert me to strangers who seem overly friendly."

Crawling fear mixed with guilt when she thought about Will Court working in the nether regions of the library at this very minute. *That's silly, Addie. A distinguished professor from Yale couldn't be a murderer, and if he were, why would he want to kill the women in her book group? Besides, he's not a stranger, he's our guest.*

"Sure, sure, Joe. Has anyone talked to the rest of the group?"

"Yes. Sheriff Glazier told me that two of the women decided to take a few weeks of vacation and are leaving the country. Another has moved in with her parents, and Millie Bailey thinks she'll move to Florida. She has a teaching job waiting for her there. They are all being carefully watched."

"This is crazy. Who would want to kill harmless women who get together twice a month to talk about books?"

"Someone with a warped mind, that's who. And don't go thinkin' that you're any safer than the others were, 'cause you're not."

"I'll tell you one thing, Joe Bolo, I refuse to live in fear. I'll be careful, but I will not sneak around looking into every corner and suspecting everyone I meet."

He took her other hand now, and held them both in his. He squeezed them tightly, and leaned down close to her face, nose to nose, to say, "You listen to me, Addie Rivers. You better be scared. You better be damned scared."

3

An escalating wind whipped and tore at the farmhouse, its keening chilling to ear, bone, and soul.

Addie gave the fire a jab with the poker to perk it up. The flames leaped high, gold and blue sparks reaching for the chimney, and she wished her spirits matched the soaring flames. She worked to hide her melancholy from Joe, and more importantly, to hide the growing panic she seemed helpless to control.

Always strong, sensible, and intrepid, although prone to romantic flights of fancy, Addie hated being afraid of anything. The events of the last few days, however, had compelled her to acknowledge that there were unseen malevolent, forces over which she had no power.

Finally, she turned to force a smile at Joe, hugged her sweater closer about her shoulders, and sat down on the sofa next to him.

"This is kinda romantic, Ad," said Joe. "Is this what you and Buck do on rainy nights? Sorry. That's none of my business, but I bet you wish Buck was here instead of me."

"Not necessarily. Buck can't miss a PTA meeting, and it's always nice being with you. We had some good times in high school, didn't we?"

"Yeah, we did, and I wish that we were on a date right now, and we were roastin' marshmallows for the fun of it, and not because you need someone to protect you."

"Well, *I'm* roasting marshmallows for fun, and I'm not thinking of you as some sort of bodyguard. You're a friend and you should visit more often."

"How was the funeral this afternoon?" asked Joe.

"Pretty bad. Millie and I sat with Jennifer's parents. We were the only members of the book group there. Maria and Sally are in London for a month. Fannie is looking for a job in San Francisco."

In the church, Buck's tall form sitting next to her should have made her feel safe, thought Addie. But it hadn't. The harsh reality of the murders of her friends had come into sharp, excruciating focus at the funeral. Buck's protective arm around her shoulders hadn't taken away the stark sadness on Mrs. Hatfield's face, or Millie's shaking hands and terror-stricken eyes. Sheriff's deputies stationed throughout, trying to be unobtrusive, but failing, had only intensified her apprehension. Safeness, sureness, the promise of a normal tomorrow had become a foreign concept, something she would never feel again.

She ached to go back two days, six months, a year, laugh with Laurel again, trade barbs with Janelle, argue with Jennifer the merits of Joyce Carol Oates.

Addie withdrew her blackened marshmallow from the fire, grabbed a graham cracker layered with Hershey Bar, smushed the sticky concoction together, and handed it with a flourish to Joe. He took a big bite, chewed with approval, and groaned with delight.

"Wow, this is dee-licious. Great idea we had. Just the thing to keep our minds off the storm, and off the loony who's offing beautiful bookish women."

As if in answer to mention of the storm, the shrill wind rattled the windows, threatening entrance, and the lights flickered off and on. Addie shivered and rubbed her hands together. The sturdy country house, this cozy room, the cheerful fireplace, and putting together the chocolate-marshmallow confection she'd made since she was a Girl Scout should be shoring her up, giving her a semblance of security. But she couldn't rid herself of a spiraling, panicking perception that her life was out of control.

"Deputy Lee Bert called right before I came over here," said Joe, "to tell me the police in Marysville have called in the FBI. He says it's hailing over there. Sure hope your mom gets home from prayer meeting okay."

"Mom hates to miss Wednesday Prayer Meeting, but she wouldn't leave until you called to say you were coming. I'm sure she'll stay at church until the storm's over. It'll give her an excuse to gossip with her friends, and they're finishing plans for the Fall Hoedown next week."

"I told you I'd make sure you were never alone until we catch this creep." He munched his s'mores, licking the marshmallow off his fingers. "I'm relieved your mom doesn't have bed-and-breakfast guests right now. I don't like the idea of strangers being around you in *any* kind of situation."

"But we do have a guest. I thought you knew. His name is Dr. William Court, and he's doing research at the library. I don't know where he is this evening."

Joe wiped his mouth with a paper napkin, stared at her in disbelief, and frowned. "You've got some guy stayin' here that you don't even know? Christ Almighty, Adelaide Rivers, you should have told me. Where is he from, and how do you know he's who he says he is? I mean, don't you think it's damned suspicious that this guy shows up here the same time as the third murder?"

"Calm down, Joe. He's a professor from Yale, and he's perfectly legitimate. I read a book of his a few years ago."

"Just because he writes books doesn't mean he isn't a murderer."

"Trust me, he's okay," Addie said. She would never admit to him her own underlying anxieties about the fascinating and mysterious Will Court.

"I want to meet him, talk to him, do some checking up on him."

Addie sighed. "Okay, if you must. If he doesn't arrive before you leave tonight, talk to him tomorrow. I hardly know the man, but I'll guarantee he won't be cooperative. He seems very much the individual, has an air of detachment, sort of a 'touch me if you can, but I'll decide who's boss here' attitude."

She realized she was talking too much, and Joe was looking at her in alarm.

"Christ Almighty, Addie, you talk like you know the man better than you say. How long has he been here?"

"Three nights."

"Hmmmm, well, if I was you, I'd be mighty careful about making quick friends with him."

"I'll be careful."

But Addie remembered the searing kiss in the library, and her rhythmic heartbeats stopped and melded together in one long, wrenching stroke that threatened to splinter her ribs. Cracker crumbs caught in her throat, and she choked, coughing, until her eyes teared.

Joe offered her water and smacked her on her back a couple of times, looking at her with concern. "Okay?"

She nodded, "Thanks, Joe. I wish you wouldn't worry about me so much."

"Have to, and I wish you would take all of this more seriously."

"I take it very seriously, but I hate all the suffocating attention. Everyone in town watches every move I make."

"I damned well hope they do. In fact, Addie Rivers, that's an awesome idea. I'm going to deputize everyone in Blue Springs. They are never to take their eyes off you."

Addie frowned. "You're teasing, right, Joe?"

"Maybe," he said. He poured another cup of coffee from the silver pot on the low mahogany butler's table before them, and helped himself to another of the s'mores Addie had prepared. "I can't deputize all of them, but I can sure tell everyone to keep their eyes open."

Somewhere out near the barn, Rags barked. Sharp pellets of rain assaulted the windows, and the angry wind shrieked like a thousand banshees. The lights dimmed, then wavered on and off again. Addie pulled her sweater closer around her shoulders.

"This big house chills down quickly. I hope the power doesn't go off for good."

"I don't think it will, but we need to be ready if it does. Maybe you should get out your kerosene lamps and candles."

Addie went to the pantry next to the kitchen, gathered a kerosene lamp and candles, and returned to the front parlor.

She paused before entering, enjoying the look of comfort her mother had created. The room, a pleasing eclectic mix of contemporary and antique furniture, was quietly elegant in whites and beiges, with accent spots of lemon and emerald. Joe, his back to her, sat on a pale beige chesterfield sofa, its plump, curved back so high that she saw only the top of his head.

The lights went off and the house was dark. With no city lights close by, the blackness outside the windows seemed impenetrable.

"Addie?" yelled Joe. The firelight outlined him standing quickly.

"Don't panic, Joe. I'm here in the doorway."

"Stay there. You'll fall over one of your mom's little stools."

"I'm fine. I grew up in this house, remember? The light from the fire is enough to get me across the room safely."

The lights flickered on, then off again. She held her breath, then laughed as they went on. "See, nothing to worry about."

Rags's barking again. Addie wished she could bring him inside, but her mother wouldn't allow the dog in the house.

She set the kerosene lamp and matches on a table near the front hall, and placed candles around the room. Joe watched her, worry in his earnest brown eyes. Sometimes she wished she'd ended up with Joe, instead of Buck.

Rags bark sounded once more, piercing high and urgent through the whine of the wind.

"Does Rags usually bark like that?"

"He is making a bit of a racket, but he'll settle down soon," she said, as she sat next to him again on the big sofa. "I'm sure it's the storm that's bothering him."

"Poor dog. Shame your mom won't let him in the house. It's cozy here by the fire." He grinned with mischief, and winked at her. "Maybe it wouldn't be so bad if your mom got delayed, and the lights went off for good."

"Joe Bolo. Are you flirting with me?"

"Yeah, wanna do something about it?"

Rags's insistent bark came yet again, and Joe put his cup down with a clatter. "Okay, that's it. Something's wrong out there. I'm going to check it out."

"Oh, sit down, Joe. You're a worry wart," she said, attempting to reassure him as well as herself.

He ignored her, and headed for the hall where his rain slicker hung on the coatrack. She followed and watched as he slipped into it, and headed out the front door.

"It's probably nothing, but I'd rather check it out than sit here all evening and worry. Keep the doors locked, and don't let nobody in but me." He gave her a wave and shut the door.

Addie usually loved the drama, the audacious blustery show of a good electric storm, but not tonight. Tonight's tempest increased her nervousness, held notes of portent that she'd rather not hear. On her way back to the warmth of the fire, lightning blazed across the sky, and threatened to explode right through the windows.

She stopped to close the curtains on the bay windows, which looked over the front lawn toward the highway. She turned on the CD player, and nodded with pleasure as Mendelssohn's *Violin Concerto in E Minor* filled the room.

Settled on the sofa again, she shucked her shoes, curled her legs under her, and snuggled into its deep comfort, searching for any measure of safety available. Rags's bark sounded fainter, while the rain pelted noisily against the glass, and small blue and orange starbursts exploded in the fire.

Acutely aware that this was the first time she'd been alone in three days, knots twisted in her abdomen, and her heart skipped erratically. *Nothing to be afraid of, Addie Rivers. Joe's just outside and the doors are locked.* Swallowing hard, she tucked herself even closer into the curve of the sofa and its arm.

It's okay. Everything is fine. Don't let this monster of a man spook you. Relax, Addie, relax.

In spite of her edginess, exhaustion soon took over. Addie's head began to nod with fatigue. The last three days had been tiring. She'd been balancing too many physical and emotional balls. Trying to keep the library services going, visiting Jennifer Hatfield's parents, attending Jennifer's funeral, consoling her own friends, calming her mother's fears, had all taken an emotional toll.

The lights went off again. Her stomach knotted, and she jolted upright. Firelight cast sinister shadows on the walls of the dim room.

"Damned if I'll turn into some witless nervous nellie," she insisted to herself. The words echoed back to her in the emptiness. Gritting her teeth with determination, she curled up again, and tugged an emerald-colored throw from the back of the sofa over her for warmth.

As her lids closed wearily, she wondered vaguely about the absence of Will Court this evening. He had been in the library every day, but had kept his distance. His presence in the rear of the library, though out of sight, had added to the stress of the past few days. The effort to restrain herself from casually wandering back to where he worked had taken all of Addie's will power. In the evenings, by the time she arrived home from her round of consolation visits, and interviews with police, Will had been sequestered in his bedroom.

Rags had stopped barking.

A shadow crossed the light between her and the fire.

Her eyes flew open, and she found Will standing near the sofa in front of her. His slouching body cast a shadow over hers. Hands in jeans pockets, strands of dark hair clinging damply to his wet forehead, he watched her.

She sat up quickly, and the throw fell off her shoulders. "You."

"Sorry, Addie. Didn't know you were in here. I was going to make myself a snack and sit by the fire. Wanted to give it a good poke before I went to the kitchen. Can't cook anything now anyway, with the power off. You all alone?"

"Mom's at—uh, prayer meeting. Joe's here, our local police chief. Joe Bolo. But he went to find Rags." Nervousness made her words come in funny starts and stops. "Did you see him?"

"Nope. Parked as close to the house as I could get, and still got drenched."

"Rags has been barking all evening, and we were worried."

Self-consciously, she gathered the throw around her shoulders, and set her feet primly on the floor, but her bare toes looked like pale sausage links against the braided rug, and she jerked them back into the fall of the throw. She shivered, whether from nerves, or from the chill of the room, she couldn't decide, but she couldn't stop. Clenching her jaws to keep her teeth from clicking, and pressing her heels hard against the rug, she forced herself to sit quietly, to not reveal any emotion.

Ear-splitting thunder shook the house with its clout, but didn't seem to ruffle Will. He sank to the floor at her feet next to the butler's table. His navy cable sweater, the same one he'd worn at the library when he kissed her, looked damp on the shoulders. His jacket must have leaked, she thought irrelevantly. His arms rested on his propped-up knees, and his intense gaze seemed to look right into her, inspecting every thought, dream, fear, weakness she'd ever had.

"Addie, are you afraid of me?"

"Of course not. I'm just a little nervous, you know, with the power off, the storm, and I went to the funeral of one of my friends today."

"Yes, I heard about that at the library this afternoon. I'm extremely sorry about your friends. It must be terrifying for you."

"I think I'm still in shock. It's difficult to conceive such evil."

"Have they formed a profile of the killer?"

"Joe says they're looking for an intelligent man, at home with books, maybe a scholar of some sort, probably attractive to women, someone who considers himself a ladies' man, and who is angry about something. Furious at a perceived slight, or devastated by a failed relationship with a woman who was perhaps an avid reader."

His eyebrows drew together, and he frowned, his mouth turned down at the corners as if he was thinking hard.

"Sounds reasonable," he finally said, and smiled. "So Chief Bolo is here to protect you, I assume, not to court you."

"Heavens, no. Everyone knows Buck and I are engaged."

"Yes, well, it's good to know you have so many protectors." He smiled again, that so very devastating, lazy, engaging smile that caused her heart to curl up and flutter like a lacy valentine. "I'd like to keep an eye on you, too."

"Oh, that's not necessary. I've got so many watchdogs around me that I can't even cough without someone saying 'Addie, dearest, are you okay?' "

They laughed together. With the laughter, the muscles in Addie's jaws yielded somewhat and stopped aching, and her knees stopped tingling as the warmth of his smile began to thaw her tension.

"I missed you this afternoon, but your friend Lulu was a help." He glanced at the table next to him. "Are those the makings for s'mores?"

"Yes."

"Thought so. You've got marshmallow on your cheek, and chocolate at the corner of your mouth." She watched in stunned fascination, unable to move, like the snake and the snake charmer, as his hand came to her face and his thumb wiped the marshmallow from her cheek. "Sticky stuff."

"Guess I missed a spot."

"Maybe this will help."

He got to his knees, and kissed the spot where the stubborn marshmallow stuck. She caught her breath as her thighs warmed and trembled, and her heart shook until it rattled her ribs. *Breathe, Addie, Breathe.*

"Ummmm, tastes good," he murmured against her cheek.

"Will," she said weakly. "I don't think this is a good idea."

"Have to get the chocolate off," he whispered, and licked at the bit of chocolate in the corner of her mouth.

Chocolate and marshmallow forgotten, the lick became a kiss, and Addie became a mindless, wanting, craving, creature of sensation. The kiss deepened, his sensual mouth demanding more, his tongue asking entrance, then entering hotly, exploring, darting, and caressing.

Addie heard herself moan and didn't care. Slowly, slowly, he disengaged his tongue, brought his fingers to her mouth and brushed them over her lips, then placed delicate butterfly kisses on her temples and closed eyelids. He slid his fingers into her hair, and whispered into her ear.

"Open your eyes, Addie."

She did, and his eyes held hers, telling her of his admiration and desire.

"From women's eyes this doctrine I derive: they

sparkle like the right Promethean fire; they are the books, the arts, the academe's that show, contain, and nourish all the world."

"*Love's Labour's Lost,* Act Four, Scene Three," she murmured weakly. "Will, it's quite obvious that we're attracted to each other, but you know I've been engaged to Buck for three years."

"Yes, much too long. If you were mine I wouldn't let three years go by without marrying you." He kissed her forehead, and said, "Methinks you don't protest enough about your so-called engagement, fair lady. I don't see much jubilation between the two of you. You happy, Addie Rivers?"

She should say yes, the word should leap from her mouth without hesitation, but it stuck in her throat as her heart rebelled. "I don't know about happiness. Is there such a thing?"

His hands cupped her face and he looked hard into her eyes. "Are you telling me you've given up on happiness?"

At the moment, Addie didn't care much about happiness or anything. All she wanted was to be close to Will again, skin close, whiskered face grazing hers, hot mouth against hers. She wanted the rough grid of his sweater scuffing her cheek. She wanted to breathe in the scent of the rain in his hair, the aroma of a rich cup of coffee enjoyed sometime this evening, and the clean, faint citrus fragrance of his aftershave. Her fingers ached to flirt with the small gold loop that glinted in his ear-lobe.

Answering his question about happiness was impossible because she was melting inside. An untamed river of wild yearning had filled the swollen mound between her legs, and tributaries flowed warmly down her legs, and up into her breasts. She was lost and she knew it.

"Answer me, Addie. Have you given up on happiness?" He kissed her lips lightly, then drew back to look at her again, the fierce light in his eyes questioning her, sweeping away any equilibrium she had left.

"I'll admit you make me wonder if I've been missing something, Will," she said shakily.

"Does this make you happy?" he asked, then kissed her again. She kissed him back, then slid over the edge of the sofa and down on the floor next to him.

"Oh, yes, it certainly does."

He nuzzled into her neck, planting soft kisses on her ear, across her collarbone, and in the hollow of her throat. Addie clasped her arms around his shoulders, and folded herself into him, breathing him in, loving the safe, solid feel of his chest, the tautness of his arms as he held her tight.

"Addie, do you want to go anywhere with this?" he whispered huskily in her ear.

Suddenly, the electricity hummed back on. Light flooded the room. Addie jerked away from him, embarrassed, feeling that a dirty secret had been exposed, and belatedly remembering that Joe might appear at any minute. Relief flooded her when she realized she had an excuse not to answer his loaded question about continuing this dangerous physical flirtation.

He raised his eyebrows quizzically, a smile on his face, and asked, "Kissing's not as much fun when you can see me?"

She laughed and relaxed back against his chest and

into his arms where she wanted to be, her head on his shoulder. Will kicked off his loafers, stretched his legs out on the floor toward the fire, leaned against the sofa, and gathered her close.

The mood was broken, but Addie felt comfortable. A newness sang within her, thrilling her in its raw beckoning call. "Come, Addie," it said, "come adventure with me, come explore life, and passion, and heart happiness, and maybe even heartache."

"Hungry?" Will asked. "I could stay here forever, but I'm starving. Haven't eaten since breakfast."

Addie wanted to stay right where she was, warm against Will's side, thinking forbidden thoughts, dreaming dreams and seeing them come true in the dance and leap of the hungry flames. But she knew Will had made a wise suggestion. Better to be busy than to stay here and give in to temptation.

"I'm not hungry," she said, "but we'll fix you a snack and bring it back in here."

In the kitchen, as Will chopped tomatoes and onions, and Addie beat eggs for an omelet, she worried guiltily about Joe. She was glad he hadn't found her kissing Will, but he should have returned long ago.

"I'm getting worried about Joe," she told Will. "He should have been back by now."

"I'll go look for him. He'd probably like some food, too. Do you have an extra slicker around?"

The back door flew open, banging noisily as it bounced against the wall. Buck rushed inside the kitchen, bringing rain and wind with him. A worried frown on his face, he gave a swift, curious glance at Will, then removed his sou'wester and slapped it against his leg. Drops of water flew everywhere, landing on the floor, on the table, and on Addie and Will.

"Thank God you're okay, Addie. Call an ambulance. I found Joe unconscious near the barn, and someone beat Rags half to death. All I could think about was running here to see if the bastard had gotten to you."

Addie's head whirled. Sick with thick, sudden fear, she grabbed the back of a kitchen chair and held on tight. "Is Joe going to be okay?"

"I don't know. I should have dragged him into the barn out of the rain, but I was afraid to move him. Rags needs to see a vet, pronto." He ran a wet hand across the top of his spiked cut, and gave Will a cold look. "Hello, Court. You been here all evening?"

"We don't have time for questions, Buck. I'll call 911 and we'll go right to the barn," said Addie, running to the pantry for slickers for her and Will.

"You're not going out in this storm," Buck declared with authority.

"I most certainly am. My dog and my best friend are out there."

Fifteen minutes later, she followed the two men as they carried Joe's sagging body toward the house. Rags had been moved into the barn and covered with dry canvas.

They laid Joe gently on the kitchen floor. Addie disregarded the other two men as she knelt beside Joe, loosened his collar, and pulled it away from his neck. She wiped the rain from his still face with a kitchen towel, and whispered encouraging words. Blood trickled from his ear and onto the floor, supplying a spreading puddle of red against the topaz tile, and mixing obscenely with the mud tracked in by all of them.

The sight and feel of dependable, stalwart, protective Joe lying vulnerable and helpless on the floor beside her cast any remaining feelings of safety and normalcy aside for Addie. She closed her eyes, dug deep, and grabbed hold of an inner core of strength she didn't know she possessed. Opening her eyes, she kissed Joe on the forehead and uttered a quick prayer.

"You're going to be all right, Joe," she told him. "The ambulance will be here shortly."

His eyes fluttered open for a second, and he tried to speak.

Addie placed her ear near his mouth.

"Addie," he whispered, his voice a faint, sibilant hiss, barely a sound at all, only a valiant effort.

She would never forget his words.

"Be careful," he gasped. "He's here, close by. It's . . . don't believe . . . he . . . what . . ."

And that had been all Joe had managed to get out. Had she understood him correctly? It was clear he was warning her that the killer was close by, of that she was sure. But how close? In Blue Springs, or in the neighborhood, or near the house? And what, or who, shouldn't she believe?

An ambulance siren could be heard in the distance. Addie sighed with relief.

"Now you can answer my question, Court," said Buck. "How long were you here this evening?"

Addie looked up at Buck in dismay. How could he be thinking about anything but Joe and Rags?

"About forty-five minutes," answered Will dismissively. To Addie, he said, "I'll go to the barn and stay with Rags until we can get him to the vet."

"Wait a minute, Court," said Buck. "You're not going anywhere until I find out where you've been all night."

Buck's belligerent tone shocked Addie. She'd never known him to be anything but pleasant and conciliatory to everyone. He could be hardheaded and stubborn at times, but was always patient and courteous with whomever he disagreed with.

"I don't have to answer to you, Harvey." Will brushed by Buck, and reached for the doorknob. "Rags is more important now."

Buck's face got red, his refined features pinched with anger. He seized the front of Will's slicker and jerked him toward his chest.

"You listen to me, Mr. Stranger in Town. I want to fuckin' know where you were tonight. For all I know you kicked Rags half to death, knocked Joe senseless, then came up here to get cozy with my fiancée."

Will's face tightened. He grabbed Buck's restraining hand, and squeezed the offending fist until Buck winced. "Let go, Harvey. This isn't the time for a fight, and Rags is alone out there."

"Will, tell him where you were tonight or he'll never let you go," insisted Addie. "He's stubborn as a mule, and determined."

"Release me, Harvey, and I'll tell you."

Buck released Will's slicker and glared defiantly at him. "Start talking."

"I don't have to tell you a damn thing, but for Addie's sake I will. I did research at Marysville Community College, then had coffee with old friends."

"I don't believe you."

"I don't care whether you believe him or not," wailed

Addie. The ambulance could be heard racing along the highway. She shoved both men, and opened the door. "Will, go to the barn, and Buck, show the paramedics where we are."

Will hunched deep into his rain gear, and headed out into the storm again as the ambulance drove up the driveway.

"I don't like that guy," said Buck to Addie. "I particularly don't like him being here with you. We'll talk about this later." He shoved his hands into his pockets and stepped out onto the porch to motion the paramedics toward the kitchen.

Twenty minutes later, Addie stood on the back porch, huddling into her slicker, ignoring her mother's pleas.

"Addie, do come in out of the rain," implored Eileen Rivers.

Her mother had returned home as the ambulance paramedics worked with Joe in the kitchen. She stood now wringing her hands in the open door behind Addie.

Soaked to the skin, Addie knew she was being foolish, but she didn't care, didn't even feel the wetness as the rain gusted in and out of her porch shelter.

The ambulance's flashing lights whirled discolike in the black, soggy night. Yellow, pink, and red, they pierced through the rain, highlighting the forms of the paramedics and Buck as they gently placed Joe's gurney into the ambulance. The specterlike forms standing around the large, official-looking vehicle only enhanced Addie's feelings of unreality, her increasing perception of encroaching danger.

"Addie, you're getting soaked," said her mother from the open kitchen door. "I insist you come in."

Addie wanted to go to the hospital with Joe, but everyone said that wouldn't be a safe idea, so she stood there feeling helpless and useless, worrying about him, and his warning words.

The ambulance tore away carrying one of her best friends, the one person with whom she'd always felt incredibly safe. Joe Bolo was pure gold, someone Addie had always counted on to come through, someone she'd taken for granted. Tears mixed with the rain on her cheeks. She dashed them away, and strained to see a figure splashing toward her through the rain and mud with a burden in his arms.

Will came carrying Rags. He headed for his car and Addie knew he intended taking Rags to the veterinary clinic himself. Something in her heart lit and took off like a firecracker in the stormy night, and she acknowledged immediately it wasn't retrievable. The exploding clarity would be forever etched in her soul, and for the moment felt glorious.

She watched as Will loaded Rags into the backseat of his car and listened to Buck's directions to the clinic. Gripping her slicker tight around her, she ran out to them.

"I want to go with you. I know the way. We'll all go together."

"No, Addie," said Buck, holding her arm tightly. "The two of us have things to discuss, and Will doesn't mind going alone do you, Will?"

Will, rain plastering his black hair to his forehead, gave Buck a peculiar look, then shrugged his shoulders, and said, "Of course not. Be happy to."

"We're imposing on a guest, Buck. This isn't right."

Will spoke up, his expression grim, but his words light. "I'll be back as soon as possible. All I ask is that you have some of your mom's hot vegetable soup ready." He got into his car, closed the door with a slam and started the engine, as if to put an end the discussion.

Addie and Buck walked through the rain back to the house, his hand clasped firmly around her upper arm.

"I'm sure Joe's going to be just fine, sweetie, and Rags is a tough old dog. We'll visit them both tomorrow."

Addie barely heard his words. All she could see was dear Joe's pale face against the bloody, muddy floor, and all she could hear were his words.

"He's close by, Addie."

4

THE ALWAYS CONVIVIAL, NOISY, lunchtime crowd at Dixie's Diner provided a semblance of normalcy for Addie, which she desperately needed. The sound of plates clattering behind the counter, and hamburgers sizzling on the griddle, and the tantalizing smell of country-fried chicken seemed somehow reassuring.

Buck and Addie sat in the corner booth Dixie always saved for them if she knew they were coming. They'd made the booth their own since high school days.

Addie viewed the meatloaf and fluffy mashed potatoes in front of her with misery. The last time she'd had Dixie's specialty was the day she and Joe had lunched here over two weeks ago. Now Joe was in a coma and she didn't feel like eating. Restless and disturbed, she stared out the plate glass window at the denuded oaks and maples on Town Square. Brown, gold, and orange leaves scuttled indiscriminately across the street and sidewalks. Though midday, the sky was gray with cloud cover.

"Eat up, honey," said Buck. "I've got a meeting with the Hoedown Committee at one o'clock."

"I know, but I'm not very hungry, and I can't attend the meeting with you anyway. I have work to do at the library."

"I've got a super idea. Since I'm committee chairman, I can schedule meetings anytime and anyplace I want to. I'll call everyone and we'll meet at the library instead of church."

"No, Buck," she said emphatically. "Donny Jim's been acting weird lately, and his aunt called to say he probably wouldn't show up this morning. I have things I need to catch up on and I don't care to have a lot of people around."

"Whatever you say, honey, but I'll be there as soon as the meeting is over." He winked at her and cut another bite of chicken steak. "With Joe in the hospital the only official protection you have is Lee Bert. The FBI seems to think he's sufficient. I don't. You know I love the kid, but he's slow as molasses."

"Everyone in town watches me, Buck."

She watched as he placed the meat precisely in his mouth, chewed his calculated number of times, she could never remember whether it was fifteen or twenty, then dabbed delicately at the corners of his lips with the napkin. She'd watched him do this a thousand times. Why was it all of a sudden irritating?

"Yes, even Dr. Court watches you. I don't like him, Addie, and I don't trust him. I particularly don't like him sleeping in the same house with you. You and your mother are defenseless out there in the country by yourselves."

"My mother likes him, Buck, and that's enough for me. She's a pretty good judge of character."

"Ha! That's what you think. Remember the time she fell for that con man's spiel about getting her house painted for half-price? He put one coat of watered-down paint on it. When it rained the paint washed right off, and the salesman was nowhere to be found."

"Everyone makes mistakes sometimes. So far Will has been very helpful. When he isn't researching or hiking, he lends Bobby Heed a hand with the chores."

Perturbed at this news that Will was making himself so at home, Buck choked on his coffee, and the hot liquid dripped off the cup and down his chin. Tiny brown spots soiled his blue and gold striped tie. Furious that he'd been so careless, he dabbed at them with his immaculate handkerchief, all the while glancing up at her with angry looks.

"Addie, I can't believe how you two have let that man worm his way into your good graces. You really need looking after, which is exactly why I feel we should be married soon. This is the first of November. How about a Christmas wedding? Six weeks should give you plenty of time to pull a few things together. Doesn't have to be fancy."

The knots in her tummy tightened, and a whining noise, like mosquitoes, droned in her ears. She shook her head to make the sound disappear, but it persisted. She drew a deep breath and released it slowly, slowly. The whining, buzzing phenomenon faded away, but left her light-headed. She lifted her fork and poked indifferently at the mashed potatoes. The golden pool of melted butter on top of the mound slid down to swim on her plate.

"What's the matter, honey? If you don't like the December idea, we can do January, maybe. But I don't want to put it off any longer than that."

Addie had an earthshaking thought. For the first time she wondered if she sincerely loved Buck. Did she really want to marry him, or had he become a habit she'd neglected to review, a rut she'd let herself travel in? They'd become a team of well-trained ponies pulling a wagonload of expectations placed there by her mother and the town.

"I'm not ready to talk . . ."

Dixie saved her. She appeared at the booth, pulled her pencil from behind her ear, and began to add up their bill. She stopped writing and stared at Addie's plate.

"Adelaide Rivers. I never in my whole life seen you leave a plate of meatloaf and potatoes. Are you sick?"

"No, no, Dixie. I'm just not hungry today."

"Well, Lord have mercy, come to think of it, it's probably them murders that are shakin' you up." She frowned, and looked at Addie with speculation. "Scares me to death thinkin' about them poor girls, and thinkin' there might be someone around here who could take a notion to kill any of us. You takin' good care of her, Buck?"

"Always have, always will." He smiled and reached for Addie's hand resting beside her plate. "Nobody's going to hurt Addie. I'll make sure of that."

"Not with you around, eh, Buck?" asked Dixie.

"Right! Things are going along like we've always planned. I like to make sure our lives are tidy and neat. Eliminates a lot of stress. In fact we were just talking about setting a wedding date."

"God help us, it's about time."

Addie smiled and refrained from pulling her hand out of Buck's grasp. Dear God, what was wrong with her? Ashamed of her traitorous reaction, she lowered her gaze to the table to regain her composure. Light beamed down from the garish fake Tiffany lamp hanging over the table and caught their hands.

The Rolex, which Buck had saved for years to buy, gleamed gold and silver on his smooth slender wrist. A different watch on another wrist flashed into her mind before she could suppress the memory. An old, but rich and luxurious leather band held the simple gold watch on Will's strong wrist. Tufts of dark hair curled over the leather, hugging the band as if they were at home there, comfortable with its feel and shape.

Remembering now the warm feel of the worn band and his skin when she'd run her fingers down his arm to catch his hand, Addie flushed with guilt.

Dixie laughed. "What's the matter, Addie, sweet? Talkin' about the wedding embarrass you? Never known you to be shy. Look at them pink cheeks, Buck. You'd think you two jest met."

Buck smiled what she called his "endearing" smile, the smile that showed everyone just how much he loved them, the smile that made everyone say he was "so charming."

Oh, my God, Addie, you have to stop this. Where is the love you felt for Buck? Has it been simply a feeling of great friendship and companionship all along? Did you fall into step with everyone's hopes and expectations because it was easier? Or is it Will Court who has muddied the waters?

No, she had to be honest with herself. She'd been

looking differently at Buck for more than a year. That's why she continued to put off the wedding. But her crazy reactions to Will Court had certainly highlighted her confusion about Buck.

"What do you hear about Joe?" asked Dixie.

"I visit every day, and he's still in a coma," said Buck. "Addie goes every day, too."

Addie was surprised at this information from Buck. She had no idea that he visited Joe so frequently. Buck had always been fond of Joe, but a bit condescending.

"Poor Joe," said Dixie. "He jest knew he could protect you, and there wouldn't be no problems. Told me so himself. Always had a crush on you, Addie. I think he still does. I'm prayin' for him. How's your dog doin'?"

Before Buck could answer for her again, Addie said, "Thanks for asking, Dixie. Rags is still in the clinic. The vet said he'd have to stay another week or so."

"I'm real sorry about what's been happenin'. It's depressing. Hell's bells, let's change the subject," said Dixie. "I hear you got a real hunk stayin' with you. That must be kind of exciting. I seen him goin' into the library a time or two. Mavis and the girls in the flower shop next door say they been using the library a lot lately."

"Dr. Will Court," said Addie, with a smile. "I wondered why Mavis and Mertie were so interested in books all of a sudden. Which reminds me, I've got to relieve Lulu."

"I'll walk you over," said Buck.

Addie waved good-bye to Buck and Lulu with relief. Buck had insisted on inspecting every inch of the library, going down every aisle, poking his nose into every closet. He'd even gone down into the foul, damp cobweb filled cellar, which was empty. Addie avoided the cellar like a dreaded toothache. She hated the spiders there, and the fetid smell, and it was useless for storage because the clammy air destroyed the books.

Finally, she was alone.

Thursday afternoons were usually slow. No children's classes, no book groups, but sometimes an occasional reader wandering in to look for a good book. Addie loved the quiet, the sense of being protected, enclosed by walls of books filled with wisdom, history, adventure, and love.

Will wasn't here.

She would have known the minute she stepped through the doors. She didn't know how she knew, but she always did. It was as if she had built-in antennae. Not only did she know when he was in the library, she didn't have to see him to sense where he was in the size-able converted house; behind the history stack, or in the reference section, or in the small galley kitchen.

Shaken at her deep disappointment in his absence, Addie shook her head in confusion. *What is happening to me? One minute I'm scared to death of him, and the next minute I want to throw myself into his arms and make mad passionate love.* She massaged her temples, trying to avert the headache she felt coming on.

Stop this! Get to work. Lots of leaves to clean up. When Donny Jim didn't show, the clean-up jobs fell to Addie. She seized the rake Buck had gotten for her from the supply closet, and headed outdoors to the leaf-li___ ed front l__ __.

In spite of its pumpkin companions, the scarecrow looked forlorn and out of place. Halloween had come and gone and he was still here. Addie poked at him with the rake, but hadn't the heart to destroy him yet. She would rake the leaves first.

The square was empty. It was that midafternoon lull when children were still in school, and Blue Springs residents were either deep in their work, or napping.

An hour later, knee-deep in leaves, hands and nose cold from the November chill, she heard a car pull up and park in the small parking area behind her. The sound of the engine was familiar, and her heart leaped into her throat. She raked furiously, ignoring the thud of a car door closing, ignoring the rustle of footsteps approaching behind her, ignoring her watery knees and rapid breathing.

The footsteps stopped. A shower of leaves fell over her head and onto her shoulders, littering the front of her red down jacket. Brushing them away, she turned to confront Will.

"Hey, you're not much help. I just put those into a neat pile."

"You sure did, and they hate it." His eyes bright with mischief, he scooped another handful into her face.

Laughing, Addie retaliated with a handful of her own and the fight was on. Flinging armfuls of leaves at each other, they battled furiously, but Will had the advantage as he advanced on Addie, backing her up into the huge pile she'd built. She stumbled and fell, laughing, deep into the center of the heap of crisp leaves. On her back, she tried to defend herself by scooping leaves in his face as he closed in on her. He grabbed her wrists and fell next to her, landing at her side, leaves flying everywhere. He propped himself on one elbow, and leaned over her, inspecting her face with a serious expression.

"I do believe, Miss Rivers, that your nose is red, your face is dirty, and your hair is full of leaves. Definitely not the appearance of a proper librarian."

Addie held her breath as he brushed leaf fragments off her cheeks, then placed a swift kiss on her cold nose. He drew back to look at her again, his face only inches from hers, and his breath warmed her chin.

"I'm sorry, Professor, if I don't live up to your idea of a proper librarian, but you certainly contributed to my disreputable state."

"Yeah, I sure did, and I have an urge to make you more disreputable."

He lowered his head and caught her mouth in a hot kiss. Addie forgot about being cold and dirty and confused. She felt vital and alive, glowing and carefree. Swiftly lost in her new feelings, she kissed him back, drawing immense pleasure from the give and play of their lips and the longing burning in her breasts. He slipped a leg over her, and his long length warmed her body, acting as if that was its sole purpose.

A car horn honked in the square, and abruptly Addie came to her senses. They were lying on the ground kissing in view of anyone who passed or anyone peering from a shop window.

"Dear God, Will, this is crazy. Please get up. Someone will see us."

That lazy, heartbreaking smile came, and he kissed her on the chin.

"No one can see us, Addie. I'm not a complete fool.

We're hidden in the middle of the leaves. Look, there's a mound on both sides."

"But someone might come up the library walk to the front door."

She pushed on his chest, and slowly, reluctantly he drew away. They both sat up, and Addie threw an anxious glance toward the street. The passing car was now out of sight, the square was still quiet, and no one seemed to be around. Will stood up and gave her a hand, helping her to rise to her feet.

"Thank you."

"No problem," he said, and gave her an unfathomable look. Was it disappointment? In her?

His eyes had lost their sparkle and now seemed to smolder. Smolder with what? Anger, impatience, hurt? His frivolity and playfulness had dissolved into a seriousness that disturbed her.

"I have to finish cleaning up here," she said. "You can go on into the library if you wish."

"No, I contributed to the mess, so I'll help you clean up."

Soon, having obtained another rake from the supply closet, Will worked at her side, gathering and bagging the legions of dry leaves. He said nothing, worked silently and efficiently, and never looked her way. Addie went through moments of sheer joy at his silent companionship, and moments of raging guilt when she thought of Buck.

The air grew colder and the skies darker as the afternoon waned, and near the end of their task he finally spoke.

"Seems a shame to stuff all these leaves into bags.

There's one pile left. Let's burn them. Leaves put on a spectacular show for us in the fall. They deserve a better end than being packed into black bags and thrown away, and surely Mr. Scarecrow has earned a roaring send-off."

The idea enchanted her. She hadn't had a bonfire in years, and suddenly wondered why. Had she become so set in her ways that she'd forgotten the delights of her childhood? Will Court's ability to call on the child in him was endearing, and she felt herself drawn deeper into the web he wove.

"Blue Springs has an ordinance about burning trash, but there's no wind today, so who gives a fig. Let's do it," she cried.

Qualms about Will, worry about Joe, fear about the killer of her friends, and guilty feelings concerning Buck all dissolved. Addie threw caution to the winds as they hurriedly stowed the bagged leaves at the curb for pick-up. They piled the remaining leaves around the scarecrow and lit a match to the artful mound.

Will laughed and put his arm around her shoulder as the leaves caught and roared with flames high into the air. Addie rested snug into the crook of his shoulder, and laughed with him. The woodsy tang of smoke soon fogged the air and drifted into the square, along with the hiss, snap and crackle of burning leaves. She felt ten years old again.

The fire began to draw a crowd; Burt Manning came from the hardware store, and Dixie with Jingles, the chef from the diner; the Simples children dropped their bikes on the lawn and danced around the bonfire; Mertie came from the flower shop; old Mr. Cartwright came to sit on the stone bench adorning the library lawn.

Caught in the romance Will had created on the square, Addie beamed with joy, loving the delighted faces of the children, the obvious pleasure of the adults, and the whispering memories crossing the lined face of eighty-year-old James Cartwright.

Gradually, she tuned into the questioning glances Dixie cast her way, and the sly, snoopy peeks Mertie was taking at Will's arm around her shoulder. She straightened and stepped away from him.

"Thank Dr. Court for the bonfire. It was his idea," she called to all of them, smiling. She waved. "I've got work to do."

Will followed her into the library. She wished that he hadn't. What must her friends think? Rebellion flared up in her, bright red and dangerous, and suddenly she didn't care what her mother or the whole darn town thought. This was her life she was living, not theirs.

"We shouldn't leave the fire unattended," she said, attempting a casualness she didn't feel.

"Jingles volunteered to keep an eye on it," Will said. He gave her another unreadable look and went to his usual table at the rear of the library.

With determination, she marched to Fiction, prepared to organize Hemingway through Millay, hoping in the process to harness and put in order her galloping fear and confusion. She climbed the ladder, reached for *The Sun Also Rises,* and heard the soft slide of his moccasins behind her. Light-headed, she squeezed the ladder rungs.

"Look at me, Addie."

"Will, I know I'm not being fair to you," she said from

her perch, whispering into the books. "But all of my life I thought that I would probably marry Buck, and suddenly you appear in my life and everything goes crazy."

"Look at me," he demanded again, "and come down off that damn ladder."

Feet and legs, behaving like feathery wisps of nothing, moved shakily down the ladder, and landed with miraculous safety on the floor next to a pair of masculine moccasins.

She turned to face him. "I've made up my mind that I have to tell Buck how I'm feeling. Even if this thing between us goes nowhere, I must be honest with Buck. If a complete stranger can come into town and turn my head so, then I'm certainly not ready to marry him."

He held her chin, and rubbed his thumb along her jaw. "Do you think of me as a stranger, Addie? I hope not. I feel as if I've known you all of my life."

"I know, Will, I feel the same way. But it's scary for me."

"Scary like I'm going to hurt you, or scary of changes and new things?"

"I'm not sure. Maybe both."

"I would never hurt you. You must know that you've become very important to me. I, too, am feeling things I've never felt before. It's quite obvious that I'm drawn to you physically," he said, and smiled softly, "but it's more than that. I love your love of books and history. I get a kick out of your sense of humor. And there's more, but I don't have the right to say any of it. Give me a chance, Addie. Give *us* a chance."

Overwhelmed, she covered the hand that held her chin, and said, "Will, I'm going to have a talk with Buck tomorrow night before the hoedown. I'll let you know how it goes."

He frowned. "Your mother invited me to the hoedown, and I accepted. I'm not sure Buck will be happy I'm there. Will that be awkward for you?"

"Maybe, a little. But I'm a big girl, and Buck is a gentleman."

They jumped at the clatter of a dustpan hitting the wooden floor, and turned to see Donny Jim watching from the end of the aisle. Waves of purple and red undulated over his face, then faded to a sheet-white, and he hurriedly bent to pick up the dustpan he had dropped.

Addie was surprised at his appearance, but held her hand out to beckon him forward. She wanted to try to explain to him the scene he had obviously just witnessed. But he shook his head at her gesture, and his eyelids fell to cover an expression she had never seen before and could not understand. He moved away, vanishing silently somewhere in the labyrinth of shelves.

"He seems completely enamored with you, almost too much so. Are you sure he's harmless?" asked Will, and he leaned over to place a small kiss on her forehead.

"Donny Jim wouldn't hurt a fly, Will. Don't worry about him."

Doors slammed, and heavy footsteps pounded into the library. "Addie? Addie, come quick."

Addie recognized Deputy Lee Bert's voice. She ran to the front and found him pacing frantically.

"What on earth is the matter?" she asked him.

The lanky power company meter-man-turned-sheriff's-deputy shook his head like a dog ridding itself of water. "Addie, get holt of yerself, don't panic or nothin'."

"Just spit it out, Lee Bert. I can take care of myself."

"It's Joe. He died, Addie, he died, he's done passed over," the young man said with a big gulp.

Addie's head whirled, her knees buckled and she sat in the nearest chair.

"No!"

Not Joe. Never Joe. The whole business was hideous enough, but now Joe had died protecting her. Would this nightmare never end?

Lee Bert knelt on one knee in front of her, and took her hands. "Can I get you some water, or do you need a hankie or somethin'?"

"No, I'll be fine. When did he die? Was anyone with him?"

"The doctors figure it was about two this afternoon. He never regained consciousness that they know of. They think he jest slipped from that coma into the arms of the Almighty. His breathin' and everything seemed good, so no one had checked on him for about an hour, and when the nurse finally did, he was gone."

"But it's almost dinner time. Why are we just hearing this?"

"The Marysville police wanted to make sure his family was informed first, and they wanted to question the staff at the hospital. They're going to do one of them autopsies, too. Want to make sure Joe died natural, with no help from anyone."

Hoping to clear her head, she raked her shaking hands through her hair, scraping the nails against her scalp until it hurt. Nothing helped. Nothing ever would. Joe was gone. Joe was gone because of her.

"Ohhhh, God, Lee Bert. He was such a good man."

She sat straight, threw her shoulders back, and wiped the tears from her eyes. "I should have been with him. I hate to think of him dying alone. Did he have any visitors, anyone who might have been with him?"

"Well, yeah." He looked behind her, frowned and nodded his head. "Him. The folk story professor. The floor nurse said he was there about one-thirty."

Addie jerked around to find Will standing behind her. She wondered how long he had been there.

"What's happened?" Will asked.

"Joe Bolo died. Lee Bert says you were there this afternoon."

"Yes, I dropped in after lunch. I'm sorry to hear this."

Lee Bert stuck his thumbs in his belt and thrust his pouch of a stomach forward. "Yeah, and the police want to talk to you. Now jest how come you would be visitin' Joe, professor? You didn't even know him."

"I was there the night he was injured, and felt partly responsible. If you must know, deputy, it wasn't the first time I visited."

Addie saw suspicion grow in Lee Bert's eyes, and gnawing dread joined the grief wreaking havoc inside of her.

"This is nonsense," said Addie. "I'm sure Joe died from his injuries. There's no need to drag anyone else into this."

She smiled at Lee Bert, trying to diffuse the tension between the men. He didn't return her smile, and Addie's skin prickled with apprehension. A pleading glance at Will did nothing to assure her.

His eyes were dark and unreadable. His lips had thinned and hardened into a grimace. Will looked angry and dangerous.

5

Twilight traced pink streamers across a darkening plum-colored sky. The Allegheny foothills in the distance had already dissolved into the night. Hoedown merrymakers wrapped their jackets close as the sharp November air pinched cheeks and hands until they were rosy.

Henry Meredith, the old gentleman sitting in the rocking chair next to Will on the Simples's front porch, had fallen asleep. His story told, he'd drained the last of his hot chocolate and nodded off. Will placed his blue pad of paper on the porch at his feet, then tugged the plaid stadium blanket covering Henry knees up over his chest, and tucked it beneath the man's straggly beard.

He rubbed his cold hands together and blew on them, sitting back to enjoy the scenery, which meant looking for Addie. Occupied most of the afternoon with Henry, the elderly man Addie had brought to the picnic for him to interview, Will had paid scant attention to the activity around him.

The porch of the Simples's farmhouse looked across a square meadow to a large weather-beaten gray barn. All afternoon, people carrying plates of food and drink had eddied in and out of the barn and across the meadow to the house. In the fading light the picnic looked as if it was winding down. They were finishing their dessert, putting their baskets together, and cleaning up. Laughing children were helped off, jumping and tumbling like joyful puppies, from the hay wagons. From the barn the strains of a fiddle tuning up could be heard.

The scene seemed bucolic; a church social on a beautiful crisp, purple, fall mountain evening, but Will knew better. Currents of anger, fear, and suspicion, some of it aimed at him, surged close beneath the peaceful, amiable surface. The specter of Joe's funeral in two days didn't help matters.

Addie had informed him briefly, before she left him with Henry, that Buck had been shocked when she told him of her interest in Will. He'd insisted her attraction was simply infatuation, and they should continue with their wedding plans. They had argued, but eventually Buck calmed down, and agreed it would be all right with him if they delayed plans for a while longer.

Will stood up to look for her. He saw her shepherding a group of children into the barn, Buck by her side. A shiver of apprehension ran down his spine, for no reason that he could think of except that he'd grown to dislike Buck. Chilled, he zipped up his jacket and jammed his hands into the pockets.

Buck may seem calm to Addie, but Will had recognized the signs of simmering anger as the school principal had greeted him. Buck Harvey was difficult to read, but years of dealing with reluctant college students, and competitive fellow professors, and years of interviewing subjects who were tentative about telling their family folk tales, gave Will an advantage. Buck's eyes had been flat, showing no emotion at all. When they'd shaken hands, Buck's hand was cold and dry. His greeting, "Hi, Dr. Court. Happy you could be with us this evening. Thoughtful of Eileen Rivers to invite you," though said with a smile and pleasant in form, was expressed in cold, clipped tones.

The one constant of the day had been the presence of Deputy Lee Bert. Lee Bert had established himself under a tree near the porch, and had kept an eye on Will, and Henry Meredith, the whole afternoon. Only the lure of the overladen picnic table had beckoned the lawman away from his self-appointed post. He'd returned quickly with two plates piled high with ribs, chicken, biscuits, and fudge cake. Will had tuned him out, and ignored the irritating surveillance.

Lee Bert approached him now, ambling along as if he'd just noticed Will on the porch.

"Well, hello, Professor. I see ol' Henry faded out on you."

"Yes, but we had a nice conversation. He had some interesting stories to tell."

"Good," said Lee Bert, nodding his head and chewing on a matchstick. "Good. I guess that means you should have plenty of stories now, huh? You'll be leavin' soon, I suppose. Huh?"

"You anxious for me to leave, Lee Bert?"

"Let's jest say that terrible things have been happenin' since you arrived, professor. Poor Joe, God rest his soul, wasn't real happy about you bein' here and I ain't either. Fact is, the folks in Blue Springs have a hard time gettin' used to smarty-pants strangers, especially those wearin' earrings. Fact is, the FBI is wantin' to question you as to your whereabouts when Joe was attacked."

"I told Buck I was in Marysville, and I'll tell the FBI the same thing," said Will.

His irritation at the distrust of this small town cop grew, and he began to be concerned at mention of the FBI. Perhaps he'd been too cavalier about the cloud of suspicion cast around him.

"And they ain't too happy about your bein' at the hospital shortly before Joe passed over."

"I'm sure, by this time, they will have ascertained that a nurse was in the room most of the time," he said, enunciating each word so that it dripped with sarcasm. "Excuse me, Lee Bert. Mrs. Simples volunteered to sit with Henry while I'm at the square dance. I have to find her."

"Sure, Professor. I know I ain't got too much smarts, not enough to catch the killer. But I'm like a dog with a bone, and I'm sure not going to let nobody get to Addie. See you in the barn." Lee Bert tipped his cowboy hat and walked away.

Mrs. Simples took up her post next to Henry Meredith, and Will headed toward the barn and the sound of music. The sky had grown dark, but a full moon shone on the milling crowd.

He knew a few people; a man he'd met at the library, Dixie and Jingles from the diner, a church friend of

Eileen Rivers, and a mountain woman he'd interviewed. They greeted him quietly, careful of being too friendly, not wanting to offend Buck, he figured. Dixie and Jingles popped a forbidden can of beer, and offered him one as he passed.

"Hey, Professor, how about a beer? The preacher's gone home," sang out Dixie. Clad in tight jeans and a frilly off-the-shoulder blouse, Dixie's ample middle-aged bottom and pillowy breasts were displayed without apology.

Everyone laughed, and others sheepishly displayed their own hidden cache of beer or wine hidden beneath the hay, or behind a post, or under a jacket. Will smiled, waved, and relaxed a little. Maybe this wasn't the prudish, puritanical crowd he'd expected.

Addie stood near the caller platform with Buck. He caught her anxious eyes on him as he stood in the doorway. He ached to reassure her that all was well, that he could handle himself among her friends. If Buck thought he had Will at a disadvantage, he'd have to think again. Will smiled to himself. He'd been raised on a farm in Iowa, and was quite at home with square dances, hayrides, picnics, and other small town rites. It had been a while since he'd done any folk or square dancing.

Yale University, and its accompanying social mores, didn't offer much opportunity for barn dances. His last fifteen years had been spent at departmental teas, faculty get-togethers, formal banquets honoring fellow professors, and occasional performances with the English Department's Jazz Band, where he played the cornet. Frequent excursions into New York City for the latest shows, dining at his favorite Italian restaurant there, or rich, stress-free days at one of the museums satisfied his need for a different pace.

At a glance he could tell the church social had metamorphosed into a carefree community wingding. Most of the children had been sent home with baby-sitters. Those who remained played with Brad and Amy Simples in the hayloft overhead. They'd made a fort with the baled hay, and placed old, stored and forgotten chairs within the waist-high walls. Baby kittens climbed gingerly over and around the bales. The children were laughing, and tossing handfuls of straw at one another.

Jingles, the diminutive short-order cook at Dixie's Diner, appeared at his side in the open doorway.

"How ya' doin', Professor?" The smoke from his pipe drifted up into Will's face. "Sure you wouldn't like a beer, some cider, maybe? We got some potent cider. It's been puckerin' up for a year now. Dern good stuff."

"No thanks, Jingles. I'm a guest of Addie and Eileen Rivers, and I want to stay out of trouble." The acrid pipe smoke wreathed around Jingles's bald head and drifted behind them out the barn door into the cold moonlit night. "Besides, I'm not too popular to begin with. Gotta be on my best behavior."

"Okay. Jest tryin' to be sociable. The ladies look real pretty, don't they?"

Several women, who were obviously square-dance regulars, wore colorful circular skirts and white blouses, while their partners wore jeans, white shirts, boots, and bow ties. Will couldn't take his eyes off Addie. She was shedding her heavy sweater in the warm barn, and like a butterfly from its cocoon she emerged in a scoop-necked sky blue dress with puffed sleeves, nipped-in waist and full skirt. Her coppery hair shone bright in the glow of the Christmas lights looping from the loft and strung throughout the barn.

"Yeah, Jingles, you're right. They sure do look pretty."

Will studied the milling crowd. Most of them looked familiar, even if he didn't know who they were. One man worried him. Young, fair-haired, pleasant faced, but dressed not quite right.

What bothers me about him? Will asked himself. His trousers were black and neatly pressed, too dressy, and his shiny shoes were all wrong.

"You know everyone here, Jingles?"

"Jest about. One or two strange faces."

Jingles seemed unperturbed that there would be people here he didn't know, so Will tried to lose his concern. His scrutiny returned like an arrow to Addie.

He saw Buck say something to her. She nodded her head and started toward Will, but Buck held her by the arm and evidently told her to stay put.

"Addie's about as pretty as they come, ain't she?" remarked Jingles.

Was it so obvious that Will couldn't stop looking at her? Did the whole town know they couldn't keep their hands off of each other?

Reluctantly, he turned his gaze to Jingles. "Yeah," he said to the grizzled old cook. "Addie's special."

"Buck's been thinkin' that for a number of years."

"Are you trying to tell me something, Jingles?"

Tiny sparks jumped from Jingles pipe as he drew heavily on it before answering Will. "S'pect so. Buck ain't too friendly when he don't get what he wants."

"Hey, Jingles. Did I hear my name?" Buck, in white shirt and string tie, appeared next to them with a cup of cider in his hand. He grinned his beautiful, charming, snaky grin. Will's hand itched to knock it off his handsome face. "Better not be talking about me, Jingles. I'll put a curse on your pancakes."

Will was fairly sure Buck hadn't heard much, but Jingles gave a nervous laugh, and said, "Heck, no, Buck. I was jest sayin' that you were the best school principal in three counties."

"Thank you, thank you. You're a good friend, Jingles." He patted the short man on his back, and held out the cup of cider to Will. "I noticed our guest hadn't been offered any of our famous cider, so I brought him a cup."

"He wouldn't take none of what I offered him," said Jingles, a small embarrassed smile rearranging his cheeks.

Buck winked at Will. "Well, now, Professor, this is not the aged cider that Jingles brews. This is your hostess, Eileen Rivers's, cider."

"Anything Eileen makes is superb," Will said. He accepted the cider, and masked his surprise and suspicion at this friendly gesture from Buck. "Thank you."

The banjo player, an elderly woman with a happy grin on her wrinkled face, plunked out some tentative notes, and the fiddler rosined his bow again. Some of the women practiced clogging, and other intricate patterns. Their stomping feet stirred up small clouds of chaff-filled dust from the planked floor.

"Gotta go," said Buck. "Addie's waiting. We're a great dancing team. I think you'll enjoy watching, Professor."

"I'm not going to watch. Thought I'd join in." He sipped the cider and relished the look of dismay on Buck's face.

"Fine, fine. Hope you can keep up." Buck nodded and waved a hand in farewell. "See you later."

Will's searching gaze found Addie again, in the corner now with a middle-aged man he recognized as the part-time handyman at the library.

Unable to speak, Donny Jim had only nodded to Will on the occasions they had encountered each other at the library. His utter devotion to Addie was sometimes painful, always sweet to observe. At the moment, she seemed to be spelling words into his palm with her finger, and Donny Jim nodded with understanding. The music tuned up fast and lively and Addie touched her friend's cheek and walked away. Will could see, even at this distance, the abject adoration in the man's eyes as he watched her join hands with Buck for the first dance.

He wondered if such devotion was healthy, but ignored his leap of anxiety as the caller instructed the group to form their first position.

"Okay, ladies and gents," he announced, "we're doin' the Red River Valley."

He called for sets of three in a circle. One man in the middle of two women, arms linked. Buck had Addie on one arm and Eileen on the other.

"Hey, there, handsome," yelled Dixie to Will. "Jingles has deserted us for those cute Bedley sisters. Come and be our man."

Will smiled, deposited his cup of cider on an upended barrel, and linked up with Dixie on one arm and Addie's friend Lulu on the other.

The hoedown music, swinging sweet and rich, filled the barn, and flowed out the barn doors into the night. The children in the loft clapped in rhythm, and the smiling caller issued his directions with benign authority.

"Hey, now you lead right down the valley," he called, tapping his foot to the rhythm, and the sets moved forward to meet a new set.

Will struggled with long forgotten patterns and steps for a time, but with concentration he eventually began to catch on and enjoyed the give and flow of the dance.

Addie's set would meet his soon.

"Circle to the left, then to the right."

The tempo speeded up and Will weaved in and out following the caller's instructions, bowing, and linking.

The air in the barn seemed warmer, and he began to perspire. In top physical shape from running, tennis, and swimming, he was surprised at the effect the dancing had on him. He caught a glimpse of Brad and Amy waving to him from the loft. He smiled back, but to his dismay found it difficult focusing his eyes on the laughing children.

Addie's blue dress flashed around and around in the crowd of swirling skirts. Her set approached. He would soon be right across from her.

"Now you swing with the gal in the valley."

Addie waited while Buck swung her mother, and took a quick glance around the circle to locate Will. Her breathing quickened.

Soon they would touch.

"And you swing with your Red River gal."

Buck swung her with expertise, and kissed her swiftly on the cheek before she passed on to the next set.

The fair-haired man, who hadn't taken his wintry eyes off her all evening, now stood next to her. Addie shuddered. She wondered if she should alert Lee Bert, Buck, or Will. *Stop this*, she told herself. *You can't allow yourself to be afraid of every stranger you meet. He's probably someone's cousin, or a visiting friend.*

"Circle to the left, then to the right."

The stranger linked her arm in his and swung her. "How are things with you, Addie?" he asked.

She gave him a weak smile, but pretended to concentrate on the dance pattern and didn't answer. He leaned down to whisper in her ear. "Everything okay?" he asked intimately.

She shuddered and felt a rush of relief as he left her and swung her mother. A quick and anxious spot check for her protective knights, should she need someone, found Will's attention riveted on her; Buck, despite making an effort to be gracious to his dance partners, glared at her, and managed to watch every move she made, while Lee Bert talked animatedly with some farmers at the large barn door.

She could signal to any one of them, she thought, but reasoned that it wasn't necessary. If this stranger was the killer, he couldn't hurt her here in the midst of all these people. After this dance was over she would voice her concerns to one of them.

"Now the girls make a wheel in the valley."

Addie joined hands with her mother, Dixie, and Lulu, and wheeled around and around until she landed in the arms of Will.

With his touch, the whole world righted, then tilted again. Safe with Will, she was now giddy with relief and excitement. The menace of the stranger dissolved into happiness at the sight and feel of Will. He linked her mother on one arm and Addie on the other. The warmth of his body heated her right side, and she sucked in the musky male scent of him, and the faint lemony aftershave he used. Wiry hair on his arms, and the side of her breast against the brawn of his upper arm bred a chain of reactions in her body that left her light-headed, and yearning for more of him.

Will gave her a reassuring, but lopsided smile, and whirled her around. It was her mother's turn. Addie stood patting her foot in time to the lively music, and tried to manage the exhilaration swirling through her.

Will lurched. Her mother laughed and caught his arm to steady him.

Had he been drinking beer as he sat on the porch with Henry Meredith, worried Addie, or had he been indulging himself with Jingles's ripe inebriating cider? Neither of those possibilities seemed likely, and the cider she'd poured for Buck to take to Will had been plain fresh apple juice variety. Though she knew Will possessed a wild and unconventional streak, she also knew he was too courtly and polite to get drunk and embarrass them.

Was he ill? No, he seemed fine now, laughing with her mother, having a good time.

"And the boys do-sa-do so polite."

Will "do-sa-doed," then grabbed Addie for a final twirl before sending them off to the next set. He managed to bring her close enough to smooth a swift palm over her breast and place a soft kiss in her hair.

Flying with excitement, Addie had forgotten Buck, but now caught a glimpse of him across the circle, frowning at her, and angry. Obviously he'd noticed the quick exchange of affection between her and Will. He cast her a malevolent look that shook her to her roots, and her happy excitement plummeted to the dusty floor to join the dancers' busy feet.

Buck had never, ever looked at her with anything but love and happiness. She hated being the cause of anyone's misery, and especially Buck's.

Face it, Addie. You've seen other things in Buck's eyes lately, things you've ignored or haven't been willing to acknowledge. You've seen ownership, and jealousy, and spite. You've seen condescending attitudes in the leaning, hovering stance of his body, and the swift jerk of his perfectly shaved chin.

"Now you lead on down the valley," sang out the caller.

The set changed again and the pattern was leading her back to the cold-eyed stranger's nosy questions, and then to Buck, whose expression had now turned to one of hurt and frustration.

The faster the music went, the faster Addie's thoughts swirled, like the twirling red, blue, and green skirts, like the spinning, smiling couples. Her thoughts and feelings flew high, then fell and whirled into confusion. She searched for Will. She caught a glimpse of Jingles playing in the loft with the children.

Something's wrong with Jingles being up there, she thought. Twirling fast now, she concentrated on keeping her balance, and tried not to place undue concern where there should be none.

She hadn't the time to figure it out, or think about Jingles and the children right now.

Will. If she could find him she would feel better. If she found Will everything would be all right.

It was then that Addie admitted to herself, with relief and exhilaration, that she loved Will Court, that she was irrevocably, romantically, and forever in love with Dr. William J. Court. She remembered the night she'd watched Will carry a dying Rags through the storm to his car, and how her heart had taken off like a fire-cracker giving brilliance to the bleak night. She relived that blinding joy now as she spotted him making his way, in a rather wobbly manner, over to the ladder lead-ing to the loft.

Again she wondered if he was sick, or drunk, or just tired? He grabbed the ladder with determination and climbed quickly, as if he had a mission.

Worry about Will left as the stranger linked his arm in hers and hugged it close to his body. His perspira-tion-soaked shirt stuck to her arm, making it slick. She gritted her teeth, but promised herself that she would be cool. She would get through this with a polite smile.

But butterflies boogied in her tummy while she smiled.

"Hi. I'm David Stowalsky," he said in a hushed voice close to her ear. "Please meet me outside the barn after this set is over. I know you're having fun, but I have something to ask you before the next dance begins."

Addie tensed, but pretended she hadn't heard him. She kept smiling, curtsying, and swinging, and smiling, smiling, smiling. While the Stowalsky man swung her mother, Addie looked again for Will.

"Fire!"

Someone yelled "fire" again, and the dancing partners began to separate and look around. Smoke could be smelled now.

A perfect silence held the crowd for a frozen moment.

Then shouts came from everywhere in the barn, and a flashing sheet of flames and roiling smoke erupted from the loft. Pandemonium broke loose.

Addie turned to look for her mother, and saw Eileen Rivers being led hurriedly out of the barn by the stranger. Her mother kept turning to look for her. Her eyes were wide with panic, and she tried to break loose from the man's grip, but he kept pushing her forward. Addie started after them, but lost sight of them as clouds of smoke enclosed her.

Her alarm at the first smell of smoke had now escalated into mounting terror at the sight of the flames and the fear on her mother's face.

Fighting terror with every ounce of courage she possessed, Addie ached to inhale deeply and calm herself, but knew she'd only be sucking in her death. The smoke had become so thick she could scarcely breathe at all. She fumbled for a tissue in the pocket of her skirt and held it over her mouth and nose.

The smoke had gathered so swiftly. The flames had flared so high and out of control in seconds.

Screaming children could be heard above the panicked din, and she remembered that Will had been heading up the ladder to the loft and the children.

She got on her hands and knees and crawled in the direction she thought the ladder was in, lowering her nose all the way to the floor where several inches of good air still remained. Coughing and gasping into her thin tissue, she began to wheeze and fight for air. The impenetrable smoke stung her nose. Excruciating pain seared her eyes.

The ladder to the loft? Where is it? Waves of blackness washed back and forth through her. For long alarming moments lucidity fled with the darkness, then returned, only to be gone again.

This is foolish, Addie. Look for the door. Get out. Will and Buck can take care of themselves.

But where is the door? There are two of them, she thought. A little one, and the big loading door. Which direction? Which direction?

She was lost.

"Will?" She thought that's what she cried out, but her voice sounded like a whistle.

"Will?" she tried again.

He was gone.

No. Someone was nearby. The pitch-black smoke yielded for a second. Was that the form of someone at her side? The inky smoke closed in again. Choking, smothering, gasping for air, Addie lay flat on the floor and sniffed for air.

Gone. It was gone. No air left. No air.

A hand touched her. Oh, thank God. Someone to help.

Nauseous from the smoke, and dizzy from lack of air, she groped for the person, but the hands moved over her and found her neck. They tightened. Addie pulled to loosen the fingers, but they were too strong. She didn't understand. Pulling her to safety? This wasn't the way. Didn't understand.

Suddenly she did understand.

This was the killer. This was the man who'd murdered Laurel, Janelle, and Jennifer. No-o-o-o. In spite of all the precautions, he'd gotten to her after all. She tried to scream for Will, for Buck, or Lee Bert. Anyone. But she knew it was too late. She was suffocating.

Grabbing, poking, tearing at the powerful fingers around her throat, Addie struggled for her life. She kicked, and heaved, and bucked, but brilliant red streaks burst across her brain, then black, then blue, then red again.

The scant air remaining in her heaving lungs would soon be gone, smothered by these lethal hands, by this man who hated her so. Why?

Too late.

I'm not ready. It's the wrong time.

Too late.

Amy Simples's thin arms squeezed his neck so tight that Will felt the sharp, fragile bones in her wrists and knees. The kitten she'd snatched up clung frantically to his shirt. The frenzied creature's claws dug into his chest, but the pain was unimportant, and was nothing compared to Will's fear. Ten-year-old Brad hung close behind them, his hand hooked rigidly around Will's belt. Brad carried a kitten, too. They hadn't time to search for the mother cat.

He thought they were almost to the loft door. Couldn't see it now, but he'd looked for it the minute he'd swept Amy into his arms. *Please, God, keep me on a straight course.*

He stumbled over an implement of some kind, probably a rake, he thought, as the handle flew up and thumped him on the knee. He grunted and righted himself, hoping he still headed in the right direction.

His head ached from the spiked cider, but fear of the fire had cleared his brain of everything but the will to survive.

He tried to give a word of encouragement to the children, but the dense smoke smothered any attempt at breathing, much less talking. They would be damned lucky if they made it to the loft door unharmed.

Thank God there was little breeze. What wind there was blew to the east of them through the window on the far side of the loft, fanning the flames to the rear of their path. The fire behind them leaped high, dropping huge clumps of fireball into the barn below.

Will refused to think of the people down there. He couldn't. Thinking of Addie caught in that flaming inferno would have rendered him useless. He was fairly sure most of the dancers got out before the fire grew vicious. As he'd scooped Amy into his arms, and given Brad and Jingles instructions, he'd seen the crowd below run for the doors.

Behind him, Jingles, ashamed and sober now, struggled in the same manner Will did. He carried one child, and another was hooked onto his belt.

Jingles was the reason Will had climbed to the hayloft.

Sick to his stomach and dizzy, Will had excused himself from dancing, and found a cool place to sit. The bale of bound hay against the barn post had been perfect. He'd had flu shots, and he'd eaten nothing that disagreed with him, and had not indulged in anything alcoholic. So why did he feel like he'd consumed five martinis?

Had Buck put something in the cider he'd given Will? *If I had finished the whole cup, I would be falling down drunk.* Could Buck have done such a stupid thing out of jealousy, or a desire to make him look bad in front of Addie? It was something a high school kid would do, immature and spiteful.

Will was trying to reason out that startling thought when he'd noticed Jingles sitting in the loft with the children. Laughing, and dancing a jig with the kids inside their fort, Jingles kept puffing on his pipe, while sparks from the pipe jumped into the dry straw all around the merry group.

Will had yelled to Jingles, but the music was too loud.

He'd made his way through the dancers and begun to climb the ladder when he heard a child voice the first alarm. He hadn't been too worried at first. Sometimes a small hay fire can be stomped out quickly, but something else stored in the barn must have ignited because the flames grew out of control in no time.

Will figured the old furniture and stored burlap bags filled with feed had caught and added to the inferno.

Like a ravenous beast, the fire ate at the barn, and everything in the barn, in starving gulps. Hungry for the air it needed to live, the fire swallowed everything in its path.

The roar of the fire swept closer. A barn owl zipped by his head, followed by three smaller ones. The frenzied flapping of their wings sent brief, whishing, welcome puffs of motion across his perspiring head.

The tempo of Amy's frightened breathing against his

neck increased. The seven-year-old panted like a tiny caged animal.

Almost there, Amy. Almost there.

The smoke cleared and the loft door, a blessed open rectangle of star-studded indigo sky, presented itself right in front of him. With enormous relief he lowered Amy to the floor, and looked down. A babble of voices traveled up from below. A shout rang out.

"There they are," yelled someone. "Harry, swing that pulley closer."

Enormous relief swept through Will as he realized the children could be lowered with the pulley. Everyone would reach the ground, and safety, relatively unharmed.

Brad, Jingles, and the other two children crowded around him as he knelt on the edge and scanned the crowd below.

Where was Addie? He couldn't find her. He spotted Eileen Rivers. The abject horror in her eyes could be seen at this distance, and he knew immediately that Addie hadn't gotten out.

Hanging on for dear life, Amy and Brad were lowered on the pulley, and Will turned to speak to Jingles.

"You make sure the other kids get down safely. I'm going back for Addie."

"You ain't doin' no such thing. There ain't nothin' left. We're damned lucky we made it, Professor. The fire's eatin' at our ass right now."

The ferocious heat of the flames seared his face as he looked behind him. The stench of singed hair on his arm stung his nostrils, as his heart shook with terror.

Jingles was right. The barn, and everything in it, was gone.

6

WHITE. White. Everything that had been red, black, blue and yellow had turned white. A misty, magic, soothing white. She had traveled to another land, another world, or dimension. Someplace with lovely fairies flowing in the air, and airy emerald trees, and blissful faces. Nice there. Happy there.

She wanted to return to that peaceful, carefree place.

She struggled against the strong arms that held her. Someone gripped her so tight to his chest that his ribs dug roughly into her cheek. His jarring stride ignited every sensitive nerve ending in her drained body.

Her throat was on fire. So sore. So sore. And she smelled bad. Burned hair. Oh, God, was her hair all gone? She tried to open her eyes, but they were swollen shut.

Whoever you are, just let go of me. Let me go. I hurt everywhere. I can't breathe. Let me go.

With horror, she remembered now the fire, and the man strangling her.

Oh, dear God, the killer hasn't finished. We're out of the barn. He's taking me where no one will ever find me. He'll rape me like he did the others.

She struggled, tried to kick, tried to bite, but she was too tired. Exhausted.

Everything went black again.

7

A THOUSAND STAMPEDING HORSES stomped across her chest, their hot hooves striking sparks through her entire exhausted body. So dry, so hurting. Addie's burning lungs heaved for air, and her throat felt like summer roof tar.

Somewhere there were voices.

A coughing spasm wracked her body until the bed shook, forcing Addie's swollen eyes open. Everything appeared blurry and fuzzy. But the ruffled, pink lace canopy over her head looked nothing like the enchanted place she'd visited when she'd passed out in the barn, so she knew she had returned to the land of the living. Mrs. Simples's fussy lace canopy was a welcome sight.

Dr. Hamilton, Blue Spring's one practicing physician, stood on one side of the bed next to her mother, and Donny Jim hovered at the other like a protecting, avenging angel with singed eyebrows and hair. His nut-brown eyes held a hard, "dare me" expression, as he searched continually around the bedroom. She followed his gaze.

The Simples family gathered anxiously in a corner. Next to them stood a grimy, red-faced Buck, who glared at Donny Jim. Will leaned against the wall at the end of her bed staring at her as if he wanted to make sure she wouldn't disappear.

Lee Bert stood wide-legged in the doorway, trying to look official and important, his arms folded across his chest. Looking over his shoulder were Jingles, Dixie, and other concerned faces.

She squeezed her mother's hand, and said, "I'm fine, Mom." Her voice sounded like a foghorn, and each word sliced her throat like a paring knife. "A little worse for wear, but fine."

Tears flowed down her mother's cheeks. "Oh, Addie, we've been so worried. An ambulance is on the way."

Buck made a move toward her, but Donny Jim lifted his arm like a traffic cop, and made a violent halting gesture with his hand.

"Now listen here, Doc Hamilton," said Buck, "I'm not going to let that . . . that . . . that retard keep me from Addie's bedside. You tell him that I would never hurt my Addie."

Doctor Hamilton sighed. "Sorry, Buck, but there's no way he's going to let you near her. Somehow, Addie and I will convince him that you won't harm her. In the meantime, relax. You can be with her at the hospital."

"What's going on, Doc?" croaked Addie, pressing her hand to her throat in an attempt to alleviate the pain.

She felt then the bruises and scratches on her neck. The terrifying confrontation in the barn with the stranger rushed back to grip her with such horror that every muscle in her body tightened like a bowstring, and her jaws clamped like a vise.

"Donny Jim saved your life, Addie. Evidently he carried you through the door on the far side of the barn. We found the two of you under the big oak tree. He wouldn't let us near you, but he was trying to tell us why. He kept putting his hands around his throat as if he were being choked, and he made awful faces, and groped at us like he might imagine a monster would."

A sob, like a bullfrog's nighttime lament, rasped through Addie's raw throat.

"What was he trying to tell us?" her mother asked.

Addie closed her eyes for a second, dredging up strength to tell them about the terrifying moments in the smoke-filled barn, then opened them.

"At first, I thought someone was trying to help me find my way out through the smoke, but they weren't. They tried to kill me, tried to strangle me." Trembling with emotion, her tortured voice broke and she couldn't go on.

Will moved toward her, but Donny Jim blocked his way.

Will raised his hands, and looked as if he wanted to shove the big mute away from him, but thought better of it. He restrained himself and leaned back against the wall.

Covered with soot, Will looked like a chimney sweep. Bloody streaks outlined rips in his shirt, and the skin on his arms had turned bright pink. His worried gaze examined her over and over again, starting at her head and following every curve, convex, and concave part of her all the way to her toes. All Addie wanted to do was stare right back at him, gobble him up with her eyes, invite him to crawl into bed with her so they could comfort each other.

"Did you see who attacked you?" asked a bristling Buck. "Who was it? It was probably Donny Jim. How do we know he's telling the truth? He tried to strangle you and then got scared that he might die in the fire, too, so he brought you out."

"Are you all right? Did he do anything besides choke you?" asked Will.

They all spoke at once.

"Can you remember anything, Addie?" asked Lee Bert. "You know, did he smell of anything, like cologne, maybe, or did he have a mole on his nose?"

Addie felt a nervous laugh trying to bubble up at Lee Bert's denseness, but it died swiftly. "Lee Bert, I couldn't smell anything but smoke, or feel anything but heat, and I sure couldn't see any moles on his face. I'm sure it wasn't Donny Jim, Buck."

"Well, who do you think it might have been, Addie, dear?" asked Buck.

"I think it was the stranger. He was a stranger to me, anyway. He asked me some odd questions while we were dancing. I think he said his name was Stowalsky, David Stowalsky."

"No, Addie, he wouldn't hurt you. Agent Stowalsky is with the FBI," said Lee Bert. "He was here to investigate, and to protect you. He's outside right now interrogating everyone who came to the hoedown."

Addie knew she had to make an effort to defuse the obviously tense standoff among her friends in the bedroom. She garnered any shreds of remaining stamina, and tried to smile. Her tense jaws ached with the effort, but she smiled at Buck, who still frowned in the corner, then motioned to Donny Jim to come close. Using every means of communication they had developed between them, she told the man that no one here would hurt her, and that he must let them come near.

He finally nodded an assent, but refused to leave her side as they loaded her into the ambulance. He rode to the hospital with her and Buck.

Will and Jingles, with burns on their arms and back, were in a following ambulance. Because of the quick thinking of Will, the children had emerged relatively unscathed.

8

ADDIE WORKED CONTENTEDLY IN the hushed library, relieved to be back at work after a week of recuperating from the physical and emotional trauma of the fire. She was alone, but she welcomed the solitude. People had been hovering around her for days like worker bees around the queen.

It was late, ten o'clock, but she had so much to catch up on.

A sound behind her startled her, and she twirled the swiveled chair around.

"Oh, Donny Jim! Lee Bert said you would be here tonight, and I forgot. Great. That makes me happy. I know I'm safe with you here."

Knowing her words fell on useless ears, Addie grinned as big as she could to convey her pleasure. Her signing skills were limited, but she tried a few words, then drew letters on the palm of his beefy hand. The two of them had worked out ways of communicating.

His soft brown eyes warmed with joy, and he nodded his head so vigorously his cheeks reddened.

"You don't have to stay right here beside me tonight," she explained to him. "I'll be fine. You dust the shelves."

He nodded and moved off down an aisle, glancing over his shoulder to check on her as he went, then finally disappeared.

The phone rang, and she sighed, running her hands through her new short haircut in frustration. It had to be either Buck or Will calling. Both of them kept such close tabs on her they were driving her crazy. Every night she said a prayer asking God to please help law enforcement find the man who had attacked her in the barn.

When she thought of the nightmare moments in the smoke her body iced with fear so real that she shook with chills. She avoided recalling the memory at all costs. Quickly, she snatched up the phone, eager to talk to the caller and forget her memories.

"Hi, beautiful librarian of my heart. Are you okay there?"

"I'm just fine, Will. Really, I am. Donny Jim is here, and Lee Bert is right outside on the bench."

"Too bad the FBI guy had an emergency. If I know Lee Bert, he's reading a comic book, or he's fallen asleep."

Addie laughed. "He takes his job very seriously, Will. This is the biggest thing that's ever happened to him."

"I know, beautiful, but I won't feel right until you get home. I'm surprised Buck isn't hovering over you," he said with a touch of sarcasm.

"He called earlier, and wanted to come and stay with me, but I told him the same thing I just told you."

There was a short silence. "I see."

"How are you feeling?" she asked him.

Confined to bed until this afternoon, with his arms wrapped in gauze, Will was getting restless.

"I'm doing great. Rags is right here next to me, and the Simples children visited again. They brought the kittens with them, and told me they sleep with them every night just to make sure they're safe. The best news came from Dr. Hamilton, who called to tell me my lungs are clear, and that I could remove the gauze on my arms. So I did, with your mom's help, and they don't look bad at all. Just have to keep salve on my arms for a few more days. Come home, Addie, or I'm coming to get you myself."

"You're supposed to be resting, regaining strength. Dr. Hamilton said you're lucky your lungs weren't permanently damaged."

"There's no way in hell I'm getting back in that bed."

"Okay," she sighed. "Just another thirty minutes, Will. I promise. Don't come. Lee Bert will bring me home in the cruiser."

He laughed. "I think you like riding in that cruiser."

"Yeah. Especially when he turns on the flashing red lights. I feel like arriving royalty."

They laughed. Will said, "Come home, princess."

"See you soon," she said, and hung up.

The pile of work on her desk soon absorbed her. Fear was shoved away until only distant edges framed her, and the tug of war between Will and Buck was forgotten for a while. Time slipped away as she studied new children's books being offered for selection next year. The town council had told her they had a lean budget for the coming year, so she had to be judicious in what she ordered.

A plaintive meow registered in her consciousness, and she wondered briefly about Coffee. He'd deserted his post at her feet. She continued working. Another meow. She raised her head and listened. The swish of something slipping across the floor came from the history section to the rear.

Odd, she thought. *Haven't I heard that sound before? Oh, sure, it's Donny Jim. He's usually so quiet, though*. In fact, Donny Jim moved so silently that he often appeared almost magically. *Kind of spooky, sometimes*, she thought.

She went back to her work, but she'd lost her focus. Concentrating had become a chore. At the sound of Coffee meowing again somewhere in the library, she dropped her pencil and stood up. It sounded as if the cat needed help, and she remembered the day she'd found him locked in the cellar.

"Darn cat. I'll bet he's in the cellar again." It was a mystery to her how the cat got in there. "Maybe Donny Jim let him in there accidentally."

She started to call out for the quiet man, but then felt foolish. They communicated so well that she often forgot Donny Jim was deaf and mute. He couldn't hear Coffee's meowing distress calls. She would have to look for the cat herself.

The heels of her loafers clicking on the hardwood floor echoed hollowly in the silent library. She passed through Non-fiction, patting a book into place here and there as she went, and arrived in History. Visibility was limited here at night. They had tried all kinds of different lighting solutions, but the area was windowless, high-ceilinged, and difficult to light. An antique Tiffany lamp, casting a weak amber glow, sat on one table.

Surprised that she hadn't caught a glimpse of Donny Jim, she glanced down each aisle as she traversed the area leading to the cellar door.

Coffee's worried wail came again.

Addie stopped dead in her tracks. Something wasn't right. Her skin crawled with the sensation. She felt it in her bones.

A sudden chill raised the fine hair on the nape of her neck, and goosebumps prickled her arms.

No. This is absurd. Donny Jim is here somewhere. He watches me like a hawk. And Lee Bert is outside. No one could have come in.

Her heart flew a rapid rat-tat-tat, thundering so hard in her ears that she could hardly hear. She grabbed hold of a nearby shelf, drew a deep breath, and released it slowly.

Yes, they could, Addie. Someone could sneak behind the bench Lee Bert's sitting on, and go around back to the old cellar door. Wouldn't take much to pry up the rotted boards.

Imagination, Addie, imagination.

She took a few steps, wishing she could find Donny Jim. He couldn't hear her, so she would have to search the library. A fine mist of sweat broke out on her forehead, and her armpits were dripping. Her chest itched where her wool sweater stuck damply to her ribs.

Suddenly, she knew she didn't have time to look for him. She had to leave the library. Now!

Coffee cried again.

She couldn't leave the poor cat locked up.

Running the last few steps to the cellar door, she yanked it open.

Coffee yowled, and leaped out straight into Addie's arms, followed by the dank cellar odor. The weight of him threw her off-balance, and she sat heavily on the floor, square on her butt.

"Ouch, cat."

The shock of it, and the heavy bundle of cat fur in her lap, kept her sitting on the floor, dulling her immediate panic to get out of the library.

Coffee purred softly, and un-catlike nuzzled beneath her armpit. He acted as if he'd been scared to death.

"What's the matter, you big scaredy-cat?"

Her voice echoing in the silence renewed her sense that something was terribly wrong here in the once friendly library, that something evil was close enough to touch. Coffee dug his claws into her shoulder and let out an unearthly howl.

Addie shivered violently, and spilling Coffee out of her lap, tried to get to her feet. But her knees were shaky, and she kept her eyes glued to the floor. She had diligently avoided looking through the yawning door into the dark dankness of the cellar stairwell. But now she was dreadfully drawn there. As if lured by things unimaginable, her gaze, on a level now with the stairwell landing, riveted on the object she'd pretended wasn't there since she'd first yanked the door open.

A foot, twisted at a grotesque angle, lay on the landing.

The foot wore a large, dusty brogan. Donny Jim's

shoes looked like that. Rising slowly, straightening to stand erect, Addie knew fear like she'd never known before. It choked her until her stomach churned, and she felt sick.

The foot belonged to Donny Jim. She knew that. And she couldn't run away and leave him there. Her feeling of aloneness enhanced ten-fold. Even Coffee had deserted her, leaping off like lightning into the safety of the brightly lit area around her desk.

With buckling knees almost dropping her to the floor, and with teeth clamped until her jaws ached, Addie bullied herself forward to the yawning cellar door.

She stepped onto the landing, grasped the stair handrail for support, and knelt to investigate.

Donny Jim's bulky body, twisted, still, and facedown, sprawled down the steps into the blackness. His broad shoulders rested solidly on a step, but his head had disappeared into the descending darkness. She couldn't tell whether he was breathing or not.

You'll have to go down there, Addie. You'll have to walk down those stairs and see what the situation is.

She fumbled for the light switch next to the door, but the old-fashioned twist knob was loose, as if someone had removed and not replaced it properly. Cautiously, placing one foot after the other, she lowered herself deeper into the darkness. Finally, breathless, stomach twisting and catching, she reached Donny Jim's head and knelt to investigate.

With a death grip on the stair railing, she ran her other hand over her big friend's burly shoulders, and then up the back of his neck. The warm, sticky residue that came off on her hand wasn't difficult to identify. Forcing herself to continue the inspection, she felt the back of his head and encountered more blood and a wound of major proportions.

Donny Jim's head had been bashed in with a weapon wielded by a powerful hand. The opening was soft and malleable. Pieces of splintered bone were mixed with a squashy substance she couldn't identify. Pus, or brains?

She gagged, and jerked her hand away.

"Addie?"

She screamed, and stumbled down the step behind her. Only her tight grip on the rail kept her from falling the rest of the way down onto the cellar floor.

Someone stood in the cellar doorway blocking the light from the library.

"Addie? What are you doing down there? What did you find?"

"Oh, thank God. It's you, Buck."

Giddy with waves of relief, she sat heavily on the step next to Donny Jim's inert head. She closed her eyes, and let her head sink back to rest against the wall behind her.

"What's the matter?" he asked.

The voice that whished out of her sounded like a tin whistle.

"Oh, God, Buck. Get Lee Bert, and call 911. Donny Jim has a hideous wound on his head. I can't tell if he's breathing."

The old wooden steps creaked as he slowly made his way down to her, and she wondered why he hadn't rushed to the phone to call the ambulance.

"Buck. Don't worry about me, I'm fine. Run, quick, call for help."

"I'm not worried about you, Addie."

His feet were on the step right above her. She crooked her neck so she could look up into his face. But Buck was so tall; his head vanished into the gloom of the stairwell.

"The lights aren't working. We need a flashlight. I can't see a thing now with you blocking the light."

"We'll be fine. I repaired the switch just now, but we aren't going to need illumination. I've got eyes like a cat. Besides, I know my way around the cellar by heart, and I've rigged the lights so they will behave as I want them."

"This is ridiculous." She stretched her hand up to him for assistance. "Help me up. We'll go get Lee Bert."

But he didn't take her hand. What was wrong with him?

Her hand fell on his shoe as she braced to stand up. Buck's shoe seemed supple and soft, like felt. It wasn't a shoe. It was a slipper. Buck wore slippers. How odd.

Buck is so impeccable. Always. Neat. Never a hair out of place. Shoes always cleaned and polished. Always a suit to church, jeans at a picnic. Why is he wearing his slippers?

The notion that he would wear slippers out in public was as mind-boggling as this devastating bloody scene with Donny Jim. Maybe she was losing it. Maybe this was another nightmare.

"I know it isn't important right now, Buck, but why are you wearing slippers?" She started to laugh, but the laugh came out a nervous giggle.

"Slippers made it easier to move around without your knowing I was in the library, dear Addie. So you wouldn't catch me watching you. You almost caught me though, the night I followed you home jogging. I never made that mistake again."

His answer came from way above her, and it seemed some disembodied voice out of the blackness. Dizzy now with the lurid unreality of the past fifteen minutes, Addie shook her head to clear it. What did he mean? Buck sounded like a different person, a stranger.

"What are you talking about?" She stretched her hand up toward him. "Here. Help me up, and go turn on the lights."

"Sure, I'll help you up, but we don't need lights. I want you to enjoy the same mystical experience your friends did. Besides, there are two small ground-level windows that reveal light to the street, and we don't want anyone to know where we are." He took her hand. "And we're going down the stairs, Addie, dear, not up."

Impatient now with his strange behavior, Addie jerked her hand from his, grabbed the railing, and pulled herself clumsily erect. On the way up her knee slid like slippery soap across Donny Jim's bloody forehead. She gagged, and her hand flew to her mouth. Too late, she realized her hand was smeared with blood, and she felt the wet imprint of her fingers across her mouth and cheek. She retched again.

"Really, Addie. I had no idea you had such a delicate tummy."

Donny Jim groaned and she bent toward him, but Buck grabbed her shoulder and yanked her erect.

"Leave him. He's close to death. Don't prolong his misery. Here, hold my list for me." He handed her a pad of paper, and gave her a little push. "Go down into the cellar, Addie."

"What's your list for, Buck?" she asked, trying to keep her voice light with inquiry.

"Notations, Addie, of people, places, and things. Happenings. Things I don't like and need to correct. Reminders of who needs watching and who upsets me. Like your Will, for instance."

She couldn't see the color of the pad she held in her hand, but she knew it was blue.

It dropped from her fingers, and made a light fluttering noise when it hit the concrete floor below.

Buck gave her another shove. "Move, Addie. I can carry you down or you can move on your own."

Fear cut through her, sharp and cold. This wasn't the Buck she knew. He wasn't teasing her. This wasn't a game. Like a stroke of lightning, the knowledge came, lucid and quick and sure.

Buck meant to kill her.

She had no time to wonder why, or to reason what had changed him, or to mourn their past. She only had time to think of the next minute. Only time to save herself.

"Why are we going to the cellar, Buck?" she asked, trying to sound as normal as possible. "We really should get some help."

"Move below, I want to show you something," he ordered, his voice cold and unemotional.

Yes, Buck seemed strangely unemotional, as if he'd left himself behind somewhere, maybe up in the light by her desk, or maybe in his easy chair at home, or maybe in his office at the school..

Stupid. Get it together, Addie. It's not important now.

"Okay, Buck. Sounds like fun." She would humor

him. "I've only been down here twice. Once when I first came to work at the library, and once last winter when I couldn't find Coffee. You know I hate the cellar, but we're playing a game, I guess."

He gave her another shove and she stumbled down two more steps. The clamminess she dreaded began to close around her. The clammy odor, which warned of molding cement, rat feces, and spider webs, stung her sinuses, and clung to her skin like moist sealing tape.

Her foot touched the basement floor and she shuddered.

"No games, Addie. Don't fool yourself any longer. We're not down here for games. I told Lee Bert that I was here to pick you up, and that he could go on home. The bumpkin yawned, and took off. So don't count on him rescuing you. He's home asleep by now. After you've made your transition, I will run out of the library for help, horrified and distraught at finding you dead in the basement." He gave a small laugh, more like a bitter bark. "Same way I pretended to find Joe that night of the storm. No one ever suspects me, so when I approached Joe that night he was happy to see me, just as you were tonight."

"You killed Joe?" Addie whispered, weak with horror.

"Yes, and unfortunately I had to give Rags a good beating in the process. When I blasted Joe over the head with my car jack, Rags attacked me."

"But why, oh, my God, why?"

"The same reason I killed your friends, Addie. They took you away from me. You never had time for me anymore."

"That's not true, Buck."

"Yes, you were growing away from me. You didn't realize it, but I did. In college we were together all the time. I thought that was the way it would always be. But when we came back to Blue Springs you began to live a life of your own, which didn't include me."

"That's not true, Buck. We do lots of things together."

"No, Addie. Not the way we used to. You spent more time with Laurel than you did me. I thought maybe you would need me more after she died. But you're so independent, you just kept on attending your book group, sometimes even going out afterward for a drink and never even thinking of me. And you went to Marysville twice to go to the movies with Janelle."

Her mind raced with precautions, escape routes, and the wisest way to gain control of the situation, while her head ached, and her midsection felt like someone had tied it in a knot. She took a step back toward the bottom stair, but slipped on the moldering, moss-covered floor, and Buck grabbed her elbow with crushing fingers.

"Whoops. I better be careful," she said, attempting a lighthearted tone through the pain. Maybe talk some sense into him, bring him back into the real world where rational people didn't kill because they were jealous or lonely. "Come on, Buck, this is silly. We're getting married, remember? Let's go upstairs and talk about this."

She couldn't see the smirk on his face in the pitch-black dank air, but she could hear it in his voice. "Don't try to charm me, little Addie. I know you too well. I carried your backpack for you in tenth grade. Remember? I was the new boy in school, and you befriended me."

"Yes, I remember."

"Joe didn't like it one bit," he said, grim satisfaction in his voice.

"Why would you want to hurt an old friend?" Panic flirted around the edges of her sanity now, and scampering, fluttering, in her chest and stomach. Her heartbeat had ratcheted up until she jerked for breath, almost belching with the effort.

Get it together, Addie.

"Don't worry, this won't hurt too much, and you're going to be much happier where you're going. Come with me."

He shoved her by the elbow, which he continued to clench with a brutal invasive hold, his fingers separating bone, muscle, and tendon. Addie bit her lip against the pain, which skated across screaming nerve endings up into her shoulder and neck.

They moved deeper into mysterious regions of the cellar where Addie had never ventured. She was lost here. This was not her venue, not her territory. Should she just humor him until she saw an opportunity to escape? How could she get away from him, trick him, seduce him, how could she do anything to save herself if she couldn't orient herself?

She began to resist him, pulling back, trying to slow their progress.

"Come, come. Don't think you're going to save yourself by balking on me. There's a box of coal here, Addie, dear. Step around it."

Coal? Then there should be a furnace somewhere.

"You seem to know your way around the cellar very well."

"Yep. You know me. I research everything painstakingly. I wanted to keep an eye on you after I killed Laurel, so I broke into the cellar one Sunday when you weren't here. Now I don't need any light. I've been here so often that I know this place like the back of my hand."

She shuddered. He jerked her so close his breath warmed her nose. Then he bruised her mouth with a hard cruel kiss. "Don't shiver like I'm repulsive, Addie. I'm not a monster. I'm simply a man who makes sure the world runs in rhythm. You have been out of rhythm. Things aren't neat anymore. We were meant to be together and you ruined it all, you made everything messy."

"Buck, you just need time to think things out. We'll be good together, you and me."

"No. I realized the night I peeked through the window and saw you roasting marshmallows with Joe that this might have to happen. I thought he was dead when I left him in the barn, and I—I thought that would be the end of your feelings for other men. By the way, Joe died a natural death in the hospital. If he hadn't, I would have finished him off. Fortunately Mother Nature finished what I started. Stop hanging back."

He pushed her harder, using both hands now to propel her forward—to what, she worried.

Upstairs the telephone rang four times, and the answering machine clicked on. She heard her voice say, "You have reached Blue Springs Library. I'm away from my desk for the moment. Leave a message."

The sound of her own voice floating eerily over her head sent a chill to her heart, and reinforced the killing knowledge that she was alone with an insane murderer.

"I switched on the answering machine before I came to the cellar door. Earlier I heard you tell Will that you would be home in about a half an hour. If he calls he'll think you're on your way home with Lee Bert."

The panic was returning. *Calm down. Calm down. Delay him.*

"Was that you in the barn at the hoedown, Buck?"

"Yes, sorry about that, but I had to leave you because I was choking, too. It never entered my mind that retard would save you. I figured you would die in there. Everybody would feel sorry for me, and all my problems would be solved."

"Buck, you couldn't hate me this much."

"I love you more than anything. But you did yourself in, Addie, when you started flirting with Will Court. Then when you told me with your own mouth that you had a crush on him, I knew I had to kill you."

"Killing me won't help anything, Buck. Eventually they will figure it all out, and then you'll go to prison, and probably be sentenced to death. Let's think this thing over. Come on, we've always been good at figuring things out together."

He laughed, and the cold, mirthless sound ran a chill up her spine.

"No more, Addie. This isn't a jigsaw puzzle, or a logic question. That's all over."

The air around them seemed to change, as it does when objects fill a vacuum and change the dynamics. She sensed a large black shape in front of them, and raised her free arm to grope in front of her.

Buck wrenched her forward. "It's the furnace, Addie. Sixty years ago, this big daddy would have been roaring with fire this time of year. Too bad the city council put in oil and wall heat. It would have been a handy way to get rid of Janelle."

A furnace. Coal. A poker, maybe there's a poker somewhere, or a shovel? Did he say Janelle?

"You brought Janelle down here?"

"No more questions. I can't be in the library too long. They'll suspect me."

His hands dug cruelly into her shoulders, and he shoved her again, leaving the furnace behind.

"Here we are. Step in to my parlor, Addie. You'll find company here."

Her groping hands found a decaying wooden wall, and an opening. A small cubby of a room probably used for coal storage. Every instinct she possessed warned her not to enter the cold, black space, which smelled of sickening evils.

She jabbed her foot backward to kick at him, and connected with his shin. He grunted and let go of one shoulder. She yanked lose from his other hand, and swung madly about to dash around him. He caught her on her second leap, to jerk her so swift and hard that she landed in a distorted heap on the floor. When she put her hand out to push away from him, she slipped flat on her stomach until her cheek smacked the floor and slid across the ancient slimy mold. A moan rolled from her, and weak tears finally came.

"Don't try that again, or I'll make this worse than I'd planned," he whispered, his voice hissing with venom. "I hadn't planned to make you suffer like the others, but if you disobey me again you'll be sorry, little Addie."

He yanked her up from the floor, and shoved her

through the opening of the small room, which she knew would be her burial place.

"Now you'll see how nice I've been. You won't be lonely on your way out of this world," said Buck softly. "I'm going to tie your wrists and ankles so you won't get any more escape notions. Then we'll have a good time, you and me, here in the dark. We've never kissed in a coal cellar before. Sit down here next to Janelle."

As he pushed down on her shoulders, she stumbled over sticks and soft things, that felt like bones and clothes, and . . . *oh, God, it's Janelle, or what's left of Janelle.*

Her scream exploded from her toes. It ripped and burned up through her body, and came out a shrieking, unearthly screech. It filled the small ghoulish room, and rang and rang throughout the cellar. It reverberated around and around and around her. All control and rational thought had fled. Buck shook her until her head bounced back and forth like a loose jack-in-the-box, but the scream wouldn't stop coming. Loud enough to wake the dead, maybe it would wake Janelle. *Yes, wake up, Janelle. Help me. Somebody help me.*

"I should have silenced you right away, but I wanted you to talk to me," he whined. "You never talk to me anymore."

He slapped her so hard he busted her lip, and blood sprayed like a fountain and ran down her chin and onto her sweater. She grabbed his hand with her teeth and bit down until she hit bone.

Buck yelled, jerked his hand away and socked her with his fist. The pain was excruciating as her teeth cracked together, and bits of enamel spewed onto her tongue. She barreled through the pain, and shoved and kicked at him, pummeling him with jabs to his stomach, and she never stopped screaming.

Oh, God, please, someone hear me!

Her throat ached with the screaming.

Buck worked to catch hold of her whirling hands and jabbing feet, and finally caught one arm in a fast grip. He punched her in the stomach. The screaming stopped, and the cellar seemed eerily still as the wind whooshed out of her, and she collapsed like a rag doll over his arm. Never letting up on his death grip, Buck yanked a handkerchief from his pocket, stuffed it into her gasping mouth, and lowered her to the floor next to Janelle.

A fold of cotton skirt fluttered onto her thigh as she was settled close beside the corpse—Janelle's skirt, probably the full red circle that she loved to wear in the summertime. Addie gagged, and fought to draw air back into her lungs, and energy back into her legs. The cloth filling her mouth made it almost impossible to breathe.

Oh, God, why doesn't he just kill me? Why doesn't he get it over with? Is he going to rape me first?

Don't give up. Fight him until the last.

He grunted as he sat astride her hips, and leaned forward to place kisses around her face, and whisper softly in her ear.

"You'll like this, Addie." His hands fastened around her throat, as he kept kissing her. "There's nothing as exquisite as a climax at the moment of death. Trust me, I know."

A grim voice cut through the darkness, "Let her go, Buck. I've got a twelve gauge aimed straight at you, and Lee Bert is right behind me."

Addie's heart flew with excitement. Will. It was Will.

Buck's hands tightened on her throat, and he moaned.

"Hit the lights, Jingles," yelled Lee Bert.

Light flooded the cellar. Dim light, but to Addie it was light from heaven.

As her eyes adjusted to the light, Buck's beastly face hovered over her, his mouth twisted with hatred, his eyes mad with jealousy. He seemed to be in a world not of theirs, and ignorant of the presence of Will and Lee Bert. Limp now, and passing out, she felt his weight yanked off her.

Will gently pulled the handkerchief from her mouth and lifted her in his arms. She had only enough strength left to place her hand on his chest near his throat. His muscles worked as he swallowed, as if he were struggling not to cry, and she felt her own tears roll helplessly down her cheeks.

Lee Bert seemed to be tussling with Buck, and as she closed her eyes with relief she heard Jingles arriving.

"You forgot, Buck, my boy, this wee town is mighty quiet after ten o'clock, and I'm baking bread at the diner," crowed Jingles. "At first, I thought it was a cat wailing, but soon changed my mind."

"I don't want to look at Janelle," whispered Addie, her eyes still closed. "I don't want to see any of this. I don't want to see Buck."

"You don't have to, sweetheart. I'm taking you out of here right now." Will held her close to his chest and walked away from the little chamber of horrors.

As they gingerly skirted Donny Jim's lifeless body on the stairs, she squeezed her eyes so tight they hurt.

"How did you know? What made you come?" she managed to get out as they entered the fresh air and bright lights of the library.

Holding her tight and secure, he carried her through the library and outside to sit on the bench by the square. Her nose tucked into the curve of his neck and shoulder, her breath warming her face, his mouth on her hair murmuring sweet nothings, Addie's world began to right itself. When she finally felt safe enough to open her eyes, she saw the big cardboard Thanksgiving turkey Mertie always put in the flower store window, and she saw the blue and yellow neon lights flicking over the diner. DIXIE'S DINER. THE BEST FOOD IN TOWN.

Will kept smoothing her hair, and kissing her forehead as he talked.

"Lee Bert told me once that he was stubborn, and he sure proved it tonight. After Buck told him to go on home because he would take you to the farm, Lee Bert did a dutiful drive around the county to check out the rest of his domain, as he always does, he told me. As he passed the farm, he decided to visit and say goodnight, make sure everything was okay with us." He laughed. "The FBI guy had laid an extra load of responsibility on him, and he was taking it super seriously.

"Anyway, Lee Bert told me his story, and we figured you and Buck should have been home by then. About that time, Jingles called and said he thought he heard screaming coming from the library and he was going to go check it out. Lee Bert and I jumped into the car and made it here in five minutes. Jingles was waiting for us at the top of the cellar steps. It was dark, and he had no weapon. Lee Bert was familiar with the layout because he used to read meters down there. So we felt our way down, passing poor Donny Jim on the way. We tried to come quietly, but it didn't seem to matter because you were fighting Buck so hard he wasn't listening for anything."

"I don't think he was expecting interference. He was awfully sure of himself." She snuggled closer. He tucked her inside of his big jacket, and she breathed in the warm, sweet maleness of Will. "Oh, Will, poor Buck. He's insane, isn't he?"

"Yes, darling."

"We'll talk about it later." She was tired. So tired.

He kissed her ear. "Addie, I love you."

"Will, are the winters really cold in New Haven?"

"Pretty cold." She heard his amusement. "But we'll have glorious summers in Blue Springs, won't we?"

"Yes, yes, yes."

ABOUT THE AUTHOR

LINDA ANDERSON is the author of *Over the Moon, The Secrets of Sadie Maynard,* and *When Night Falls.* A mother of five grown children, she lives in South Florida with her husband. "Writing is a gift that brings me great joy, for which I'm very grateful. I hope my stories bring the same joy to my readers."

You may write to Linda Anderson:

      c/o Pocket Books
      Publicity Department
      1230 Avenue of the Americas
      New York, NY 10020-1586

'TIL DEATH
DO US PART

═══

MARIAH STEWART

to
Kate Collins,
with love

1

He slid the delicate tool—made for such purposes and readily available if one knew where to look—between the doorjamb and the frame, listening carefully for the sound of the lock slipping aside. Pushing open the door only far enough to allow him entrance into the town house, he stepped into the dark silence, trying to figure out just how much time he would have to first locate, then disengage, the security system. The small metal marker on the front lawn had told him whose system protected the premises and being well familiar with that company's product, he knew he could disable the mechanism in the blink of an eye. Once, of course, he located it.

He dropped his shoes, which he'd removed outside before he'd picked the lock, then walked straight through the kitchen, down a short hall, and directly into the foyer, taking no pains now to keep quiet. She wasn't at home, and wouldn't be for at least another two hours. This was Wednesday. One of her gym and dinner-out-with-her-friends nights. She never arrived home much before eleven. That gave him more than enough time to complete his task.

It took only seconds to turn off the alarm, which was, as he'd have bet his last nickel it would be, right there inside the front door. And then he was free to take his time.

He stood in his stocking feet on the plush carpet in the cool of the darkened living room, taking care not to stand too near the large window, where plants of every height and variety crowded the sill. He smiled, having suspected that a country girl like her would surround herself with as much greenery as possible.

Shining his flashlight around the room, he set out to acquaint himself with his surroundings. The sofa was a pretty floral, the pair of wing back chairs covered in a coordinating plaid. A handsome armoire covered part of one wall. With one finger, he slid the door over, then peered inside to find a large-screened TV—not so large as to be excessive, he noted—a VCR and a stereo. Shelves of videos—some of which were classic black-and-white films—and stacks of CDs, classical composers and classic rock. Nothing more contemporary than Santana's latest.

That was his Valerie.

Nothing too far out for *his* girl.

The coffee table held a number of small items, and he leaned closer to take a look. Small porcelain shapes, so many that she must have been collecting for a long time. He scanned the array quickly with the flashlight. One shape in particular caught his eye. Smiling—surely it was a sign—he slipped it into his pocket.

The old rolltop desk stood open, a pile of mail to one side. He paused to thumb through it, noting where she shopped and what she bought. A card handmade with childish fingers and signed in childish scrawl—*we miss you from Eric and Evan*—sat next to an antique inkwell.

Photographs poked out of an envelope, and he looked through those as well. In one, she stood on the front steps of an old cabin, a little boy on either side of her like matching bookends. In others, she wore a dark blue bridesmaid's dress and posed with others similarly clad. He studied these closely, taking note of the veil worn by the bride and the cascading bouquet of white roses and some other white things, he couldn't tell exactly what but they looked elegant. Then there she was in a group shot in front of a Christmas tree. He wondered who the man was who stood so close to her right side, one arm casually draped over her shoulder. Frowning, he replaced the pictures, closed over the envelope, and tucked it into his back pocket.

He padded up the steps to her bedroom, which, he knew from watching her these past few months, would be at back of the house. Once he'd closed the door and drawn the drapes tightly, he felt free to turn on the lights.

Again, he smiled. All was so very tasteful. He nodded his approval of the queen-size sleigh bed with its matching dressers of dark wood. The small oriental accent rug with its deep crimson flowers on a background of taupe. The quilt folded neatly to stretch across the end of the bed. The small chair that stood in one corner of the room. The dense sage green carpet under foot. All totally classy, like the lady herself. All neat as a pin, not a thing out of place anywhere.

Well, of course there wouldn't be. He'd suspected that she would take great care with her things, and she obviously did.

He poked his head inside the green and white bath-room and took a quick look around. Fluffy, pure white towels hung from shiny chrome rods, and an oversized brandy snifter filled with colorful soaps stood atop a small wicker table. He studied them for a long moment, then dipped his hand into the glass and took one—a pale pink rose—and added it to the porcelain trinket in his jacket pocket, for no particular reason except that he wanted it.

Opening the walk-in closet, he searched for an inte-rior light, then reached in to touch the dresses that hung on the bar to the right of the door. He stepped inside and trailed his finger along the hangers. She obviously favored silk, as so many of the garments were of that fabric. Several things he'd seen her wear, and those he gathered in his hands, pressed his face into their cool-ness, seeking her scent. Then, reminding himself of his purpose, he stood back as if taking inventory. There was not nearly the quantity one might have expected, con-sidering who she was. Once again, he nodded his approval. Success had not made her careless with her money nor had it made her overly materialistic. What she had was certainly of good quality—some designer pieces, he noted—but for the most part, her wardrobe was quite modest.

He pulled one dress after another from the rack, hold-ing them up as if studying their style, then checking the size on the label of each. After taking care to return each to its place, he turned his attention to the boxes that were stacked on the floor and lined one entire wall.

Shaking his head slowly, he smiled somewhat indul-gently.

She sure did love her shoes.

He opened the box nearest him and parted the tissue to reveal a tall leather heel of dark brown which he caressed briefly before returning it to its box. Leaning closer to read the notations written on the ends of the boxes with black marker, her grinned broadly. Leave it to her to mark every one of them clearly with their contents.

He scanned the boxes until he spied one that held promise, the third one down in the second stack. A white high-heeled sandal.

He pulled the box out and opened it, lifted a shoe and held it up for inspection. It was, in fact, a white, high-heeled, strappy, dressy sandal of some fabric that felt like silk. Judging from the soles, the shoes had barely been worn.

Perfect. Absolutely perfect.

He paused, considering this unexpected bounty.

His original quest had been merely to determine size, but here was something even better. He tucked the shoe box under one arm.

He tidied up the stack, then turned off the light, but not before he'd run his hands over several more of the dresses nearest the door, stroking their length as if they graced her body.

With one backward glance from the doorway, he glanced around the room to make sure that nothing was amiss. Then, convinced that all was as he found it, he bounded down the steps two at a time, pausing at the bottom to look back up and imagine her standing there. He reached into a pocket for the small plastic bag and opened it, tossing a handful of the contents toward the vision at the top of the steps. At the back door, he put his shoes back on, then, his mission accomplished, left as quietly as he'd arrived.

2

"I'D LIKE TO REPORT A BREAK-IN."

Valerie McAllister cradled the telephone between her head and shoulder, all the while tapping the fingers of one hand impatiently on the steering wheel of her car.

"Yes," she told the officer on the other end of the line, the third one she'd been transferred to in less than two minutes, "I'll hold . . ."

Her eyes darted from one side of the darkened street to the other, watching for movement in the shadows, but all was still.

"Well, actually, I'm not exactly certain that anything was taken," she said hesitantly. "But I do know that the security alarm was turned off. . . . Yes, I am absolutely positive that I set it before I left the house this afternoon. . . . No, I didn't go beyond the entry. As soon as I realized that someone had been there . . . you mean, besides the fact that the alarm wasn't working?"

She listened impatiently, her sense of indignation growing. In spite of the officer's skepticism, she knew she'd set that alarm. And besides, once she'd pushed the door open and stepped into the foyer, she had just known that something was not right. It had been as if the air inside her town house had been disturbed—not only touched, but tainted—by an outsider.

There'd been a pricking at the back of her neck, an instinctive warning, even as she'd turned on the small lamp that sat on the table under the alarm. She'd turned slowly, the hair on her arms rising, as she searched the shadows that fell over the living room to her left. To the kitchen at the end of the short hall. Up the stairs, straight ahead, and beyond.

She'd backed out of the open door and snapped it behind her in an attempt to close in anyone who might still be lurking there. With uncharacteristic carelessness, she had waded through the knee-high shrubs that had been planted between her tiny porch and that of the town house next door. She'd leaned on the doorbell, waited, then leaned again, but there'd been no response. Bruce, her neighbor, must have taken his dog, Prudence, for one last evening walk. A glance at the house to her left, where no lights shone from within, told her that her neighbors on the other side were out as well. Seeking safety, she'd hurried back to her car, locked herself in securely, and dialed 911 on her cell phone.

And there she sat, anxiously awaiting the someone from the police department who would be there soon, as the voice on the phone had promised.

Valerie had never been the victim of a crime before. Over the past ten years, as a sought-after print model, she'd traveled from her home in the Montana hills to the most celebrated cities of the world, from New York to London to

Lisbon, Paris to Rome, Rio to Hong Kong, without being mugged, robbed, or assaulted in any way. She'd lived in Manhattan for several years without incident. Yet here she'd been in California for barely six months, living in one of those small towns that sat just outside of Los Angeles County that boasted a low crime rate, and already the sanctity of her home had been violated.

Well, it could have been worse, she concluded. I could have been home when the break-in occurred, and no telling what might have happened then.

And, she reminded herself, she still didn't know what, if anything, had actually been taken. She sincerely hoped that whomever had been in her house that night had not had a penchant for photography. She'd left most of her equipment on the dining room table, in plain sight, the night before.

Two shapes appeared in the light of the street lamp. Bruce Miller, her neighbor and an aspiring actor, rounded the corner, holding a long red leash, the end of which was attached to the collar of a large, fluffy dog. With a sigh of relief, Valerie unlocked her door and stepped into the street.

"Hey, Val," Bruce called to her, struggling to hold onto the leash when the dog spied his buddy Val and took off in her direction. "You're late tonight."

"I've been home for awhile," she said as she walked toward him, putting out her hands to greet the bouncing mop of fur that was Prudence, the Old English sheepdog that shared Bruce's town house.

"Something on the radio that you just had to hear the end of?" He handed Val the leash, since Prudence was intent upon showering her with affection.

"Actually, I was waiting for the police to get here," she told him as Prudence pranced around her in a wide circle, much like a giant cat. "I think I've had a break-in."

"What?" Bruce exclaimed.

"Someone was in my house. When I came home tonight, I opened the door and stepped inside, and the first thing I noticed was that the security alarm was off."

"Maybe you . . ."

"Please. Don't say it." She held up one hand as if to halt his words. "I did not forget to set it. It's the last thing I do before I leave. I distinctly remember that I did, in fact, set it this afternoon."

"What was taken?"

"I didn't go past the foyer, so I didn't have a chance to look around. I just knew that someone had been there, but I didn't know if they were still lurking inside, so I came out to the car and called the police. I was just sitting out here waiting for an officer to show up."

As if on cue, a dark sedan rounded the corner and pulled over to the curb, stopping nose-to-nose with Val's car. A tall, densely built man stretched out of the car and stepped onto the sidewalk, nodding to Val and Bruce as he did so.

"Is this Thirty-seven Meadow Circle?" he asked.

"Yes. Are you with the police department?"

"Detective Rafferty, ma'am," he replied.

"I'm Valerie McAllister. I'm the one who called about the break-in." She handed the leash back to Bruce. "At least, I think there was a break-in."

"I'll take Prudence inside," Bruce told her as he led the dog in the direction of their door. "Come over when you're finished if it's not too late, and I'll make you a cappuccino and Pru can show you what she learned in doggie school this afternoon."

"Did you see anyone?" the detective asked as Valerie approached him.

"No. I didn't go in. I left as soon as I realized that someone had been in there."

"So you don't know what, if anything, was taken?"

She shook her head.

"That was quick thinking." He smiled at her. "There's always the chance that you surprised someone who was still there."

"I was afraid that might be a possibility."

The detective was tall and good-looking, with light brown hair and a smattering of freckles across his nose. His pleasant smile and polite manner immediately put Val at ease.

"Shall we go inside?" Val asked as she headed toward the walk.

"Let me go in first and take a look around." He followed her up the walk.

"Is the door locked?" he asked as they approached the narrow covered porch.

"Yes. I have the key," she said, holding up the key ring to the light to find the right one. She slid it into the lock and turned the door handle, pushed the door open, and stepped aside.

"Just wait here for a minute, if you don't mind," Detective Rafferty told her as he moved past her into the foyer.

"Shouldn't you call for back-up or something?" she found herself whispering.

He drew a gun that had been previously hidden behind a light brown sport jacket.

"I'd be real surprised if anyone was still here after you opened the front door. Is there a back entrance?"

She nodded.

"Just give me a minute to take a look around."

Valerie stood directly in the haze of the overhead porch lamp, and watched as the lights in her town house came on. First the living room, then minutes later, a faint glow could be seen at the top of the stairs.

"Just as I thought," the officer said as he came down the steps. "Whoever was here is long gone. Come on in and we'll see if we can tell what's missing."

Val's first concern was for her camera equipment, and now that the house was safe to enter, she made a beeline to the dining room where she'd left several bags holding expensive cameras and numerous lenses on the table that she rarely used for dining. Relieved to find that all was as she'd left it, she turned her attention to the rest of the house.

Over the next two hours, accompanied by the detective, Val scoured every room. When she stepped into her bedroom, she experienced the same tingling along her spine she'd felt when she'd first opened the front door, though nothing appeared to be disturbed on the second floor. She was beginning to wonder if there had been a break-in after all.

And then she heard the faint crunching sound under her feet.

She bent down and picked up the tiny white grains. "Rice." She held her hand out to the detective. "It's rice . . ."

"Had you dropped . . ." he began.

"I don't have rice in my house. I don't eat it." She

looked up at him, baffled. "Why would someone leave *rice* on my floor?"

"I don't know." Rafferty picked a number of grains from the steps and dropped them into an evidence bag. "Let's take another look around downstairs."

The first item that she'd positively determined to be missing from the living room was the Limoges wedding cake box made of porcelain that had been sitting in the middle of the coffee table as part of a collection. She was positive of this, she told Rafferty, because she'd placed it there only two days earlier, when she'd brought it back from the jeweler where she'd taken it to have the hinge repaired.

"I'd accidentally dropped it a few weeks ago," she said. "The jeweler called on Friday to let me know it was ready to be picked up, but I was out of town and wasn't able to get there until Monday. Why would someone steal something so insignificant, yet leave all of that expensive camera equipment in the dining room?"

She paused in front of her desk and frowned.

"Miss McAllister?" Rafferty inquired, following her gaze.

"The photos are missing."

"The photos?"

"There had been an envelope of photos there on the desk. I was looking at them this morning, thinking about having a picture of my nephews enlarged and framed as a gift for my sister-in-law's parents."

"Are you sure you didn't drop them into one of the desk drawers, or maybe carried them into another room?"

"No. I left them right there." In spite of her assurances, she opened and closed all the desk drawers to prove that the photos were not there. "Why would anyone steal photographs?"

"With all due respect, Miss McAllister, yours is a pretty well-known face. If someone had taken pictures of you, it really wouldn't be so surprising."

"They weren't all of me. There were pictures of my brother and his twin boys that his wife sent to me. And several that she recently came across that had been taken at her family's home several Christmases ago. And some photos from their wedding. Nothing of any interest to anyone other than family."

"Still, you being a model, I'm not all that surprised that someone lifted pictures of you, though you'd expect that more as an incidental loss, you know, if the TV or the VCR had been taken as well." Rafferty told her as he stood in the open doorway, preparing to leave. "Look, it's pretty late. If it's all the same to you, I'll stop back tomorrow to make a formal report. And maybe between now and then, you'll discover something else that is missing. It's odd that someone would go to the trouble of breaking into your home, disabling your security system, and then not take anything of value."

"I don't have much jewelry." She shrugged. "And I don't keep money in the house, ever. And except for my cameras, there just isn't that much here to steal."

"Well, someone thought there might be."

"Someone went home disappointed."

"Not to make you uncomfortable, but have you noticed anyone following you, or received anonymous phone calls in the middle of the night?"

"No." She shook her head. "Nothing like that."

"It was just a thought. Sometimes, with people like yourself, especially women like you—well-known, beautiful—well, sometimes people follow them. . . ." he said awkwardly.

"You mean like a stalker?" She shook her head again. "No. No, Detective. There's been nothing like that."

"I only bring it up because sometimes that type of behavior can lead to more overt actions, like a break-in. Often there's nothing significant found to be missing, but just as often, there might be something obscure, but personal. . . ."

"I'll take another look around and I'll let you know."

"In the meantime, I'll see to it that a black and white makes the street and the alleyway out back part of his regular run."

"Thank you. I appreciate that," Val said as the detective turned and walked toward his car.

It was just after midnight, too late to take Bruce up on his offer of cappuccino and dog tricks. She locked the door behind her, reset her alarm—for all the good it had done tonight—and reminded herself to call another security company in the morning. The system she had was obviously ineffective and could be overridden with the right code.

She went upstairs and turned on the bedroom lamp. Could she sleep in this room, knowing someone had been there just hours earlier? She didn't think she could.

From the bedside table, she took the book she'd started reading on the plane back from the photo shoot she'd completed last week in Hawaii, and removed the old quilt from the bottom of the bed. She went into the guest room in the front of the house and plopped the quilt over an arm of the wide, overstuffed chair that stood in the corner facing the door. After turning on the lamp that stood behind the chair, she locked the door, snuggled into the chair, tucked the quilt around her, and pretended to read.

There were times, like now, when Valerie regretted ever having left the small Montana town where she'd grown up. And yet, at age eighteen, just out of high school, there hadn't been much of anything to keep her there. Her mother was long gone, having left home when Val was a baby. Between bouts with the bottle, her father, a long-haul truck driver, spent most of his time coming and going as he pleased, and hadn't seemed interested in providing much of a home for Val and her older brother, Cale. They'd been raised by their grandmother, who'd moved them into the small house in one of the lesser of Larkspur's neighborhoods. She'd died right before Cale's eighteenth birthday, and while she'd done the best she could for her grandchildren, there just hadn't been many jobs in a small town like Larkspur, Montana, for a woman her age. It never failed to amaze Val that somehow, her grandmother had managed to keep food on the table and oil in the tank in the winter. After she passed away and Cale had left for college on a baseball scholarship, Val divided her time between the little green house, and the home of her best friend, Eliza Hollister, who just happened to be the sister of the woman Cale had married just two summers ago.

Valerie wondered what her life might have been like had she grown up in a home like the Hollisters', where both parents were always there for their children, where love and hugs were freely distributed, where wonderful aromas always greeted you when you came in the back door after school, where there was always food and warmth and laughter, where people always cared about you, no matter what.

Even Val had been cared about in that house. Too ashamed to admit even to Cale when he called home from college that their father had not returned in months, Val had become adept at hiding the fact that she was pretty much on her own that last year of high school. And while the school administration had been fooled, Val was never really sure if Mrs. Hollister had been. How else to explain the fact that Eliza so often had an extra lunch in her locker ("My mother remembered that you liked chicken sandwiches, Val, so she sent an extra.")? Or those times, when heavy snow had been predicted, that Liza always seemed to need help with a school project that would necessitate Val going to the Hollisters' after school? And if she was snowed in there and had to stay for a few days, well, at least she had a warm bed to sleep in and the promise of wonderful meals until the storm passed and the roads were cleared.

Val never thought back on those days without an ache in her throat. Mrs. Hollister had been her fairy godmother, and certainly more of a mother than her own had ever been. There had been countless ways in which Catherine Hollister had quietly come through for Val in times of need.

Val shifted in her seat, remembering the senior ball, when she'd declined a date because there was no chance of being able to buy a dress fancy enough for the occasion. Somehow, Mrs. Hollister knew, and when she made over one of her older daughters' many dresses for

Eliza to wear, she made one over for Val as well, insisting it was no more trouble to cut down two than one.

Val had never had a dress as perfect as that strapless number—pale gold satin with a full skirt— fitted to her perfectly by Mrs. Hollister's capable hands. To this day, Val could close her eyes and hear the *swish* it had made when she walked. It still hung in the back of her closet, after all these years, a reminder of Catherine Hollister's loving heart, and the way it had made Val feel to know that someone had cared enough about her to make certain that she had a dress to wear to a school dance.

Val had left high school with no particular plans, no money for college, no clear goals or skills. Most of her energy that last year had gone to surviving while managing to stay out of the child welfare system. A graduation trip to the east coast—a gift from her brother, who had just that summer left college to sign a contract to play major league baseball for the Baltimore Harbormasters—had led to a chance introduction to a photographer, a cousin of the team owner, who'd begged to take Val's picture. Two weeks later, while still pondering what to do with her life, Val had received an excited call from the photographer, who'd shown her pictures to a friend who worked for a major modeling agency in New York. How soon could Val get to New York? the photographer wanted to know. His friend wanted to meet with Val as soon as possible to see for herself if Val had what it would take to become a top model.

Despite her protests that she'd never thought of such a career—she'd never thought she was *that* pretty—but lacking any other prospects that summer, Val had gone to New York, met with the modeling agency, and before she knew it, was on her way to London for her first assignment. At five feet six inches tall, Val was too short for the runway, but with her dark hair and pale green eyes and features that were just enough short of perfect to give her a look that was slightly exotic, she'd photographed beautifully. Soon she found herself in demand, and making more money than she'd ever in her life dreamed possible.

No one was more surprised by her success than Val.

And while her agent continued to assure her that she was getting hotter by the week, and even as her business manager continued to invest her money, secretly Val wondered just how long it would be before someone figured out that she was just a girl from the hills who'd gotten lucky.

Sometimes, like now, when she was feeling nostalgic, Val would think back to those early days and wonder what would have happened if she hadn't gone to Baltimore that summer. If she'd stayed at home and maybe gotten a job at one of the two boutiques in town. Where might she be now? Married to a cowboy, most likely, with a couple of kids.

Not so bad a life, with the right cowboy, she mused.

Of course, back in those days, there'd only been one cowboy who'd caught her eye. And a trip back to the hills just two years ago had proven that he still could. Eliza's older brother, Schuyler—Sky—had always treated Val in the same manner in which he'd treated Eliza, like they were pesky little beings that needed to be tolerated and kept from getting underfoot.

So different from his manner at the wedding of his

sister and Val's brother just two summers ago, when Sky had apparently noticed—finally!—that Val was all grown-up.

She'd planned to stay for a while after her brother's wedding, had thought that Sky, in his own quiet way, was hoping she would. Though they'd known each other all their lives—Sky and Cale had always been best friends—Val and Sky had spent precious little time together as adults. That week, it seemed they were together every day, every night, enough for her to realize that the crush she'd had on him from the time she was fifteen was growing into something more. They'd barely begun to explore just what that might be, when a call from Val's agent sent her unexpectedly to Rome for almost two months, then to Africa for several weeks. By the time she got back to Montana, Sky had left for the valley and the farm he and his brother had taken over from their grandfather. While debating whether or not to follow, she'd been called for a shoot in Brazil. She'd repacked her bags and headed for the airport, gone before Sky had even been aware she'd be there.

Val drew the old quilt around her, chilled in spite of the warm California night, and wondered where Sky Hollister was right at that moment, what he was thinking about. And if he ever thought about her.

3

"Val? Are you there?" Derek Marx's voice popped from Valerie's answering machine in short, emphysemic puffs. "Pick up if you're there. This is important."

"Yes, Derek, I'm here." Val resisted a sigh as she picked up the receiver. Her agent was the last person she felt like speaking with at that moment. Calls from him this late in the day could only mean one thing.

"How's the weather?" he asked, as if he'd be expected to make small talk.

"Lovely." Val decided to cut to the chase. "Where to this time?"

"The Florida Keys," he told her, then added because he knew she would ask, "Another swimsuit shoot."

"Derek, it's July. Last week we did parkas and ski wear."

"And this week you'll do tropical vacation wear. Sorry it's so last minute, but I just got the call five minutes ago. They had someone lined up for the shoot but she had a death in the family and the agency isn't willing to wait a week while she buries her father. All heart, you know what I mean?"

"I know what you mean." This time, Val did sigh. "All right. What are the arrangements?"

Val wrote the next morning's flight information on the white erasable board that hung on the wall next to the phone in her kitchen. When she'd finished with her call, she hung up and turned to Detective Rafferty, who'd leaned against the kitchen counter, waiting patiently for her to complete her call.

"I'm sorry for the interruption," she apologized. "Now, what else do we need to do here?"

"Actually, nothing," the detective told her. "We have your fingerprints—and mine, too, of course—for elimination. I'll go back to the station and compare the prints I lifted here today and run them through the computer and see if we connect with anyone. Then I'll let you know if we have a suspect."

"And if we don't?"

"Then we have nothing to go on unless we get very, very lucky."

"How do we get very, very lucky?"

"Someone gets arrested for something, starts talking about something he heard from someone on the street, thinking to make a deal. Or we catch the right guy by accident and he decides to tell us his life story. . . ."

"Right. I won't hold my breath waiting for you to call to tell me that someone pulled over for running a stop sign has come clean and confessed that he stole the little porcelain wedding cake from my coffee table and lifted a bunch of family photos," Val said wryly. "Do you see that happening?"

"You never know what people will come out with if they think it will help them."

"What you're saying is that the chances are slim that you'll find the person who broke into my home."

"Possibly. Unless, of course, he decides to come back."

"Why would he come back?" Val frowned. "Once should have been enough to convince him that there's not much of great value here, except the stereo and television and my cameras, which would be a pretty obvious heist. Frankly, I don't understand why he didn't take them the first time."

"Maybe you startled him when you opened the front door," Rafferty said, then hesitated, as if debating, before adding gently, "Maybe it was someone just trying to get close to you. Someone who wanted to have something of yours . . ."

"Don't even suggest that." She shivered. "That just totally gives me the creeps."

"I'm sorry. I'm not trying to scare you, but you do need to be aware that a lot of women are stalked."

"No one has been stalking me," she told him flatly. "I'd have known if someone was watching me."

"Don't kid yourself. If he's really good, you wouldn't know."

She shivered again and rose. "Sorry. There's been no one following me, no one hanging outside my house, no anonymous phone calls . . . none of the things you read about that are associated with stalkers."

"Stalkers don't all follow the same pattern, Ms. McAllister. Some are smarter than others. But look, let's see what we get after we've run these prints through the system. For all we know, the guy who did this was picked up at midnight on a B and E in Beverly Hills. Let's not get ahead of ourselves, okay?" Rafferty said as he collected his equipment.

"Good point." Val nodded, then followed him to the front door.

"I'll give you a call as soon as we have something. In the meantime, try to be aware of the people around you. If you see anyone acting suspicious, give me a call. A car seems to be following you, you let me know. Strange phone calls, anything out of the ordinary, call me."

"I'll be leaving first thing in the morning for some work out of town," she told him as she opened the front door, "but you can leave a message on my answering machine if you need to get in touch. Or if it's really important, Bruce, next door, has the number of my cell phone." She paused, as if thinking, then said, "I should probably give you that number now, in case something comes up and you can't get Bruce. His hours are erratic, since he's waiting tables while he's waiting for that sit-com he's hoping for."

"Oh, another out-of-work actor, eh?"

"Bruce is really very good," she said as she went to her desk and tore a page from small notepad upon which she wrote the number of her cell phone. "He does a killer stand-up routine. He should be doing television. And I'm absolutely positive that sooner or later, someone will recognize his talent and he'll be pulling up stakes out here and hauling Prudence off to Malibu."

Val handed the slip of paper to the detective and added, almost as an afterthought, "Bruce also has a key in case you need to get back in for any reason."

"He has a key? To your house . . . ?" Rafferty asked.

"Yes." She nodded. "I'm sometimes gone for weeks at a time. Bruce brings in my mail, waters my plants, generally keeps an eye on things."

"Does he also have the code for your security alarm?"

"Of course. How else could he . . ." She paused, then folded her arms across her chest with open indignation. "Are you suggesting that Bruce was the person who was in here last night?"

"It's not out of the question."

"It's absolutely out of the question. Why would he have done such a thing? He's free to come in anytime he wants when I'm not here."

"I wouldn't be so quick to dismiss him."

"Sorry, you'll have to look somewhere else. Bruce has been in this house a hundred times. He never left the trace of . . . of *violation* that I felt when I opened that door last night. Sorry, detective, but you'll have to work a little harder than that to find the intruder. Besides the fact that Bruce had no motive and respects my privacy too much, he wasn't home last night. As a matter of fact, he arrived home at the same time I did. I was speaking with him, if you recall, when you got here."

"Ms. McAllister, I don't mean to upset you. I just think we need to explore all the options at this time."

"My next-door neighbor is not an option."

Recognizing defeat when he met it, the detective shrugged and said, "I'll give you a call after we run these prints and I'll let you know if we have others."

Val stood inside her front door and watched the detective walk to his car. She'd already gone inside and closed the door behind her by the time he'd turned to wave good-bye.

The tinny bell over the door jangled as it opened to admit the customer. The woman behind the counter looked up and smiled absently before returning to the paperwork she had almost completed.

"I'll be with you in a minute," she called to him with little enthusiasm. It was late in the afternoon on a day when business had been very slow. She didn't expect the newcomer to be adding to that day's cash receipts.

"No hurry," he assured her, as he glanced around the small shop as if trying to decide where to begin.

Handing the receipt to the customer she was waiting on, the saleswoman walked around the corner to where he stood. "Now, is there something I can help you with?"

"Well, I'm here to pick out something for my fiancée," he told her.

"We sell only wedding dresses here," she said.

"Yes, yes, I know that." He nodded. "That's what I'm here for."

Seeing her puzzlement, he added, "My fiancée is out of the country on business, and we'd decided to get married in two weeks and since she won't have time to look for a dress, I told her I'd pick up her dress for her."

"Oh, I see. So it's up to you to take care of all the details while she's gone." She patted his arm reassuringly. "What is your fiancée's name?"

"What difference does that make?" he asked.

"Why, so I can get her dress for you from the back. And I'm assuming you have a sales slip."

"Oh, no, no, you don't understand." He shook his head. "She hasn't bought the dress. I'm here to do that."

"Your fiancée sent you to pick out her wedding dress for her?" The woman's eyes grew wider.

"Yes. I know it sounds odd, but we'd decided to get married, then unexpectedly, she was called off on business, and rather than change the date—her father is very ill, you see—she asked me if I'd mind getting her dress and veil for her."

"She must trust your judgment very much. And she must be *very* busy." Louise's eyebrows were still raised. No matter how busy a woman might be, when had any bride ever been too busy to pick out her own wedding dress? She'd never heard of such a thing.

"Yes, to both." He smiled agreeably. "So, a small size, a four I think she said. Something not real fancy, she prefers things on the simple side. . . ."

"Did she give you a price range?" Louise asked.

He smiled patiently. "Price will not be an object."

"I see." Louise beamed. She might yet salvage this day. "In that case, come this way. Just last week I received a small shipment from New York. Perhaps you'll find something there that you like. And you said you wanted a veil?"

"Yes." He nodded.

"Will her hair be short, or long, up or down?"

He paused to ponder, then said, "Long. Down, I think."

"Perfect." Louise said. "I have just the thing. . . ."

4

He STOOD IN THE SHADOWS, watching. Waiting.

Shifting his weight from one foot to the other, then glanced at his watch. She should be here. It was time.

It was past time.

She'd told him that her evening flight from Florida was scheduled to land at nine-fifteen. The flight had been on time, he'd checked that, of course. It was now moving toward eleven.

What was taking her so long?

He wanted desperately to clear his throat, but dared not make a sound, lest a chain reaction of barking dogs spread along the row of town houses ending who knew where. Everyone, it seemed, owned a dog these days. He just couldn't risk setting them off. He had a job to do.

And it was time.

Just when he began to feel somewhat desperate—perhaps her shoot had been held over until the next day and she'd changed her flight plans?—he heard the sound of the car door slam. Leaning forward ever so slightly to enable him to see through the dense foliage without being seen himself, he saw her open the rear passenger door and pull out her travel bag. This she slung over her shoulder, then hopped up that one flagstone step from the sidewalk to the walkway leading directly to her door. As always, he was mesmerized by her long-legged stride and easy gait and the nonchalant beauty of that face.

It was a shame, really.

But he had no choice. Anyone could see that.

She passed by his hiding place, and the scent of her drifted to him on a soft evening breeze. He closed his eyes, just for a moment, to savor it before reminding himself that he had a job to do. Soon enough, there'd be time—endless time—to drink her in, in every way. They just had to get through *this* to get to *that*.

Someday, he hoped, she'd understand.

With new resolve, he went on full alert.

Now at her doorstep, he heard her sigh of exasperation when she realized that her outside light—the one over her small porch—had gone out. He heard her there in the darkness, shuffling her travel bag from one shoulder to the other. Heard her keys jangling in her hand . . .

NOW.

He emerged with barely a sound through the long, thin blades of tall ornamental grasses, but at his passage they had shifted slightly, disturbing the stillness just enough to alert her.

"What . . ." She half-turned, but he was there, in one smooth motion. Fingers closed around her throat until the darkness closed in from every side and she slumped to the ground. A flash of a knife, quick and sure.

And in that moment, Valerie McAllister's life changed forever.

By the next morning, the gruesome story of the vicious attack on the beautiful young model whose flawless face had been slashed by an unknown assailant seemed to be everywhere, with various degrees of embellishment. How she'd been left to bleed to death on her own front doorstep. How only the barking of her neighbor's dog and that same neighbor's quick thinking had saved her life.

Details at noon. Then again at six. And again at eleven.

The first thing an awakening Val became conscious of were the tubes in her arm and in her nose and in other places that were flat-out uncomfortable to think about.

The second was the stinging tightness, the burning on the left side of her face.

The third was the aching pressure that seemed to circle her throat like a too-tight neck chain.

She raised a hand to her face, to touch the spot where the stinging began, and winced at the pain.

Gingerly her fingers traced the throbbing line that began an inch from the corner of her eye and ended just below her left ear.

Stitches.

Her mind blurred.

Stitches running up the side of her face.

Would there be a scar? Gently her fingers sought to assess the damage.

"Val?"

At the sound of her brother's voice, Val jumped, unaware that the exploration of her wound had been witnessed.

"Cale?" She forced her eyes to focus. "What are you doing here?"

"Waiting for you to wake up." He rose from his chair and took two steps to the bed, reaching gently for the hand that had been trying to count stitches and held it between his own.

"Isn't it still baseball season?" Val asked, trying to pinpoint place and time. "Is it still July?"

"Yes, it's still July," Cale assured her.

"Aren't you supposed to be . . . doing something baseball?" Her groggy mind tried to remember just what that might be.

"Not this week," he told her. "I took a few days off."

"How can you do that if it's still baseball season?"

"Oh, they'll get along just fine without me. Probably haven't even noticed that I'm gone," he assured her. "That's the beauty of being one of several assistant coaches, see. No one's really sure who you're assisting at any particular time."

Val tried to swallow, and wondered why it hurt so much to do so.

"What happened to me?" Val whispered.

"We were hoping you could tell us." A deep voice came from the doorway.

Val shifted somewhat to look around Cale to see Detective Rafferty nearing the foot of the bed.

"Hi," she greeted him quietly.

"How are you doing?" the detective asked.

"Apparently not as well as I'd like to be." She turned to her brother and said, "Cale, this is Detective Rafferty. He investigated the . . ."

Val paused, recalling that she had neglected to tell

her brother about the break-in at her town house the week before. She hadn't wanted to worry him or Quinn.

"Yes, we've met. And don't bother to try to cover it up. We heard all about the break-in. Why didn't you tell us?" Cale's eyes narrowed.

"I didn't want you to worry," she told him. "I thought it was just a random thing, and when the person realized that I had nothing worth stealing, he left. I didn't want to make a big deal out of it."

"Well, it's a big deal now. In all the papers." Cale's wife, Quinn, came into the room, carrying a cardboard tray of cold drinks in tall paper containers and several sandwiches wrapped in cellophane.

"Quinn, you're here." Val tried to smile, but the muscles on the left side of her face were uncooperative and sore.

"Of course, I'm here." Quinn McAllister leaned over her sister-in-law and smoothed the tangle of hair back from the right side of Val's face.

"Where are the boys?" Val frowned, referring to Cale's twin sons, now six, a product of his brief marriage to a former Miss Tennessee.

"We shipped them off to my parents two weeks ago," Quinn told her. "They'd wanted to spend some time being real cowboys with their uncles and their grandparents this summer, so we packed 'em up and shipped 'em out for a few weeks of ridin' the range and sleepin' under the stars."

Val tried to laugh, but the pain in her throat brought tears to her eyes.

"Why does my throat hurt so much?" she asked.

"Ms. McAllister, don't you remember what happened?" Rafferty asked.

She shook her head, as if trying to clear it.

"Why don't you tell us what you *do* remember?" Quinn suggested.

"I remember driving home from the airport. Getting out of the car. Walking up to my front door . . ." She paused, frowning. "The light was out. The one over the porch. I remember wondering why it was so dark. I had a flashlight in my purse, but I couldn't find it, so I thought I'd just fiddle around with the key until I found the lock."

Val closed her eyes, as if forcing the scene to replay in her mind.

"I heard something . . . like a *shimmer* . . ." She said, her voice lowering an octave with each utterance. "Soft . . ."

"We think he must have been hiding behind those tall grasses near the side of the building," Rafferty told them. "That might have been what you heard."

"Yes," she nodded. "Almost like a really soft breeze, but . . . yes, it could have been the grasses."

"What else do you remember?" Cale asked. "Did you hear anything else? Did you see anything at all?"

She shook her head. "No."

"Then . . . ?" The detective sought to urge her on.

"I'm not sure. Someone was behind me. There was a hand over my mouth. Then here . . ." Her hands reached toward her throat. "Hands around my throat . . . couldn't breath . . ."

"That's all?" Rafferty asked.

"That's the last thing I remember. Black spots before my eyes, then bright lights, then nothing at all . . ."

"You never saw anyone?" Rafferty continued his questioning.

"No one," she told him.

"Any impressions you might have about your assailant?"

Val frowned again. "Seems as if there should be, somehow, but, no . . ."

"No idea of how tall, how heavy . . . ?"

She closed her eyes again, forcing herself back to that moment when she first realized that she was not alone on the walkway.

"He would have been tall," she rasped, her throat raw now from the effort to speak. "When he grabbed me from behind and pulled me back, I hit his jaw or the side of his face with the top of my head."

"What else?" Rafferty leaned closer, as if to urge her on.

"Strong. His arms were strong. He had no trouble at all even though I know I struggled. His hands went right for my throat and that's just about the last thing I can remember." She touched her fingers to her throat gingerly. "That's why it hurts so to talk. He was strangling me. . . ."

"And fortunately, he wasn't able to do more than give you a sore throat."

"Did he cut my face?" Valerie attempted to frown, but the effort pulled at the stitches. "Why don't I remember anything about my face being cut?"

"You don't remember anything about that at all?" Cale asked.

"No. Nothing. Not pain, not . . . anything. Why?"

"Would he have cut your face after he strangled you?" Quinn said, a puzzled look crossing her face. "Why would he have done that?"

"We don't know that he did," Rafferty pointed out.

"I think most people would remember something like having their face slashed, Detective." Quinn turned to him. "And if Val doesn't remember, I'd have to think that maybe it's because she wasn't conscious at the time."

"Maybe, subconsciously, she's choosing not to remember," Rafferty offered.

"Maybe he just didn't want her to feel it," Cale said. "But then that sort of muddles the theory that he was strangling her and only stopped because he was interrupted, doesn't it?"

"Ms. McAllister, are you sure you don't recall anything else?" Rafferty persisted gently. "Nothing at all about seeing a knife at any time . . ."

Val shook her head. "The last thing I remember is hearing a dog bark someplace far away as I started to black out."

"It wasn't so far away," Rafferty told her. "It was right next door."

"Prudence? Bruce's dog?" Val asked.

"Yes. She may have saved your life. She started barking, then the dog on the other side barked. . . ."

"Tell Bruce I owe Pru a very large box of her favorite treats," Val whispered.

"We'll do that." Cale reached over and patted Val's hands. "Now, if Detective Rafferty is finished, why don't you try to get a little more sleep, and rest your throat?"

Val's eyelids fluttered at the mere suggestion, and she nodded dreamily. "Just for a minute . . ."

She appeared to drop off, then half-opened her eyes and asked, "The cut on my face . . . how bad is it?"

The silence, as both her brother and his wife tried to decide what to tell her, told her all.

"Oh." Val's spirits visibly lowered.

"It's going to take some time to heal, Val," Quinn responded a bit too quickly. "It will be a while before they'll know. . . ."

"Before they'll know just how bad the scar will be?" Val completed the thought when Quinn hesitated to do so.

"Let's give it some time to heal, honey," Cale answered softly.

"Will I be able to work again?"

"I think it's a little early to worry about that."

"That bad, is it?"

"Val, they really don't know just yet how it will heal, but it doesn't mean your career is over. Not by a long shot," Quinn assured her.

"It's okay," she told her brother as she stopped fighting the fatigue and allowed herself to drift off. "It's okay. . . ."

"How do you think she'll react when she's really conscious of what's going on?" Quinn stood behind her husband and worked at the knot of tension that always plagued his right shoulder whenever he became anxious.

"It's hard to say," Cale replied thoughtfully. "Val has always said that modeling was no more than a means to an end for her. I don't know that she ever enjoyed the work all that much. It was a job, albeit one that paid extremely well and allowed her a lot of freedom. Allowed her to travel to wonderful places. Gave her a chance to develop a skill."

"A skill?" the detective asked.

"Gave her an opportunity to learn photography from some master photographers. I've been telling her for the past four or five years that she should think about exhibiting some of her pictures. She really has a great eye for composition. But modeling is something she fell into at a very early age and stuck with it because, well, because she did well with it. Frankly, I think she's more comfortable on the other side of the camera."

"Really?" Detective Rafferty's eyebrows raised. "I'd have thought . . . I mean, there are thousands of women who'd do just about anything to do what your sister does."

"Detective, my sister and I came from a really poor background. These days they'd call it disadvantaged. Back then, they just called it poor. For Valerie to have found something that pays her the kind of money she makes for doing little more than standing still and just being her naturally beautiful self was nothing short of a miracle. As much as a miracle as it was for me to be able to play professional ball all those years."

"Interesting." Rafferty nodded. "I did, as I mentioned, cover the break-in at her town house. She certainly doesn't appear to live the celebrity life, if you know what I mean. Her house seemed very, well, the word *modest* comes to mind."

"Val has never been extravagant. She tends to save more than she spends, and has a very good business manager. He's made some excellent investments," Quinn told him.

"My sister has a terrible fear of poverty, detective. Having lived with very little for a very long time, well, I think Val's always saving for that rainy day. You know, when she can't work anymore."

"That day may have arrived," Quinn said softly.

"What about other family members?" The detective turned a page in his notebook.

"None," Cale told him.

"Parents?"

"No idea of where either of them are. Our mother left us when Val was a baby. Our father was a long-haul trucker who had a deeper bond with the bottle than he ever did with either of us. I haven't seen or heard from him in years."

"That's surprising that you never heard from him." Rafferty looked up from his notes. "Both of you being well-known in your fields, you being a bit of a celebrity. You'd think he'd have been in touch. You know, 'my son, the professional ball player.' 'My daughter the model.' "

"I didn't say that I *never* heard from him." Cale's eyes narrowed. "I said I haven't seen or heard from him in years."

"How do you know he hasn't contacted your sister?"

"Valerie and I are close, Detective. She would have told me."

"She didn't tell you about the break-in at her house," Rafferty reminded him.

"That's different. Believe me, if our father had contacted her, she'd have told me."

"So there's no other family. How about friends that you think we should talk to?"

"I don't know that Val had that many close friends, except for my sister, Eliza, and she lives in Portland," Quinn responded. "I don't recall ever meeting any friends other than Bruce the times when I visited. There were two women that she went to the gym with one afternoon every week. They'd work out then go for dinner."

"Names?"

"Caroline something. I don't remember that I knew the name of the other woman. Bruce would probably know."

"How about the men she dated?" Rafferty asked as he scribbled a few notes.

"I don't think there was any one man in particular. Actually, I don't think she dated all that much, now that I think of it." Cale turned to his wife. "Quinn, did Val ever talk to you about who she dated?"

"No. I always had the impression that she didn't go out much," Quinn responded. "Though I was never sure if she told me that hoping that I'd pass it on to Sky."

"Sky?" Rafferty raised an eyebrow.

"My brother, Schuyler. He and Val have always sort of had a . . . I guess *understanding* is the best way to describe their relationship."

"What kind of understanding?" The detective continued to write.

Cale and Quinn exchanged a long look, then Quinn said, "Neither of them ever said anything, but I just always had the impression they were, well, waiting for each other, somehow."

"And your brother lives where?"

"Back in Montana. Part of the year, he lives at the ranch where we grew up. The other part, he works a farm that our grandparents owned."

"Ranch, huh? Sounds like a real cowboy."

"Actually, both of my brothers are cowboys." Quinn smiled. "And they're both quite proud of it."

"I'm sure they are." Rafferty closed his notebook with a snap.

"So, can you tell us what is being done to find the person who did this to my sister?"

"We have several officers working on it, looking for leads, keeping their ears to the street," the detective said, "But there's not much else we can do until she comes around again. I'll need to talk to her friends. The people she works with."

"I can get the number of her agent and her business manager for you," Cale offered.

"That will help. But I'm also hoping that she'll remember something else. Maybe there's someone who stares too long at the gas station, the supermarket, the gym. A delivery boy . . . a neighbor . . ." He paused, then added, "The next-door neighbor seemed to get on the scene pretty quickly."

"You said the barking dog had alerted him."

"*He* said the barking dog alerted him."

"Then I'm certain that's exactly what happened," Quinn told him.

"He was the only one seen around, same as the night of the break-in," Rafferty told them.

"That's out of the question. Bruce would never hurt Valerie." Quinn frowned.

"I don't know how badly the assailant wanted to hurt her. Let's face it, with a knife sharp enough to have cut her face the way it did, he could have killed her. The weapon made an almost scalpel-thin slice. She has no other wounds. Why? If you're going to attack someone, why just cut the face?"

"Because cutting her face would could ruin her career," Quinn answered without thinking.

"Right."

"So maybe it's another model, someone who thinks that Valerie is in her way," Cale said.

"That's a possibility that we'll be exploring," Rafferty told them. "But I still don't know about this neighbor."

"Why would you suspect Bruce?"

"Well, you know, this guy's an actor. Actors are a dime a hundred out here. Tough to get noticed, tougher still to get any press at all, for a guy like him. But since your sister's attack, he's been interviewed by all the local television stations and the major newspapers. How he rescued the beauty from the beast, that sort of thing . . ." Rafferty frowned.

"You think he did it for the attention?" Quinn asked incredulously.

"I think it's an angle worth pursuing. He's sure gotten a lot of press these past forty-eight hours."

"I don't believe it. Not for a second. Bruce is her friend." Cale stood and folded his arms over his chest. "Sorry, Detective, but I think you're looking in the wrong place."

"Actually, we're looking everywhere. We have as many men on this as we can spare. That's just one possibility. Certainly we'll pursue every angle. But this guy next door, he had opportunity—that lightbulb had been unscrewed, he could have easily done that—and he knew her routine. He knew when she'd be back, since he was the one taking in her mail, that sort of thing. He has a key to her house."

"Then why didn't he wait inside and attack her then?"

Cale asked. "Why didn't he attack her in her sleep? If he had a key, he could have done this at any time."

"If his motive was to garner attention for himself, as a hero, he'd have to have set it up in a way that he had an out. And the barking dog gave him that out."

"I'm not following you," Quinn said.

"If his plan was to attack Valerie when she came in that night from the airport, but not to hurt her in a way that threatened her life, then he would need an excuse to have cut the assault short. Now, it's a very logical scenario if you're the assailant, you start the attack, there's some commotion, the dog next door starts barking to beat the band. You figure someone's going to come to investigate. So you run away, the neighbor comes out, sees the attack, runs back inside the house and calls 911." He paused in the telling. "This is a logical progression of events."

"So why do you think it didn't happen that way?"

"It just seems that the attack was over too soon." Rafferty shrugged. "Something about it just doesn't sit well with me. But we'll see what else we can learn when our victim here can give us some information."

"Well, if you have questions to ask her, better plan to spend some time here tomorrow or the next day, because after that, all your interviews will be done by phone." Cale told him.

"What do you mean?"

"I mean that the doctor told us that if she woke up today, she'd most likely be able to leave day after tomorrow, assuming there are no complications. I plan to have her out of here as soon as possible. So if all goes well, Valerie will be on her way to Montana by Saturday."

The detective frowned and appeared to be about to speak.

"That's not negotiable, Detective Rafferty. My sister needs time to recover, in a place where she's going to be safe. Val and I jointly own a cabin in Montana, right up an old mountain road from my in-laws' place. Unless there are medical reasons to prevent the trip, my wife will be taking my sister there this weekend. So if I were you, I'd plan on stopping by tomorrow to spend some time with Val, since it's going to be a while before she comes back to California."

Rafferty frowned.

"But you understand that if someone does intend on harming her further, we can't watch her from here."

"Frankly—and with all due respect—I think she's safer at home."

Quinn nodded. "My parents are close by and my brothers will be keeping an eye on her. We've all discussed it, and it's been decided. Val is going home."

"So I guess your job is to find the person who assaulted her here, and keep him here." Cale offered his hand to the detective to indicate that today's interview was over. "But in the meantime, Detective Rafferty, as soon as we get the green light from the doctors, my sister is going home."

5

QUINN MCALLISTER GLANCED across the front seat of the car she'd rented in Lewistown, Montana, and wondered whether or not she should awaken her sister-in-law for this last leg of their drive to Larkspur, and beyond, to the High Meadow Ranch, Quinn's family home. In the distance, she could see the Big Snowy Mountains rising, and a smile crossed her lips. There was no place on earth quite like Montana—particularly, to Quinn's way of thinking, like this part of Montana. She never came back without feeling that rush of gratitude, every time, for all the years she'd spent there.

"As close to heaven as you can get on God's green Earth." She murmured her father's expression without realizing she'd spoken aloud.

"My heart catches in my throat every time I look at those mountains," a voice from the passenger side whispered.

"Ah, she awakens." Quinn reached over to pat

Valerie's arm fondly. "I was just wondering if I shouldn't give you a little pinch to bring you around."

"I must have known I was home." Val stretched her legs out before her to ease the kinks. "I can't imagine how I managed to fall asleep again after having slept all the way from Los Angeles to Billings. And then from Billings to Lewistown. And then from Lewistown to here."

"Well, we could start with the fact that you just got out of the hospital this morning after four long days. And let's face it, your body must be a little weakened by your ordeal."

"Well, I'm glad I woke up when I did. I'd hate to miss the view." Val leaned back in her seat and added, "I miss it enough as it is."

"Do you ever think about coming back for good?"

"Sure." Val nodded. Like every day . . .

"Me, too. I keep thinking about someday maybe Cale and I can build a house a little farther down the mountain from my folks. A little closer to town might be nicer for the boys. Growing up, we Hollisters always felt so isolated from everyone and everything that was happening in Larkspur." Quinn smiled at Val. "Of course, you and Cale grew up in town and were close to the action all the time, so you didn't really miss anything, I guess."

Val merely smiled. The things that she and Cale had missed growing up in town ran along the lines of heat in the winter and an occasional meal, but some memories weren't worth bringing back.

"I think about the cabin a lot." Val pushed those times firmly behind her, where she believed they belonged. "I thought I'd be spending much more time here than I have. I didn't expect to be working so much, this past year in particular."

"Well, now you'll have some time off."

"Maybe all the time in the world," Val muttered, then sat up in her seat as the car rounded a bend in the road. "Can't you just *feel* what it was like here a hundred or so years ago? Can't you just see the covered wagons, hear the thunder as the endless herds of buffalo ran across the prairie?"

"Well, with the exception of the fact that there are more cattle now than bison, and that there's more hay growing than prairie grass, I don't imagine it's changed all that much."

"Big Sky," Val said fondly. "Oceans of blue over miles of golden plains. I never feel as small, as insignificant, as I do when I'm here."

"I feel that way when I'm up in the mountains. Like I'm less than a spot. Like ten of me could dance on the head of a pin."

Quinn made a left onto a narrow two-lane road that would take them into the town of Larkspur. On both sides of the road, the prairie spread out as far as the eye could see, dotted here and there with splotches of red, yellow, and blue wildflowers.

"I wonder if the boys are still down at the farm," Quinn said as if to herself.

"The boys?"

"Trevor and Sky are taking turns with three of our Dunham cousins working our grandparents' farm, since my granddad passed away, remember? They put in a few hundred acres of wheat this past spring, like Grandpa used to do. Gramma hasn't decided what to do with the farm in the long run. She doesn't think she wants to stay there but doesn't want to sell the property, either. I think she's hoping that one of the boys will want it. For now, they're taking turns with the fields and the livestock, and she's staying with my aunt Charlotte."

"I guess it's keeping everyone pretty busy."

"That's an understatement. Farming or ranching is tough enough. Trying to do both is ridiculous. I told Sky that the other night, but they feel they owe it to Grandpa to keep the farm going. At the same time, they recognize that Dad isn't getting any younger, either. And of course, Sky decided to try his hand breeding horses last year."

"Sounds like he's got a lot on his hands right now," Val said as if distracted.

"He does. He said . . . oh, look, Val, there's Sandy Osborn. Mom said she's buying out Mr. Hiller's old warehouse and she's going to put some boutiques in there."

"In Larkspur?" Val's eyebrows raised. "Who does she think will shop there?"

"Oh, haven't you heard? The Marshalls sold their farm to a developer who's putting in a bunch of mini-ranches on something like ten acres each. I hear he already sold a dozen or so of them."

"All to city people?"

Quinn nodded.

"It's driving the old-timers like my dad crazy because some of these folks are bringing their mountain bikes up into the hiking trails and turning them into mud holes. It's got people so riled up around here that Dalton, my sister CeCe's fiancé, is thinking about running for public office."

"My." Val smiled a crooked half-smile. "That's a lot of news to be coming out of Larkspur all at the same time."

Quinn laughed and slowed down as they approached the town limits.

"Is there anything you need? Would you like me to stop anywhere in town while we're here?"

"No, no, thank you," Val responded just a beat too quickly. "There's nothing I need."

"Well, if you think of something later, you just let me know, and I'll run in and pick it up for you," Quinn said, ignoring the flash of panic that had crossed Val's face.

Val doesn't want anyone to see her, Quinn realized. *She'd been fine in the airport, where she didn't know anyone, but here, at home, she probably doesn't want anyone to feel sorry for her.*

"Thank you, Quinn," Val said simply, her anxiety deflating as quickly as it had risen within her.

Val had tried to protest the trip to Montana, but there was no arguing with Cale. There was no other place where she would be as safe as she'd be there on the mountain, he'd told her bluntly, with the Hollisters to look after her while the police sought her assailant. Only her pleading had gotten him to agree to let her stay at the cabin rather than at the High Meadow Ranch. Val just couldn't bear the thought of others looking at her, at least until she got used to looking at herself. And that might take a while.

As the car rounded the first sharp turn that led up into the hills, Val's fingers sought the side of her face, the tips following the jagged trail from stitch to stitch. When she'd taken her first long, hard look at herself in the hospital, she'd been sickened by what she saw. The angry red slice held together with what could have passed for fishing line was closer to her hairline than she'd first suspected, but its prominence had still come as a shock. The nurses who'd cared for her had been wonderful about not expressing pity, but it had been there, in their eyes. *Such a shame . . .*

At last here, in the hills, she wouldn't have to face anyone but Quinn's family, and Val would do all she could to avoid even the Hollisters for as long as she could.

There had been no words to tell how grateful Val was to hear that Sky was taking his turn at his grandparents' farm just then. She'd dreamed too many times about coming back—coming back for good—and finally having time to find out just what it was that had been lurking under the surface between the two of them for so long. She just hadn't figured on coming back this way, with a track running along the side of her face and purple bruises ringing her throat like an ugly strand of pearls.

No, better that Sky was at the farm, the longer the better. Maybe by the time he came back, the scar would have begun to heal and she wouldn't look so . . . so disfigured.

In the side mirror, the hillside flowed behind them like a golden cloak. If she had been driving, she'd have stopped right back there and gotten her camera out of her bag and shot a roll of film trying to catch the way the sun played off that butte down there to the south. Then there was the way the wildflowers dotted the landscape like embroidery on an old quilt. Maybe one day soon, she told herself, she'd come back down on her own and perhaps recapture just that same effect of color and light and shadow.

Dust blew up in pale swirls as the car left the paved road and headed up the dirt drive that would lead to the High Meadow.

". . . can't wait to see those little boys. I can't even tell you how much I missed them," Quinn was saying as she began to make her turn.

"Oh. Quinn." Val reached out a hand and tried not to panic. "Would you mind if . . . I mean, please, let me out here and I'll walk up to the cabin."

"Valerie, what's wrong?" Quinn stopped the car, not bothering to pull over to the side of the road. There was little need for concern for on-coming traffic up here.

"I just . . . I'm just tired. Do you think your mother would mind if I didn't . . . if I went to the cabin instead of to the ranch?"

"Well, of course everyone is looking forward to seeing you, but I'm sure they'd understand if you're tired from the trip. Of course my mother wouldn't mind." Quinn leaned over and took Val's hand. It was shaking. "And you just close that door. Of course, I won't have you walking up to the cabin. For heaven's sake, Valerie, close that door."

"I know how anxious you are to see the boys. . . ."

"It will take me five minutes to get you settled," Quinn assured her as she turned the car around and headed back up the gravel road that led farther up the hill. "You can see everyone tomorrow, if you're feeling up to it."

Valerie nodded, not knowing just when she'd be feeling up to it, but relieved that it didn't have to be now. Not now. Not yet . . .

Quinn stopped the car gently in front of the old log

cabin that sat nestled in a stand of pines. Leaning on the steering wheel, she told Val, "I have such fondness for this old place."

"I guess you do." Val smiled, recalling that it was here, at her ancestor Jedidiah McAllister's cabin, that Quinn and Cale, once high school sweethearts, found each other again after many years of being apart. The reunion had been touched by a bit of magic, Val recalled, Quinn insisting that she'd been led to the cabin through a blinding snowstorm by the spirit of her great-great-great grandmother, Elizabeth Dunham.

Val wondered if perhaps a little of that same magic lingered, if Elizabeth's magic worked for Hollister in-laws as well.

"If you'll pop open the trunk, I'll just grab my bags," Val told Quinn, "so that you can just turn around and head back down to the ranch."

"Are you sure you don't need some help?"

"I'm fine. I only have these two bags and my camera gear." Val slammed the trunk lid and walked back to the front of the car to lean in the window.

"Be sure to tell your mom and dad I send my love. I'll see everyone as soon as I get my feet on the ground."

"Well, go on in, then, and get yourself settled." Quinn blew her a kiss. "Call down to the ranch if you think of anything you need or want."

"I will. I promise." Val stepped back from the car and watched Quinn make a tight turn around on the narrow lane, then waved as her sister-in-law passed by on her way back down the hill.

Swinging her travel bag over her shoulder, she turned and took a good look at Jedidiah's old cabin. Made of log and stucco a hundred years and more ago, the cabin had withstood many a fierce winter storm by virtue of its precise craftsmanship and its sheltered location, tucked in as it was in a dense grove of pine trees that served as a sort of fortress on the north and west sides. It was just three years ago that Val, city-weary from living in New York for almost seven years, and starved for the hills, had decided to bring the cabin into the twenty-first century. To this end, she'd had electricity brought up and had running water installed so that she could have a real bathroom and kitchen. New heavy wool area rugs, new furniture, new everything had made their way on trucks up the narrow road. Delighted with the results, Val had spent every spare moment there that first year. The second year, too, she had come often, wanting to take advantage of all the activity surrounding Cale and Quinn's wedding. But over the past ten months, her career had taken off like a shot, and she'd been so busy that she'd had scant days off since early spring.

The thought occurred to Val then that, had it not been for the assault, she probably wouldn't have gotten there this summer, either.

She was thinking about this as she walked up the steps to the narrow porch that ran across the front of the cabin. Setting her bags down, Val rummaged in her purse for her keys, but then realized that the door was open just a tiny bit. Hesitating, she took two steps back without even realizing she had done so, then sighed, remembering *where* she was. If she were anyplace but *here,* a partially opened door would give her pause after the trauma of the past week. But the cabin was her sanctuary. An open door here meant that someone had opened it for her as a gesture of welcome. She pushed on the door and it swung all the way back, inviting her to enter. Gathering her bags, she stepped inside, using one foot to kick the door closed behind her.

Sure enough, on the coffee table sat a stack of current magazines. Someone had taken the time to dust all of the surfaces, and the rugs appeared newly vacuumed. The windows had been opened to allow the scent of pine to drift in and drench her senses, reminding her, in the event she'd forgotten, that she belonged nowhere on this earth if not here. It was the only place where Val had ever felt at home, the only place she ever longed to return to.

On the small maple dining table that overlooked the woods, an ivory envelope bearing her name stood propped against a vase of cobalt blue glass holding a handful of wildflowers. Recognizing the handwriting as that of Catherine Hollister, Quinn's mother, Val opened it, and scanned the message.

> *Our dear Valerie, welcome home!*
> *Please let us know what you'll need for your stay and we'll be happy to pick it up for you.*
> *We've missed you.*
> C. H.

How like Mrs. Hollister, Val thought as she folded the note and tucked it back into the envelope, to offer to pick up something as if she had only to pop down to the corner store. Out here, the corner store was miles away. Following her nose, Val went into the kitchen and found a still-warm huckleberry pie on the counter. She looked inside the refrigerator, and found eggs, milk, butter, and even cream for her morning coffee.

"Mrs. C., you will never change," Val murmured aloud. "And I love you for your thoughtfulness."

Promising herself a slice of that fabulous pie as soon as she changed, Val carried her bags into her bedroom at the back of the cabin and sat down on the edge of the bed. Here, too, she could see Mrs. Hollister's touch. The bed was turned down and sported fresh sheets, and Val knew that the bathroom would have been tidied up and clean towels would be piled on the top of the wicker hamper.

Val sat on the edge of the bed and knew that there was nothing she could ever do to repay Catherine Hollister for all the many ways over the years she'd made Val feel as if she mattered. Coming on the heels of the past week, the loving gestures the older woman had made on Val's behalf caused emotions to spill over and seek release in the form of hot tears that streamed down her face. It was the first time since the attack that Val had really been alone, and the first time she'd permitted herself a good cry. Val wept for the terror she'd felt during those few moments when her assailant had her in his grip. She wept for the pain he had inflicted on her. She wept for the feeling of violation, for the anguish of having been victimized. And she wept for her lost career.

Oh, the doctors had assured her that plastic surgery could do wonders, but Val knew that by the time the wound had healed enough for surgery on the scar, she'd be yesterday's news. This wasn't a business where you could drop in and drop out. And if she did go back, would her assailant come looking for her, maybe to finish her off this time? Maybe she was better off out of the limelight.

Maybe Cale was right. Maybe she was safer here. . . .

She lay back upon the soft pillow and rested her head for only a moment. The windows were open, the curtains drawn back and an easy breeze blew in, coaxing her to close her eyes for just a moment. To relax, and to leave her worries back in L.A., where they belonged. . . .

She hadn't meant to fall asleep, but the minute she closed her eyes, she just drifted. She awoke from a dreamless sleep to find that the sun now slanted in through the windows at a much different angle, and the cool of the afternoon was beginning to settle in.

And that she had company.

"Oh, my God, Schuyler Hollister, you damn near gave me a heart attack." Val scrambled to sit up.

"Whoa, Val, calm down." He walked toward her from the open door and sat down next to her and attempted to take her hands.

"How long have you been here?" she demanded.

"Just a few minutes. How are you?"

"Fine. I'm fine." Suddenly terribly conscious of her wound, she wondered how she could get him to leave without seeing the left side of her face. "I thought you were at your grandparents' farm."

"I was. But when I heard about what happened . . . and Quinn said she was bringing you home, I . . . well, I wanted to be here when you got here," he told her, and she knew that he meant it.

But her face. She couldn't let him see her face.

"Well." Val cleared her throat. "Thanks for stopping by. I think I'll be . . . I'll be taking a shower now. So thank your mom for . . ."

He moved closer to her on the bed and reached out a hand to touch her face. When she pulled away, he cradled her chin, then without a word, turned her face, wound side, toward his.

"Sky, stop. Please don't," she asked, a flood of panic rising, though she did not move away.

"I just think we need to get this out of the way as soon as possible, Val. I can see you're self-conscious about how you look, but . . ."

"Self-conscious! Sky, my face was sliced open with a scalpel. I've got enough stitches running along my hairline to knit a sweater for a small child. I look in the mirror and I don't even recognize myself. . . ."

She was trembling now, and he eased her into his arms.

"Shhhh, Val. Hush." He comforted her, rocking her slightly against his broad chest. Then, when he felt she was ready to hear it, he stroked her back and said, "Valerie, you are—now and always—the most beautiful woman I ever knew. That scar on your face doesn't change a damned thing."

"That scar has changed everything," Val whispered.

Nothing that really matters has changed, Sky could have said, to assure her. But knowing that timing was everything, and that *now* was not the time for that particular conversation, he patted her twice on the back before pulling her onto her feet and pointing her toward the door.

"It might interest you to know that out there on that

little dining table, there's a plate of meat loaf and mashed potatoes that my mother sent up for you. I have been instructed to stay here until you have eaten every bite."

"Your mother's meat loaf?" Val stopped in the doorway. "Her mashed potatoes with the little tiny pieces of chopped onion . . . ?"

"The same." Sky draped a casual arm over her shoulder and walked her to the large open room that served as both living room and dining room.

"I have had dreams about your mother's meat loaf, Sky."

"Well, dream no more, miss," he said, pulling a chair out and gesturing for her to sit.

"Oh, it smells like heaven." Val grinned in spite of herself as she removed the heavy foil that covered the plate and leaned close to take a long whiff. "What does she put in here that makes it smell so good?"

"You'll have to watch her sometime and find out," Sky said as he went in search of a fork for her. When he returned a moment later, she asked, "Will you sit with me while I eat? Will you stay for a while?"

"I'll stay for however long you want me to," Sky said as he pulled up the chair next to her and sat. "I have all the time in the world. . . ."

He punched the wall with an angry swing, then ignored both the resulting pain and the blood that ran from a knuckle to pool in his hand.

"SHIT!" he screamed, and punched the wall again.

They had taken her. Who were they to have taken her away from him?

He forced himself to take deep breaths, leaned against the wall and concentrated on calming himself. Nothing good was ever born of anger, his mother used to say. And she was right. Of course, she was right. She was always right.

He punched the wall again.

Five minutes later, he was in his car, willing himself to stay within the speed limit. He couldn't afford to call attention to himself this day. He had errands to run and things to do in preparation for his trip. There was no time to spare.

First stop, the dry cleaners, where he picked up his neatly pressed tuxedo, bought special for the occasion at a consignment shop not far from Beverly Hills. He'd have preferred to have bought new, but this one looked as if it had never been worn, and besides, he himself would only wear it this one time. After all, a guy only married the girl of his dreams once.

The second stop was at the ATM machine, where he cleaned out his savings account. Must have cash for the trip, he reasoned. He did have credit cards, of course, but all things considered, cash was harder to trace.

He walked from the bank to the florist shop across the street. A little bell tinkled merrily as he opened the door. A good sign, he thought, that little bell.

"How may I help you?" A young man emerged from the back room carrying a tall, narrow metal bucket overflowing with some purple flower.

"I need a bouquet."

"Anything particular in mind?" The young man opened one of the glass refrigerated compartments and placed the bucket on the center rack. "A mixed bouquet, perhaps? We have some lovely summer mixes already made up." He pointed to a selection of vibrantly colored flowers in a container near the cash register.

"No, something white."

"Roses perhaps?"

"Maybe." He peered through the glass doors where the purple flowers had been set, unsure of just what protocol might be. There didn't seem to be much of a variety of white flowers. It occurred to him then that perhaps one just did not walk into a florist's shop and order a bridal bouquet to be made up on the spot. Was one supposed to do this in advance?

"What I actually wanted, well, was something that would make a . . . a wedding bouquet." There. He got it out.

"A wedding bouquet?"

"Is that a problem?" His eyes narrowed. Why should that be a problem?

"Well, no, of course not. But usually, you know, the bride orders her flowers. . . ."

"The bride in this case is out of the country on business and asked the groom to take over." He forced a grin and pretended to throw up his hands as a sign of helplessness.

"Oh, I see." The young man chuckled. "Well, then, tell me when you need them, what the color scheme of the wedding will be. . . ."

"Color scheme?"

"You know, what the bridesmaids are wearing."

"There are no bridesmaids. She is wearing a white dress, I am wearing a black tux." He fairly snapped. "And I need them now."

"I'm afraid I don't have much of a selection in white right now." The young man backed toward the counter as if spooked. "Perhaps if you stopped back on Thursday . . ."

"I don't have until Thursday." He ran his long fingers through his hair. "The wedding is Thursday."

"Anything I could give you today, would be wilted by then." The shopkeeper leaned an elbow on the counter. "Unless you want to pick them up that morning."

"The wedding is out of state."

"Well, then." The young man's eyes brightened, understanding now his customer's dilemma. "I think we want to consider silks. I have something in the back that's absolutely stunning."

Silks? Did he mean fake flowers? Fake flowers for his bride?

Before he could protest, the young man had re-emerged from the back carrying a large bouquet.

"Isn't this elegant? I made it for a bridal show we did last weekend." He held it up for inspection. "It's got your roses, your stephanotis, your orange blossoms . . . all made from the finest silk, absolutely one of a kind, designer quality. And one of the nicest things about it is, your bride will always have it. It will never fade or wilt. It will make a lovely keepsake of your special day."

He touched the petals of a rose tentatively. "Do people actually buy these, instead of fresh flowers?"

"Oh, absolutely," the shopkeeper crowed, closing in on the sale. "They've become very popular over the past ten or so years."

"Really?"

"Absolutely. And since I made this for a show, instead of a customer, I can give it to you at a special price."

"I wasn't looking for a bargain." He stiffened slightly at the suggestion.

"I wasn't implying that you were." The shopkeeper forced a smile. The price had just gone up another twenty dollars.

"Well, it would probably travel better than fresh flowers."

"Oh, absolutely."

"I'll take it."

"Shall I wrap it, then, since you said you're traveling with it?"

"That would be fine. Thank you." He sighed a sigh of relief. One more detail tended to.

"My pleasure. I'll wrap it in a way that none of the flowers can get crushed. Now, while I do that, tell me about the wedding. Where did you say it would be?"

"In Montana." He smiled, his sense of calm returning. "On a quiet hillside in Montana . . ."

7

VALERIE STOOD in front of the bathroom mirror and tried to decide if the floppy straw hat made her look carefree and country, or silly and immature. The important thing, she reminded herself, is that it could keep her face in shadow, the only hope she had to obscure the scar which, while healing, was doing so at its own leisurely pace. She craned her neck, studied the jagged line and acknowledged grudgingly that the doctors had done a pretty decent job of putting that side of her face back together again. And, as Sky had reminded her the evening before, she was really lucky that no nerves had been severed, that the muscles were intact.

Everyone seemed intent on assuring her that the scar would be barely noticeable. Sky's easy dismissal of its importance aside, both his brother, Trevor, and Trevor's twin sister, CeCe, had stopped at the cabin after dinner her first night back to welcome her home. Both of them had commented on the fact that they'd expected the scar to be so much worse after all they'd heard on the news.

And the very next morning, Mrs. Hollister had appeared at the cabin door with a basket of fresh, warm muffins and Val's two nephews in tow. Before she'd been able to protest, Mrs. H. had tucked Val's hair behind her ear to take a good look at the subject scar, and had nodded as if in approval.

"Why, your doctors have done a fine job, Valerie. Once the redness fades and those stitches disintegrate, and you can put a little makeup on, you'll be hard-pressed to tell where the cut was. You're a very lucky young woman."

Val had fought back a sharp retort. The last thing she felt right about then was lucky.

And while Val understood that everyone meant well, it was pretty clear to her that the scar couldn't be much more noticeable if it was blinking neon. The fact that everyone insisted on assuring her that it would barely be noticeable made her feel patronized. Even the doctors up in Lewistown she'd seen yesterday, on referral from her surgeon in Los Angeles, had assured her that the gash was healing wonderfully, yet anyone could see it was huge and red and ugly.

Besides, Val noted, everyone isn't standing on *this* side of the mirror.

Still, it was impossible to stay annoyed at any of the Hollisters for very long. Mrs. H.'s excellent cooking and loving heart aside, CeCe and Trevor still treated Val as if she were just another of their younger siblings, just as they always had. There was something comforting in this, Val acknowledged.

And then of course, there was Sky, who definitely did *not* treat her like a little sister.

Thank God.

Over the years, Val and Sky had sparred with each other, flirted with each other, teased each other. After the marriage of her brother to his sister, Quinn, there had almost seemed to be some sort of understanding between them, though neither of them had spoken of it. They'd not had the luxury of time to explore what might have been building between them before her workload had exploded from *in demand* to *frenzy*. She'd barely had a weekend free.

Until now, she reminded herself. Now, all of her weekends would be free—weekdays, too, most likely— probably for a very long time. And most of them, for the foreseeable future anyway, would be spent right here in Jed's cabin, with an occasional appearance at the High Meadow Ranch. Her presence at dinner the night before had made that clear. More a summons than an invitation, Mrs. H. had sent Sky up to the cabin with the instructions to accept no excuses.

It had been Val's first time out with a group since the attack, and though she'd dreaded it, she couldn't come up with a good enough reason not to go. Besides, she reminded herself, it was something she'd have to do sooner or later, and while *later* would have suited her just fine, *sooner* it had turned out to be. She just couldn't say no to Catherine Hollister.

All in all, it had been fine. Better than fine, Val had to admit. And before the night was over, she'd found herself so engrossed in conversation that, for a while, she'd forgotten herself and had not put her head down when all at the table had turned to her when she'd offered a comment or two on this or that. And though she'd planned on slipping out as soon as the meal had ended, she'd stayed to have coffee and dessert on the wide deck that overlooked the pastures where sheep grazed and the barn where the Black Angus had settled in for the night.

The conversation drifted from the best breed of sheep for wool—they all agreed that rambouillet was the finest—to the need to diversify beyond sheep and cattle to make the ranch more self-sufficient.

Val had settled in and sipped at her coffee, savoring the night and the conversation and the sense of belonging that had always seeped inside her when she was under this roof.

"Val, if you need something to read, I have a few books upstairs I've recently finished that you might enjoy," CeCe offered.

"Thanks. That's one thing I didn't think to bring with me. I'd appreciate a loan." Val smiled gratefully at the thoughtful gesture.

"I'll run upstairs and get them for you while I'm thinking of it." CeCe excused herself to seek out the books.

Evan and Eric, Cale's twin sons, ran noisily up the steps with mason jars filled with lightning bugs, which they brought to their aunt Val to admire.

"Look at 'em all." Eric held the jar up in front of her face. "We never find this many in Maryland."

"I've got more than you do." Evan held his jar up to compare.

"No, you don't," Eric protested.

"Yes, I do."

"Boys, it seems to me that you both have more than enough," Val told them. "Now, why don't you just set those jars on the railing there and open the lids so the lightning bugs can fly away?"

"It's too early. I want to catch more."

"It's almost time for your showers, guys," Quinn told them from the doorway. "Do as Aunt Val said, then come in to get cleaned up for the night."

"Gramma and Aunt CeCe let us stay up till eight . . . *nine* o'clock," Eric told his stepmother pointedly.

"Well, Gramma and Aunt CeCe are much nicer than I am. Let's go, buckos." Quinn stepped onto the deck, her arms crossed over her chest. "And besides, we need to have a little talk about the two of you going off up into the hills by yourselves."

"We knew where we were going," Evan told her. "Honest. We weren't lost."

"*Lost* is not the issue, guys." Sky sat down in the chair next to Val. "No one thought you'd get lost. Don't either of you remember what I told you about what you might come across up in the hills this time of year?"

"Mountain lions," Eric said. "Rattlesnakes."

"Wolves and bears," Evan added.

"Guys, you have to take this seriously. The momma bears are very protective of their babies." Trevor joined the conversation, leaning against the deck railing and lifting a jar of lightning bugs as if inspecting them.

"We know what to do if we see a bear, Uncle Trev," Evan assured him. "You make lots of noise to scare them away, or you run up the nearest tree."

"And if you can't get to a tree, you fall on the ground like this." Eric dropped to the deck and curled into a ball, clasped his hands behind his neck, and played dead.

"All well and good, but you really don't want to be in that situation. A bear can take an arm or a leg with one swipe of that big paw, whether you've rolled into a ball or not," Sky reminded them.

"Did you ever see one, Uncle Sky?" Eric asked as he uncurled himself. "Did you ever see a real bear?"

"Several times. I was very lucky that I was never chased by one."

"Sunny was chased by one once," CeCe said, referring to their sister, Susannah, as she eased around Quinn, who stood in the doorway. "Elizabeth saved her."

"Elizabeth is a ghost," Eric told Val, as if she didn't know, though of course she'd heard the legend. How Elizabeth Dunham, Catherine Hollister's great-great-great-grandmother, a full-blooded Cherokee, had lived in a tiny cabin for years after her beloved husband Stephen had died and was said to still walk the hills.

"How did she save Aunt Sunny?" The boys sat at her feet.

"She stood in front of Sunny so that the bear couldn't see her."

"Didn't the bear see Elizabeth?" Eric asked.

"Apparently not."

"Is Elizabeth a real ghost or not?" Evan asked, his eyes narrowing, adding, "My teacher says there are no ghosts."

"She's sort of what we think of as a ghost," Quinn answered. "But not a scary one. And she only comes around when someone in the family is in trouble. And whether or not ghosts really exist, well, all I can tell you is that I saw her with my own eyes."

"You did?" The boys were wide-eyed.

"I did," Quinn nodded solemnly.

"What did she look like?" Evan leaned forward.

"She had black hair that she wore in one long braid over her shoulder. It reached almost to her waist. And she had a blanket around her." Quinn gazed out across the landscape, remembering.

"What did she do, the time you saw her?" Eric asked.

"She led me through a terrible snowstorm to Jedidiah's cabin once. That was the day I met you boys, remember?"

"You didn't tell us you came there with a *ghost*." Eric scowled. "Why didn't you let us see her?"

"I think you were sleeping when I got there."

"You should have called her back."

"She doesn't come when she's called. She just appears when she thinks someone needs help."

"You're making that up," Evan accused.

"No, she's not," Catherine Hollister joined the conversation. "I've seen Elizabeth more times than I can count."

"I've seen her, too," CeCe added. "One time when Liza was little, I took her swimming in Golden Lake. On the way home, a mountain lion started following us. We were so scared, I just didn't know what to do. Then, the next thing we knew, Elizabeth was there. We followed her down to the stream and crossed it where she did, but the mountain lion didn't follow us."

"Wow. A real ghost in the hills." Eric nodded to his brother. "Cool."

"So even if a bear did try to follow us, Elizabeth would know that we were in danger and come and save us." Evan turned to Quinn. "So what's the problem?"

"The problem is that you can't rely on a spirit showing up," Quinn told them.

"And here's another thing you need to know about." Trevor joined them. "The rattlesnakes are really bad this year. I've seen dozens of them. I can't recall ever seeing so many. Last week I'll bet there were a dozen or so sunning themselves on that outcrop of rock up there beyond Jed's cabin."

"That makes me about as nervous as a long-tailed cat in a room full of rocking chairs." Eric nodded solemnly.

"Now where did you hear that expression?" Sky laughed.

"From Charlie," Eric admitted.

"It figures. Charlie's from Texas. And that sounds like Texas to me." Trevor got up and lifted one small boy under each arm. "Come on, fellows, I'll carry you in for your momma."

"We don't want to. . . ." The boys' wails trailed behind them all the way through the house.

"So much for the tranquillity of the hills." Quinn laughed as she followed them inside.

"Oh, I almost forgot." CeCe glanced at her watch. "I was supposed to call my cousin Alexa at eight. I need to let her know what time to be at the dressmaker's on Saturday for the fitting of her bridesmaid dress."

CeCe excused herself.

"I swear there should be a ban on more than one family wedding in any given year." Catherine shook her head. "First my nephew, Christian—he was married last month—then my niece Selena announced that she was getting married at the end of July. And then CeCe and Dalton in September . . . my nerves can't take it all."

Catherine paused for a moment, then sighed. "I forgot to tell CeCe that the caterer called this morning. Excuse me," she said somewhat absently and she, too, went into the house and closed the door.

"Tired?" Sky leaned over and stroked the back of Val's hand.

"A little." She nodded.

"Come on, then." He helped her to her feet. "I'll take you back to the cabin."

Sky's battered old pickup was parked out near the barn. Cautioning her to watch her step, Sky took Val's hand and led her across the uneven ground behind the house, where years of ranch equipment and trucks of various weights had rutted the earth. He opened her door and gave her a gentle assist up into the cab, then climbed into the driver's side without comment. The radio came on with the ignition, spewing static. He turned it off with one hand while he backed the truck from its parking place.

The moon was high, and generously shed its soft glow across the hills. A golden stream of pale light led from the Hollisters' barn to the old dirt road that led to the McAllister cabin. Sky drove slowly, making small talk, until they reached the cabin.

"You can just let me off here," Val told him as he parked along the side of the dirt road.

"I'll walk you up," he said, turning off the ignition and hopping out before she could protest.

He was there to offer his hand even as she opened the door. She took it and hopped down, landing in the circle of his arms, where she stayed for a very long minute. Then, as if following a script she'd known by heart all her life, she raised her face to his, inviting his kiss.

Sky leaned down and met her mouth with his own, softly, so softly, as if fearful of causing her yet more pain. Holding onto his collar, Val pulled him closer still, and this time he responded to her demand with a kiss that all but took her breath away.

Later, after she'd gotten into bed and pulled the thin cotton blanket around her, she closed her eyes and tried to recall what it had felt like to have him kiss her like he really meant it. She marveled at how just the mere pressure of his lips on hers had caused such heat to spread down to the soles of her feet. She had fallen asleep thinking about how good it had felt, how it was about time that they finally began to explore exactly what had been hanging between them for the past few years, and how maybe just this once, reality had a good chance of proving to be better than fantasy.

8

SKY SLOWLY MANEUVERED THE PICKUP up the hill, humming along with the tape that played almost inaudibly. Basically a shy man, he was comfortable with silence surrounding him. But he knew that everyone did not share his ease, and wondered if Val had been hoping for a livelier conversation the night before. The last time he and Val had spent any amount of time together alone, there had seemed to be so much more to say. But that was almost two years ago, before her face had appeared on so many of those magazine covers. How much might she have changed since then? He hadn't spent enough time alone with her these past days to call it.

But last night, just about the time he'd started wondering about it, she'd rolled down her window and reached her right arm into the night, raising her open hand as if to catch the moonlight, much as a child might do, and said, "Remember the time Liza and I went camping up near the lake and you and Cale and your buddies dressed up in sheets and came up to scare us?"

And in her laughter, he'd heard the same girl he'd known most of his life, that same girl who'd caught his eye the year she'd turned eighteen. And he remembered that same girl who had, the following year, come home for that first visit since she'd moved to New York. Beneath her big city polish and new, designer clothes, he'd sensed both restlessness and vulnerability, and in her smile, he'd found none of the confidence one would have expected from a young woman who was clearly going places. She'd seemed less excited about her new life than resigned to it, almost reluctant to discuss it, appearing more interested in Liza's experiences as a college freshman than in her own as an up-and-coming cover girl who'd already been photographed in some of the world's most exotic locales. She'd seemed vaguely disconnected from her success, as if baffled by it. The thin layer of fear hidden beneath her insecurity had touched him then, and it touched him now.

Sky'd known about the poverty that the McAllisters' had endured as children. Hadn't Cale once confessed, in the mist of his best year as a professional baseball player, that despite his success, he was never without the fear it could all be taken from him in a heartbeat? In Val, Sky recognized that same hesitancy, that reluctance to believe that all might, in the end, be well. In the tentative eighteen-year-old just trying her hand at a very sophisticated game, it had not been unexpected. In the woman, a ten-year veteran of that game, it came as a surprise.

And yet, for as long as Sky had known Val, he'd never known her to be consciously aware of her beauty, perhaps because it had taken so many years to assert itself.

His earliest memories of her were as a very spindly eight- or nine-year-old who, in worn shorts and bare feet, had sat on the top bleacher at the ball field, watching as her big brother played little league baseball. Her presence there had been a constant, he couldn't recall that she'd ever missed a game. And afterward, Cale would walk her home in the dark to their tiny house across town before returning to the ball field to celebrate a win or commiserate a loss with his teammates. But always, Cale's skinny little sister came first.

Sky could recall in perfect detail the exact minute when he'd noticed that Val wasn't a skinny little kid anymore.

It had been the summer before her senior year in high school. Sky had been a junior in college and reluctant to come home anymore than he'd had to, college life offering so much more than what was to be found at the High Meadow. He'd been hoping to get a job on the rodeo circuit like several of his friends were planning on doing, but there was no end to the work that had to be done on the ranch, and his father had other plans for him. Up until that summer, Sky had never thought of Valerie as much more than his friend's little sister or his own little sister's best friend. He'd had no way of knowing that while he was off at college, she'd been busy growing up.

And grow up, she had, and done a damned fine job of it, too.

There'd been a party for Liza's eighteenth birthday, a sleep-over with all her friends from town. The plan had been for the girls to picnic and swim in the afternoon, and return to the High Meadow for a barbecue. The girls were due back at the ranch by five, but when, at six-thirty, they still had not arrived, Mrs. Hollister had sent Sky up to bring them back. When he arrived at the lake, the girls were all still swimming, and he'd stood on a rock and with two fingers to his lips, whistled to his sister to get her attention, then signaled that their mother wanted her and her friends to start on home. Liza had waved to let Sky know she'd gotten the message and would comply. He'd turned to walk back to his truck just as the girl closest to shore had stepped out of the water and onto the grassy slope. She'd reminded him of that painting, the one where the woman was walking out of the sea, and he'd stood staring, mesmerized by her beauty and her natural grace, his mouth growing dry.

His face flushed crimson when she'd waved and smiled, and he'd realized that the rush of lust had been inspired by Valerie McAllister. He hadn't had one thought of her since then that had not been accompanied by that same stab of heat. There was something about her, her physical beauty aside, that had captivated him then and there and had never really let go. Oh, there'd been plenty of women in his life, all right. Especially those years he'd spent roping cattle and playing at being a rodeo hero back before he'd had to take his part running the ranch. The young ladies sure did go for that cowboy mystique.

But ever since Val had come back to renovate old Jedidiah's cabin, he'd found less and less of what interested him in the bars down in town or up in Lewiston. She'd come again for Cale and Quinn's wedding, and the time they spent together that week had seemed like a promise given, though no such words had been exchanged. There had just been an air of certainty about them when they were together, and he'd known then that when she was finished doing what she'd been doing, she'd be coming back home. And he'd be waiting for her.

He'd just never figured that she'd be coming back like this, wounded and afraid, the victim of some random act of violence, the kind that had never seemed to hit so close to home, until now. He'd been sickened at the news that she'd been attacked, sickened at the thought of anyone harming her in any way. It had been all he could do when he'd gotten back from two weeks on the Dunham farm not to take off for California as soon as he'd heard, find the person who had hurt her, and beat the living stuffing out of him. But of course, by the time Sky'd heard, Val was but two days away from being flown back with Quinn, and Cale had asked him to wait.

And so he waited at the High Meadow for his sister to bring Val home. Quinn had warned them all that Valerie was most self-conscious of the cut on her face, but even that had not prepared him for the viciousness of the wound. For her own sake, Sky had decided that the direct approach would serve best, and so he'd forced her to let him look at the cut, made her see that he did not flinch nor was he repulsed by the way she looked, as her eyes had told him so plainly that she feared he might be.

How anyone could have done that to her was beyond Sky's comprehension.

But what had all but broken his heart was her fragility. One look at her face and Sky knew that Valerie would not be leaving the hills to return to her old life even once the healing process was complete. She'd come back there to lick her wounds, literally and figuratively, because it was home. It was where she belonged.

But beyond all that, Sky knew—had known for years—that she belonged with him. He hated that her retirement had been forced upon her, that the choice had been taken from her but that was the hand she'd been dealt. It would be up to her now, how she'd play it out.

Sky parked the truck along a row of aspen trees and rolled up the window despite the heat. The bugs had been fierce this summer, and he hated the thought of getting back into the car later this afternoon and finding the cabin filled with all manner of flying devils. He took the picnic basket by the handle and swung it out, slammed the door behind him as he made his way to the front of the cabin.

"Val," Sky called through the open screened door.

"Come on in," Val answered from the kitchen. "I was just starting to make some iced tea to take along with us."

Sky held up a Thermos jug and grinned. "My mother made some this morning."

"And lunch, too, dare I ask?" Val pointed to the picnic basket.

"She referred to it as a snack," he told her.

"Let me guess," Val said. "A little fried chicken. A little salad. A couple of biscuits she made this morning. A few cookies . . ."

"I see you've done the Catherine Hollister picnic tour of Golden Lake before." Sky nodded.

"Oh, but not for years." Val grinned. "I'm delighted to see that the menu hasn't changed."

"I hope you have your bathing suit on under those shorts," Sky said. "It's going to be hot this afternoon, and that cool mountain water is going to feel really good after a long hike."

"I'm prepared," she assured him. "And frankly, that long hike will feel really good to someone who's been inactive for the past few weeks. I'm looking forward to the walk and the swim."

They left by the front door, Val taking care to make certain that the screened door was shut tightly, though not locked. It was only ten in the morning, but the sun had already begun to bake the hills. Val began to regret her earlier decision, obviously not a good one, to leave her straw hat with its wide, sheltering brim back at the cabin. She'd stood before the mirror, tying it this way and that, trying to cover the red streak that twisted down the side of her face. She had given up with a sigh, and tossed the hat across the room. There was no point in trying to pretend that her face was intact. It wasn't. And there was no sense in pretending that it didn't matter, because it did. There was nothing she could do about it, so she tied her hair back in a ponytail and searched for her sunglasses, reminding herself that she'd spent months pining for the sights and sounds of the hills. As long as she was here, she'd indulge in them. If she could share them with Sky, so much the better.

Sky linked his fingers through hers and set off up the well-worn trail toward the lake.

"I remember one time when Liza and I were little, Trevor told us that if we startled a bear up here, it would turn around and eat us both," Val said, "so we always sang at the top of our lungs all the way from the top of your driveway until we got to the lake."

"Ever see a bear?"

"Nope." She shook her head. "We never did, so I guess all of that off-key singing must have worked."

They paused where the trail crested, giving them a view out over a shallow valley.

"My granddad told us that the Crow Indians used to camp down there," Sky told her. "We used to find arrowheads and all sorts of things after a big rain."

"Cale told me that Old Jed had a Crow wife," Val said softly. "Maybe he met her right down there in that valley."

"I remember Cale mentioning that, that he had an ancestor who'd married a Crow woman and who'd gone into the hills by himself after she and their baby son had been massacred by some white soldiers."

"I don't remember that part." She frowned. "About them dying. I wonder where Cale heard that."

"I think he looked it up in the library for a paper he did in high school. We had to write about our family's ties to the area, if we had one."

"I wonder if he made that up," she murmured. "It's too sad if it's true."

Sky shrugged. "You'll have to ask your brother. Though I do seem to recall he did have an A on that paper."

"What did you write about?" she asked.

"About the Dunhams searching for gold in the streams on the other side of the hill. About how they found the silver mines instead. And about how the silver paid for the spread that my great-grandparents had down on the other side of town."

"The farm that you and Trevor are working this summer."

He nodded.

"It's been in our family for over one hundred years. After my grandfather died, my grandmother started to worry about what would become of the farm, what would happen to their animals. So Trevor and I, and two of our cousins, agreed to share the work to keep things going for a while. At least until a decision could be made about what to do with it."

"It's wonderful that you have such a close family," Val said. "That the four of you would get together and rearrange your lives for your grandmother's sake."

"We couldn't have her being worried at her age." He shrugged as if there was no personal sacrifice involved for any of them, though Val suspected there must be. "And besides, we all love that farm. You know, we all spent so much time there, growing up. I'm starting to realize that I love farming as much as I love ranching. Maybe more. And besides, having the farm on which to grow grain is great for the ranch."

He held her forearm to steady her as they began their descent from the top of the rise to the lake shore.

"One of the reasons why ranching has become so expensive, is that it costs so much to bring in feed. Dairy herds, for example, are just about non-existent out here these days—it's cheaper to ship milk in than it is to feed the cattle. Years ago, when we were little, my dad tried his hand with a small herd, but it was labor-intensive and not profitable. He ended up keeping a few milk cows for our own use, but after experimenting with several types of livestock, decided that the wool-producing sheep were his best bet." He grinned as he helped her down the uneven staircase of rock. "Meat producing animals were out, since my mother couldn't face raising animals to be sent away to slaughter."

"Then I guess raising sheep for their wool was a good move."

"We've done well with it." He nodded. "My dad supplies exclusively to Pandora Mills. The arrangement simplifies things, takes a lot of pressure off him, because he knows he has a steady market. And last year, we decided we'd try our hand at breeding horses."

"I didn't notice that there were more horses at the ranch," she said as they sat on an outcrop of rock that overlooked the crystal clear below.

"They're mostly at the farm. We're breeding thoroughbreds and quarter horses." Sky grinned and added, "Not necessarily to each other."

"You're breeding to sell?"

"Yes. The quarter horses go mostly for rodeo stock, and the thoroughbreds, well, we're hoping to get a few that are fast enough to race on the tracks back east."

"Why back east?" she asked.

"Because that's where you'll find most of the best tracks and the biggest purses." Sky scanned the line of trees across the lake and pointed to the left. "Look there, there's an eagle at the top of that last pine."

Valerie raised a hand to shield her eyes from the sun and following Sky's sight line, located the large bird where it sat preening.

"I can't remember the last time I saw such a sight," she told him.

"Then you've clearly stayed away too long."

"Not much argument there." Val nodded.

He touched her arm and drew her attention to the eagle who had left its perch. They sat in silence, watching the majestic bird take flight to soar across the lake, over the heads of the two who sat watching below.

"Why did you?" Sky asked when the eagle had disappeared.

"Why did I what?"

"Stay away so long."

"I hadn't intended to." She frowned. "It just seemed that things began to move so fast. 'Val, they want you in Milan.' 'Val, you need to be in Rio next week.' 'Val, you'll be three weeks in Australia.' "

"Tough being so popular."

There was a faint undertone of sarcasm that Valerie did not miss.

"It's my living, Sky," she said gently. "It's how I support myself."

"And then some, I'd imagine," he noted.

"Yes, and then some. Some for those rainy days. Some for when the time comes that I no longer have work." A worried look crossed her face. "Like now."

"Has someone told you that you won't work again?"

"No, but . . . well, let's be honest here." She tried to laugh but it sounded hollow, brittle. "There are few calls for a model with a zipper running down the side of her face."

"It's really not as bad as you think it is," Sky assured her, "and besides, didn't the doctors tell you that you need to give it time to heal?"

"Yes. It will heal. But it won't disappear." Val stared at

her hands for what seemed to be a long time. Then, she sighed and looked up at Sky and said, "I'm lucky that I was able to make enough money over the past ten years that I could afford to invest some of it. I guess one of these days soon I'll need to call my business manager and see where all that stands. I didn't expect to need to be drawing from it now, but I'm glad I have it. And I have the cabin, so I'll always have a place to live. My expenses are very low here."

"You don't think you'll be going back to California?" he asked, trying hard not to sound as eager as he was to believe that, this time, she'd be staying for a while.

"I'll go back to pack up my apartment, but I don't want to live there anymore. Without work, there's nothing to keep me there."

He could have told her that her assumption that she'd not have work was probably premature, but he let it pass.

"What's going on with the investigation?" Sky asked. "Have you heard anything at all from the police department? Any suspects?"

"I called the detective who is handling the case, Detective Rafferty, but he wasn't in, so I left a message for him to call me on my portable phone. The last I heard, he was still looking at Bruce, my next-door neighbor, as his prime suspect, which is ludicrous."

"Why?"

"Because he just wouldn't do something like that. He just doesn't have it in him to be that violent. Besides, the guy who attacked me was tall and strong. Bruce is tall, but he isn't that strong."

"How do you know?"

"What do you mean, how do I know?" She frowned, annoyed with the question.

"Sometimes, under certain circumstances, people exhibit a strength that they might not normally have."

"You mean, like in attacking someone, your adrenaline might start flowing in the heat of the moment?"

"Something like that."

Val shook her head. "You just don't know Bruce."

"You haven't known him all that long yourself," Sky reminded her. "You've only been out there, what, six months?"

"It doesn't matter," Val insisted. "Bruce is not a physical person. I'm hoping that the police have come to the same conclusion and that they're looking for the person who really did attack me. And I'm hoping that someone will call me back soon—the detective, Bruce. Hell, even my agent—I've left messages for all of them and haven't heard from a soul yet."

"I'm sure you'll hear from someone sooner or later."

"I hope so." Val sighed. "I'd feel a lot better knowing that they've found the person and locked him up."

"You don't feel threatened here, do you?"

"Oh, no, not here." She smiled up at him, and another bit of his heart was hers. "This is the only place where I do feel completely safe."

"Good. We want you to feel safe here. You are safe here." Sky ran his hand through the long tangle of her dark hair. "And we want you to stay."

"Are you part of that 'we,' Schuyler Hollister?"

"A big part of that 'we.' " Sky leaned down and, cupping her pretty face in one hand, kissed her pretty mouth, which was so soft and perfect that he kissed her again.

He was just getting into serious kissing when she jumped.

"What?" he asked. "Did I hurt your face?"

"No, no," she said.

"Then what?"

"I just for a minute . . . just . . . well." She appeared somewhat flustered. "Just for a minute, I felt like someone was watching us."

Sky turned and looked up the hill behind them.

"Val, who do you think could be out here? There's no one around for miles, literally," he reminded her. "My brother left for the farm last night, and my sisters left early this morning to go shopping in Lewistown with my mother. There isn't anyone else up here."

"I guess I just got jumpy," she told him. "Talking about the man who attacked me, knowing that he's still out there . . ."

"Still out there in California, Val. Not here."

"I know, I know." She nodded. "I just got spooked."

"Let's take a swim," Sky suggested, "and then we'll walk up to Elizabeth's cabin and have our picnic up there."

"That sounds like a plan." Val nodded.

She stood and stripped off the T-shirt that covered the top of her bathing suit, then stepped out of her shorts and toed off her sneakers.

"I can still beat you to the raft." She pointed out toward the middle of the lake where a wooden deck, tied to a post, floated.

"You could never out-swim me," Sky scoffed.

"Try and catch me." Val laughed as she slid carefully

down the smooth side of the rock to the grass below, and strode, on long legs, to the water. She walked in till the lake was almost to her hips, then dove forward, and with strong strokes, headed for the raft.

It felt so good to have the water gliding off her skin, to feel the sun on her back, to stretch her arms and legs and test their strength. While in the autumn, Golden Lake was in fact golden from the larch trees that framed the southern end of the lake, in mid-summer, the lake was purest blue. She raced through it and felt her muscles begin to burn just slightly, and slowed her pace. Still, she reached the raft before Sky did, and pulled herself up onto its edge. And there she sat, watching him swim toward her in long even strokes.

When Sky reached the raft, he pulled on her feet to bring her back into the water. Encircling her waist with his hands, he drew her close, and kissed her, causing that old tingle to start back down her spine again. What could she do but kiss him back?

The sweetness of him flowed through her, and she moved herself back through the water, just slightly, to lean her back against the rough hardness of the raft. Twining her arms around his neck, she pressed against him, wanting to feel his skin against her own. Sky's hands slid down her back to rest on her hips, and she felt, more than heard, the soft intake of his breath as her body melted into his own.

This is just about where we left off last time, she reminded herself of the week before Cale and Quinn's wedding. *Just about this close. Just about this intense.*

The same sensations she'd felt then flooded through

her now, as Sky's tongue traced the inside of her bottom lip and splinters of want sped through her, head to toes.

"Here we are again," he whispered.

"I was just thinking that same thing."

"So where do we go from here, Val?" he asked, his brown eyes warming now with the reflection of the sun off the lake.

"I guess we just see where it all leads," she said carefully.

"Not good enough." Sky shook his head. "We tried that once, and it led nowhere. I'm not willing to let you drift away again."

"What do you want me to say, Sky?"

"I guess I want you to acknowledge that what's between us is not something casual. That it's too important to leave to chance. That it's worth taking time with."

Val looked up into eyes that had gone dark and smoky.

"It's worth taking time with." She nodded. "It's well worth whatever time it will take."

And time, she reminded herself as his lips found hers again, was one thing she had plenty of right then.

9

His first thought as he followed Route 191 South outside of Lewistown in his rented SUV was, when they called Montana Big Sky country, they meant BIG sky. It was almost intimidating, seeing how wide and how high overhead it stretched. Why, there was prairie ahead for miles, as far as the eye could see, and out here, with endlessly open countryside, that was pretty damned far.

Then there were those mountains in the background, surrounding all like a moat made by a giant's hands. Rocky outcrops—buttes, he figured, recalling all those cowboy movies he'd watched over the years—rose solidly here and there, seemingly out of nowhere. It was, in fact, a breathtaking land, with breathtaking views on every side. He'd just never imagined it to be so, well, so *damned big.*

He'd bought a map just that morning at the airport, and though he'd pretty much memorized the names of the roads and the appropriate turns he would have to make, he found himself pulling over to the side of the road to double-check. This wasn't an area where one would want to take a wrong turn. Lost out here would mean lost for real, and who knew for how long?

Leaning over the console, he grabbed a bottle of water from the cooler that sat where a passenger's feet might. Twisting off the cap, he downed a few long swallows while he consulted the map. All appeared well so far. He was right where he wanted to be, and making good time, too. He'd make it to Larkspur by midmorning and he'd check into that little motel that the guidebook told him was right outside of town. Then maybe he'd have some time to scope out the lay of the land, get his bearings so that tomorrow he'd not be worrying about finding his destination.

He had big plans for tomorrow.

Dropping the bottle into the cup holder, and putting the car into drive, he eased back onto the two-lane road. Up ahead on the left, wire fencing enclosed a herd of buffalo, and he stopped in the middle of the roadway to gape at the lumbering beasts. Ugly things, he shook his head in disgust, with all that dirty fur and those humped backs, but they sure do make you feel like you're back in the Wild West. There was something very cool about driving through the prairie and coming across a herd of buffalo, watching them roam. Just like that old song said. Unconsciously he began to whistle that old song, wishing for just a moment that he was astride a horse instead of behind the wheel of a rented Jeep.

The moment of nostalgia passed, and he gunned the engine, drawing dull gazes from several of the animals closest to the fence.

The town of Larkspur was there before him without warning, and he braked quickly to avoid exceeding the posted twenty-five mile speed limit. Pretty town, he observed as he drove past the tidy business district. Not much activity, with its few shops and fewer restaurants, but a nice enough place.

A sign with an arrow pointing down a side street indicated that the regional high school was off to the left. On a whim, he turned and drove the four short blocks to the school, which sat back off the road at the apex of a long and wide circular drive. He followed it halfway up, then stopped under some aspens and, motor still running, sat for a few long moments, just staring at the building.

She had gone to school here. She'd walked up those steps, maybe sat under these very trees. Had she played sports, he wondered as his gaze drifted toward the athletic fields across the road. There was so much he still needed to learn about her, but, of course, they would have plenty of time to get to know each other. They'd have eternity.

After all, marriage was forever.

He started the car and drove back toward town. Anxious now to see her, he'd check into his room, grab a bite to eat, then head on up to the hills to see what he could see.

10

VALERIE STOOD IN THE DOORWAY and watched the lights from Sky's pickup fade as he drove down the hill through the pitch dark of midnight. With no light but the stars overhead, she leaned back against the door and sighed. In spite of all that had happened to her, the break-in, the assault, the surgery, the uncertain status of her career—in spite of it all, she felt more light-hearted than she had in . . . well, she was hard-pressed to remember when she had ever felt that good. She felt younger, more contented, than she had in years.

She and Sky, after all these years, had finally landed on the same bit of ground at the same time, wanting the same thing. It was nothing short of miraculous. She raised the fingers of one hand to the side of her face, and touched the ragged scar. Blessing or curse, she wondered.

Grinning because she just felt so damned good, she took a deep breath of mountain air and closed the door behind her. After an afternoon of lazing in the sun, they'd joined the Hollisters for dinner on the wide deck, where tables had been set up to seat one and all—fourteen of them that night. The food had been wonderful, and the affection so freely offered had wrapped around her like a hug. But it was the light in Sky's eyes that had let her know for certain that she was exactly where she was supposed to be.

Funny, she thought as she turned out the porch light and slid over the latch on the front door, how she'd been all around the world but had never found what had been waiting for her right here. Dorothy had said it best, Val mused as she turned to snap off the lamp on the table behind the sofa. There is no place like home.

A spot of something white across the room caught her eye, and curious, she went to the small dining table to see what it was. She'd reached her hand out to pick it up when she realized just what it was that rested there in the middle of the table. A chill ran up her spine as she stepped back as if to distance herself from the small porcelain Limoges wedding cake. The same small porcelain wedding cake that had been stolen from her apartment.

Beneath her feet, something crunched. She did not need to look to know it was rice.

Val ran for the door and unlatched it, leaning over the porch railing and watching as the lights from Sky's truck disappeared around that last bend. Her heart pounding, she ran back into the cabin and relocked the door.

He knew where she was and he had found her.

He had been here, in her cabin.

He had invaded her sanctuary. Taunted her with the undeniable truth that she wasn't really safe anywhere.

Not even here.

She pulled down the window shades with shaking hands as if to block out the dark and whatever might lay hidden by it. Then, forcing herself to gather her wits, she realized that help was only a phone call away.

"Sky," she whispered aloud. "I'll call the ranch and he'll answer the phone. He should be just getting in . . ."

Val hurried into the kitchen for the phone that she'd earlier left on the counter near the small vase of wildflowers she'd picked on her way back from the picnic at the lake. The blue glass vase sat alone on the counter.

With frantic eyes, she scanned the kitchen, but the phone was nowhere to be seen.

The bedroom, then. I must have taken it in there while I was getting dressed for dinner. . . .

But it was not on the bed, nor the dresser, nor the little nightstand. Not in the bathroom, nor the living room. The phone was nowhere to be found. It took a few long moments for her to realize that he'd probably taken it with him.

If in fact he had left at all. . . .

For the first time, it occurred to her that he could still be inside.

Barely breathing, Val's eyes scanned every corner of the front room. Grabbing the black wrought iron poker from the fireplace, she pulled open the closet door.

No one.

On the quietest of feet, she tiptoed back down the hall, sweat beading on her lip as she eased into the bathroom and pushed aside the shower curtain.

No one.

Taking a deep breath, she went back into the bedroom and checked that closet, under the bed, then repeated the drill in the second bedroom.

No one.

Grateful to find that he was no longer in the cabin, Val stood in the hall, debating her next move. She was isolated, with no phone and no means of getting down to the High Meadow, except to walk. And only a fool would go out into the black of night and stumble down the hill not knowing who is out there, maybe waiting for her to do exactly that.

The nagging knowledge that he'd been here, that he'd gotten so close, terrified her, and she crept back into the bedroom and closed the shades there was well. Then, wrapping a blanket around her shivering body, she curled up against the headboard, and waited in the dark for morning.

An insistent blue jay jawed outside Val's window and the sound of its chatter broke through the sleep that had been so long in coming. Her eyes flew open and darted furtively about the room. Convinced that she was in fact alone, she cautiously left the bed and crept into the front rooms. All was as she'd left it the night before, and for a long moment, she wondered if perhaps she had dreamed that she'd found the little wedding cake on her dining table. But no, there it was, right where she'd dropped it the night before. She stared at it across the room, but couldn't bring herself to touch it. She left it there, on the floor, and went back into the bedroom to find her shoes. She'd trek on down to the High Meadow. It was early, but someone would be awake. Grabbing her sunglasses from the edge of the dresser, she left the bedroom at the back of the cabin and walked straight to the front door. When she opened it, she was face to face with a visitor.

"Hello, Valerie," he said softly.

"Detective Rafferty?" Her head tilted slightly to one side, her eyes widening somewhat in surprise.

"Daniel," he told her pointedly. "It's Daniel."

Taken off guard by his casual manner, she took a half-step backward.

He smiled charmingly, then lifted the two suitcases that sat at his feet. "Aren't you going to ask me in?"

Val's brows knit together in a frown.

What exactly was wrong with this picture?

"Ah . . ." She hesitated long enough for him to step around her. Her gut reaction—to slip behind him and run out the door—was thwarted when, with one foot, he slammed the door.

The sound jarred her senses like a shot.

"You act as if you're surprised to see me." Rafferty dropped one suitcase on the floor and opened the second, a garment bag, and draped it across the sofa. From where she stood, Val could see that something long and white rested inside.

"Well, yes. Yes, I am." She nodded, the confusion that was building inside her now touched with the first trace of fear.

"Detective . . ." she began.

"Daniel," he corrected her.

"Daniel. What are you doing here?"

"Why, I've come to claim my bride," he told her calmly.

"Your bride?" Val repeated flatly.

"Oh, come on, now, Val," he said indulgently. "You don't have to pretend that you don't know."

"Don't know?" Her voice caught in her throat. Dare she ask?

"That we were meant for each other, of course. Meant to be together. I knew it the first time I saw you jogging in the park."

"You watched me jog?"

"Every day. At least, every day that you weren't off someplace working. You've been working way too much, Valerie." He shook his head. "But after today, all that will change."

"It will?" She took another small step backward.

"After today, we'll always be together." He flashed a brilliant smile, "Always and forever. For better or for worse. Through all eternity."

Val stared blankly at the stranger before her.

"Oh, I have something for you. Something special for you."

The detective turned his back and Val stood there, dumbly, watching him, trying to make sense out of his presence and everything he'd just said.

"The florist assured me that you'd love these. Well, I told him that you'd rather have fresh flowers, but there was a logistics problem there."

He flipped the suitcase onto a chair with the same ease with which he'd toss a magazine. He opened it and drew out a box which he handed to her.

"Go ahead, open it." He smiled benignly, and added, "Sweetheart."

Cringing at the endearment and struggling to control the shaking of her hands, she took the box and placed it on the table, walking around to the far side to put some distance between them.

"Open it," he said again, the smile intact, but the voice hinting at firm command.

Val unwrapped the box, and parted the tissue. Beneath the several layers of thin paper lay a silk bouquet of white flowers.

"Oh," she exclaimed.

"Do you like them?" His eyes narrowed as he watched her face.

"Oh. Yes. They're . . . they're beautiful," she stammered.

"Good. I wanted you to like them." He nodded. "The florist said that lots of brides were using the silks instead of the fresh flowers, so I thought it would be okay. And besides, he said you'd like it that the flowers would last forever. You'd like that, wouldn't you?"

A weight seemed to land in Valerie's chest. Was he kidding? He had to be kidding. . . .

But one look at his face . . . the calm and happy smile, the eyes slightly glazed over . . . told Val that her worst fears were right on the money.

"It's a beautiful day for a wedding, don't you think?" He turned to point to the window, then realized that the shades were all drawn. He walked to the nearest window and pulled up the shade to let the early morning sun drift in.

"See?" he said, then added merrily, "Happy the bride the sun shines on today."

Valerie stared at him, her heart beginning to pound wildly.

"Now, make your sweetie a cup of coffee, then go put on your dress." He stood before her, his hands on his hips, a man who obviously was accustomed to having his orders obeyed. The small handgun strapped to his side and visible when his jacket flapped aside probably went a long way to assure that. She knew it was having an effect on her.

Val nodded and went into the kitchen.

"I'll be right back," she told him.

"I'm coming with you." He followed her into the small kitchen, stopping at the back door and checking to make sure it was locked.

"Don't want you having any last minute jitters." He smiled. "Everyone says brides are skittish on their wedding day."

Val poured water into the top of the coffeemaker, wishing he'd stop saying that. Her wedding day? Over her dead body.

She winced inwardly, realizing that that could be a possibility. The man was obviously mad, delusional. Enough to believe she wanted to marry him. That she would marry him. What would he do if she told him, flat out, that she had no intentions of playing into his fantasy? Might he not kill her, right then and there?

The coffee began to drop into the glass pot as she turned to get a mug from the cupboard.

"You were the person who attacked me," she said as casually as she could force the words out.

"I know, sweetheart. And I'm sorry that that was necessary." He shook his head slowly. "And truthfully, this isn't the way I intended things to happen."

"What did you think was going to happen?" She tried

to sound calm, rational. Talk to him. Find out what he's thinking. . . .

"Well, I thought that we'd work together to find your stalker, and over time, I knew you'd come to see that we were meant for each other. That you'd fall in love with me just as I'd fallen in love with you. I didn't expect you to leave California, Valerie. You weren't supposed to leave."

"Why did you cut my face?"

"Well, sweetheart, I just couldn't have you traveling all over the place without me, having all those other men staring at you, could I? I just had to put an end to that. You were meant to belong to me. Only to me. And now you will. After today, we'll always be together. That's what God intended." He frowned. "I think you'll see that this is really the best for both of us."

The coffee had completed its short run into the pot, and she poured it into the mug.

"You know how I take my coffee?" he asked.

"Black?" She tossed off the response without thinking.

"Right." He beamed. "See how you just *knew*?"

Valerie cleared her throat, wondering how she could distract him so that she could . . . could what? Hit him over the head with something? Not a smart move when he is armed and I am not, she reminded herself.

"Great coffee," he told her. "Aren't you going to join me?"

"Sure." She poured herself a cup then snapped off the dial on the coffeemaker.

What does one do when trapped in a remote cabin with a mad man who believes you are destined to be his own true love? Do you fight? Flee?

What if he shows no sign of letting you out of his sight, is much bigger and stronger than you are, and has a gun? Then what do you do? Do you play along with him, hoping for a chance to escape, to outsmart him?

"I know you're dying to see your wedding gown." He smiled.

Her wedding gown?

Val stared at him blankly.

"Now, you didn't think I'd come all this way to marry you and not bring you something special to wear, did you?" He gestured to the door. "Now, come on out here and bring your coffee, and I'll show you. I think you'll love it, Val. It's a designer gown. The woman in the shop said it came from New York. . . ."

Rafferty led Val back into the front room of the cabin and pointed to the fireplace that ran along the outside wall.

"You just stand right there, and I'll show you." He turned his back and for one second Val's eyes searched desperately for something substantial enough to smack him over the head with.

There was only the lamp, and he was between her and it.

"Here we go." He bent over the open suitcase and lifted the plastic garment bag that held the white something she'd glimpsed earlier. "You have to admit, it's a beauty."

He held up the dress for her inspection.

"Yes." She nodded. "It's a beauty."

"And I'm pretty sure it will fit you," he told her. "It's a four. Your size."

How would he know that?

"And of course," he added, "you need shoes."

He handed a shoe box to her. She was startled to see the box was from her own closet, held her own shoes.

"You've thought of everything," she told him.

"I tried to, baby," he said as he dipped back into the suitcase. "Here's your veil. The woman in the shop said this style was suited for long hair worn down. I want you to wear your hair down."

He held up a gossamer veil that was attached to a headdress covered with white silk flowers.

"She said you'd want to pull your hair back from your face," he continued as if he hadn't seen the look of growing revulsion on her face.

"When . . . ah . . . when is the ceremony?" she asked, wondering how much time she might have. Sky would be picking her up at eight to drive her into town to do some grocery shopping. It was just barely seven.

"As soon as you can get into that dress."

"Wh . . . Where are you . . . are we doing this?"

"Well, we could do it right here, in the cabin. But it's such a beautiful day, maybe an outside ceremony would be nicer. I'll even let you pick the place, since you know the area so well."

"Someplace outside?"

"Right. Maybe someplace where we can look out over the valley. Or maybe someplace that overlooks the lake. I walked up there yesterday, by the way. It sure was a breathtaking view." His face clouded over and his eyes went dark. "Who was the man, Valerie?"

"The man?"

"The one you went to the lake with yesterday." He leaned closer, his jaw tight.

So someone had been watching after all. . . .

"Valerie." Rafferty's voice could draw blood. "I asked you, who was the man?"

"Oh. Him." She waved a hand as if to brush away a fly. "He's just my sister-in-law's brother."

"It looked like you were awfully close there for a while. Too close."

"I . . . I had a cramp in my leg." She forced a smile. "He helped me to work it out."

"Why were you alone with him?"

"Oh, he's like a brother to me," she said as if to dismiss Sky's importance. "He's Cale's best friend. I've known him all my life."

"You won't see him after today." His voice dropped a few octaves and he reached out a hand to touch her hair. It took all of Valerie's willpower to not slap his hand away and run for the door.

Think, her frightened brain demanded. *Think* . . .

"Who is going to marry us?" Get him talking about his plans, make him relax. . . .

"Why, *we're* going to marry us. We don't need someone to bless our marriage, Valerie," he told her solemnly. "A love like ours is a blessing unto itself. We'll exchange our own vows." He patted his pocket. "And I have our rings right here."

"I see."

"I knew that you would." Rafferty held up another plastic bag.

"My tuxedo," he announced proudly.

"It would appear that you really have thought of everything."

"Absolutely." Daniel Rafferty reached back into the

suitcase and took out a bottle of wine. "To toast each other with after we became man and wife."

"I don't have champagne glasses here," she told him, fighting an urge to retch.

"Anything you have is fine," he assured her. "Sweetheart."

Val gritted her teeth and nodded.

"Well, I think we'd better get started, don't you?" he picked up the garment bag containing the long white dress and handed it to her. "Will you need help getting into this?"

"No, no," she assured him. "I'll be fine."

If she appeared to be a willing participant, would he be more likely to let his guard down?

"Well, you just call me if you do." He gestured for her to go down the hallway to her bedroom as if he were at home there.

The dress bag containing the gown draped over her arm like a lead weight. She was halfway down the hall when he called her name. She turned back at the sound of his voice.

"You forgot your shoes." He walked toward her and placed the box into her hands.

"Thank you," she whispered.

His fingers touched her face and she fought with every ounce of her will to not flinch.

She backed down the hall to her bedroom door. When she finally was able to close the door behind her, she slumped back against it, trying frantically to figure out a way to escape.

"Valerie," he said from the other side of the door, and she nearly jumped out of her skin at the sound of his voice.

She dropped the dress on the floor and ran to the closest window and sought to open it.

"Don't do that." The cool voice spoke from the door she'd not heard open. "Don't . . . do . . . that."

"I . . . I need some air." She swallowed hard. "Daniel."

He stared at her, his eyes cold and flat.

"You were going to run away."

"No, no . . . I . . ." She backed toward the wall as he stepped into the room.

"Your wedding dress is on the floor, Valerie. That's no way to treat something you cherish."

"It must have slid off the bed when I turned to open the window," she said, forcing down the tremble in her own voice. "Now, if you'll excuse me, I'll get dressed."

"Don't try to run away from me, Valerie," he said stonily.

"I wouldn't do that, Daniel." She met his eyes. "After all, this is our wedding day. Why would I run?"

His smile was very slow in coming.

"That's my girl." He walked to her and leaned down, kissing the side of her face. She fought the grimace that threatened.

"It won't take me long," she said through clenched teeth. "I promise."

"All right, then. I'll just be right outside the door, Val." He ran his hands up and down her bare arms, raising gooseflesh every place he touched. "I'll be putting on my tux, right out there on the other side of the door."

She nodded, and closed the door gratefully as soon as he passed through it, and cursed the fact that she'd never had locks installed on the inside doors.

Val pulled her T-shirt over her head and unsnapped

the top of her denim shorts, then turned to the bed where the white dress lay. Unzipping the bag, she removed the gown. It was beautiful, with rows of seed pearls on lace and a gently scalloped neck. It was a dress that, under other circumstances, would have been a delight. But for Val, it had all the appeal of a shroud. She turned and twisted to zip up the back, all the while looking for something, anything, that she could use as a weapon, but there was nothing. She had nothing but her wits, and they seemed to be failing her.

Think, her voice screamed inside her head. There has to be something. Something . . .

"How're we doing in there?" Rafferty asked from the other side of the door.

"Fine. Almost ready." She dumped the contents of her handbag onto the bed. Was there nothing there that she could use?

Not even a nail file.

Damn.

She glanced at her watch. It was almost seven-thirty. A half-hour more and Sky would be at the cabin. But Daniel had a gun, and Val had absolutely no doubt that he wouldn't hesitate for a second to use it.

"Sweetheart, are you ready?"

"Almost," she said, the panic beginning to rise within her. She had to think of something. There had to be something. . . .

Without warning, he opened the door.

"You're beautiful." He sighed. "Just as I knew you'd be."

"Thank you," she whispered, her heart sinking.

"Need help with pinning on your veil?"

"I'm afraid I don't have any hair pins."

"The sales lady gave you some. Didn't you look in the box?" His hands slipped into his pants pockets, and she could see that under his tuxedo jacket, the handgun was in place. The groom was apparently taking no chances.

"I . . . I left the veil in the front room," Val told him.

"Well, slip into those shoes and come on out, and I'll help you with it." He smiled and held out his hand. With a sinking heart she followed him down the hallway.

"Have you decided where you'd like us to exchange our vows?" he asked when he leaned over her to secure the veil in place.

"I . . . I haven't had much time to think about it."

"There must be a place that's special to you." He dipped his hands into his pockets, and once again she saw the flash of metal.

"Daniel, why do you have a gun with you?"

When he didn't respond, she said, "It isn't the one you had with you when you came to investigate the break-in. That one looked bigger."

"I bought this one special for the occasion," he replied.

Along with the gown and the bouquet? Valerie shivered.

"It's for us, darling." He held up the small handgun.

"For us?" And in that moment, Val realized that neither of them would be coming back down the hill after the ceremony had concluded.

"Why?" she whispered. "Why, Daniel?"

"I'm sorry, sweetheart, but it's really the only way. You understand."

"No. No, I don't understand."

"Valerie, it's the only way that I can be sure that we'll always be together. We're supposed to always be together."

"But we can be. We can be together. . . ."

"No." He cut her off. "No. They'll always be looking at you. They'll always be wanting you."

"But, Daniel, I won't want anyone but you. I won't look at anyone else. Not ever. We can live happily together. . . ."

"I can't take that chance, Valerie." He shook his head slowly.

She was staring at the door, wishing with all her might that it would swing open and that Sky would come in and rescue her. But the door remained closed, her jacket hanging on the back and her old boots standing on the floor right next to her camera bag.

"Daniel," she said as an idea slowly—oh so slowly— formed in her head.

It was such a long shot.

"Yes, my love?"

"What about pictures?"

"Pictures?" He frowned.

"Pictures of our wedding." She smiled up at him.

"I . . . I hadn't thought of pictures." The omission clearly bothered him. He'd been so certain that he'd covered every base.

"Look, I have my equipment here. I can set up the camera on a tripod, and use a remote control to take some pictures. And when Cale sees them, he'll realize that we'll always be happy together."

"Then you do understand."

Val nodded. "It's the only way to keep our love pure. Eternally pure."

He beamed. He knew she'd come around.

"Then certainly, let's take your equipment. Do you have film?"

"I have rolls of film. Enough to fill a whole album." She pointed to the door where the bag stood.

"Great. Let's get going." He paused when he reached the door. "Have you decided on a place yet?"

"I . . . yes. Yes, I did," she told him.

"Is it someplace special?"

"Oh, it's very special," she assured him.

But how to let Sky know where they'd gone?

"Oh, for heaven's sake, Daniel." Val sighed as if exasperated. "I don't have a bit of makeup on."

"You don't need makeup, sweetheart. You're just naturally beautiful without it."

"Thank you. But I really would like to dash into the bathroom, just for a little lipstick. I don't want to appear pale in the pictures. I'll just be a minute."

"I'll be counting the seconds."

I'll just bet you will, Val thought as she rushed down the hallway and into the bathroom. She lifted the small basket of makeup from the window ledge and rifled through the tubes and containers for a red lipstick. Finding it, she traced the outline of her mouth, then with shaking fingers, wrote upon the mirror, and prayed that Sky would find it.

"Val?" She heard Daniel in the hallway.

"All done." She smiled as she stepped out to meet him and closed the bathroom door behind her.

Taking his arm, she led him back toward the front room. There was only one more thing she needed to do.

Stopping at the front door, she picked up her leather boots and began to slip off the dressy heels.

"What are you doing?" He frowned. "You can't mean to wear cowboy boots with your wedding dress."

"Oh, it's just until we get to where we're going." She looked up at him with what she hoped would pass for an adoring gaze. "I appreciate that you went to all the trouble to bring my sandals, but I won't be able to walk up the hill in anything so delicate. I'll bring these with me." She held up the sandals.

"Oh, all right, then." He nodded. "Ready?"

"Ready as I'll ever be." She blew out a breath that she'd held way too long and handed him the bag holding her equipment.

She grabbed her bouquet, and tucked her tripod under her arm. She wished it was heavy enough to bash him with.

Val followed Rafferty out the door, knowing that she had one chance to get it right. She could only hope that Mother Nature was feeling real cooperative that morning.

She'd never understood the concept of dying for love. Living for love, now *that* she understood.

She thought of Sky and his whiskey dark eyes and his easy smile and the possibility that she might never see him again.

Live for love, she told herself sternly.

Live.

11

THE MORNING WAS WELL ON ITS WAY TO BEING A HOT ONE, the sun having risen early, when Sky knocked on Valerie's cabin door. When she did not appear to let him in, he turned the knob and pushed the door aside.

"Valerie?" he called.

He stepped inside and called again. "Valerie?"

Maybe she was in the shower.

He stood in the hallway, but heard no sound of running water.

Sky poked his head into the kitchen. An empty cup stood on the counter, a trace of black coffee pooled in the bottom. Sky frowned. Val drank her coffee light, never black.

Had she had a visitor already this morning?

Where could she have gone off to? And with whom?

He walked back into the front room, and noticed the suitcase standing at one end of the sofa. He opened it up, and found several items of men's clothing. Val hadn't mentioned that she'd been expecting a visitor the night before.

"Val?" Sky called again toward the back of the small house.

A chill settled in the back of his brain, and he went back down the hallway and flung open her bedroom door. A red T-shirt and a pair of shorts lay discarded on the floor. Not like her to be messy with her things, he noted.

He pushed open the bathroom door, and stared at the writing on the mirror.

Jed's rock.

Jed's rock? Sky frowned. What in the world would she being doing at Jed's rock? Hadn't Trevor told her just a few nights ago how bad rattlers were this year?

He started toward the door when his glance fell upon a white object lying on the floor. Picking it up, he turned it around and around in his hands. A wedding cake. It was hinged and opened, like a box.

Hadn't Val said that her intruder had taken nothing but a box shaped like a wedding cake?

And there, on the floor. Was that a scattering of rice?

"Shit," he said aloud. "Shit."

He bolted through the door and left it standing open, stopping at his pickup only for the hunting rifle that he left under the front seat, and headed off in the direction of Jed's rock. He hoped he wasn't too late.

"Here?" Rafferty climbed to the center of the large boulder. "Is this good?"

Valerie took a long look at the outcropping of rock that hung over the valley, all the while searching the nooks and crannies for movement. The sun was warming, but apparently not quite warm enough to coax out the reinforcements.

"Wait a minute," Val called to the eager groom. "It will take a few minutes to set up and then to get the aperture adjusted correctly for the light." She flashed a broad smile to reassure him.

"How long will this take?" he asked.

"Not long." Val set up the tripod about eight feet back from the rock.

"Why is this such a special place?" he asked.

"There's a story about how my ancestor, Jedidiah McAllister, stood on that rock and watched the Crows set up camp down in the valley below." She reached in the bag for the remote for her camera; at the same time she studied a deep pocket in the rock. "He fell in love with a Crow woman and they married and had several children, I forgot how many."

"Did they live together in the cabin?"

"No. They stayed mostly with her people. The story is that Jed went hunting buffalo with her brothers, and when he returned, he found that the camp had been attacked by soldiers and his entire family had been massacred."

"That's terrible." Rafferty frowned. "Valerie, what are you doing?"

Trying to figure out a way to wake up those rattlers without making it obvious.

"Just trying to get everything set up right." She dove back into her bag, hoping against hope that she had packed the small light she sometimes used. Her fingers closed over it happily.

Now, if the battery pack is in there, I have a chance to pull this off. . . .

Yes!

"What's that?" Rafferty asked, clearly anxious to get on with it.

"It's a portable light," she told him with a smile. "It's battery operated so that I can use it anywhere and take the shots I want even if the light isn't just right."

Rafferty looked around at the bright sunny day.

"There's plenty of sunlight," he pointed out.

"But it's casting shadows that I don't want in our photos." She hooked the light to the battery pack and turned it on, then let it drop to the ground, its beam focused on a crevice about a yard from Rafferty's right foot. "Now I'll drop the film in and we'll be ready to take some pictures."

She took her time loading the camera, keeping one eye on the break in the rock. The shadows were beginning to move, slowly at first. Then there, right there . . . a scaly face appeared, drawn to the warmth of the light.

A little more . . . just a little more . . . come on, handsome . . . just another foot or so . . .

"I'm going to take one or two shots of you by yourself," she told him, "so stand up straight and smile. . . ."

Val raised the camera to her face and focused on the rattler. A second head now poked out to investigate the source of heat.

She snapped off the first shot.

"I think I want you to take a step to the side."

"This way?" he asked, stepping to the left.

"No, I think just a little to the right might do it." The camera still to her face, she watched the larger of the two snakes begin to coil. The second one followed its lead.

"Val, do you hear . . ." Rafferty called to her.

He didn't get to finish the sentence. The first snake

struck right at the ankle. The second struck at the back of his calf.

Stunned, he looked down. Then, barely flinching, he reached for his handgun and shot both snakes before turning back to the spot where Valerie had stood only seconds before.

She was gone.

"You bitch," he said softly, calmly.

He stepped off the rock and sought the path they'd taken from the cabin. His right leg was beginning to burn. In old cowboy movies, snakebites were treated by sucking the poison out. Well, he'd have to be a damned contortionist to do that, given the location of the bites. He'd tend to *them* when he got down the hill. For all the mystique about them, he wasn't really sure that rattlesnakes were all that poisonous. He'd never heard of anyone actually dying after being bitten.

"Valerie, stop playing games," he called out. "We both know that this is inevitable, so come back here and let's do this."

The only sound was that of a bird at the top of a far-off tree.

"Come on, now, Valerie." Rafferty stood still, the gun dangling from his right hand, as he sought to get his bearings where the path branched off into a Y.

"I think the lady has had second thoughts," said a voice from close behind.

"Don't try it," the voice warned as Rafferty began to spin around.

But his training and years on the street had served the detective well. Sky never saw the elbow until it smashed into the middle of his face.

"Stupid son of a bitch," Rafferty hissed. "Who do you think you're dealing with?"

He lowered the gun to Sky's head.

"No, don't!" Valerie screamed. "Don't."

"I can't think of one good reason not to blow his brains out." Rafferty looked up to see his bride—the hem of her dress a bit tattered—standing before him.

"I'll marry you," she told him, "I promise. I'll do whatever you want."

"I know you will, Valerie."

Rafferty attempted to line up Schuyler in his sight, but his head was beginning to buzz. His leg had grown numb as the venom began to move through his bloodstream, and his arm began to feel disconnected from his body. He managed to squeeze off a shot, but it missed his target by nearly a foot.

Valerie lunged for Sky's rifle, but Rafferty blocked her way.

"You wouldn't even want to think about that," he said unsteadily.

He reached for her, his left hand closing over her throat. He attempted to hold on to her, but his grip lacked strength.

The last things that Detective Daniel Rafferty would know, the last memory that he would take with him into the next world, was the sound of the rifle's blast, and the force that threw him back onto the ground like a broken doll.

12

Thin fingers of sunlight slipped through the narrow blinds, making a hazy trail across the carpet. Valerie turned over and pulled the thin blanket up to her chin, not quite asleep, not quite awake.

From somewhere in the distance a phone rang and sleepily she reached an arm out to answer it, hands blindly searching on the nightstand. The ringing stopped and Val wondered vaguely who had picked it up. It was then that she realized that she wasn't in her own bed in her town house, and she opened her eyes. The room was familiar, but one she hadn't slept in for years. Liza's room at the High Meadow.

She sat bolt upright when she realized where she was—and why—and fought back a wave of nausea. It had been less than a day since a man had fallen dead at her feet, and the memory sickened her. That it had been Sky who fired the fatal shot—gentle Sky, who had never raised a hand to anyone, who rarely even raised his voice in anger—was almost incomprehensible.

The entire afternoon and evening seemed to have passed in a blur. The sound of the gun like an unexpected clap of thunder, loud enough to make Val's knees quake in the aftermath of its deafening blast. The look of sheer surprise on Daniel Rafferty's face. The rapid spread of red across the front of his crisp white shirt. His stumble and fall to the ground, the dense thud as he hit it, face first. Sky taking Val back down to the High Meadow and turning her over to his mother, while he and his dad, Hap, called the sheriff. Val sitting in the living room of the ranch house wrapped in an old quilt, shivering in spite of the summer heat, trying to make sense of what had happened. Sheriff Brown bringing the body down from the hills and sending it along to the county coroner, then staying a while himself to ask about Val's relationship with the deceased. . . .

And later, still, Catherine insisting that Val stay there at the ranch for a few days. Val had been more than happy to comply. She simply wasn't ready to spend a night alone in the cabin.

Val wondered if Daniel Rafferty had a family, and what they would think when they found out what had happened. She glanced at the clock on the dresser across the room. Eight A.M. Perhaps they already knew.

Would they blame Val? Or Sky? Or might they somehow have known that something was not quite right?

Val desperately wanted—needed—a hot shower, wanted to wash it all away, the sights, the sounds, the smells. After foraging in Liza's dresser for an old, forgotten sweatshirt and a pair of shorts, she headed for the small bathroom that the Hollister girls had all once shared on the second floor of the ranch house. She turned on the hot water and let it fill the room with steam before stepping in and lowering her head, allowing the little spikes to first work on the muscles at the back of her neck, then on her left shoulder, which ached where she'd hit the ground the day before.

The aches and pains were insignificant, Val reminded herself, when one considered that, had all gone according to Rafferty's plan, she'd be on a slab at the morgue by now. In her heart, she couldn't help but feel sorry that Daniel Rafferty was dead, but not so sorry that she'd have sacrificed herself or Sky or their future together for his sake.

Val shivered again, and cranked the hot water up just a little higher.

Twenty minutes later, Valerie padded down the steps in bare feet. While she could fit into Liza's clothing, her feet were and always had been two sizes smaller than Val's.

Voices were heard in the kitchen, and Val followed them to find Sky at the old worn table with his parents.

"There you are." Catherine jumped up when Val entered the room. "How did you sleep, honey?"

"Much better than I'd have expected," Val assured her.

"You okay?" Sky asked with clear concern.

"All things considered, I'm better than I have any right to be."

"I'm glad to hear that, honey," Hap pulled out a chair for her and gestured for her to sit.

"We had pancakes, Valerie." Catherine went to the old white stove and turned a burner on. "I saved some batter so that you could have some when you got up."

"Thank you," Val said, knowing it would be fruitless to protest. Catherine had already poured batter into the frying pan.

"Here's your coffee." Sky brought her a mug of fragrant dark liquid, then passed her a small white pitcher covered with little red flowers.

"Liza's pitcher," Val said without thinking.

"Oh, my, Valerie, do you remember that pitcher?" Catherine turned and smiled.

"I was with Liza in Reynold's Drug Store when she bought it for you." Val nodded. "It had a little sugar bowl that went with it."

"I can't believe the sort of things that you women remember." Hap shook his head as he pushed back from the table to answer the phone that was ringing again.

"He's just covering for the fact that he was the one who broke the sugar bowl." Catherine nodded toward her husband.

Val sipped at her coffee and sniffed at the aroma from the frying pan, caught Sky's eyes and smiled. Sitting there in a well remembered room, surrounded by people who cared about her, was balm to her ragged nerves. There was a tranquility to the morning, even in the aftermath of what had happened the day before. The contrast was almost staggering, surreal, and made her feel lightheaded.

The storm had preceded the calm, she was thinking, as Hap hung up the phone.

"That was Sheriff Brown, again," Hap told them.

"Again?" Val raised her eyebrows.

"Third time he called already this morning." Hap nodded. "The first time, he called to assure us that no one would be charged with Rafferty's death."

"Why would someone be?" Val asked. "It was self-defense."

"It's just a formality," Hap assured her. "The second time was to tell us that the department Rafferty worked for in California called back a little while ago. He'd called them last night to tell them what had gone on up here yesterday. Well, they sent someone out to this fellow Rafferty's apartment."

"And?" Sky asked when his father hesitated.

"And . . . they found that his walls were covered with pictures of Val. Some that he cut from magazines, some that he'd apparently taken himself."

"What?" Val's cup nearly slid from her hands.

"There were pictures of you everywhere, they said. Walking down the street, looking in a shop window, getting into your car, walking a dog, sitting on a deck. . . ."

"The deck behind my town house." Val's skin crawled.

"And some photos of you in a wedding."

"Cale and Quinn's wedding." She looked up at Sky and grimaced. "The pictures that were stolen from my house. He answered the 911 call. He came and made the report. All the while he had the photos. He had the little porcelain box. And a pair of my shoes."

"They also found a journal he'd been keeping. He'd been planning this for some time, Val. He apparently felt you and he were somehow destined to be together."

Sky sat down next to Valerie and rubbed the back of her neck. In his eyes, she felt she could see her true destiny. But had Rafferty felt the same way, looking at her?

Catherine sat a plate of pancakes in front of her and put out a knife and fork.

"Then, that last time that the sheriff called, he wanted to warn us that the California press caught on to this story. He said they can't answer the phone fast enough down there, that we should expect an onslaught of reporters from all over."

"When . . . ?" Catherine met her husband's eyes from across the room.

"Within the next few hours."

"Val, if there's a place you can go to stay—to sort of hide out for a few days, you might think about heading there this morning," Hap said.

"The cabin was always the place I'd go to when I needed sanctuary," Val told them. "There's never been anyplace else. I could go to Liza's—I told her when she called the other night that I'd be coming for a visit real soon."

"Sooner or later, someone will think to look for my sister," Sky said as he took her hand. "When you've finished eating, we'll run up to the cabin and grab your things. I know just the place where no one will think to look. . . ."

The pickup bounced over the ruts in the dirt road, and Val was glad that the coffee she'd brought with her was safely in one of those cups that had a nice, tight lid. Val turned off the air-conditioning and rolled down the windows to listen to the sound of the long, thin reeds of grain that lined the road on either side and shivered in the late morning breeze. The sky was china blue and cloudless, the wheat still green, the barn off to the left a deep red, and the old farmhouse, still a quarter of a mile away at the end of the lane, was a cheery yellow.

The colors lay vivid against each other and the sun, now nearing its midpoint in the sky, shed a graceful glow over all.

"This is the most beautiful place I've ever seen," Val told him. "It takes my breath away."

"I thought you might feel that way." Sky slowed the pickup and tried—unsuccessfully—to avoid yet another large hole.

"Are you sure your grandmother won't mind?"

"She'll be delighted to have helped. You wait and see. She'll be sending someone over loaded down with strawberry preserves before the day is over."

They reached the end of the drive, and Sky stopped the truck. Val hopped out, took a deep breath, and hugged herself.

"You're looking better," Sky said as he wrapped his arms around her from behind.

"I'm feeling better." Val leaned back against his chest.

"Val, if there had been any way to have saved you without killing him . . ."

"I know."

"I never killed a man before," he said softly. "I never believed there could be any force powerful enough to make me take a life. But in that split second when I realized what he was going to do, I knew that I'd do anything—anything—to keep you safe. There wasn't even a choice. I just couldn't let him kill you. I love you too much, Val."

"I love you, too, Sky. I think maybe I always have."

"It's been a roundabout course we've taken to get to each other, wouldn't you say?" He gently rubbed the side of her face with his own.

"Ummm," she agreed. "But the point is, we got there. And look at us, Sky. We're both alive. We're here, together, in the most beautiful place on the face of the earth."

"Now, wait a minute. All of the places you've been— Paris, London, Hawaii, all those islands . . ."

"Can't hold a candle to this place," she insisted. "No other place even comes close."

"Then there's a chance you could get used to it?"

"Well, gee, holing up here for a few days could be a sacrifice." She nodded slowly.

"I mean, beyond just laying low until the press loses interest."

Val turned in his arms to look into his eyes.

"I'm thinking of taking over the farm for good, Val. My cousin Will and I are serious about breeding some fine quality horses here. It won't be a part-time thing. Can you give up what you've had—the travel, the . . ."

She placed a finger to his lips.

"In a heartbeat."

He raised her fingers to his lips and kissed all ten of them.

"Farming's not an easy life."

"I don't imagine it is. But after the week I've had, it might not seem so bad." She smiled up at him.

"Come on then." He kissed the tip of her nose and took her by the hand. "It's time you met my babies."

He pointed to a pasture where several colts stood watching on spindly legs. "We have a few that hold great promise. . . ."

They walked toward the fence, Sky pointing out the stallion he'd bought from a famous ranch in Texas to serve as stud for a mare he'd bought in Kentucky.

"Wait right here, and I'll bring her over to meet you."

Val leaned against the fence and watched Sky stride across the field to the large chestnut mare he'd identified as his favorite. The horse nuzzled at him and began to follow him back toward the place where Val stood waiting. The sun spread out across the landscape in golden strands of light.

A golden afternoon, Val thought, filled with golden promises.

Of a life to share.

A love to live for.

Truly, a love to live for.

ABOUT THE AUTHOR

MARIAH STEWART is the award-winning author of nine contemporary romances and three novellas, all for Pocket Books. A three-time nominee for Romantic Times Career Achievement Award for Contemporary Romance and a winner of *Romance Times* Reviewers Choice Award for Best Contemporary Romance of 1999, she has been called "one of the most talented writers of mainstream contemporary fiction in the market today." *Brown-eyed Girl,* her first romantic suspense, was a bestseller in 2000. *Voices Carry*—also romantic suspense—was a February 2001 release. She is the recipient of the Golden Leaf Award (New Jersey Romance Writers), the Award of Excellence (Colorado Romance Writers), and the Dorothy Parker Award for Excellence in Women's Fiction (Reviewer's International), and is a four-time finalist for the Holt Medallion. A native of Highstown, New Jersey, Mariah Stewart lives in a century-plus Victorian country home in a Philadelphia suburb with her husband of twenty-two years, two teenage daughters, and two golden retrievers. She is a member of Novelists, Inc.; the Valley Forge Romance Writers; and the Romance Writers of America. Write to her at P.O. Box 481, Lansdowne, PA 19050, or at MariahStew@aol.com.

POCKET STAR BOOKS
PROUDLY PRESENTS

NO WAY OUT
ANDREA KANE

Available November 2001
from
Pocket Star Books

Turn the page for a preview of
No Way Out . . .

April 14
Leaf Brook Mall
Westchester County, New York

Wrong place. Wrong time.

She had to get out of here.

Julia gritted her teeth as she fought the crowd surging back and forth through the mall. She shoved her way to the door leading to the twelve-story parking garage. Wall-to-wall people. Everything was called a grand opening. This felt more like Mardi Gras in New Orleans.

Coming here today had been stupid. The Stratfords were enveloped by spectators, surrounded by members of the press. And the mayor was flanked by his father and brother—a clear message that the Stratfords represented a unified front. Even Julia's desperation hadn't been enough to get her through. She'd have to find another way.

Taking an elevator wasn't an option. There was already

a huge line, and, as each car opened, Julia could see they were all filled to capacity. The stairwell wasn't much better, but it was her only choice. She scaled each level as quickly as she could, wincing as the deejay's music rocked the concrete walls and vibrated through her head.

Eventually, the throng of people began to thin out and the music began to fade as she put more distance between herself and the celebration. She was worried sick and frustrated as hell. If what she suspected was true, an hourglass was running out. It was up to her to stop the flow of the sand.

She exited the stairwell on the eleventh floor, where she'd intentionally parked her car to avoid the pandemonium. Reflexively, she groped for her keys as she walked.

The screech of tires was what alerted her.

Her chin came up just as the silver Mercedes blasted around the corner, bearing down on her with lightning speed.

She knew she was its target. She also knew why.

Her hunch had been right. And she was about to be silenced.

A frozen moment of fear paralyzed her. Abruptly, it shattered. A surge of adrenaline jolted through her, and she tried to jump out of the way.

She couldn't make it.

She felt the stunning impact, and then a dazed awareness as she was hurled through the air. The concrete floor came rushing up to meet her.

Brian, she thought, shards of pain piercing her skull. *Who's going to save Brian?*

Look for

NO WAY OUT

the thrilling paperback from

ANDREA KANE

New York Times **bestselling author of** *Run for Your Life*

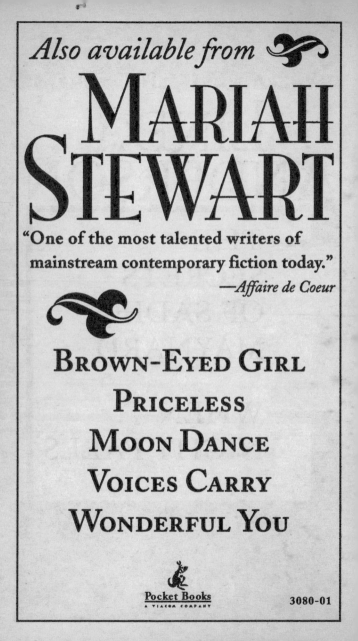